W9-AAQ-546
MOUNTAIN VIEW
PUBLIC LIBRARY

THE BLUE ROOM

THE ACCOMPLICES

THE BLUE ROOM

two novels by GEORGES SIMENON

THE ACCOMPLICES

A HELEN AND KURT WOLFF BOOK

HARCOURT, BRACE & WORLD, INC., NEW YORK

First edition

Library of Congress Catalog Card Number: 64-22674

Printed in the United States of America

The Blue Room is a translation of *La Chambre bleue,* and was translated by Eileen Ellenbogen.
The Accomplices is a translation of *Les Complices,* and was translated by Bernard Frechtman.

THE BLUE ROOM

CHAPTER

I

"Have I hurt you?"

"No."

"Are you angry with me?"

"No."

It was true. For the present, everything was true, because he was living through it now, at this moment. He accepted it all without question, not attempting to understand, not foreseeing the time when he would learn that there had been something to understand. Besides being true, everything was real; herself, the room, Andrée naked still on the ravaged bed, her legs apart, a few drops of semen clinging to the dark hair, shadowy between her thighs.

Was he happy? If anyone had asked him, he would have said "yes" unhesitatingly. He felt no resentment toward Andrée for biting his lip. In the context of their love-making, it had its place, and, naked as she was herself, standing in front of the washbasin mirror, he dipped the towel in the cold water and dabbed his lip.

"Will your wife question you?"

"I don't think so."

"Doesn't she ever?"

What they said scarcely mattered. Lightheaded, their bodies still tingling, they exchanged words for the joy of it, as people do after making love.

"You have a beautiful back."

There were little pink spots here and there on the towel, and in the street an empty truck bounced on the cobblestones. On the terrace, people were talking. Only an odd word here and there reached them clearly, making no sense.

"Do you love me, Tony?"

"I think so."

He said it teasingly, though without a smile, for he was still dabbing his lower lip with the damp towel.

"Aren't you sure?"

He turned to look at her, and noticed with pleasure the drops of semen, his semen, recalling the intimate union of their bodies.

The room was painted blue; "washday blue" as he had once described it to himself, remembering his childhood and the little muslin bags filled with blue powder which his mother used to dissolve in the washtub for the final rinse, just before taking the household linen into the field and spreading it to dry on the shining grass. That must have been when he was five or six years old, and there had been a kind of magic for him in the blue that turned the linen white.

Years later, some time after his mother's death—when even her features had become blurred in his memory—it occurred to him to wonder why the whiteness of the linen should matter so much to people like themselves, who were so poor they had nothing to wear that was not patched and darned.

Were these his thoughts at this moment? That, he was to find out later. The blue room was at once washday blue and sky-blue, the blue of a hot August afternoon sky, just before it is tinged with pink deepening to red by the setting sun.

It was a day in August, August 2nd. It was late afternoon. At five o'clock gilded clouds, light as whipped cream, drifted over the top of the station, leaving its white façade in shadow.

"Could you spend the rest of your life with me?"

The words scarcely registered, or so it seemed at the time. He noticed them no more than shapes and smells. How could he guess that he was to live through this scene ten times, twenty times, more times indeed than he could count, each time in a different frame of mind, seeing it each time in a different light?

Over a period of months, he forced himself—sometimes of his own free will, sometimes at the bidding of others—to recall everything, down to the smallest detail.

Professor Bigot, for instance, the psychiatrist appointed by the Examining Magistrate, was to press this point, watchful for his reactions:

"Did she often bite you?"

"Occasionally."

"How many times?"

"In all, I only met her eight times, at the Hôtel des Voyageurs."

"Eight times over a period of twelve months?"

"It was eleven months . . . Yes, eleven . . . It was September when it all started . . ."

"How many times did she bite you?"

"Three or four, maybe."

"During intercourse?"

"I think so . . . yes . . ."

Yes . . . No . . . Today, as it happened, it was afterwards. He had moved away from her and was lying on his side, looking at her through half-closed eyelids, dazzled by the brilliant light that enveloped them both.

It was hot outside in the station square. In the room,

with the sun full on it, it was hot too, and the heat seemed a living, breathing presence.

He had pulled the shutters to, but with a foot-wide gap between them so that through the open window they could hear the bustle of the little town, a far-off jumble of noise, like a distant choir, punctuated by sharp, clear sounds, such as the voices of the people on the terrace.

A short while ago, during their ferocious love-making, these sounds had flowed in to them and become one with their bodies, their saliva, their sweat, the whiteness of Andrée's belly, the darker tones of his own skin, the strip of light that split the room down the middle, the blue walls, the glinting mirror, the smell of the inn, a somewhat rural smell, a blend of wines and spirits being served in the lounge and stew simmering in the kitchen, mingled with the faintly musty smell of the fiber mattress.

"You're a handsome man, Tony."

She said this every time, always at the same point, lying on the bed as he moved about the room or fumbled for a cigarette in the pocket of his trousers, which were slung over the back of a wicker chair.

"Are you still bleeding?"

"It's almost stopped."

"If she asks about it, what will you say?"

He shrugged, seeing no cause for anxiety. To him, living for the moment, nothing else mattered. He felt good, at peace with the world.

"I'll say I bumped into something . . . I know . . . the windshield . . . Having to jam on the brakes suddenly . . ."

He lit his cigarette, which had a distinctive flavor. In reconstructing this conversation, he was to recall a smell that stood out from the rest, the smell of trains. A freight train could be heard shunting in a siding, and, from time to time, there were short blasts from the engine whistle.

Professor Bigot, red-haired, small and skinny, with fierce beetling eyebrows, was to hammer home his point:

"Did it never occur to you that she might have a motive in biting you?"

"What motive?"

Later, his lawyer, Maître Demarié, was to revert to this:

"I believe these bites could be turned to our advantage."

They would not leave it alone, but he could only repeat that he had not given another thought to his bitten lip. How should he, when he was wholly absorbed in living? What, in fact, had he been thinking about? Nothing, that he was aware of. He had answered Andrée carelessly, saying the first thing that came into his head, believing that words were weightless things, to be borne away on the wind.

One afternoon, at their third or fourth meeting, after telling him, as usual, that he was handsome, Andrée had added:

"You're so handsome, I wish we could make love right out in the open, in front of everyone, there in the Place de la Gare."

He had laughed, though the notion had not seemed to him so very strange. He never wanted to shut out the world, even while she was in his arms. He took in everything, the bustle, the voices, the play of light on the walls, even the footsteps on the pavement and the clink of glasses on the terrace tables.

Once, a brass band had played through the streets, and it had been fun making love in time to the music. Another day, during a violent storm, Andrée had insisted on having the shutters folded back and the window wide open.

Had it been anything more than a kind of game? He, at any rate, had seen no harm in it. She was naked, sprawled across the bed in a deliberately abandoned attitude. It was her way, the minute they were inside the room, to throw aside all reserve, all modesty.

Sometimes, after they had undressed, she would murmur with a kind of mock shyness which was not intended to deceive but was just a move in the game:

"I'm thirsty. Aren't you?"

"No."

"You will be later. You'd better ring for Françoise and order something to drink."

Françoise, the servant, was about thirty and, having worked in cafés and hotels from the age of fifteen, was past being surprised at anything.

"Yes, Monsieur Tony?"

She called him Monsieur Tony, because he was the brother of her employer, Vincente Falcone, who, as landlord, had his name painted on the front of the inn, and whose voice could now be heard on the terrace.

"Did you never suspect any ulterior motive in her behavior?"

What he lived through in that half hour—no, less than that, just a few minutes of his life—was to be shattered into fragments of sight and sound, each of which would be scrutinized microscopically both by himself and by other people.

Andrée was tall. He was not conscious of it in bed, but she was two or three inches taller than himself. Though of local stock, she had the dark, almost black, hair of a Southerner or an Italian, against sleek, white, translucent skin. Her figure was shapely, a shade on the heavy side perhaps, and her flesh—breasts and thighs especially—was firm and smooth.

At thirty-three, he had known many women. With no other had he experienced the intensity of pleasure that he had known with her; a total fulfillment, spontaneous, animal, with no aftertaste of revulsion, awkwardness, or lassitude.

Quite the contrary. After two hours spent in the fullest enjoyment of one another's bodies, neither would be in any hurry to dress, prolonging their physical intimacy, savoring their well-being, their contentment not only with each other but with everything about them.

Everything was precious. Everything had its place in

their pulsating universe, even the fly that settled on Andrée's belly, which she watched with a contented smile.

"Could you really spend the rest of your life with me?"

"Of course . . ."

"Can you be so sure? Aren't you a little afraid?"

"What is there to be afraid of?"

"Can't you just see us together, day after day?"

These words, too, would return, so lighthearted today, but a few months from now, so menacing.

"We'd get used to it, in time," he said without thinking.

"Used to what?"

"To one another."

He was guileless, innocent. Nothing mattered but the present. A virile male and a warm female had enjoyed one another to the full, and if Tony ached a little afterwards, it was a healthy and pleasurable ache.

"Good Lord! There's the train."

It was not he who had spoken. It was his brother outside. As though the words were a signal, Tony went mechanically to the window and stood in the strip of scorching light between the shutters.

Could he be seen from the terrace or the square? It was unlikely, since, to anyone looking in, the room would seem dark. Anyway, he was not worried. They were on the first floor. The most that anyone looking up could see would be a man stripped to the waist.

"When I think of all the years I've wasted because of you!"

"Because of me?" he echoed, smiling.

"Well, I wasn't the one to walk out, was I?"

They had been at school together from the age of six. But it was not until they were both over thirty, both married that . . .

"Seriously, Tony . . . If I were free . . . ?"

Had he been listening? The train, invisible behind the white station building, had stopped, and the passengers were beginning to file through the door on the right, where a uniformed ticket collector was checking them out.

"Would you get your freedom too?"

Starting up again, the engine let out a shrill whistle, drowning all other sounds.

"What was that you said?"

"I asked you whether, in that event . . ."

He had half turned his head toward the blue walls of the room, the white bed and Andrée's body, but out of the corner of his eye he caught a glimpse of something that made him turn back to the window. In the anonymous crowd of men and women, one carrying a baby in her arms, another tugging at the hand of a little girl, he had recognized a face.

"Your husband . . ."

In that moment of time, Tony had become a different man.

"Nicolas?"

"Yes."

"Where is he? What's he doing?"

"He's crossing the square."

"Is he coming here?"

"Definitely."

"How does he look?"

"I can't see. The sun's in my eyes."

"Where are you going?"

For he was gathering up his trousers, his underwear, his socks, his shoes.

"I mustn't stay here. So long as he doesn't find us together . . ."

He was not looking at her now. Suddenly he cared nothing for her, for her body, for anything she might say or think. Panic-stricken, he took one last look out of the window, then rushed from the room.

Nicolas would certainly not have got on that train, especially with his wife away in Triant, unless he had some very pressing reason.

On the dark staircase, with its worn treads, it was cooler, and Tony, his clothes over his arm, climbed to the second floor and made toward a half-open door at the end of the corridor, where he found Françoise, in black dress and white apron, changing the sheets on a bed. She looked him up and down, then burst out laughing:

"Well, if it isn't Monsieur Tony! Have you had a row?"

"Shhh . . ."

"What's going on?"

"Her husband . . ."

"Caught you, did he?"

"Not yet. But he's on his way here."

He dressed feverishly, listening intently, expecting to hear Nicolas's listless tread on the stairs.

"Go and see what he's up to, and be quick about it. I must know."

He was fond of Françoise, a thick-set sturdy girl with laughing eyes, and she returned his affection.

The room had a sloping ceiling, the papered walls were patterned with pink roses, and a black crucifix hung above the walnut bedstead. There was a crucifix, too, in the blue room, a smaller one, hanging over the fireplace.

He was not wearing a tie, and he had left his jacket in the car. The caution that he and Andrée had exercised for almost a year now was suddenly proving useful.

Whenever they met at the Hôtel des Voyageurs, Tony left his truck in a quiet old street, the Rue des Saules, parallel to the Rue Gambetta, whereas Andrée parked her gray Citroën in the Place du Marché, about five hundred yards away.

Through the skylight he could see the forecourt of the inn, with stables at the far end, and chickens scratching about in the paddock. On the third Monday of each month, a cattle fair was held next to the engine sheds, and country people came to Triant in large numbers from the surrounding districts, many riding in old-fashioned farm carts.

Françoise, taking her time over it, was coming up the stairs.

"Well?"

"He's sitting on the terrace, and he's just ordered lemonade."

"How does he look?"

This had been Andrée's first question, too.

"I couldn't say, I'm sure."

"Has he asked about his wife?"

"No, but from where he's sitting, he can keep an eye on both entrances."

"Any message from my brother?"

"You're to slip out the back way, across the used-car lot behind the filling station."

He knew the way. Having scrambled over a five-foot wall, he would land behind the Chéron Garage. Beside the pumps, in the Place de la Gare, was a narrow lane leading to the Rue des Saules and emerging between a pharmacy and Patin's bakery.

"What's she doing?"

"I don't know."

"Couldn't you hear anything in there?"

"I didn't listen."

Françoise had no great liking for Andrée. Because of her own affection for him, she was possibly a little jealous.

"You'd better not go through the lounge. You might meet him on the way to the toilet."

In his mind's eye, he could see Nicolas, with his bilious complexion, his expression always either sad or sullen, sitting at a table on the terrace with his glass of lemonade, when he should have been standing behind the counter of his grocery store. Most likely he would have asked his mother to take over from him before leaving for Triant. What had he said to her? What excuse had he found for breaking the habit of a lifetime? What did he know? Who had told him?

"Did it never strike you, Monsieur Falcone, that there might have been an anonymous letter?"

The question was put by Monsieur Diem, the Examining Magistrate, whose diffidence Tony found disconcerting.

"No one in Saint-Justin knew about our affair. Even at Triant, no one knew, except my brother and sister-in-law, and Françoise. We were very careful. She used the residents' entrance, in the Rue Gambetta. That was where the staircase was, so she didn't have to go through the bar to get to the room."

"You could trust your brother, of course?"

He could not help smiling. Not trust his brother? He would as soon have mistrusted himself.

"And your sister-in-law?"

Lucia loved him almost as well as she loved Vincente, though of course in a different way. She was, like them, of Italian parentage, and family loyalty came first with her.

"What about the servant?"

In love with Tony Françoise might be, but it was not in her to write an anonymous letter.

"There is one other person . . ." stammered Monsieur Diem uncomfortably, looking away from Tony, so that the sun shone full on his rather bushy hair.

"Who?"

"Can't you see? Think back to our last interview. You repeated a conversation . . . Do you wish the clerk to read you the transcript?"

Reddening, he shook his head.

"Andrée? It's unthinkable."

"Why?"

But that lay far in the future. At present, he was following Françoise down the stairs, treading like a cat so that the wooden boards would not creak. The Hôtel des Voyageurs dated back to the days of the stagecoach. Tony stood for a moment outside the blue room, but there was not a sound to be heard. Could that mean that Andrée was still lying there naked on the bed?

Françoise led him to the end of the L-shaped passage, and pointed to a skylight opening onto a ledge under the sloping roof.

"There's a pile of straw to your right. It's a safe drop. You won't come to any harm."

The hens cackled as he landed in the courtyard, and a few seconds later he was over the wall at the far end, in among a jumble of derelict cars and scrap iron. An attendant in white overalls was filling a car at the front. He did not turn around.

Tony threaded his way through the cars, found the lane, noticed a strong smell of stagnant water and farther on the smell of new bread from the air vent behind the bakery.

In the Rue des Saules at last, he got into his truck, which bore the inscription, in black lettering on a pale yellow ground:

Antonio Falcone,
Tractors—Agricultural Machinery.
Saint-Justin-du-Loup.

A quarter of an hour earlier, he had felt at peace with the whole world. How to describe the uneasiness which now took possession of him? It was not fear. He saw no reason to suspect a trap.

"When you saw him coming out of the station, didn't it worry you?"

Yes . . . No . . . A little, Nicolas being what he was, a creature of habit, a sick man, always fussing about his health.

Making for the road to Saint-Justin, he skirted the town to avoid the Place de la Gare. From one of the bridges, an entire family was fishing in the River Orneau, including a little girl of about six who had just landed a fish, and obviously did not know how to get it off the hook. Parisians for sure. In the summer they were everywhere; there were some at his brother's place too. In the blue room, a little while back, he had recognized the accent among the voices drifting up from the terrace.

The wheat had been harvested a fortnight back, and the road ran between stubble fields, vineyards, meadows in which cows were grazing, the tawny cows of the region, with their near-black faces.

Saint-Severin, a couple of miles farther on, was a tiny village—just one little street with a few farm buildings clustered round it. Then, on his right, there was Sarelle Wood, named after the adjoining hamlet, screened from view by the trees.

It was here, only a few feet from the rutted road that, in September of the previous year, it had all started.

"Tell me about the beginning of your association."

He had been asked these same questions at Police Headquarters in Triant, first by the Sergeant, then by the Inspector, then by a Chief Inspector of the Forensic Branch at Poitiers. That was before Judge Diem, the skinny psychiatrist, and his own lawyer got to work on him in preparation for the final ordeal before the President of the Court of Assize.

Week after week, month after month, the same words were to be repeated, by different voices in different places, as spring gave way to summer, and summer to autumn.

"The real beginning, you mean? We've known each other since we were toddlers, living in the same village, going to the same school. Later, we went to first communion together . . ."

"I'm referring to your sexual relations with Andrée Despierre. Had you been intimate before?"

"Before what?"

"Before she married your friend."

"Nicolas wasn't my friend."

"Well, let us say comrade or, if you prefer it, schoolfellow. Her maiden name was Formier, and she lived in the Château with her mother . . ."

It was not a real château. There had been a château once on the site, just opposite the church, but all that was left of it was a few outbuildings. It had probably been destroyed in the Revolution, but still, more than a hundred and fifty years later, it was always known as the Château.

"Was there intimacy, before her marriage?"

"No, your Honor."

"Not even a flirtation? Did you never kiss her?"

"It never even occurred to me."

"Why not?"

He just stopped himself from replying:

"Because she was too tall."

And it was true. He could not imagine this tall, languid girl making love, any more than if she had been a statue.

Besides, she was Mademoiselle Formier, the daughter of Doctor Formier, who had died in a concentration camp. Was this the real reason? He could think of no other. He and she had belonged to different worlds.

When they came out of school, their satchels on their backs, she had only to cross the playground to reach her home in the heart of the village, while he, with two other boys, walked to La Boisselle, an outlying hamlet—if a cluster of three houses can be called a hamlet—near the Orneau bridge.

"When you came back to Saint-Justin four years ago, to make a home for your wife and child, did you renew your acquaintance with her?"

"She was married to Nicolas, and worked in the grocery store with him. I did buy things there occasionally, but it was usually my wife who . . ."

"Quite. But I should be obliged if you would now tell me how your affair with her began."

It was here, just here, at the edge of Sarelle Wood. It was

not the day of the monthly cattle fair at Triant, nor was it market day. Both were held on a Monday, though there was also a smaller market on Wednesdays. He attended regularly, since he depended for his livelihood on the good will of the local farmers.

Nicolas, as the Judge knew, was subject to fits and therefore did not drive. It was Andrée who drove into Triant every Thursday in the Citroën, to order what was needed from the wholesalers and chain stores.

Every other Thursday she spent the whole day in town, so as to fit in a visit to the hairdresser.

"Surely, in the course of four years, you and she must have met quite often."

"Yes, now and then we did. One always meets people from Saint-Justin at Triant."

"Did you speak?"

"Just a formal greeting."

"From a distance?"

"Sometimes from a distance, sometimes not. It varied."

"And that was all?"

"I may have inquired after her health or her husband's once or twice."

"Had you nothing in mind?"

"I don't understand you."

"It has clearly emerged during this inquiry that, in the course of these business trips up and down the country, you had a number of amorous adventures."

"A few, like anyone else."

"Did it happen often?"

"Whenever I got the chance."

"With your brother's servant, Françoise, for instance?"

"Once. It was just in fun. Nothing but a joke, really."

"How do you mean?"

"I met her on the stairs one day—I don't really remember much about it—she dared me . . ."

"You mean it happened on the staircase?"

"Yes."

In their eyes, it seemed, he was a depraved monster one minute and a kind of Holy Fool the next. Why?

"She didn't take it seriously, and neither did I."

"All the same, you had intercourse?"

"Certainly."

"You never felt like repeating the experience?"

"No."

"Why not?"

"Perhaps because of Andrée. It was just after that . . ."

"Didn't this woman, your brother's servant, resent it?"

"Why should she?"

How to put into words the difference between living through an experience, and stripping it bare layer by layer afterwards? Feelings and motives were imputed to him that he did not recognize. He was losing his bearings, no longer sure of what was true and what was false, no longer able to distinguish right from wrong.

That September meeting, for instance. Almost certainly it must have been on a Thursday, since Andrée was on her way back from Triant. Probably she had been held up at the hairdresser's or somewhere, because she had set out later than usual, and it was already growing dark.

As to him, he had been invited to join some of his customers for drinks and, unavoidably, had had quite a few glasses of the local wine. Left to himself, he scarcely ever drank, but in his line of work it was not always politic to refuse.

He was in good spirits, a little lightheaded, much as he had been just now in the blue room, as he stood stark naked in front of the mirror and dabbed at the blood on his lip.

It was dusk, and he had just switched on his headlights when he saw Andrée's gray Citroën by the side of the road. Andrée herself, in a light dress, was signaling him to stop.

He did stop, of course, as anyone would.

"Am I glad to see you, Tony!"

She used the familiar *tu* of their childhood.

Later, they were to ask him, as though laying some charge against him:

"Were you on those terms already?"

"Of course, since our schooldays."

"Go on."

At this point, for some inscrutable reason, the Judge made a note in the margin of the typescript in front of him.

She said:

"I would have to have a puncture, the one and only time I haven't got a jack. I had such a load, there just wasn't room for it so I left it at home. You've got a jack, haven't you?"

It was still very warm, and he was in his shirtsleeves, so he did not have the bother of taking off his jacket. He remembered that he was wearing an open-necked shirt with short sleeves, and blue drill trousers.

What choice had he but to start changing the wheel?

"Have you a spare?"

It was pitch dark before he was done. Andrée stood beside him, handing him the tools.

"You'll be late getting home for dinner."

"Well, you know how it is with my work. I'm often held up."

"Doesn't your wife mind?"

"She knows it's not my fault."

"Where did you meet her? Paris?"

"Poitiers."

"Is that where she comes from?"

"From a village nearby. She worked in the town."

"Do you like blondes?"

Gisèle was fair-haired, with delicate translucent skin which warmed to pink at the least thing.

"I don't know. I've never given it a thought."

"I wondered if you were scared of brunettes."

"Why should you think that?"

"Because, in the old days, you kissed pretty nearly every girl in the village except me."

"It was an oversight, I daresay."

He was making light of it, wiping his hands on his handkerchief.

"Would you like to kiss me sometime?"

He stared in amazement, and just stopped himself from stammering:

"Why?"

He could not see her clearly in the dark.

"Well, would you?" she repeated, in a voice that he scarcely recognized.

He remembered the little red lights on the back of the car, the smell of chestnut trees, then the smell, the taste of Andrée's mouth. With her lips pressed against his, she seized his hand and guided it to her breast, which he had not imagined to be so round and full and warm with life.

And this was the woman he had compared to a statue!

A truck was coming toward them and, to avoid its headlights, they stepped back, still locked together, into the ditch at the edge of the wood.

There, Andrée was suddenly taken with a fit of trembling such as he had never before encountered in a woman, and pressing against him with all her strength she whispered:

"Will you?"

They were in each other's arms on the ground, among the long grass and the nettles.

He had not told the police or the Judge. Only Professor Bigot, the psychiatrist, knew the truth, and he had dragged it out of him piecemeal: that it was she who pulled her skirt up to her waist, she who tore at her bodice to bare her breasts, she who urged in a voice so hoarse that it was like a death rattle:

"Kiss me, Tony!"

It was she who had taken possession of him, and there was triumph as well as passion in her eyes.

"I never dreamed she could be like that."
"What do you mean?"
"I thought she was reserved, frigid, like her mother."
"And she didn't seem embarrassed, afterwards?"

Lying motionless in the grass with her legs apart, lying as she had done that afternoon in the hotel bedroom, she had said:

"Thank you, Tony."

He believed she meant it. She was submissive, docile, almost childlike.

"I've waited so long, you know! I wanted you even when we were schoolchildren. Do you remember Linette Pichat? She had a squint, but that didn't stop you from chasing after her for months."

She was a schoolteacher now in the Vendée region, but still came home to her parents for the holidays.

"I caught you together once. You must have been about fourteen."

"Behind the brickworks?"

"You haven't forgotten?"

He had laughed.

"I haven't forgotten, because it was the first time."

"For her too?"

"I've no idea. I was too inexperienced to judge."

"I hated her! For months I used to lie in bed at night trying to think of a way to make her suffer."

"And did you?"

"No. I just prayed that she would be taken ill or disfigured in an accident."

"Don't you think we'd better be going?"

"Wait, Tony. No, don't get up! The roadside is all very well, but there must be somewhere else where we could meet? I'm in Triant every Thursday."

"I know."

"Maybe your brother . . . ?"

The Judge was to remark:

"So, it was all settled that evening?"

It was hard to tell whether he was being sarcastic.

On August 2nd, the Judge had not yet come into his life. He was on his way home. It was not dark, as it had been in September. To the west, the first streaks of red were showing in the sky, when he found his way blocked by a herd of cows, and he had to crawl behind them for ages before he got a chance to get by them.

A hamlet in a hollow: Doncoeur. A gentle slope, more fields and meadows, a great expanse of sky, a hump in the road, and then a clear view of his brand-new house, built of pink brick, his daughter Marianne sitting on the doorstep, and at the bottom of the field behind the house, the silver-painted shed—with his name spread across it in the same black lettering as on the truck—where the agricultural machinery was stored.

Marianne recognized the car when it was still some way off. He saw her turn toward the door and guessed that she was calling out: "Here's Pap!"

She would not say *"Papa"* like other children, and sometimes impishly, and perhaps because she was a little jealous of her mother, she would call him "Tony."

CHAPTER

2

The house, to his left, was halfway down a slope, with a garden all around, and a field separating it from the old, gray house with the slate roof where the Molard sisters lived. Beyond was the blacksmith's, and then, a hundred yards lower down, the village, with proper streets, terraced houses, little cafés and shops. The local people did not call it a village: to them it was a town, a large town of sixteen thousand inhabitants, not to mention the three adjoining hamlets.

"Have you been in a fight, Pap?"

He had forgotten Andrée's bite.

"Your lip's all swollen."

"I bumped into something."

"What?"

"A lamppost, in Triant. See what happens when you don't look where you're going!"

"*Maman!* Pap bumped into a lamppost . . ."

His wife, wearing a check apron and holding a saucepan, came from the kitchen.

"Is that right, Tony?"

"It's nothing. See for yourself."

Mother and daughter were so much alike in appearance that it was almost uncanny to see them side by side.

"It's been so hot, you must be worn out."

"It wasn't too bad. There's an urgent job I must see to in the office."

"Shall I plan a late dinner?"

"No, I should be through by half-past six."

They dined early because of Marianne, who was always in bed by eight. She too was wearing an apron, with little blue checks. She had recently lost her two front baby teeth, and the gap gave her an almost pathetic look. It was as though, for a few weeks, she was both child and little old woman.

"Can I come with you, Pap? I'll be quiet, I promise."

The study, with its rows of white wood shelves stacked with prospectuses and green box-files, faced the road, and Tony watched anxiously for the Citroën to drive past.

Next door was what the architect called the living room, the largest in the house, intended for use as both sitting room and dining room.

For the first week, Gisèle had shuttled back and forth with the dishes, forever getting up from the table to see to things on the stove. It was an impractical arrangement, and they now ate in the kitchen.

It was spacious and bright, with an adjoining room which was used for washing and ironing. It was well planned and always spotlessly clean and tidy.

"Your wife, I gather, was a good and efficient housewife?"

"Yes, your Honor."

"Is that why you married her?"

"I didn't know it when I married her."

It was like a play in three or rather four acts. First, Saint-

Justin, his own house, and the Police Sergeant followed by the Inspector, tormenting him with questions that were utterly incomprehensible to him at the time. Next, Poitiers and Inspector Mani, who pinpointed dates and times, and drew up a schedule of his comings and goings.

These people, the junior police officers especially, were not interested in his thoughts or feelings, since their private lives were not so very different from his.

With Judge Diem, with the psychiatrist, with his own lawyer even, things were to be quite different. When there was a hearing before the Examining Magistrate, for instance, Tony was brought from the prison in the police wagon, and driven back there in the same car immediately afterwards, while the Magistrate went home for lunch or dinner.

He felt more uncomfortable with Diem than with any of the others, perhaps because they were almost of an age. The Judge was a year younger than himself, and had been married eighteen months longer. His wife had just had her first baby. The Judge's father, who had no private means, was chief clerk in the Social Security Department, and Diem had married a typist. They lived modestly in a flat with three rooms and a kitchen, in the newer part of the town.

Surely they ought to have been able to understand one another?

"What exactly were you afraid of that night?"

What could he say? Of everything. Of nothing in particular. Nicolas would not have left the shop in his mother's charge and boarded the train, without good reason. He had not gone to Triant just to sit at a table on the terrace of the Hôtel des Voyageurs and drink lemonade.

When Tony rushed out of the blue room, Andrée was still lying naked on the bed, and seemed in no hurry to move.

"Did you believe Nicolas capable of violence?"

"No."

All the same, he was a sick man, a broody introvert from childhood.

"That day in Triant, did you think he might be armed?"

He had not thought so.

"Was it your family you were anxious about?"

There was no common ground on which he and Diem could meet. They did not speak the same language. They were on different wave lengths.

He was pretending to work, with a pile of bills in front of him and a pencil in his hand. From time to time, for the sake of appearances, he would mark some item with a cross.

His daughter, sitting at his feet, was playing with a little toy car that had a wheel missing. Across the lawn, behind the white fence, some twenty yards from where he sat, he could see the road, and beyond it a meadow, and the backs of the village houses with their back yards and tiny gardens where the dahlias were in flower. In one, a huge black-centered yellow sunflower stood out vividly against a gray wall, next to a water tank.

Coming into the room, he had glanced automatically at the clock and noted that it was a quarter to six. At twenty past six, Gisèle came in to ask:

"Can I start serving dinner?"

"Could you wait another moment? I'd like to get this out of the way before dinner."

"I'm hungry, Pap!"

"I shan't be long, honey, but, if you like, you and *Maman* can start without me."

Now, suddenly, he was panic-stricken, but it was not the same panic as had driven him to bolt, clutching his clothes, up to the second floor of the inn. It was a physical anguish, a contraction of the heart, a sudden fever, which impelled him to get up and stand at the window.

His hand shook as he lit a cigarette. His legs seemed to give way under him.

A presentiment? He spoke of it, or rather was induced to speak of it by the psychiatrist, Professor Bigot.

"You had never felt anything like it before?"

"No. Not even when I had the car accident and was nearly killed. Even though that time, when I came to, sitting in a field without a scratch, I cried like a child."

"Were you afraid of Nicolas?"

"He always gave me the creeps."

"Even in your school days?"

Mercifully, just as the hands of the clock came together on the half-hour, the Citroën appeared at the top of the rise. They drove past the house, Andrée at the wheel with her husband beside her, but neither so much as glanced in his direction.

"Gisèle! I'm ready when you are."

"Right away. Go and wash your hands, Marianne."

They had sat down to dinner as usual: soup, a ham omelette, salad, a camembert, and, for dessert, apricots.

The windows overlooked the kitchen garden, planted and tended by his wife and himself, where Marianne would squat for hours pulling up weeds.

The runner beans had grown to the height of the poles. In the chicken run, behind the wire netting, some dozen white Leghorns were feeding, and moving shapes could be discerned in the darkness of the rabbit hutches.

On the surface, the day was drawing to its close like any other summer day. A warm breeze was coming in through the open window, with an occasional gust of cooler air. The fat blacksmith Didier was still hammering at the forge. The countryside was peaceful, quietly settling down for the night.

Professor Bigot's questions were nearly always unexpected:

"Did you feel, that night, that she was lost to you?"

"Who? Andrée?"

He was taken aback, for that was not how he had felt.

"You had been involved for eleven months in what it is surely no exaggeration to call a wild passion . . ."

That was not how he would have described it. He had

desired Andrée. After a few days without her, his memories of their tumultuous and searing hours together would grow to an obsession, memories of her smell, her breasts, her belly, her wantonness. Often, in bed beside Gisèle, he would lie awake for hours tormented by fantastic longings.

"What about going to the movies?"

"What day is it?"

"Thursday."

Gisèle was a little surprised. As a rule, they went to the movies once a week, in Triant, which was only ten miles away.

The rest of the week, Tony worked in his study, and his wife did the dishes and then came to sit with him, occupying herself with sewing or darning his socks. From time to time they would exchange a few words, generally about Marianne, who was to start school in October.

On occasion, they would sit outside in the back garden, watching the darkening sky, the moon above gray roofs and red roofs, the trees, dense somber masses, the rustle of their leaves almost stilled.

"What's on?"

"An American film. I saw the poster. I can't remember the title."

"If you feel like it. I'd better let the Molards know."

When they went out in the evening, one of the two Molard sisters always came in to keep an eye on Marianne.

Léonore was the elder of the two. She and her sister Marthe were both in their late thirties, but they might have been any age. The passing of the years would merely accentuate their old-maidishness.

They had round, moonlike faces, with smudged features. They wore identical dresses, coats, and hats, as though they were twins.

They went to holy communion every morning at seven o'clock—often they were the only communicants—and never missed vespers or evensong.

They were a great help to the Abbé Louvette, tending

the church, keeping the altar bright with flowers, looking after the cemetery, watching over the dying and laying out the dead.

They were dressmakers and could often be seen at their window, sewing, with their fat tabby cat dozing on the sill.

Marianne did not like them.

They had a nasty smell, she said.

It was true that there was a kind of mustiness about them, the mustiness of the dry goods shop and the church, with a whiff of the sickroom thrown in.

"They're ugly!"

"If they didn't come in to look after you, you'd be left all alone in the house."

"I'm not scared."

Gisèle smiled. He had never seen a smile quite like hers, the corners of her mouth twitching very slightly, as though she were trying to hold it in.

"Would you describe her as reserved?"

"Yes, your Honor."

"What exactly do you mean? Secretive, would you say?"

This endless wrangling over words!

"I wouldn't say that. She didn't like drawing attention to herself. She didn't want to be in the way, to be a nuisance. She asked nothing of anyone."

"Was she always like that—even as a girl?"

"I think so. For instance, after the movies or a dance, if she was thirsty she wouldn't mention it, to spare me the expense of buying her a drink."

"Did she have many friends?"

"Only one, a neighbor, an older woman. They used to go for long walks together."

"What was it about her that attracted you?"

"I don't know. I've never really thought about it."

"You felt safe with her, was that it?"

Tony, staring blindly into the Judge's face, was trying desperately to understand, to explain.

"I thought she would make . . ."

The right word eluded him.

"A good wife?"

That was not quite what he had meant, but he let it pass.

"Yes," he said.

"Did you love her?"

And since he made no answer:

"Did you want to go to bed with her? Were you intimate before marriage?"

"No."

"Did she attract you physically?"

He had married her, so she must have attracted him.

"What about *her*? Did she love you, do you think, or was it just that she wanted the status of a married woman?"

"I don't know. I think . . ."

Suppose he had asked the Judge that same question. What would his answer have been? They got on well together. What else was there to say? Gisèle was clean, hardworking, self-effacing, a homemaker, the right person in the right place.

He had been glad to get home that night, and, except for Andrée, he had never been seriously involved with a woman, apart from the odd casual encounter, when occasion offered.

"Are you asking me to believe that you never contemplated divorce?"

"It's the truth."

"Not even toward the end?"

"Never, at any time."

"Yet you told your mistress . . ."

Then, suddenly, before he knew what he was doing, he was hammering the desk with his fist, glowering at the little Judge, and shouting:

"Don't you see, I didn't say anything—not really! She did the talking! She was lying naked on the bed. I was standing naked in front of the mirror. We had just . . . But you know that as well as I do. At such times, words don't mean a thing. I scarcely heard what she was saying. Look! For a time, quite a long time, I was watching a bee . . ."

Up to this moment, he had forgotten the bee. Now he recalled it clearly, remembering that he had actually opened the shutters wider to let it out.

"I just nodded—I didn't mean to commit myself. I was thinking of other things."

"What, for instance?"

It was disheartening. He could not wait to get back to his police wagon, with its bars and padlocks, where no one bothered him with questions.

"I don't know."

Gisèle had gone next door to let the Molard sisters know, leaving him to put Marianne to bed. Afterwards, as always after being with Andrée in Triant, he had taken a shower and changed his underclothes. There were three bedrooms and a bathroom on the first floor.

"If we have more children, we can put the boys in one room and the girls in the other," Gisèle had said, when they were planning the house.

Six years later, there was still only Marianne, and the third bedroom had been in use only once, when Gisèle's parents came to Saint-Justin for a holiday.

They lived at Montsartois, five miles from Poitiers. Germain Coutet, handyman-plumber, was a thick-set gorilla of a man, with a ruddy complexion and resonant voice, who began every sentence with:

"I always say . . ."

or

"The way I see it . . ."

From the very first day, it was clear that he was envious of his son-in-law, of the bright, orderly office, the up-to-date kitchen, and, most of all, the silver-painted shed where the machinery was stored.

"I still think it's not right for a working man to set up on his own."

He uncorked his first bottle of red wine at eight in the morning, and drank unceasingly through the day. He was always to be found in one or another of the village bistros, and his thundering voice was audible from the street. He did not get drunk exactly, but always grew more dogmatic, even aggressive, as the day wore on.

"Which of us two goes fishing every Sunday? You or me? You see? Which of us gets three weeks' holiday with pay? And which of us is able to take it easy at the end of the day, because he doesn't have to bother his head with a lot of figures?"

His wife, fat and passive, with a distended stomach, always let him have his own way. Did this perhaps explain Gisèle's reserve?

Toward the end of their stay, there had been some altercations, and the Coutets never returned to Saint-Justin.

Having arranged for the Molard sisters to keep an eye on Marianne, Gisèle found time to put away the dishes and change at leisure. Her movements were light as a breath, serene and unhurried, so that it always seemed as though her work got done by magic.

One last good night to Marianne in the warm darkness of her room. The Molard ladies, downstairs, were already bent over their sewing.

"Have a good time."

It was the familiar routine. They had been through it so many times that they no longer noticed it.

The engine started up. Side by side in the front of the truck, they drove off. Behind them, in the village, a man was still digging his garden, but most people were sitting out of doors enjoying the cool of the evening. No one spoke, but one or two had their radios switched on indoors, and the sound echoed in empty rooms.

For a time, they drove in silence, thinking their own thoughts.

"Tell me, Tony . . ."

There was a long pause, and he felt a sharp pang, wondering what was coming.

"Don't you think Marianne has been looking rather peaked lately?"

The child had always been thin, with long arms and legs, and she had never had much color.

"I asked Dr. Riquet about it today, when I ran into him outside the grocer's . . ."

Had it surprised her to find Nicolas absent, and his mother in his place behind the counter? Had her curiosity been aroused?

"As he says, there's plenty of good fresh air here, but children need a change sometimes. He suggests taking her to the seaside—when we can manage it, of course—next year maybe?"

No one was more surprised than himself at the suddenness with which he made up his mind.

"Why not this year?" he countered.

She scarcely dared hope that he meant it. Since their move to Saint-Justin, they had not been able to afford a holiday, for the summer was Tony's busiest time. They had bought the land with their savings, but it would be some years yet before the house and the shed were paid for.

"Do you think we could manage it?"

In the first year of their marriage, when they were still living in Poitiers, they had taken their one and only holiday: a fortnight at Sables-d'Olonne. They had rented a furnished room from an old woman, and Gisèle had cooked their meals on an alcohol stove.

"I doubt if we'd be able to get in anywhere now. Everything is booked up by August."

"We'll go to a hotel. Do you remember that hotel right on the beach, not far from the pine woods?"

"The Roches Grises! No, the Roches Noires!"

They had dined there one night to celebrate Gisèle's

birthday, and had eaten enormous soles, and drunk muscatel, which had made them a little tipsy.

Tony was far from regretting his decision. It was a means of cutting himself off from Andrée and Nicolas, at least for a time.

"When were you thinking . . . ?"

"We'll talk about it later."

Before committing himself to a specific date, he would have to speak to his brother. It was, in fact, as a pretext for calling on Vincente that he was taking his wife to the movies. He drove past the Hôtel des Voyageurs without stopping, turned into the Rue Gambetta, and found a parking space a few yards from the Olympia. The street was crowded. By their clothes, their walk, and the way they looked at the lighted window displays, one could pick out the Parisians from the local people at a glance.

They always had the same seats, in the circle. In the intermission, after sitting through the news, a documentary, and a cartoon, he suggested:

"What do you say to a beer at Vincente's?"

The terrace was crowded, but Françoise found them a table, which she wiped with the cloth she carried over her arm.

"Beer for two, Françoise. Is my brother around?"

"At the desk, Monsieur Tony."

In the yellowish light of the café, men were playing cards, regulars whom Tony had seen hundreds of times in that same corner, with the same spectators crowding round them, commenting on the play.

"Well?"

His brother answered in Italian, which was unusual. They had both been born in France, and had spoken Italian only to their mother, who had never been able to learn French.

"I don't know exactly what happened, but I don't think there's anything to worry about. He was there, on the terrace . . ."

"I know. I saw him from the window."

"Ten minutes after you left, she came downstairs, as calm as you please, as though she hadn't a care in the world, and as she passed through the café she called out:

" 'Please thank your wife for me, Vincente!'

It came over loud and clear, for her husband's benefit. She had her handbag over her arm, and she went straight out of the door. Just as she was turning into the Rue Gambetta, she gave a start as though she had suddenly caught sight of Nicolas, and said:

" 'Well, of all things! What brings you here?'

She sat down at his table, and I couldn't hear any more."

"Was there a row, do you think?"

"It didn't look like it. At one point, in fact, she got her lipstick and compact out of her bag and sat there calmly touching up her make-up."

"What about him?"

"It's hard to tell with him. I mean, when have you ever seen him laugh? She got away with it, I'd say, but if I were in your shoes . . . Is Gisèle with you?"

"She's on the terrace."

Vincente went out to her. It was a mild, clear night. An express train roared through the station at top speed. In the Rue Gambetta, Gisèle laid her hand on her husband's arm, as she always did when they were out walking.

"Is your brother doing well?"

"It's been a good season. The tourist trade is building up nicely."

Vincente had not bought the building, only the business, as the former landlord, now living in retirement at La Ciotat, was unwilling to sell.

Starting from nothing, the two brothers had done well for themselves, leaving their early struggles a long way behind.

"Did you see Lucia?"

"No. She must have been in the kitchen. I didn't have time to go in and say hello."

Not for the first time, he felt a twinge of uneasiness. Although she knew he had been in Triant that afternoon, she did not ask him whether he had seen his brother then.

There were times when he wished she would ask questions, awkward though they might be. Was it conceivable that she should take no interest in his life outside the home, in spite of all she had learned about the business through helping him with his bookkeeping and monthly accounts?

Was it that she suspected nothing, or that she preferred to keep her suspicions to herself?

A bell shrilled in the movie, and they quickened their step as other patrons of the Olympia tumbled out of the little bar next door.

On their way home, in the dark interior of the car, driving through fields and farms, black and white in the beam of the headlights like the movie, he said abruptly:

"It's Thursday."

Thursday. Just saying it brought a flush to his cheek, evoking as it did Andrée's soft flesh, her sprawling legs, the dark patch of hair, the droplets of semen.

"We could go on Saturday. I'll phone the Roches Noires tomorrow. If they have two rooms . . . or we can make do with one, if they put up a small bed for Marianne . . ."

"What about the business?"

"I can always leave you and come back for an hour or two, if anything urgent crops up here."

It was going to be all right. He felt as though a great weight had been lifted from him, and realized for the first time how close he had come to disaster.

"We'll have two weeks, just the three of us, taking it easy on the beach."

Suddenly, thinking of his daughter, he was overpowered by a great wave of tenderness, and he hated himself for not having noticed how pale she was. He had failed his wife too, though in less obvious ways. Why, for instance, could he not pull up at the side of the road and, with his arms around her and his cheek against her breast, say to her:

"I do love you, you know."

This was what he wanted to do, what he had often wanted to do. But he had never done it. What had held him back? Shame? Fear of being misunderstood, of seeming to beg forgiveness for his sins?

He needed her. Marianne too needed her mother. And, under pressure from Andrée, he had repudiated them both. True, he had only been listening with half an ear, as he dabbed at his lip with the damp towel. But now their words re-echoed in his head with painful distinctness—he could even measure the pauses.

"You have a beautiful back."

How absurd! Imagine Gisèle going into ecstasies over his back or his shoulder blades!

"Do you love me, Tony?"

In the overheated, sex-laden atmosphere of that room, it had all sounded quite natural, whereas now, in the cool of the night, with the motor purring, the words, the tone of voice, seemed unreal. He had neatly evaded the issue, or so he thought at the time, with his insincere:

"I think so."

"Aren't you sure?"

Had he really imagined that this was some kind of game, blind to the fact that it was anything but that to her?

"Could you spend the rest of your life with me?"

She had repeated the question in a different form within minutes. Had she not asked it in that same room on previous occasions?

He could hear himself replying:

"Of course!"

He had tossed it off, in a lightheaded and lighthearted mood. She had been quick to detect a note of flippancy, and had refused to be put off:

"Can you be so sure? Aren't you a little afraid?"

He had played up to her, fool that he was:

"What is there to be afraid of?"

The conversation repeated itself in his head, word for word:

"Can't you just see us together, day after day?"

Day after day, she had said, not night after night, as though she intended that they should never leave their bed.

"We'd get used to it in time."

"Used to what?"

"To one another."

And here was Gisèle in the darkness beside him, her eyes on that same stretch of road, with those same trees and telegraph poles springing up out of the night and vanishing into it, all in a second. He wanted to take her hand, but dared not.

One day he spoke of it to Professor Bigot, who chose to see him in his cell rather than the prison infirmary. Although the warder brought a chair for him, he always sat on the edge of the bed.

"You loved your wife? Is that what you mean?"

"Yes," Tony said dully, with a helpless gesture.

"But there was some kind of barrier . . ."

He had never dreamed that life could be so complicated. What did the psychiatrist mean by a barrier? Marriage was like that, wasn't it?

"Why did you have no more children after Marianne?"

"I don't know."

"Did you not want them?"

Far from it! He would gladly have had six, a dozen, a houseful of children, as they had in Italy. As for Gisèle, she had talked of three, two boys and a girl, and they had done nothing to prevent it.

"Did you have frequent intercourse with your wife?"

"At the beginning, mostly."

He was perfectly open, not attempting to conceal anything. He had entered into the spirit of the thing, and was no less anxious than his various interrogators to arrive at the truth.

"For a while, when she was pregnant, of course . . ."

"Was that when you began going with other women?"

"I should have done that in any case."

"You mean, you couldn't do without it?"

"I don't know. Aren't all men the same?"

Professor Bigot was a man of about fifty, with a grown-up son studying in Paris, and a daughter recently married to a hematologist with whom she still worked as a laboratory assistant.

The psychiatrist, a rather slovenly man, wore cheap, loose-fitting suits, often with a button dangling, and he blew his nose incessantly, as though he had a permanent cold.

How to make him understand about that drive through the night? Nothing significant had occurred. He and Gisèle had scarcely exchanged a dozen words. He had been certain then that she knew nothing, nothing at any rate of what had happened that afternoon; in all probability, indeed, nothing at all of his relations with Andrée, though she might have got wind of some of his other escapades.

Yet, during that ten-mile drive, he had felt closer to her, more bound to her, than ever before. He was on the verge of saying:

"I need you, Gisèle."

He needed her at his side. He needed her trust.

"When I think of the years I've wasted because of you!"

It was not his wife's voice, but Andrée's, deep, a little hoarse, as though she had a lump in her throat. She was reproaching him for having gone away as a boy of sixteen, for having left the village to learn a trade elsewhere.

He had gone to Paris and had worked in a garage until his call-up for military service. He had never given her a thought. As far as he was concerned, she was that great, tall girl who lived in the Château, whose father was a local hero.

A cold, superior girl. A statue.

"What are you laughing at?"

For he was laughing, there in the car, or at least chuckling.

"I was remembering the film."

"Did you enjoy it?"

"Quite. They're all much the same."

A statue come to life in the strangest fashion, with far-seeing eyes, demanding:

"Tell me, Tony, if I were free . . . ?"

It was common knowledge that Nicolas was a sick man and would not make old bones, but it was a far cry from that to talking about him almost as though he were dead already! He had pretended not to have heard.

"Would you get your freedom too?"

The train whistle had shrilled deafeningly.

"What was that you said?"

"I asked you whether, in that event . . ."

What would his answer have been if he had not just then spotted Nicolas among the crowd pouring out of the station into the square?

The lights were on downstairs in the house. The Molard sisters, always with an eye on the clock, must have gathered up their sewing and put on their outdoor things, anxious to get home, because they were used to going to bed at nine o'clock if not earlier.

"I'll put the car away."

She got out and went into the house by the back door, while he drove the truck into the silver-painted shed, drawing up beside the monstrous machines, garish in their red and yellow paint.

He reached the house just as the two old maids were leaving.

"Good night, Tony."

"Good night."

Gisèle looked about her, to make sure nothing was left lying around.

"Would you like a drink, or a bite to eat?"

"No, thank you."

Later, he was to relive this moment. Had she perhaps been hoping for some word or sign from him? Was it possibly that she had sensed some threat hanging over them?

As a rule, when they came in from the movies, she went straight upstairs to listen for the sound of Marianne's breathing.

"I know it's silly," she had once admitted. "It's only when I've been out, I feel somehow that no harm can come to her when I'm there to protect her."

She had corrected herself:

"When *we're* there to protect her. When I'm away from her, she seems so vulnerable!"

She would bend low over Marianne, with a look of strain, until she could feel the child's breath on her cheek.

He could find no words. They undressed facing one another, as they did every night. Childbearing had broadened Gisèle's hips, but otherwise she was thin, with pale, sagging breasts.

How could he make other people see that he loved her when, for all that he needed desperately to pour out his heart to her that night, he had been incapable of making her see it?

"Good night, Tony."

"Good night, Gisèle."

It was she who always turned out the bedside lamp. The switch was on her side, because she was first up in the morning, before first light in the winter.

Was there a fractional hesitation, an unspoken hint that it was still not too late? He held his breath.

Click!

CHAPTER

3

He was not high-strung. That much they had discovered at Poitiers, after he had been subjected to test after test, first by the prison doctor, then by the psychiatrist, and finally by that extraordinary woman, the psychologist with the gypsy eyes, who seemed to him alternately ludicrous and frightening.

Indeed, what really amazed them, and possibly shocked them a little, was his placidity. At the trial, in fact, someone—the public prosecutor or one of the other lawyers—called it "callous and insolent indifference."

He did, it was true, hold himself in check most of the time, keeping up his guard, waiting on events rather than helping them forward.

Those two weeks at Sables-d'Olonne had been happy weeks, surely? Happy, and at the same time a little sad, because, every now and then, a sudden wave of anxiety would break over him, and his wife and child could not but sense it at times.

Like most summer visitors, they breakfasted on the terrace, Marianne in her red bathing suit, and by nine o'clock all three were down on the beach, spreading out their things on the patch of sand which, from the first, they had appropriated for themselves.

It had taken them no more than a couple of days to fall in with the routine and rituals of the place, getting to know their neighbors in the dining room of the Roches Noires, exchanging smiles with the old lady and gentleman at the table opposite, who had taken a great fancy to Marianne. And she in her turn was fascinated by the old man's beard.

"If he doesn't watch out, he'll get his beard in the soup!" Night after night she watched him, convinced that sooner or later this was bound to happen.

Morning and afternoon, the same people were there under the beach umbrellas all around them: the blonde who, having anointed herself lingeringly all over with sun-tan oil, lay on her stomach all day, shoulder straps dangling, reading; the people from Paris, with their ill-mannered brats, who put out their tongues at Marianne and shoved her about in the water.

Gisèle, unaccustomed to idleness, was knitting a pale blue jersey for Marianne to wear at school, and her lips moved as she counted the stitches.

Had this seaside holiday really been such a good idea after all? He played with Marianne, taking her into the water up to her waist, and, with his hand under her chin, gave her swimming lessons. He also tried to teach his wife, but the minute she was out of her depth she lost her head and groped for him, flailing the water with her hands. Once, swept under by a sudden wave, she had given him a look in which he thought he could detect fear. Not fear of the sea. Fear of him.

For hours at a stretch, he seemed contented and relaxed, playing ball with Marianne, walking with her to the end of the pier. Together, the three of them explored the narrow streets of the town, visited the cathedral, took photographs of the fishing boats at anchor and of the Sablais women, with their pleated skirts and varnished clogs, in the fish market.

There were some ten thousand people leading much the same kind of life, and whenever there was a storm they all hastily gathered up their things and swarmed into hotels and cafés.

At times he was withdrawn and remote. For what reason? Was it perhaps that he felt ashamed of having run away from Saint-Justin, where Andrée might be signaling to him in vain?

"As to the signal, Monsieur Falcone . . ."

After a few weeks at Poitiers, he could no longer remember which questions had been put by Judge Diem and which by the psychiatrist. Sometimes they asked the same questions, in other words or in a different context. Did they collate his various statements before each interview, in the hope that he would trip himself up in the end?

"When was it decided that your mistress would signal to you in this way?"

"That first night."

"In September, you mean, after the roadside encounter?"

"Yes."

"Who suggested it?"

"She did, as I told you before. She wanted something more convenient than the edge of a wood, and my brother's place was the obvious choice."

"And the towel? Was that her idea too?"

"Her first suggestion was that she would put something in the shop window, where I could spot it easily."

There were two display windows, crammed with groceries, dishcloths, aprons, boots. The Despierre shop was in the main street, almost next door to the church. One had to pass it to get from one end of the village to the other.

Inside, it was dark. The two counters were cluttered up with goods. There were casks and crates stacked against the walls, and hams hanging from the ceiling. And rows of shelves, stacked high with jars and bottles, drill trousers and wicker baskets.

Of all the smells associated with his childhood, the smell of this place was the one he remembered best, impregnated with kerosene as it was in those days, when the outlying farms and hamlets were without electricity.

"What did she propose putting in the window?"

"A package of starch, she thought. Then it struck her that her husband might easily move it without her knowledge while she was otherwise occupied, in the kitchen perhaps."

How could they imagine that, just by seeing him for two or three hours a day over a few weeks or even months, they could begin to understand lives so different from their own? Not only his life and Gisèle's, but Andrée's, Madame Despierre's, Madame Formier's, the life of the village, the comings and goings between Saint-Justin and Triant. To explain the blue room to them, let alone anything else, he would need . . .

"In the end, it was decided that on Thursdays, if she was going to be able to meet me at the inn, she would hang a towel out of the window to dry."

The window of their bedroom, hers and Nicolas's. For they did share a room. Above the shop were three narrow windows with guardrails. One could see into the shadowy bedroom from the street, a brownish wall with a lithograph in a black and gold frame.

"So that, every Thursday morning . . ."

"I went past the house."

Who was to say that, while he was lounging on the beach in his bathing trunks, Andrée had not signaled for help, leaving the towel flapping on the rail day after day? True, he had seen them in the Citroën on their return from Triant, but as to their state of mind, he was completely in the dark.

"I was wondering, Monsieur Falcone, whether, when you suggested this holiday to your wife . . ."

"It was just after she'd mentioned that Marianne was pale."

"I'm aware of that. Let's say you saw your chance and leaped at it. An excellent opportunity to lull her suspicions, to reassure her, by playing the devoted husband and father, the family man? What do you say to that?"

"You've got it all wrong."

"Do you still maintain that your object was to get away from your mistress?"

How he detested that word, but he had to put up with it.

"More or less."

"You had already made up your mind not to see her again?"

"I hadn't made up my mind about anything, not really."

"In the months that followed, did you see her at all?"

"No."

"What about her? Did she not put out the signal?"

"I don't know. From then on, I never went near her house on a Thursday morning."

"And all this for no better reason than that, one afternoon, you saw her husband walk across from the station to the hotel for a glass of lemonade on the terrace? Yet here, according to your own story, was the woman with whom you had known ecstasies of physical love such as you had never dreamed of? In your own words, if I'm not mistaken, it was a revelation."

It was true, though he could not remember putting it in quite those words. There were times, during their stay at Sables-d'Olonne, when, resist it as he might, the blue room haunted him, and he clenched his teeth with longing. At times, he was touchy and unreasonable, snapping at Marianne for the least thing; or he was abstracted, staring at nothing with glazed eyes.

Gisèle would give the child a warning look as though to say:

"Take no notice. Your father has a lot on his mind."

Did it make things any better for them that a second later he would be a different man, gentle, long-suffering, affectionate almost to excess?

"Would you describe yourself as ambitious, Monsieur Falcone?"

It needed thinking about. It was not a thing that he had ever asked himself. Were there really people whose lives were devoted to self-examination, to gazing at themselves in a mirror, as it were?

"It depends on what you mean by ambitious. When I was twelve, I wanted a bicycle, so I took any job that came along, after school and in the holidays. When I was older, I wanted a motor-bike, and I went to Paris. When I married Gisèle, I began thinking about a business of my own. My firm in Poitiers imported tractors and so on from America. They came in sections, and we assembled them. It was a good living."

"Your brother followed much the same course, didn't he—dabbling in one thing and another, and eventually deciding to set up on his own?"

Was there any real analogy between the two cases?

The suggestion had come not from Judge Diem but from Professor Bigot, who spoke slowly, as though he were thinking aloud.

"I wonder whether the fact that you were the children of Italian parents, foreigners in a French village . . . your father was a bricklayer, I believe . . . ?"

For a whole afternoon, the Judge had interrogated the old man, Falcone, who had been summoned from his cottage in La Boisselle.

"What do you know about your father?"

"He came originally from a very poor Piedmontese village, Larina, about twenty-five miles from Vercelli. Up there in the mountains, there just isn't enough food to go around, so most of the boys emigrate, as my father did, at fourteen or fifteen. He came to France with a working party to build a tunnel, I don't know which one, but it was somewhere near Limoges. Afterwards, he moved about, working on other tunnels."

It was hard to talk about Angelo Falcone, whom everyone at Saint-Justin called Old Angelo, for he was not quite like other men.

"He traveled all over France, north, south, east, and west, and, in the end, settled in La Boisselle."

The strangeness of the place lingered in Tony's memory. La Boisselle, situated some two miles from Saint-Justin, was a disused monastery built of stone blocks taken from the ancient fortress which had originally stood on the site, and even now, overgrown with weeds, there were sections of the old walls still standing, and parts of the moat, full of stagnant water, where he used to catch frogs.

The monks were probably an agricultural community; the central precinct was surrounded by old buildings—stables, workshops, and wine presses.

The Coutant family occupied the greater part, with a dozen or so cows, some sheep, two cart horses, and an old billy goat that chewed tobacco. There were a few habitable buildings which they did not use themselves, and these were let to tenants.

They formed a little heterogeneous community, comprising the Falcones, a Czech family, and an Alsatian couple with eight children.

"Your father was getting on in years by the time you were born."

"He was forty-three or so when he went home to his village in Piedmont, and brought my mother back with him."

"You mean, he felt the time had come for him to marry, and he went back to his own people in search of a wife?"

"That was it, more or less, I imagine."

His mother's maiden name had been Maria Passaris, and when she came to France she was twenty-two years old.

"Was it a happy marriage?"

"I never heard them quarrel."

"Your father kept on working as a bricklayer?"

"It was his trade. There was nothing else he could do or wanted to do."

"You were the first child, and your brother Vincente was born three years later."

"And then there was my sister Angelina."

"Does she live at Saint-Justin?"

"She's dead."

"You mean, she died in childhood?"

"At six months. My mother had gone to Triant, I don't know what for. Before she came to France, she'd never been away from her village. Here, because she couldn't speak the language, she seldom left the house. That day in Triant, she must have got out on the wrong side of the train by mistake. She had the baby in her arms, and they were run down by an express train."

"How old were you?"

"Seven. My brother was four."

"So it was your father who brought you up?"

"Yes. When he got home from work, he did the housework and the cooking. I didn't know him well enough to be able to tell whether he was much changed after the accident."

"What do you mean?"

"You know quite well what I mean. You've talked to him, haven't you?"

Tony was on the defensive now.

"Yes."

"Well, what did you make of him? Are the local people right? Is he, as they say, simple?"

The Saint-Justin people did not say "simple-minded."

The old-fashioned "simple" was good enough for them. As to Bigot, he was obviously embarrassed, and contented himself with a vague gesture.

"I wonder if you were able to get anything out of him. As for my brother and me, he wouldn't say a word to us for years on end, except when he had to. He's seventy-eight now, and he lives alone in the house where we were born, and still does a few odd bricklaying jobs here and there.

"Vincente and I both offered him a home with us, but he wouldn't hear of it. There's only one thing he really cares about, and that's his miniature village. He's been building it in his little bit of a garden for the last twenty years. The church is barely three foot high, but it's complete down to the smallest detail.

"It's got an inn, and a town hall, and a bridge over a running stream, and a water mill, and every year he puts up a couple of new houses. Apparently, it's an exact scale-model of Larina, where he and my mother were born."

He was keeping his real feelings to himself. His father was a bovine, slow-witted man, who, until he was well past forty, had lived alone and grown accustomed to solitude. Tony could understand why he had gone back to Larina to look for a wife.

Angelo Falcone had, in his way, loved Maria Passaris, who was young enough to be his daughter. But he had given no outward sign of it, for words and demonstrations of affection were foreign to his nature.

After losing his wife and baby daughter, Angelo Falcone withdrew into himself for good, and it was then that he began building the quaint toy village in the garden.

Suddenly, with conviction, Tony said:

"He's not mad!"

Some people, he knew, thought otherwise, including perhaps Professor Bigot himself.

"I'm not mad either!"

"There's never been any question of that."

"Then why go on and on? How often have we been

through it all before? Six times? Seven? Is it because the papers are saying I'm a monster?"

But this was in the future. Staying at the Roches Noires, they virtually lived on the beach. There was a taste of sand in their mouths, and they were always finding sand in their beds and their pockets.

It rained only twice in the whole fortnight. The sun permeated their skin and dazzled their eyes until their heads swam, especially when they had stared too long at the white-crested waves rolling in slowly, one after another, from the open sea, scattering a brilliant shower of droplets as they broke.

Marianne got a touch of sunstroke. After a day or two, Tony was so brown that when he undressed at night the shape of his bathing trunks showed white on his skin, like a transfer. Only Gisèle, who kept to the shade of the beach umbrella, looked no different.

What meanwhile was happening at Saint-Justin, in the Despierres' gloomy shop? And, at night, in the bedroom, where Andrée and Nicolas undressed face to face?

Had she hung the towel with the pink border over the window bar, like a storm signal? Was it not probable that Nicolas's stony-faced mother had borne down on them from across the garden, to take things into her own hands, to get even at last with her daughter-in-law?

How could these people at Poitiers, policemen, magistrates, doctors, not to mention the formidable lady psychologist, hope to get at the truth, when they had so little knowledge of people like the Despierres, the Formiers, and the many others who had played a significant part?

And, for that matter, how much did they know of Tony? Somewhat less, one would think, than he did himself.

Madame Despierre was, without doubt, Saint-Justin's most respected citizen. She commanded greater respect and awe than the mayor himself, rich cattle-dealer though he was. In this village, where generation after generation of men and women went to the one school, and all the inhabitants had known their contemporaries since childhood, there were nevertheless few who ventured to call her "Germaine," let alone use the familiar *tu* when speaking to her. She was Madame Despierre to everybody.

Though his memory must be at fault—for she was only in her early thirties when he was first sent into the shop by his parents to buy groceries—he remembered her with gray hair, no less gray than it was now. Behind the counter, wearing a gray smock, she had seemed all gray, except for the chalk-white oval of her face.

He remembered her husband, a runt of a man in pince-nez, with an irresolute manner and a timid expression. He too wore a gray smock which flapped about his ankles.

At times he would be seen to stagger, and then his wife would drag him into the room behind the shop and shut the door, while the customers exchanged knowing glances and shook their heads.

Tony had heard talk of fits long before he understood that Despierre was an epileptic, and that behind that closed door he was on the floor in a convulsion, his teeth clenched, his body contorted, his chin spattered with foam.

He remembered his funeral procession, which he and the other schoolchildren had followed in single file, all except Nicolas, who, as chief mourner, walked beside his mother.

They were said to be very rich and very mean. In addition to a number of houses in the village, they owned two large farms, leased to tenant farmers, not to mention the hamlet of La Guipotte.

"Tell me, Monsieur Falcone, why did you choose to settle in Saint-Justin after an absence of more than ten years?"

Had he not told them why? They had repeated the same questions so many times over that he was no longer sure. He had very likely contradicted himself more than once, since he himself did not know all the whys and wherefores.

"Perhaps it was because of my father."

"You saw very little of him."

About once a week. Old Angelo had come to the house a couple of times, and had been manifestly ill at ease. He was overawed by Gisèle, whom he regarded as a stranger. Tony, realizing this, had got into the habit of calling at La Boisselle of a Saturday evening.

The door was left open, the lamp unlit. Frogs could be heard croaking in the stagnant pools, and the two men sat together in their wicker chairs not saying a word.

"And then there was my brother in Triant."

"It had nothing to do with Andrée? You're quite sure of that?"

"Not again!"

"You were aware of her marriage to your school friend, Nicolas?"

No! It had come as a complete surprise. The Despierres and the Formiers were worlds apart, and although the two mothers were more or less of an age, they had nothing in common.

While Madame Despierre was a typical *nouveau riche* of peasant stock, the wife of Doctor Formier, like so many of her kind, was a provincial *bourgeoise,* fallen on hard times but still resolutely keeping up appearances.

Her father, Monsieur Bardave, a notary at Villiers-le-Haut, had been, like his father and grandfather before him, on friendly terms with the local gentry—a frequent guest at their bridge and shooting parties—and brought up to regard himself as one of them.

He had left his children penniless. Doctor Formier, too, had been unable to provide more than a pittance for his wife and daughter. Though they lived in the Château, and dressed like townspeople, they did not always have enough to eat.

Which of the two, Madame Despierre or Madame Formier, had instigated this strange union? The grocer's widow, driven by social ambition, or possibly even spite? The *bourgeoise,* bent on securing her daughter's future, believing that it would not be very long before the bride found herself a rich widow?

"It would appear that Nicolas suffered a good deal from bullying at school."

Another of those half-truths. It was inevitable that a sickly boy, prone to intermittent stomach-ache, unable to join in games with the others, should be a target for derision. The tough boys called him a sissy, a scaredy-cat, a cry-baby tied to his mother's apron strings. Unable to defend himself, he made matters worse by tattling to the headmaster.

Tony had not been among his tormentors. Not perhaps because he was better-natured than the others, but rather because, as a foreigner, he was himself something of a misfit.

On two occasions, once during break and once as they were coming out of school, he had defended Nicolas against his attackers, though at the time he had been unaware of the boy's infirmity.

His first seizure, when he was twelve and a half, had occurred without warning, in the middle of a class. He had fallen with a thud on the wooden floorboards, and, as all heads turned at the sound, the master had banged his desk with a ruler.

"Stay where you are, all of you!"

It was spring. The chestnut trees in the playground were in flower. There had been an infestation of cockchafers that year, and the boys had been fascinated by them, as they flew clumsily about the classroom, colliding with walls and windowpanes.

In spite of the master's prohibition, the children gaped at Nicolas, all of them ashen with fright, and several feeling sick. It was a terrifying experience.

"Out into the playground, all of you!"

This had been the signal for a general stampede, but a few boys, bolder than the rest, crept up to the window and saw the master stuffing his handkerchief into Nicolas's mouth.

Madame Despierre was summoned in haste by a panting boy, and arrived wearing her familiar gray smock.

"What are they doing?" the other children asked those gathered at the window.

"Nothing. They've left him lying there. He must be going to die."

More than one boy had an uneasy conscience that day.

"Did he choke on something he ate, do you think?"

"No, it's a fit. They say his father had them too."

"Is it catching?"

After a time—a quarter of an hour or half an hour later, was it?—Madame Despierre came out, leading her son by the hand. Nicolas looked dazed, but otherwise much as usual.

He had never had another fit at school. As a rule, Tony gathered, he could feel an attack coming on, sometimes several days beforehand, and his mother kept him at home.

It was never mentioned in the presence of Madame Despierre and was a forbidden subject in the shop. Though no one could quite say why, it was generally felt that there was something shameful about this illness.

Nicolas had not gone to the senior school in Triant, and he had been exempted from military service. He had never set foot in a dance hall or owned a bicycle or motor scooter, and he did not drive the Citroën himself.

Sometimes he would not utter a word for a week at a time, but would stare at people with somber, mistrustful eyes, as though he suspected them of wishing him ill. He drank neither wines nor spirits, and could digest nothing but invalid food.

Had not the thought of him disquieted Tony, that September evening, as he looked at Andrée, half naked by the roadside?

"Did you never, even half consciously, envy him his wealth?"

He shrugged. True enough, before he knew about his illness, before that first fit at school, he had envied him, as any child would: because of the jars of rainbow-colored sweets, the biscuits in the glass-topped containers which, he imagined, Nicolas could dip into whenever he pleased, whereas he could afford only the cheapest sweets, and even those only as a rare treat.

"When you learned of the marriage, did you not feel that he had, in a sense, bought Andrée, or rather that his mother had bought her for him?"

Possibly. On first hearing that she had married a man whom she certainly could not love, he had despised "the statue" a little. On reflection he had felt sorry for her. Though he too had sometimes gone hungry as a child, it was different for someone brought up in a château, with a position to keep up.

What the marriage settlement had been, he did not know, but the two mothers being what they were, there must have been some hard bargaining on both sides. They lived almost opposite one another. The Château was to the right of the church, next to the presbytery. Across the square, on the corner of the Rue Neuve, was Despierre's Grocery, backing on the town hall and the school.

It had been a splendid white wedding, followed by a banquet at the inn. People still talked about it. The couple had not gone away for a honeymoon but had spent their wedding night in the room over the shop which they had occupied ever since.

Madame Despierre had moved into a bungalow overlooking the garden, and was thus living within twenty yards of her son and daughter-in-law.

At first the two women worked together in the shop, and the mother-in-law cooked for them as before. A local woman, an old crone who wore men's shoes, came in every day to do the housework.

All eyes were upon them, and it was soon observed that

Madame Despierre and Andrée never addressed a word to one another except in the matter of business.

Before long the older woman was going home for meals, and after a few months she was no longer seen in the shop or the house, though her son never missed going across the garden to see her two or three times a day.

Did this mean that Andrée had triumphed, having planned from the start to elbow out her mother-in-law by degrees?

Eight times he had been with her in the blue room, but had never thought to ask her about it, perhaps because he preferred to shut his eyes to that side of Andrée's life, and to think of her as he knew her best, naked and unfettered.

He had a confused sense of being in possession of some vital knowledge, which he could not put into words. It had to do, he believed, with the words spoken on August second, that notorious August second which, in his innocence, he had simply lived through, with no inkling of the probing and sensation-mongering to come, the newspaper headlines and front-page spreads.

A reporter on one of the great Paris newspapers had coined a phrase which was to be taken up by all the rival papers: "The Frenzied Lovers."

"Would you like to spend the rest of your life with me?"

"Of course," he had replied.

He did not deny it. It was he who had told the Judge of the conversation. It was the way it was said that counted, the tone of voice. He had not meant it. The words were without substance. In the blue room, everything was insubstantial, unreal. Or rather, it had a reality of its own, distinct and separate, incomprehensible to anyone outside.

He had tried to explain this to the psychiatrist. He had thought at the time that he was getting through, but a little later Bigot made some remark which showed that he had not understood in the least.

If Tony had seriously considered living with her, he would not have said:

"Of course."

He had no idea what he would have said, but he knew that he would have expressed it differently. Andrée had not been taken in, why otherwise should she have pressed him further?

"Can you be so sure? Aren't you a little afraid?"

"What is there to be afraid of?"

"Can't you just see us together, day after day?"

"We'd get used to it in time!"

"Used to what?"

Was this the way people talked in real life? Would he ever have said such things to Gisèle? It was a game to her as much as to him, as she lay there spread-eagled, satiated.

"To one another."

That was just it. It was only in bed, in the blue room, redolent of their bodies, of their frenzied love-making, as the journalist put it, that they were anything at all to one another.

They had never been anything to each other outside that room, except for that first time when they had made love among the long grass and nettles on the edge of Sarelle Wood.

"If you didn't love her, how do you explain . . . ?"

What did they mean by love? Professor Bigot claimed to be a scientist: he ought to be ready with a definition. His daughter had recently married. What kind of love did she feel for her husband?

And the little Judge, Monsieur Diem, with his tufts of unruly hair? His wife had just given birth to their first child, and doubtless, like most young fathers, like Tony himself, the Judge sometimes got up in the night to give the baby its bottle. What kind of love did he feel for his wife?

To make them understand, he would have had to tell them things that one does not talk about, putting into words feelings such as he had known at Sables-d'Olonne.

"Why did you choose to go there, rather than to some seaside resort in the Vendée or Brittany?"

"Because that's where we went the first year we were married."

"So your wife may have thought you were prompted by nostalgia, that you were proposing a kind of sentimental pilgrimage? Isn't that just how you would have behaved if your motive had been to allay her suspicions?"

It made his blood boil, but he gritted his teeth and said nothing. It was useless to protest.

How could he tell them about that last day by the sea? First, the morning . . . stretched out under the beach umbrella with eyes half closed, he took a quick look at his wife every now and then as she sat in the striped swing-chair, intent on finishing the light blue pullover.

"What are you thinking about?" she had asked him.

"About you."

"What about me?"

"That it was a lucky day for me when I met you."

It was not the whole truth. Behind him, Marianne was looking at a book, making up captions for the pictures, pretending she could read. The sound of her voice prompted the thought that not so many years from now she would fall in love, marry, and leave them, to share her life with a man.

A stranger, in fact, because it takes more than a month or two, or even a year or two, for a husband and wife really to get to know one another.

This was what had led him on to Gisèle. He had been observing her, serious and contented, at her knitting, and was himself trying to guess her thoughts when she asked him what he was thinking.

The fact was that he had no idea what she felt about him. What did she make of him, he wondered, of his looks, his manners, his actions?

They had been married seven years. He tried to picture

them together in the future. Little by little, they would grow old. Marianne would grow up. They would see her married, then, one day, she would announce that she was pregnant, and, once the child was born, its father would take precedence over them.

And that, surely, would be the crowning moment of their lives, the moment when after long years of propinquity, of learning about one another, of accumulating memories—the memories of this morning among them—he and Gisèle would love one another in the fullest sense.

His wife must have been thinking along the same lines, for a little while later she said, speaking very softly:

"I can't get used to the idea of Marianne as a schoolgirl."

And he had got as far as marrying her off!

The child was quick to respond to the indulgent holiday atmosphere, and kept her father on the go. That afternoon, especially, she did not give him a minute's peace.

The tide was low, the sea a long way off, out of reach. For over an hour, Marianne had him helping her build an enormous sand castle, or rather she gave the orders and he did the work, and like old Angelo in his garden, she kept thinking of something more she wanted; earthworks, a moat, a drawbridge.

"Now let's go and look for shells to pave the courtyard and the paths."

"Watch out for the sun. Put your hat on."

They had bought her a Venetian gondolier's hat at a market stall.

Gisèle had been afraid to add:

"Don't wear your father out!"

Each carrying a red pail, father and daughter had combed the beach from end to end, with heads down, peering for the glint of a shell in the brownish sand, occasionally tripping over the legs of a sunbather or just escaping being hit by a beach ball.

Had he felt that he was fulfilling a duty, doing penance for some sin of omission or commission? He honestly did not know. What he did know about that walk in the sun with his daughter, punctuated by the sound of her sharp little voice, was that it had been at the same time touching and painful.

He was at once happy and sad. Not on account of Andrée and Nicolas. He could not remember having given them a thought. Happy and sad as life itself was the way he would have chosen to express it.

They had walked almost up to the Casino, close enough to hear the music. They had come a long way from the beach, or so it seemed to them as they started back, to Marianne especially, who was beginning to drag her feet.

"Are you tired?"

"A bit."

"Would you like a ride on my back?"

She had laughed, showing the gap in her teeth.

"I'm too big."

It had been her favorite game when she was two or three. That was how he had always carried her up to bed at night.

"People would laugh at you," she said a little wistfully.

He had hoisted her up, and because she clung to his hair with both hands, he walked along with a pail in each hand.

"Am I too heavy?"

"No."

"Is it true that I'm skinny?"

"Who said you were?"

"Roland."

Roland was the blacksmith's son.

"He's a month younger than I am, and he weighs forty-nine pounds. I only weigh forty-two pounds. I got weighed on the grocer's scales, just before we came away."

"Boys are heavier than girls."

"Why?"

Gisèle watched them coming toward her. She looked thoughtful and perhaps a shade anxious. He put his daughter down on the sand.

"Help me put down the shells."

"That's enough, Marianne. Your father is here for a rest. He'll be back at work the day after tomorrow."

"I didn't ask him to carry me. He wanted to."

They exchanged looks.

"It's her last day, too," he said indulgently, making light of it.

She said no more, but gave him a look that plainly said, "Thank you."

Thank you for what? For having given up two weeks of his life to them?

Surely it was the most natural thing in the world?

CHAPTER

4

He was sometimes kept waiting in the passage outside the Judge's door, on a bench, handcuffed, between two police guards, not regular warders whom he knew, but different ones each time.

He no longer felt humiliated, no longer raged inwardly. He watched the people, as they came and went, prisoners and witnesses waiting outside other doors, robed lawyers with great flapping sleeves like wings, and did not flinch when some stared at him with avid curiosity and others deliberately turned their backs on him.

Inside the Judge's room, his handcuffs were taken off, and at a sign from the Magistrate the guards retired. Diem, apologizing for having kept him waiting, held out his silver cigarette case. It was a well-established ritual.

The paintwork and furnishings were shabby and none too clean, as in a railway station or government office, with greenish walls, a black marble mantelpiece supporting a black clock which had stopped at five minutes to twelve, years ago probably.

Sometimes the Judge would begin by saying:

"I don't think I shall be needing you, Monsieur Trinquet."

The clerk, who had a brown mustache, would gather up his papers and leave, to get on with his work in heaven knows what corner of the building, and this meant that the interview would not be concerned strictly with questions of fact.

"I take it you understand why I find it necessary to put questions to you which may seem to have no bearing on the case? You must see that I have to acquaint myself with your background, to fill in the gaps in your personal file, so to speak."

He could hear the noises of the town and, through open windows across the street, could see people going about their daily business in their own homes. With the Judge, Tony was free to get up from his chair, to stretch his legs whenever he felt like it, to pace up and down the room, or stand for a few minutes at the window watching the people in the street.

"It would be helpful, for instance, if I could form a picture of your normal working day."

"Well, of course, it varies from day to day and from season to season. A lot of my time is taken up with the various fairs and markets in my area."

Realizing suddenly that he had been using the present tense, Tony, with a faint smile, corrected himself:

"Was taken up, I should say. I went to most fairs within a radius of about thirty miles, including Virieux, Ambasse, and Chiron. Do you want a complete list?"

"That won't be necessary."

"On fair days, I always made an early start, sometimes as early as five in the morning."

"Did your wife get breakfast for you?"

"She made a point of it. Besides going to the fairs, I

spent a lot of time demonstrating machinery to farmers, and doing repairs and maintenance. And some days, customers would call on me, and we would talk business in the shed."

"Let's take an average day."

"Gisèle would get up first, at six o'clock."

She would creep out of bed without a sound and tiptoe to the door carrying her salmon-pink dressing gown. A few minutes later he would hear her below stoking the boiler. She would then go into the garden to throw a handful of meal to the hens and feed the rabbits.

At about half-past six he would come down, having hastily run a comb through his thick hair, but still unwashed and unshaven. In the kitchen, the breakfast things were already set out. There was no need of a cloth, because the table had a formica top. There were only the two of them; Marianne was never awake at that hour. They let her sleep as late as she liked.

"Until she started school, that is. Then we had to wake her at seven."

"Did she have to be taken to school?"

"Only for the first couple of days."

"Did you take her?"

"No, my wife did. It was convenient for her, because she was able to get what she wanted in the village at the same time. Ordinarily she went in at about nine, to get what she needed from the baker, the butcher, and the grocer."

"The grocer? Was that Despierre's?"

"It's virtually the only decent grocer's in Saint-Justin."

Inside the shop, with its low ceiling, there were always at least half a dozen women standing about gossiping while waiting to be served, especially in the morning. He had once compared the shop to a vestry, though he could not remember why.

"Did you ever do any shopping for your wife?"

"Only in Triant or one of the other towns, if she happened to need something they didn't keep in the village."

He realized that there was more to these seemingly innocuous questions than met the eye, but this did not prevent him from answering them as truthfully and accurately as he could.

"You never shopped at Despierre's?"

"Once in a couple of months, maybe. I remember going one morning when my wife was cleaning house, and another time when she had flu."

"When did she clean the house?"

"On Saturday."

As with most other people, Monday was washing day; Tuesday or Wednesday—depending on the weather and how long the linen took to dry—was ironing day. This was common practice in the village, and there were days when there was not a garden or courtyard without its clothesline hung with pegged garments and linen.

"What time did the mail come?"

"We didn't have delivery. The train called at Saint-Justin at seven minutes past eight in the morning, and the mailbags were taken straight to the post office. Being right at the far end of the village, we were last on the postman's round and wouldn't have got our letters till midday. It suited me better to collect them from the post office. I often got there before they'd finished sorting. When I had the time I waited, otherwise they kept my mail for me."

"We'll come back to that. Did you use to walk?"

"As a rule. I only took the car when I had business outside the village."

"How often would that be? Every other day? Twice a week?"

"More like every other day, except in the middle of winter. There was always much less traveling around for me in winter."

There was so much that they did not understand: the details of his work, the rhythm of the seasons, the cycle of cultivation. For instance, when they got home from Sables-d'Olonne, the fairs were in full swing. Then, immediately afterwards, there was the grape harvest, followed by the autumn plowing, so that, one way and another, he was overwhelmed with work.

That first Thursday, he had deliberately avoided going to the Rue Neuve to see whether Andrée had hung the towel out of the window. He had already explained this to Judge Diem, who, however, had his own views on the subject:

"You had decided not to see her again?"

"It would be wrong to say that I had *decided* anything."

"Were you perhaps influenced by the fact that she had communicated with you by other means?"

This time, he had been at fault, and had realized it as soon as he opened his mouth. Too late. The words, already formed, were out.

"I had no communication from her."

It was not for his own sake that he had lied, nor, consciously at least, for Andrée's, but from a kind of loyalty or manly decency.

During this interview, Tony remembered, it was raining, and Monsieur Trinquet, the clerk, was in his place at the end of the table.

"You returned home from Sables-d'Olonne with your wife and daughter on August 17th. On the first Thursday after that, contrary to your usual practice, you did not go to Triant. Was that because you were afraid of a meeting with Andrée Despierre?"

"It may have been, though 'afraid' isn't quite the word for it."

"To proceed: the following Thursday you had an appointment at your brother's inn with a Monsieur Félicien Hurlot, secretary of a farming co-operative. You lunched with your client and then drove straight back to Saint-Justin, without so much as setting foot in the market place. Was this also because you wished to avoid the risk of finding yourself face to face with your mistress?"

What answer could he give? The truth was that he himself did not know. During all those weeks, he had been numb, confused, incapable of self-analysis, still less of making any kind of decision.

What he could truthfully affirm was that he had thought of Andrée not as he had known her in the past months, but almost as a stranger, and that he had spent more and more time at home, as though impelled to remain close to his wife and child.

"September 4th."

While the Judge was speaking, Tony was searching his memory for anything significant attaching to that date.

"On September 5th, you received the first letter."

He flushed.

"What do you mean? I don't know of any letter."

"It was addressed to you in block capitals and postmarked Triant."

"I don't remember."

It was too late to retract now, he felt. There was nothing for it but to keep on lying.

"Monsieur Bouvier, the postmaster, made some remark to you about this particular letter."

Diem, extracting a paper from the file, read:

" 'I said:

" 'That looks to me like an anonymous letter, Tony. That's how anonymous letters are always addressed.' Doesn't that recall anything to you?"

He shook his head, abashed: he was so bad at telling lies, blushing, staring blankly into space so that his eyes might not betray his discomfiture.

The letter, though unsigned, was, nevertheless, not strictly speaking, anonymous. Like the envelope, it was written in block letters, and was very brief:

"Everything is fine. Don't worry."

"You see, Monsieur Falcone, I am convinced that the person who wrote that letter and posted it in Triant disguised the handwriting to conceal his or her identity, not from you but from the postmaster. It follows, therefore, that the writer was someone from Saint-Justin, someone whose normal handwriting would be familiar to Monsieur Bouvier. The following week, there was a further letter, in outward appearance identical with the first.

"The postmaster made a joke of it. 'Well! Well!' he said. 'Maybe I was on the wrong track. This begins to look more like an affair of the heart.' "

The second letter was as succinct as the first:

"I haven't forgotten. I love you."

He was so badly shaken that henceforth he dared not go near the Rue Neuve, and when, as often happened, he had to collect some urgently needed spare part from the station, he always made a deliberate detour.

He had spent several weeks restlessly driving from market to market, from farm to farm, or at home, in dungarees, working in the shed.

More often now than in the past, he would cross the field that separated the shed from the house, to find Gisèle busy peeling vegetables or scrubbing the tiled kitchen floor, or upstairs dusting the bedrooms. With Marianne at school, the house seemed empty. At four o'clock, when she was due home, he felt drawn toward the house and would go into the kitchen, where his wife and child were having their tea, facing one another across the table, each with a pot of jam in front of her.

This was a detail which was to be recalled later, more than once. Marianne only liked strawberry jam, whereas her mother, who was allergic to strawberries—even in jam they gave her a rash—preferred plum jelly.

In the early days of their marriage, he had teased Gisèle about her taste in food, which often made him smile.

Because of her golden hair, her pale skin and oval face, people frequently remarked that she had an angelic look.

But she only liked pungent foods: pickled herrings, salads flavored with garlic and liberally dressed with vinegar, and strong cheeses. Often she would be chewing at a large raw onion as she worked in the vegetable garden. On the other hand, she never touched sweets or pastries. He was the one with the sweet tooth.

This was not the only anomaly in their domestic life. His parents had brought up his brother and himself in the Italian way, as practicing Roman Catholics, and he had many childhood memories of church organs, of women and girls after Sunday morning Mass, in silk dresses, scented, their faces dusted with rice powder for this one special day.

He knew every house, every stone in the village, and could still identify the milestone which he had used as a footrest one day when his shoelace came undone as he was on his way home from school. But best of all, he knew the church with its three stained-glass windows behind the candle-lit choir stalls. The other windows were of plain glass. Those three bore the names of their donors, and the name Despierre figured in the one on the right, which had been presented by a grandfather or great-grandfather of Nicolas.

He still went to Mass on Sunday, taking Marianne with him, but his wife stayed at home. She had not been baptized. Her father claimed to be an atheist, having never read anything in the whole of his life but four or five novels by Zola.

"I'm only a working man, Tony, but let me tell you this —the Revolutionary calendar . . ."

In other families, it was the other way about. The men accompanied their wives as far as the church door, then made for the nearest bar, where they stayed drinking until the end of the Mass.

"Thinking back to that month of October, Monsieur Falcone, do you honestly claim that you were not expecting some new development?"

Nothing specific. It was, rather, a sense of discomfort such as one feels before an illness. October had been a very wet month. Tony had been forced to wear his riding breeches and high laced boots the whole time, his winter outfit in fact, except for the brown sheepskin coat.

Marianne was thrilled with school, and talked about it incessantly at meal times.

"Have you no recollection of the third letter either? Monsieur Bouvier's memory is better than yours, it seems. According to him, you received it, like the others, on Friday, on October 20th or thereabouts."

It had been the shortest and the most disquieting:

"Soon! I love you."

"You burned these notes and the later ones, I presume?"

No. He had torn them into tiny fragments and thrown them into the Orneau. The brownish river, swollen by heavy rains, was littered with fallen branches, dead animals, and every sort of rubbish.

"If my experience is anything to go by, you will soon realize that you cannot persist in denying knowledge of these letters. Except on this one point, I have been impressed by your candor in answering questions. It would surprise me if your legal adviser did not urge you to adopt the same attitude in regard to the letters, because, as things stand, you are denying yourself the opportunity of enlarging on your thoughts and feelings during those last few days of October."

It was an impossibility. His state of mind was never the same from one hour to the next. He had tried not to think, and had sensed that Gisèle, puzzled and perhaps a little anxious, was watching him. She had never again asked him what he was thinking about.

She would say listlessly:

"Aren't you hungry?"

He had no appetite. Three times, he had got up at dawn and gone out to gather mushrooms in the meadow that separated their land from the blacksmith's forge. He had picked them right at the far end, where the cherry tree was. He had sold a number of tractors, including two to the Virieux Agricultural Co-operative, who leased them out to small farmers, and who had ordered a combine harvester for the same purpose, to be delivered the following summer.

It had been a good year, and would have enabled him to repay a substantial part of the mortgage on his house.

"To proceed to October 31st. What were your movements on that day?"

"I drove to Vermoise about thirty miles away, where one of my customers was having trouble with his tractor. I worked on it for several hours before I was able to find what was wrong, and I had lunch at the farm."

"Did you return home via Triant? Did you go to see your brother?"

"It was on my way. I usually stopped for a chat with Vincente and Lucia."

"Had you spoken to them of your anxieties, or hinted at a possible, if not probable, change in your life?"

"What change?"

"We'll come back to that later. You returned home and you had dinner. Afterwards, you watched the television, having bought a set two weeks previously. I quote from your statement to the Inspector of County Constabulary. Did you go up to bed at the same time as your wife?"

"Of course."

"And you were unaware of what was taking place that night, within a few hundred yards of your house?"

"How could I have known?"

"Aren't you forgetting the letters, Falcone? True, you deny their existence, but I am bound to take them into account. The following morning—it was All Saints' Day—you set out for the church, hand in hand with your daughter, at about ten o'clock."

"That's right."

"You therefore went past the grocer's."

"The shutters were down, as they always were on Sundays and holidays."

"Were the upstairs windows shuttered as well?"

"I didn't look up."

"Because you had lost interest in Andrée Despierre? Because you considered your relations with her at an end?"

"I think so."

"Or was it that you had no need to look up, because you knew what to expect?"

"I didn't know."

"There was quite a crowd gathered outside the shop."

"There were always a lot of people about in the square before and after High Mass."

"When did you learn that Nicolas was dead?"

"Just before the sermon. As soon as he was in the pulpit, Abbé Louvette asked the congregation to join him in prayer for the soul of Nicolas Despierre, who had died in the night, aged thirty-three."

"What were your reactions?"

"It was a great shock to me."

"Did you notice that, after this announcement from the pulpit, several people turned around to stare at you?"

"No."

"I have here a statement from Pirou the tinsmith, who is also a special constable, that they did so."

"It's possible, though I can't see how anyone in Saint-Justin could have known."

"Known what?"

"About my relations with Andrée."

"You hurried home after Mass, not even stopping to visit your mother's grave."

"My wife and I had arranged to go to the cemetery in the afternoon."

"Didier, the blacksmith, your next-door neighbor, caught up with you in the road and walked part of the way with you. He said:

" 'Of course, it was bound to happen sometime, but I never expected it would be so soon. I know one person who won't shed any tears!' "

"He may have said something of the sort. I don't remember."

"Because you were too overwrought to pay any attention?"

What could he say? Yes? No? He could not put it into words. He had been stunned. All he could remember was that he had hold of Marianne's small hand in its woolen glove, and that it had started raining again.

The ringing of the telephone on the Judge's desk broke into the interrogation, and a long conversation ensued, during which there were references to a man called Martin, a jeweler's shop, and an unco-operative witness.

From what he could hear of the conversation, Tony concluded that the caller must be the Public Prosecutor, a self-important man whom Tony had seen only once, for half an hour, and whom he found alarming.

Diem did not alarm him. His feelings toward him were different altogether. So little was needed, Tony felt, to enable them to understand one another, possibly even to be friends, but that little persistently eluded them.

"I apologize, Monsieur Falcone," he said, replacing the receiver.

"Don't mention it."

"Where were we? Ah, yes, you had returned home from High Mass. You told your wife the news, I presume?"

"My daughter did. As soon as she was in the door, she let go my hand and flew into the kitchen."

The house was full of the familiar Sunday smell, the smell of roasting meat which Gisèle, crouching in front of the oven, was basting. They always had roast beef on Sundays, studded with cloves, and served with peas and mashed potatoes. On Tuesdays, the beef was boiled with vegetables.

He had not realized, at the time, how much the settled habits of their daily life meant to him.

"Can you recall your daughter's actual words?"

"She was very excited. She said: '*Maman!* Very important news! Nicolas is dead!' "

"How did your wife take it?"

"She turned to me and asked: 'Is it true, Tony?' "

He was lying again, or at least not telling the whole truth, and he could not look the Judge straight in the eye. The truth was that Gisèle had turned pale, and almost dropped the wooden spoon she was holding. His distress had been equal to hers. After an appreciable pause, she had whispered, addressing no one in particular:

"He served me himself only yesterday morning."

This, he did not mind telling the Judge. He could have gone on to repeat the rest of the conversation, for there was no harm in it, but he chose not to do so. Marianne had intervened:

"Shall I be going to the funeral?"

"Children don't go to funerals."

"Josette did."

"That was because it was her grandfather's."

She had gone into the next room to play, and it was then that Gisèle, avoiding her husband's eye, had asked:

"What will Andrée do?"

"I've no idea."

"Oughtn't you to call and offer your condolences?"

"Not today. It will be soon enough on the morning of the funeral."

"It must have happened yesterday evening or during the night?"

She had been unlike herself all the rest of that day.

"What about the next day, and the days after that?" persisted the little Judge.

"I was out almost the whole time."

"Did you inquire as to how Nicolas had met his death?"

"I didn't set foot in the village."

"Not even to collect your mail?"

"I went to the post office, no farther."

Diem consulted his papers.

"I see that, although the grocer's was shut on All Saints' Day, it was open on the morning of All Souls' Day."

"It was the custom, in the village."

"Who was serving in the shop?"

"I don't know."

"Did your wife not buy anything at Despierre's that day?"

"I don't remember. Probably she did."

"But she didn't mention it?"

"No."

What he did remember was that it had rained, and the trees had swayed in the wind, and Marianne had been difficult, as she always was when she was kept indoors by bad weather.

"I will outline the course of events in the grocery. For several days, Nicolas Despierre had shown signs of nervousness and taciturnity, which usually preceded an attack.

"At such times, according to Doctor Riquet, who prescribed for him, he took a sedative tablet every night.

"On October 31st, his mother, having dined at home, called to see him at about eight o'clock, while Andrée was busy with the washing up. She complained of feeling unwell, saying that she thought she might be in for an attack of flu."

Tony knew all this, having heard people talking about it.

"Are you aware, Monsieur Falcone, that, as it happened, Doctor Riquet was away that night visiting his sister, who was ill in Niort, and that he did not return to Saint-Justin until the following day?"

"I didn't know that."

"I understand that he was also your family doctor. You must therefore know that he scarcely ever left the village, and rarely took a holiday. On the previous day, toward noon, he called at the grocer's to see Nicolas and inform him of his movements."

With his shaggy beard, the doctor looked like a sheep dog, and he was not above dropping in at the Café de la Gare for a game of cards and a glass or two.

"Consider his absence in conjunction with Madame Despierre's attack of influenza. You see what I'm driving at? At three o'clock in the morning, your friend Andrée telephoned the doctor's house, as though she were unaware of his absence. There was no one to answer the telephone but the servant girl, as Madame Riquet had gone with her husband. She did not then call a doctor from Triant, but instead went across the garden in her dressing gown to waken her mother-in-law, and by the time the two women got back to him, Nicolas was dead."

He listened, feeling uncomfortable, not knowing how to take it.

"Madame Despierre, seeing that she had come too late in any event, decided that there was no point in fetching another doctor out to the village, and it was eleven o'clock the following morning before Doctor Riquet saw Nicolas.

"Bearing in mind the case history, Doctor Riquet after a cursory examination signed the death certificate. Subsequently, he was able to satisfy us that, given the medical facts, nine out of ten doctors would have done the same in his place.

"In spite of this, however, by the following morning the village was buzzing with rumors. Were you not aware of this?"

"No."

This time, he was telling the truth. It was only much later that he had learned, to his astonishment, that even then his name was being linked with Andrée's all over Saint-Justin.

"You know country people better than I do, Monsieur Falcone. You must realize, therefore, that rumors of this kind seldom reach the ears of the people concerned. As for public servants and police, they are always the last to hear them.

"For months, no one was prepared to speak, until the pressure of events loosened their tongues. Even then, Inspector Mani and I found most witnesses guarded in their statements.

"With patience, however, we finally overcame these difficulties, as you can see from this bulky file, a copy of which has been sent to your lawyer. I daresay Monsieur Demarié has discussed it with you."

He nodded. The truth was that even now he was baffled. During the whole eleven months, he and Andrée had taken every possible step to keep their relationship secret.

It was not merely that Tony had avoided setting foot in the grocer's shop except when he was compelled to do so, but that, whenever he did go in, he addressed himself to Nicolas rather than to his wife. When they happened to run into one another in the crowd at Triant market, he would greet her with a distant nod, nothing more.

Except for that roadside encounter in September, they had never been together anywhere but in the blue room, and they had always arrived separately, leaving their cars a long way from the inn, and using different entrances.

Neither his brother nor his sister-in-law had betrayed their trust, of that he was sure. He was equally confident that Françoise had kept her mouth shut.

"So widely known was your association that, at the funeral, you were stared at by everyone, and your wife came in for a good many pitying glances."

He had sensed this, and it had terrified him.

"It's hard to tell how these rumors start, but when they do, nothing on earth can stop them. First reactions were that Nicolas's death had come at an opportune moment for his wife, and that it must have been a relief to her.

"Then, someone remarked on the doctor's absence that night, a providential circumstance for anyone wanting to get rid of the grocer and make it appear that his death had resulted from an epileptic seizure.

"Had he been called in earlier, while Nicolas was still

alive, Doctor Riquet would probably have reached a different conclusion."

All this was perfectly true. He had no answer to it.

"There was a good deal of comment, too, on the fact that at the funeral you chose to stand right at the back, as far away from your mistress as you could possibly get, and this was generally thought to be a subterfuge on your part."

He wiped his face with his handkerchief, for he was bathed in sweat. For months he had lived in a fool's paradise, never suspecting that he was being spied on, that everyone in Saint-Justin knew that he was Andrée's lover, and that the whole village was agog to see what would happen next.

"In all sincerity, Falcone, do you really imagine that your wife could have been ignorant of what everyone else knew? Surely, she too must have been expecting developments?"

He shook his head, but without much conviction, for he no longer knew what to think.

"Supposing she had known of your relations with Andrée, would she have said anything to you?"

"Possibly not."

Certainly not. It was not in her nature. Witness the fact that she had never alluded to those other adventures which she did know about.

Not for the world would he have lived through that winter again, and yet he had never before felt so closely bound to his wife and child, never been so keenly aware of the three of them as a unit, never experienced such a sense of intimacy, almost like an animal with its female and cub, huddled together in a burrow.

In spite of the bright colors they had chosen for the rooms, the house now seemed gloomy and oppressive. He carried on his business reluctantly. It went against the grain to leave home, for he sensed danger, and was fearful of what might happen while he was away.

"You did not see your mistress once during the whole of that winter, Monsieur Falcone?"

"I may have caught sight of her in the distance. But I can swear I never saw her to speak to."

"You didn't meet her at your brother's place?"

"Of course not."

"Did she not signal to you repeatedly?"

"I only saw the towel once. I was especially careful to keep away from the Rue Neuve on Thursdays."

"But you did go there on one particular Thursday. When was that?"

"At the beginning of December. I was on the way to the station, and I took the shortest route. I was surprised to see the towel on the window bar, and I wondered whether it had been put there deliberately."

"You did not go to Triant that day?"

"No."

"Did you see the Citroën?"

"Not then. I saw it later. I was in my office, and I heard a couple of blasts on the horn, and saw Andrée drive past. It was a kind of greeting, I suppose."

"Did your brother tell you she had been to the inn?"

"Yes."

"Did he tell you that she went straight up to the blue room and that, according to Françoise, she had undressed and lain on the bed waiting for you for half an hour or more?"

"Yes."

"What message did she leave with Françoise?"

"It was to say that she absolutely had to see me."

"After she had waited half an hour for you, how did she seem? Did Françoise say?"

"She confessed that Andrée had frightened her."

"In what way?"

"She couldn't explain."

"Did you discuss the matter with your brother?"

"Yes. He advised me to drop it. Those were his very

words. I told him it was over and done with long ago. He said:

"'Over and done with for you, maybe. Not for her!'"

The steady downpour of rain continued well into December, flooding the low-lying fields, and was followed by hard frosts, then, on December 20th or 21st, by snow. Marianne was bubbling over with excitement, and, first thing every morning, she ran to the window to make sure the snow was still there.

"I do hope it doesn't melt before Christmas!"

It would be her first white Christmas. In previous years, there had been rain and frost. Now that she was at school, she referred to herself with pride as a big girl, and she had helped her father decorate the Christmas tree, and arranged the plaster shepherds and lambs around the Crib all by herself.

"You say you knew nothing of what was going on at the Despierres'?"

"I knew, because my wife told me, that the old lady was back in her old place in the shop, and that the two women were still not on speaking terms."

"Was there not some talk of a lawsuit?"

"I overheard some people discussing it in a café."

His work sometimes took him into the little village cafés. They were dark, gloomy places for the most part, where men would sit talking and drinking for hours on end, growing noisier as the day wore on. There were six cafés in Saint-Justin, though three of them were virtually empty except on fair days.

"Would you yourself have been surprised if they had gone to court?"

"Your Honor, I swear I never gave it a thought."

"All the same, you knew what was going on?"

"No more than anyone else. People were saying that old Madame Despierre, for all her cunning, had bought a pig in a poke, and that in the long run Andrée had got the best of the bargain."

"Was that a fair assessment, would you say?"

"How should I know?"

"In the eleven months of your relationship, did your mistress never tell you that a joint-estate settlement had been agreed on as a condition of her marriage?"

"We never talked about her marriage."

The truth was that they had talked very little, and it would have been better for them had they not talked at all. Witness the fact that Judge Diem was harking back yet again to that last Thursday in the blue room.

"You did, nevertheless, discuss your future together."

"It was just talk. It didn't mean a thing."

"Not to Andrée either? Are you quite sure? I must remind you that, two months before her husband's death, she was already planning for the time when she would be rid of him."

He was about to protest, but Diem forestalled him:

"Not in so many words, perhaps. Still, that was surely the implication when she asked you what your attitude would be if she were a free woman."

He would have given anything, an arm, a leg, an eye, to wipe out that exchange of words, for everything to be as though it had never taken place. It was shameful to have listened to her without revulsion. He loathed that other Tony standing in front of the mirror, dabbing at the blood on his lip, proud of his naked body caught in a beam of sunlight, vain at being admired for his virile good looks, proud of his semen oozing from a woman's body.

"Would you like to spend the rest of your life with me?" And a little later:

"Are you still bleeding?"

Oh, yes, she was very pleased with herself for having bitten him, so that he would have to go home and show himself to his wife and child with the mark of their love-play upon him!

"If she asks about it, what will you say?"

She was Gisèle, and he had spoken of her as though she were of no importance.

"I'll say I bumped into something . . . I know . . . the windshield . . . Having to jam on the brakes suddenly."

He was so well aware of the treachery of these words that when Marianne, not Gisèle, had asked him about his swollen lip, he had told a different story, substituting lamppost for windshield.

"Could you really spend the rest of your life with me?"

What would have happened if the train whistle had not sounded, as though to warn him, when she had said in her throaty voice:

"Tell me, Tony . . . If I were free . . ."

How he had come to detest the words!

"Would you get your freedom too?"

How could he tell the Judge that those words had re-echoed in his head all through the winter, that they came back to him as he sat at table in the kitchen with its steamed-up windows, that he was even saying them over to himself at the same time as his daughter was unwrapping her toys under the Christmas tree.

"The grocery store in the Rue Neuve," Judge Diem went on implacably, "the houses, the farms, the hamlet of Guipotte are now owned jointly by the two women, and Andrée Despierre is legally entitled to have the whole estate put up for public auction, with a view to collecting her share of the inheritance."

A long brooding silence followed, then:

"It was a subject of general interest in Saint-Justin, was it not?"

"I believe so. Yes."

"Was it not said that old Madame Despierre would never allow any of her property to fall into the hands of strangers? Was not that why she was working in the shop again, even though it meant being cooped up with the daughter-in-law, whom she detested, and to whom she never addressed a single word? The power of decision rested with Andrée, and Andrée would decide nothing without you."

He started involuntarily, and a hot denial sprang to his lips.

"I am merely repeating what was common gossip at the time. No wonder you were stared at. Everyone was waiting to see whose side you were on. Old Madame Despierre belonged to the village. In spite of her reputation for meanness and hardheadedness, she was still one of them.

"It was different with Andrée. They had always resented her condescending manner, and tolerated her only because they revered her father's memory.

"As for you, not only were you of foreign origin, but you had left the village and stayed away for ten years. Inevitably, people wondered what you had come back for."

"Where does all this get us?"

"Nowhere in particular. Opinion was pretty evenly divided. A good many people believed, in spite of everything, that Andrée would sell out, even if it meant a lawsuit, and that she was only waiting to lay hands on the cash to leave Saint-Justin with you at her side.

"The one person everyone was sorry for was your wife, in spite of her shyness, which prevented her from making friends in the village. Do you know how someone described her: *'A gentle little lady for whom nothing is too much trouble.'* "

Diem smiled and tapped his papers with his forefinger.

"Everything I have told you today is on record here, in black and white. In the end, it all came out. I repeat, your lawyer has copies of all the documents. He was entitled to be present at these interviews. He elected, with your approval, to let you speak for yourself."

"It was what I wanted."

"I know, though I still cannot understand why."

There was no need to explain that it was the same as when he went to confession: the priest behind the grille did not trouble him, but he would have been tongue-tied in the presence of a third person. Diem, for all his show of bewilderment, understood this so well that whenever there were delicate personal matters to be discussed, he sent his clerk out of the room.

"And now, Monsieur Falcone, what have you to say about the last two letters, those you received at the end of December and on January 20th?"

CHAPTER

5

His lawyer, too, was insistent about the letters.

"Why try to hide the truth in this instance, when you have been so honest about everything else? There is no doubt that you received these letters. You can't expect anyone to believe that they were an invention of the post-master at Saint-Justin."

Like a naughty boy who has told a fib and is too proud to admit it, he repeated:

"I don't know what you're talking about."

In his case, it was not pride, but rather a dying flicker of loyalty to the blue room. He had never intended to marry Andrée. Even if they had both been free, both unmarried, it would never have entered his head to make her his wife.

Why not? He had no idea.

"You were frightened by the intensity of her passion, was that it?" suggested Professor Bigot.

"It must have been a shock to you, that September night at the edge of the little wood, to discover that the woman you called the statue, whom you believed to be distant and proud, was capable of such unbridled sexuality."

"I was surprised."

"Flattered too, no doubt, because, as events have shown, she was sincere in claiming that she had loved you ever since you were both schoolchildren."

"I felt responsible in a way."

"Responsible for this passion of hers?"

"Not exactly. I felt I owed her something. Let me put it this way. When a stray cat follows you home, mewing appealingly all the way, and then settles on your doorstep and refuses to budge, you can't just leave it to fend for itself. It's not an exact analogy, of course, but it's as near as I can get."

Bigot appeared to understand. This interview took place during Tony's second or third week in prison. Emergency security measures were needed the first time he was summoned to the Courthouse, to deal with the pressmen, the photographers, and the onlookers crowding the main staircase.

Just as he was about to step into the Black Maria, the Governor, alerted by a telephone call from the Public Prosecutor's office, hurriedly ordered him back to his cell, where he was kept waiting for nearly an hour.

When he was brought out again, the uniformed police guards had been relieved by Inspector Mani and another plain-clothes officer. The prison car was no longer standing in the courtyard. It had been sent on ahead with a couple of prisoners picked at random, to divert the crowd.

He was driven to the Courthouse in an ordinary car without distinctive markings, and taken inside through a little door at the back.

They kept up this game of hide-and-seek for a fortnight. Public opinion, inflamed by the press, was hostile to him, and there had been threats of violence.

Now, at the end of two months, most of the journalists from Paris and other large towns had left Poitiers, and only the local reporters and Press Agency representatives remained.

From time to time he had seen pictures in magazines and newsreels of accused men pushing their way through a crowd, surrounded by police, to get to court or prison, with an arm up to shield their face.

He was one of them now, except that he did not try to hide his face. They all had the same look, the bewildered look of men cast out by society, for no reason that they could understand. Was that how he looked?

He kept a cool head. In the presence of the Magistrate, he did not behave like a hunted man. He answered questions to the best of his ability, like a conscientious schoolboy, taking a pride in the truthfulness and accuracy of his replies, except on the subject of the letters. He was convinced that to give way on this point would lead him into endless trouble.

He had received the December letter on New Year's Eve. The snow had frozen over by then, and crunched underfoot. People were already calling out, "A happy New Year," and "All the best," to acquaintances in the street.

The sky was clear, and there was a sharp nip in the air. The children had turned the Rue Neuve into a slide and were hurtling down it one after another. The postmaster had handed him his mail without a word, and Tony, as usual, had glanced through it before leaving the post office.

"Happy Our Year."

The pain in his chest, the spasm, had been more violent this time. He felt mystified and at the same time threatened by the message. The words had been deliberately chosen, that much was obvious. But what did they mean? What did "our" mean? That the coming year was to be "their" year? Was that what Andrée was thinking?

He had burned that New Year's Eve message, because the Orneau, whose banks were covered with a film of ice, was almost dry.

The next morning, all three of them had gone to wish

old Angelo a Happy New Year. His father had scarcely spoken to them, and had never once looked at Marianne. Tony believed he knew why. Was it not because she reminded him of the wife and child he had lost?

In the afternoon they had gone to see his brother, as they did every year, because on New Year's Day, as on any other, it was work as usual for the innkeeper.

Very early that morning, Tony had gone down to the kitchen and, finding his wife alone there, had put his arms around her and held her close for a long time, with her head resting on his shoulder.

"Happy New Year, Gisèle."

Had she sensed the unwonted depth of feeling behind the words? Had she shared his anxiety, his fear that happiness was not to be for them in the coming year?

"Happy New Year, Tony."

As she spoke, she looked at him and smiled, but because it was such a tentative smile, it saddened rather than cheered him.

Now that Marianne was at school, he and his wife were alone together for their midday meal. Many of the children went to the school from farms several miles away, and as they could not get home in the middle of the day, lunch was available on the premises. Marianne, who adored school, had begged her parents to let her stay and eat in the canteen.

"It's a phase. I'm sure she'll change her tune before the year is out."

It was not always easy for Tony, sitting opposite Gisèle, to hide his preoccupation. What did they talk about? Silence was what they both feared, so they talked of anything and everything, saying the first meaningless thing that came into their heads, and when words ran out, the emptiness of the silence startled them.

The last letter had made things even worse. Andrée had issued what amounted to an order as well as a sharp reminder of the promise she believed he had made to her. It consisted of just three words, written in huge letters which took up the whole sheet of paper:

"Over to you!"

As always, he had opened the letter in the post office, at the desk with the bottle of violet ink, the broken pen, the piles of telegraph forms and leaflets. Afterwards, he could not remember how he had behaved, but his distress must have been obvious, since Monsieur Bouvier, watching from his counter, had asked, with real concern:

"Bad news, Tony?"

And the postmaster was later to remark to the Examining Magistrate:

"I'd never seen him look like that. He was like a man who had received the death sentence. He didn't answer, but just stared at me, or rather through me, and then suddenly rushed out, leaving the door open behind him."

It was fortunate that, because he had several farms to visit, he had his car with him that day. Disregarding his business appointments, he had driven for hours, staring fixedly at the road ahead, not caring where he was going, trying desperately, against his better judgment, to read some more reassuring meaning into the three words.

But Andrée's intention was all too plain. The words could only mean: "Your move."

"When I think of all the years I've wasted because of you!"

She was not prepared to waste any more. Now that she had got possession of him, she was at last about to realize the dream of her childhood, her girlhood, her womanhood.

Was it really credible that she had waited so long for Tony, shutting out everything that might distract her from her obsession?

The psychiatrist seemed to believe it. Maybe this was not the first case of its kind in his experience.

In those three short words, she was telling him, once and for all:

"I've done my part. Now it's up to you to do yours."

And if he did not? The underlying threat was unmistakable. He had not protested when, as he stood with his back toward her, she had said:

"Tell me, Tony . . . If I were free . . . ?"

She had been free for two months now, though how this had come about he did not know and did not want to know. Free and rich. She was free to do what she pleased with her life, and no one had any right to interfere.

"Would you get your freedom too?"

He had not replied. Surely she knew in her heart of hearts that he had deliberately avoided replying? Admittedly, there had been the strident, angry shriek of the train whistle. It was just possible that Andrée might have deceived herself into thinking that he had said "Yes," or mistaken a turn of his head for a nod.

"Over to you!"

Assuming that she took his co-operation for granted, what action did she expect him to take?

Divorce proceedings? Did she expect him to go to Gisèle and announce point-blank . . .

It was unthinkable. He had no fault to find with his wife. He had married her of his own free will. This had been no unbridled mistress whom he had wished to make his wife, but Gisèle, exactly as she was, and if anyone imagined he had found her modesty displeasing, they were very much mistaken.

One did not spend one's whole life in bed, in a room shimmering with sunlight, experiencing the savage frenzy of naked passion.

Gisèle was his companion, Marianne's mother, the one who got up first in the morning to light the fire, who kept the house clean and bright, and who asked no questions when he came home to her.

They would grow old together, drawing closer to one another with the years, sharing a common store of memories. In years to come, when they were beginning to grow old, he fancied, they would sometimes talk about the past:

"Do you remember your grand passion?"

Perhaps, in the serenity of old age, Gisèle might permit herself a full, radiant smile.

"I don't know that it was all that grand."

"You didn't see yourself as you looked when you got back from Triant."

"I was young in those days."

"Fortunately, I knew what kind of man you were, even then. I always trusted you, though there were times when I was frightened. Especially after Nicolas died, and she was free all of a sudden."

"She did try . . ."

"To persuade you to get a divorce? You know, I sometimes wonder whether she didn't love you more than I did."

He would put out his hand to her in the dusk. For he imagined this little scene taking place on the porch of their house, late on a summer evening.

"I'm sorry for her. Even in the old days, I sometimes pitied her."

And this was the woman who, in three brutal words, was ordering him to have done with Gisèle!

"Over to you!"

The more he turned the words over in his mind, the more sinister they seemed. Andrée had not got a divorce. Nicolas was dead. She alone had witnessed his agony in the bedroom over the shop. She had waited for him to die before going out across the garden to call her mother-in-law.

Was divorce really what she had in mind for him?

"Over to you!"

Now and then, as he drove along blindly and purposelessly, in his car, he cried out furiously:

"Over to you! Over to you! Over to you! Over to you!" What was he to do, to dispel this nightmare? Should he go to Andrée, walk boldly into her house and tell her outright:

"I'll never leave my wife. I love her."

"And what about me?"

Would he have the courage to reply:

"I don't love you."

"But . . ."

What if she were able to read his mind? She was capable of saying, with a look of defiance:

"You didn't stop me from killing Nicolas."

He had suspected it from the first. So had Gisèle. And most people in the village. It was merely suspicion. No one could say what had really happened. Maybe she had done no more than fail to go for help as he lay dying.

He had had no hand in it.

"You know very well, Andrée, that . . ."

There was no escape from her, even by leaving Saint-Justin with his family. He was still paying for the house, the shed, the quipment. His business was just beginning to prosper, enabling him to provide comfort and a decent life for his family.

It was irrational, incredible. At length he had stopped at an inn for a drink. His abstemiousness was so widely known that the woman behind the bar, who kept one eye on her baby playing on the floor while attending to the customers, gave him a worried look. Later, she too was to give evidence.

The country people had at first refused to speak, but they were no match in the end for the doggedly persistent Inspector Mani.

"Do you wish me to read the postmaster's statement concerning this final letter?"

"There's no point."

"Are you suggesting that he was lying, that he made up the whole thing, including the fact that you forgot to shut the post-office door?"

"I'm not suggesting anything."

"One of the farmers with whom you had an appointment that morning telephoned your house to find out why you were late. He asked your wife when he was to expect you, and she told him you were on your way. Is that correct?"

"Very likely."

"Where were you?"

"I don't remember."

"On the whole, I should say that you had a remarkably good memory. At the Auberge des Quatres Vents you drank brandy, not beer or wine—you who so seldom drank spirits. You had four glasses, one after another, then you looked at the clock behind the counter and seemed surprised to find that it was midday already . . ."

He had driven very fast, so as to be home in time for lunch. It had not escaped Gisèle that he had been drinking. This had irritated him momentarily. Just because she was his wife, did that give her the right to watch him the whole time? He had had enough of being spied on! Admittedly, she hadn't said anything, but her silence was worse than reproof.

It was a free country! He was a grown man and answerable to no one! And, whether his wife liked it or not, he was master in his own house. Who was the breadwinner, he would like to know? Did he not flog himself to death just for the sake of giving them a better life? Did they not look to him for everything?

She was silent, and, at the other end of the table, he was silent too. From time to time, he gave her a furtive, somewhat shamefaced glance, for he knew in his heart that he was at fault. He ought not to have had those drinks.

"You know how it is, I can't help myself. It doesn't do to give offense to a customer."

"Talking of customers, Brambois telephoned."

What on earth had made him tell her a lie? Lying humiliated him, filled him with resentment.

"I was held up somewhere else. There wasn't time to go to the farm."

"Over to you! Over to you! Over to you!"

There she was, sitting opposite him, eating whatever it was they were having, deliberately avoiding his eye because she sensed his irritability.

What did Andrée expect him to do? Kill her?

There, it was out. At last, he had faced the truth, buried for too long in the turmoil of his mind. Did he not, to some extent, owe this to Professor Bigot's boring by slow degrees into the depths of his mind?

Needless to say, he had not told him everything. In spite of the evidence, he had persisted in denying all knowledge of the letters.

Be that as it may, on that day, the day of the last letter and the four glasses of brandy, the raw, stinging local marc, 65 proof, he had asked himself that question over lunch with his wife.

Was that what Andrée was asking of him? That he should kill Gisèle?

Suddenly, without warning, his drunkenness took a maudlin turn. He was to blame. He had an overpowering longing to beg forgiveness. He stretched across the table to take his wife's hand.

"Look! You mustn't be angry with me. I know I'm a bit tight."

"You'd better go up and rest after lunch."

"I've upset you, haven't I?"

"Of course not."

"I know I have. I don't treat you as I should."

He felt intuitively that he was treading on dangerous ground.

"Are you angry with me, Gisèle?"

"What for?"

"You worry about me, don't you?"

"I want you to be happy."

"Do you think I'm not happy? Is that it? Haven't I got everything? I have the best wife in the world, a daughter the very image of her, whom I adore, a lovely house, a flourishing business. Why shouldn't I be happy, I'd like to know? Right! What if I do worry a bit sometimes? It's not as easy as people imagine for a fellow born in a shack with no electric light or running water to start up in business on his own. We've traveled a long road since I met you in Poitiers. I was little better than a laborer in those days."

He talked and talked, working himself up.

"I'm the happiest of men, Gisèle, and if anyone dares to say otherwise, you can tell him from me he's lying. The happiest of men, do you hear me?"

Tears were streaming down his face, and he was choking back a great sob. He rushed out of the room and up the stairs, and locked himself in the bathroom.

She never referred to it again.

"You must forgive me for repeating the question, Monsieur Falcone. For the last time, did you receive those letters?"

Tony shook his head, as though to say that he had no choice but to stick to his denial. It was what Diem had expected, and he turned to his clerk.

"Bring in Madame Despierre."

If Tony was startled, he gave little sign of it, much less, at any rate, than the Magistrate expected. This was because, to everyone in Saint-Justin, there was only one Madame Despierre, Nicolas's mother. No one would dream of calling his wife by that name. She was Andrée to everyone, except the very old, for whom she was the Formier girl.

He wondered what the old woman could possibly have to say about the letters. The prospect of meeting her face to face was distasteful, that was all. He had risen to his feet automatically. He stood waiting, looking toward the door.

And suddenly it was open, and he was face to face with Andrée. She was followed by a fat man who looked as though he liked his food, and police guards, but Tony saw no one but her, in a black dress which made her white skin seem even whiter.

She was looking at him too, intently, her expression composed, her features softened by a vague smile. It was almost as though she were calmly taking possession of him, swallowing him whole.

"Hello, Tony."

Her throaty voice, a little hoarse, enveloped him. He did not say, "Hello, Andrée," in reply. He could not. He did not want to. He acknowledged her greeting with an awkward little nod, and then turned toward Diem as though for protection.

"Take off the handcuffs."

Still smiling, she held out her wrists to the policeman, and Tony heard the double click that he knew so well.

He had not noticed, the few times he had seen her after Nicolas's death, that she was wearing mourning. Her face had filled out in prison, and she had put on a little weight, so that her clothes were molded to her body, and she was wearing black stockings, which he had never seen her wear before.

The police guard went out, and for a second no one seemed to know what to do. They all stood irresolutely in the tiny office, with the sun blazing full on them. The clerk was the first to move, settling down to his paper-work at the end of the table. The fat man looked around him in surprise and said:

"What's happened to my colleague Demarié?"

"Monsieur Falcone did not wish him to be present, though he has informed me that, if he has changed his mind and wants him here for this meeting, he will be in the building until six o'clock, and I can send for him at any time. What do you say, Monsieur Falcone?"

He gave a start.

"Do you wish me to call in your lawyer?"

"What for?"

Whereupon, Judge Diem and Maître Capade went to the window, where they stood arguing points of law in an undertone. Tony and Andrée, still on their feet, were barely a yard apart. He could almost have touched her. She was still gazing at him with childlike wonder, as though she had been given an unexpected present.

"Tony . . ."

It was barely a whisper, a shaping of his name with her lips. As to him, he turned his head away, and it was a relief when the legal discussion was concluded and the Magistrate drew up a chair for the young woman.

"Please sit down. You too, Monsieur Falcone. You take this chair, Maître."

When everyone was seated, he rummaged among his papers and drew out a small diary with a shiny black cover, of the kind sold in the grocer's shop.

"Do you recognize this book, Madame Despierre?"

"As I have already told you, yes, I do."

"You have, as you say, identified it already. I shall, however, be compelled to repeat a number of questions which have been put to you before, and I must remind you that although your answers were taken down for the record, you are entitled to retract or modify any previous statement, if you so wish."

Tony had never seen him so formal, pompous even. Maybe it was because he was speaking in the presence of her lawyer. Riffling through the diary, he said:

"Most of the entries here do not concern us. I refer to such things as shopping lists and appointment with your dentist or your dressmaker. This is last year's diary, and in it you have indicated your meetings with Tony Falcone by a line drawn under the relevant date."

How could he have foreseen that this diary would ever be produced as a vital piece of evidence, or that, had he known what was in it sooner, he would have been cleared of one charge, at least?

"On a previous occasion, you will remember, I questioned you about the circled dates which occur at monthly intervals."

"And I told you that they were a record of my periods."

She said it without a trace of embarrassment. Similarly intimate questions had been put to Tony a few weeks back.

"Everyone in Saint-Justin," Judge Diem had said, "believed Nicolas to be sterile if not impotent, and it is a fact that, in eight years of marriage, his wife had borne him no children. Furthermore, Doctor Riquet confirms that, in all probability, Nicolas was sterile. Did you know that?"

"I'd heard it said."

"Right! Now, will you please think back to the very detailed account you gave me of your meeting on August 2nd in the blue room, as you call it, at the Hôtel des Voyageurs, from which it would appear that on no occasion when you had intercourse with your mistress did you take any steps to safeguard her against pregnancy."

Seeing that he did not reply, the Magistrate continued:

"Was this your practice, also, in other extramarital affairs?"

"I don't know."

"Do you remember a woman by the name of Jeanne, a farm worker employed by one of your customers? Inspector Mani got a statement from her, though it is not on the record, and we have undertaken not to call her as a witness at the trial. You had intercourse with her on three separate occasions. The first time, during intimacy, seeing that she appeared nervous, you whispered to her:

" 'Don't worry. I'll withdraw in time.'

"I presumed that this was your usual habit. If you deny it, I shall call other witnesses with whom you had intercourse."

"I don't deny it."

"In that case, will you explain why with Andrée Despierre, and only with her, you did not take even the most elementary precautions?"

"It was she who . . ."

"Do you mean, she referred to the matter?"

No. But the first time, when he was about to withdraw, she had held him very close. Surprised, he had almost blurted out: "Aren't you afraid?"

That time at the roadside near Sarelle Wood, he might have expected that she would do whatever was necessary when she got home. Later, at the Hôtel des Voyageurs, he had realized that she was doing nothing about it.

If he did not at first grasp the connection between this question and the crime with which he was charged, he was not to be left in ignorance for long.

"Let us suppose, for the sake of argument, that you and she had made up your minds to be united at all costs. In that case, why bother with contraception? What did it matter if Andrée were pregnant? I put it to you, Monsieur Falcone, that it would not have made the slightest difference, unless it were to bring matters to a head sooner than was intended."

That interview had left him utterly crushed, and, looking back on it later, he concluded that the Judge could not know what it was to have a mistress.

Today, it seemed, Judge Diem was not interested in pursuing this subject.

"Let us turn to the entry for September 1st. I see that you have marked this date with a cross. Will you please tell us what that means?"

Self-possessed as ever, she looked from the Judge to Tony with an encouraging smile.

"That was the date of my first letter."

"Be more precise, please. To whom was that letter addressed?"

"To Tony, of course."

"What prompted you to write it?"

"When my husband followed me to Triant on August 2nd, I knew that he must suspect something, and I dared not go to Vincente's again."

"In other words, you made no further use of the agreed-on signal?"

"That's right. Tony was terribly shaken when he spotted Nicolas in the Place de la Gare. I wanted to put his mind at rest, in case he imagined I was in serious trouble."

"What exactly do you mean?"

"He might have thought that Nicolas had made a scene or turned violent, or that he had told his mother about us, and that they were making things difficult for me, or heaven knows what. But, as it happened, I had no difficulty in persuading him that I had some perfectly innocent reason for being at the inn."

"Can you remember what you wrote in the letter?"

"Certainly: 'Everything is fine.' And I added 'Don't worry.' "

Diem turned to him:

"Do you still deny having received this letter, Monsieur Falcone?"

Andrée turned to stare at him in surprise.

"Why should you deny it? You did get my letters, surely?"

He was utterly bewildered. She could not be entirely oblivious to the danger. She must see that she had fallen into their trap.

"Let us proceed. You may change your mind later. The next date marked with a cross is September 25th. What can you tell me about this second letter?"

She needed no time for reflection. She knew them by heart, just as she knew by heart every word that had been said in the blue room on the afternoon of August 2nd.

"It was just a greeting: 'I haven't forgotten. I love you.' "

"According to your recollection, then, you wrote 'I haven't forgotten,' not 'I haven't forgotten you'? You are quite sure of this?"

"Yes. I hadn't forgotten."

"What was it that you had not forgotten?"

"Everything. Our love. The promises we had made to each other."

"Now we come to October 10th, twenty days before your husband's death, to be precise. At a previous interview, you recited the contents of this third letter: it read: 'Soon! I love you.' What exactly did you mean by 'soon'?"

Still unruffled, Andrée replied, with a quick reassuring glance at Tony:

"That we should soon be able to start meeting again."

"How was that?"

"I had managed things so that Nicolas had got over his suspicion."

"Was it not rather that you knew he had not long to live?"

"I've answered that question twice already. He was a very sick man. It was an even chance whether he would drag on for years or go out like a light. Only a few days earlier, Doctor Riquet had said as much, and not for the first time, to his mother and me."

"When was that?"

"During one of his attacks. They were becoming more frequent, and, at the same time, his stomach trouble was growing worse."

Tony listened, astounded. He could almost have believed that the whole lot of them, including Andrée and her lawyer, who was nodding in agreement, had cooked up this farce between them. His head was buzzing with questions, questions that the Judge ought to be putting to her, but which Diem seemed rather to be deliberately avoiding.

"That brings us to December 29th, almost to New Year's Eve, in fact, and we find another cross beside the date in your diary."

Without waiting to be asked, she recited the words:

"Happy Our Year."

She added, with a hint of pride:

"I thought about it a lot. It's ungrammatical, I know,

but I wanted to emphasize that the coming year was to be our year."

"What do you mean?"

"Have you forgotten that Nicolas was dead?"

She brought this up as though it were the most natural thing in the world, and still with the same horrifying self-possession.

"What you mean to say is that you were free?"

"Obviously."

"And that, therefore, there was nothing now to prevent the coming year from being, in the fullest sense, your year, yours and Tony's?"

She nodded, more self-satisfied and complacent than ever. Once again, instead of challenging her statement, Judge Diem let it pass, and produced another diary similar to the first.

Tony realized for the first time that he was not the only one to have spent hours at a stretch in this office, during the past two months. Admittedly, his lawyer had told him that Andrée had been arrested, after he himself had been in custody for ten days or so. Inevitably, therefore, she must have been interrogated. But he had never given serious thought to the implications. It had not occurred to him that her statements would be taken just as seriously as his, if not more so.

"That leaves one more letter, Madame Despierre, the shortest but the most significant of them all. It contains three words only."

Andrée, as though she were proudly throwing down a challenge, broke in:

" 'Over to you!' "

"Will you please explain, as precisely as possible, just what you intended to convey."

"What could be plainer? As you said yourself, I was free. I only had to wait until I was out of mourning . . ."

"One moment, please! Was it because you were in

mourning that you did not resume your meetings after your husband's death?"

"Partly. And partly because there were legal matters in dispute between my mother-in-law and me, and I thought that, in case it should come to a lawsuit, the less talk there was about my private life the better."

"I take it, then, that after All Saints' Day you did not hang the towel out of the window again?"

"I did once."

"Did your lover keep the appointment?"

"No."

"You went up to the room?"

Brazenly, she replied:

"I undressed as usual. I was sure he would come."

"Was there anything particular you had to say to him?"

"If I had had anything to say to him, I should not have waited for him naked."

"Were there not things you needed to discuss?"

"Such as what?"

"Among other things, how he proposed to set about getting his freedom."

"That was decided ages before."

"On August 2nd?"

"Earlier than that."

"He had agreed to a divorce?"

"I'm not sure divorce was mentioned in so many words, but that's what I understood."

"Do you hear that, Falcone?"

She turned to him, wide-eyed:

"You don't mean you haven't told them!"

Then, to the Judge:

"I don't see what's so extraordinary about it. People get divorced every day. We love each other. Even when I was only a little girl, I loved him, and I only married Nicolas because Tony had left the district, and I never expected him to come back.

"When we found one another again, we both realized that we could never be parted."

He wanted to get to his feet and shout at the top of his voice:

"No! No! No! Stop it! It's all lies! It's a trick!"

He remained seated, too stunned to speak. Did she realize what she was saying? Her manner was matter-of-fact, unemotional, as though everything were quite straightforward, as though there were no tragedy, no mystery about it.

"When you wrote the words 'Over to you!' what did you have in mind?"

"To remind him that I was waiting . . . that the rest was up to him . . ."

"Up to him to seek a divorce?"

She hesitated for a second, deliberately perhaps, before saying:

"Yes."

Before putting his next question to Andrée, the Judge looked meaningfully at Tony, as though to say:

"Listen to this. You'll find it interesting."

And, in a dispassionate tone of voice, without a trace of sarcasm or flippancy, he said:

"Did you not consider the distress you would be causing Gisèle Falcone?"

"She would have shed a few tears, and that would have been the end of it."

"How do you know? Did she not love her husband?"

"Not the way I did. That sort of woman is incapable of real love."

"And her child?"

"That's just it! She would have found consolation in her daughter, and provided they got something in the way of regular maintenance, they wouldn't have had a bad time of it."

"Do you hear that, Falcone?"

The Judge no doubt realized that he had gone too far and regretted it, for Tony's expression was frightening, almost inhuman in its anguish and hatred. He rose slowly from his chair, his face set, his eyes staring, like a sleepwalker.

His arms, ending in tightly clenched fists, seemed preternaturally long. The fat lawyer, who had glanced toward him in idle curiosity, leaped to his feet to get between him and his client.

As for Diem, he made an urgent sign to the clerk, who ran for the door.

Though it seemed intolerably long-drawn-out, it had all happened in a matter of seconds. In no time, the police guards were in the room, roughly handcuffing Tony. And there they stood, awaiting orders. The Judge looked from his prisoner to Andrée, uncertain what to do next. Andrée showed no sign of distress, but merely looked bewildered.

"Honestly, Tony, I can't see why you . . ."

But, at a sign from the Magistrate, she was hustled out of the room. Her lawyer had her by the arm and was marching her firmly out. But she turned back protesting:

"You know very well you said yourself . . ."

They were prevented from hearing the end of the sentence by the door closing behind her.

"I apologize, Falcone. I had no choice. In a minute or two, as soon as the way is clear, you can go back to the prison."

That night after dinner, Judge Diem spoke of it to his wife:

"Today, I had to bring about the cruelest encounter I have ever witnessed in my whole career. I hope I never see another like it."

As for Tony, back in his cell, he had no sleep that night.

CHAPTER 6

For two days he was in a kind of stupor, though he was roused from time to time by a spurt of rage, which drove him to fling himself about the cell at the risk of cracking his skull against the wall.

It was the weekend, and presumably everyone had gone away to the country.

Surprisingly, he had, from the start, adapted himself readily to prison life, content to obey the rules and the orders of his guards.

It was not until the third day that he began to feel abandoned. No one came to see him. There was no mention of driving him to the Courthouse. He listened expectantly to the sound of footsteps in the corridor, and got to his feet whenever they stopped at his door.

It was not until later that he realized that the streets were silent, almost free of traffic, and at four o'clock he was told by one of the warders that that Monday was a public holiday.

At ten o'clock on the Tuesday morning, Maître Demarié was ushered into the cell. He was sunburned. Unhurriedly, he got his papers out of his brief case, spread them out, sat down, offered Tony a cigarette, and lit one himself.

"These last three days must have seemed very long to you, I suppose?"

As Tony did not bother to reply, but waited with an air of indifference for him to go on, he gave a little cough.

"I have received a copy of the transcript of your last interrogation and your encounter with Andrée Despierre."

Did he believe in his client's innocence, or had he not yet made up his mind?

"I should be misleading you if I said that things were going well for us. This business of the letters is a disaster, and the fact that you denied their existence won't help with the jury. Was the Despierre's account of them correct?"

"Yes."

"I should be obliged if you would tell me just one thing: truthfully now, when you persistently refused to admit the existence of this correspondence, in spite of all evidence to the contrary, was it to spare your mistress or because you considered the letters damaging to you?"

What was the good of trying to explain? It is comforting to believe that people act as they do in all circumstances for this or that specific reason. The first time the letters were mentioned, he had lied on impulse, and it had not occurred to him that they would question the postmaster.

It only dawned on him gradually, over a period of weeks, that Inspector Mani and his staff were working prodigiously day after day, visiting countless people in their homes, going over the same ground time and time again, until the witnesses could be persuaded to speak out.

Was there a single person in Saint-Justin, a single farmer in the whole district, one man who regularly attended local fairs, the Triant fair in particular, who had not put in his word?

The pressmen had played their part, too, and the newspapers were full of gossipy personal interviews with local people.

"I had a brief word with Diem, and he gave me to understand that you were profoundly distressed at this encounter. It seems that, for once, your self-control deserted you. Andrée, on the other hand, displayed cool self-assurance throughout. No doubt she will repeat the performance at the Assizes."

Demarié was doing his best to shake him out of his apathy.

"I sounded out the Judge, though his opinion won't carry much weight once the preliminaries are completed. He makes no secret of the fact that he has a liking for you. All the same, I could swear that, in spite of having studied you closely for the best part of two months, he still hasn't made up his mind about you."

What was the point of all this chatter, this tedious verbiage?

"By the way, I ran into Bigot, too, quite by chance, on Friday evening at a bridge party. He took me into a corner and passed on a rather curious piece of information. But unfortunately, it's come too late.

"You did admit that with Andrée you did not take the same precautions as you normally did with other women, and that she took none either, and implied that you had not worried your head about it, all of which will suggest to the jury that the prospect of fathering her child did not greatly worry you."

Tony was listening now, wondering what was coming next.

"Andrée, as you know, recorded the dates of her periods in her diary. It occurred to Bigot that it might be interesting to examine them in conjunction with the dates of your meetings in Triant during the eleven months of your relationship. Diem had not thought of this. Neither, I must admit, had I.

"Can you guess what emerged from this comparison? I'll tell you: every one of your meetings, without exception, took place during the 'safe period,' when your mistress could not conceive.

"In other words, Andrée Despierre was taking no chances, a point which would have told in your favor but for your own earlier statements. I'll make use of it all the same, but it won't carry the same weight."

Tony had sunk back into his former lethargy, and the lawyer thought it wiser not to press him further.

"I understand that you will be going to the Courthouse this afternoon."

"Will she be there?"

"No. You'll be alone this time. Do you still not want me to be present?"

What was the use? Demarié was like all the rest. He understood no more than they did. His intervention could only be an added complication. Tony, in spite of everything, had been pleased to hear that the little Judge liked him.

He saw him again at three o'clock in his office. It was drizzling outside, and a dripping umbrella stood in the corner, probably the clerk's, since the Judge drove to Court in a large black Citroën.

Diem was not sunburned. Tony learned the reason why when he said, without preamble:

"I took advantage of the long weekend to go right through the papers again from beginning to end. How do you feel now, Falcone? I'm afraid it will be a long session today, because we have reached Wednesday, February 17th. Please give me an account of your movements that day, in the fullest detail if you can."

He had been expecting it. He was surprised afresh at each interview to find that they had not reached it yet.

February 17th was the end, the end of everything. He had not foreseen it, even in his worst nightmares, yet, afterwards, he saw that it was inevitable, fated.

"Will it help you if I put specific questions to you?"

He nodded. Left to himself, he would not have known where to start.

"Did your wife get up at the usual time?"

"A little earlier. It rained all that Tuesday morning, so the washing wasn't dry till late afternoon. She planned to spend the whole day ironing."

"What about you?"

"I was downstairs by half-past six."

"Were you alone together at breakfast? Did she ask about your movements that day? Try to be as accurate as you can."

Diem had the transcripts of his earlier statements spread out in front of him, the earliest statements of all, elicited from him by Gaston Joris, the police officer at Triant, with whom he had often had a drink at his brother's place, and, shortly afterwards, by Inspector Mani, a Corsican.

"I had told her the night before—Tuesday night, that is —that I had a very full day ahead, and that I should not be home for lunch and might be late for dinner."

"Did you tell her where you were likely to be throughout the day?"

"I just mentioned the fair at Ambasse, where I was to meet a customer, and a repair job waiting for me at Bolin-sur-Sièvre."

"Isn't that outside your area?"

"Bolin is only about thirty miles from Saint-Justin, and I was beginning to extend my range."

"Were you aware, at that time, that you would not in fact be going to these places?"

"What I said was partly true."

"At seven o'clock you went up to wake your daughter. Did you often do that?"

"Almost every day. I used to wake her when I went up to wash and shave."

"You wore your best suit, a blue suit which was usually kept for Sundays."

"That was because of my appointment in Poitiers. I wanted to look my best to impress Garcia."

"We'll come back to that later. When you got downstairs again, your daughter was in the kitchen, getting ready to leave for school. Before setting out for Ambasse and Bolin-sur-Sièvre, you had to call in at the post office, and then collect a parcel from the station."

"That was the piston I needed for the repair job at Bolin."

Two or three times he had glanced mechanically toward the empty chair facing the desk, and eventually it dawned on Diem that this was the chair in which Andrée had sat the week before.

This chair—it was a very ordinary chair—appeared to have been left exactly where it had stood on the Friday, and as this seemed to worry Tony, the Judge, under cover of walking about the room to stretch his legs, pushed it back against the wall.

"You offered to drive your daughter to school in the truck?"

"Yes."

"Wasn't that unusual? Was there any reason why you should make a particular fuss over her that morning?"

"No."

"Did you not ask your wife whether she wanted anything from the village?"

"No. I told the Inspector I didn't. I was leaving the house when Gisèle called me back. She said: 'Do you mind getting me two pounds of sugar and a couple of packages of soap powder from the grocer's? Then I shan't need to get dressed.' Those were her exact words."

"Did you often do the shopping for her?"

Did he really have to go into their domestic routine yet again? He had been through it all once with Inspector Mani. As in most other households, a day seldom went by but they needed something from the shops, the butcher's or pork butcher's, for instance. As the service was slow in these shops, Gisèle never bothered him with errands if she could help it. "It's not a man's job," she used to say.

On that particular Wednesday, she was anxious to get to the ironing as soon as possible. The previous day, they had had leg of mutton, and there was some left over, so she did not need anything from the butcher. There was thus only the one errand.

"So you set out with your daughter."

He could still see Gisèle on the doorstep, reflected in the driving mirror, wiping her hands on her apron.

"You dropped Marianne at the school gates and went on to the post office. What did you do next?"

"I went into the grocer's."

"How long was it since you had last been there?"

"Two months or so."

"You did not go there at all after you received the last letter, consisting of just the three words: 'Over to you!'?"

"No."

"What were your feelings, Monsieur Falcone? Distress? Apprehension?"

"Not exactly. I would have preferred not to meet Andrée, especially with other people looking on."

"Were you afraid of giving yourself away?"

"I was embarrassed."

"Who was in the shop when you went in?"

"There was some kid or other—I didn't pay much attention to him—and one of the Molard sisters, and an old woman whom everyone calls La Louchote because of her squint."

"Was old Madame Despierre there?"

"I didn't see her."

"Were you kept waiting?"

"No. Andrée said at once: 'What can I do for you, Tony?' "

"So she served you before the other people? Didn't anyone object?"

"It was the usual thing. Men are served first in most shops.

"I said:

" 'Two pounds of sugar and two packages of soap powder.'

"She got the things from the shelves, and then said:

" 'One moment. That plum jelly your wife ordered a couple of weeks back has just come in.'

"She went off to the storeroom and came back with a pot of jam—the same make as we usually had at home . . ."

"Was she away long?"

"Not very long."

"A minute? Two minutes?"

"No longer than I would have expected."

"The time it would take her to fetch the pot of jam and bring it to you in the shop? Or as long as she would need, say, to get it out from under a pile of things?"

"Somewhere between the two. I don't know."

"Did Andrée Despierre appear agitated?"

"I avoided looking at her."

"All the same, you must have seen her. At any rate, you heard her voice."

"I think she was pleased to see me."

"Did she say nothing more to you?"

"As I went out, she called after me: 'Have a good day, Tony!' "

"Did you notice anything unusual in her manner?"

"I wasn't paying much attention at the time. It was just an ordinary day, like any other."

"And afterwards, looking back on it?"

"I thought she did perhaps sound especially affectionate."

"Was Andrée often affectionate toward you?"

Was he not bound to tell the truth?

"Yes. It's hard to explain. It was a special sort of affection. It reminded me of the way I sometimes felt about Marianne."

"Maternal?"

"That's not quite it. Protective would be closer to it."

"It would appear, from your account of events, that you were the victim of a remarkable chain of coincidences. Coincidence number one: your wife takes the somewhat unusual step of sending you to the grocer's instead of going herself. Coincidence number two: a certain make of jam, which no one eats but herself, is out of stock for several days. A fresh stock conveniently arrives on the day you go into the shop, and a jar of it is handed over to you. Coincidence number three—to which, incidentally, Inspector Mani attaches a good deal of significance: on that day of all days you do not go straight home, but first call at the railway station."

"I had ordered the piston by express delivery . . ."

"And that's not all. The station building at Saint-Justin, like most other buildings, is four-sided. There is the front, used by passengers entering and leaving the station; the back, which abuts onto the main road; the south side, with a door leading to the stationmaster's office; and the north side, in which there are no doors or windows. A solid, blank wall, in fact. And it was beside this wall that you parked your truck."

"If you saw the layout for yourself, you would realize that it was the obvious place."

"The stationmaster, who was up to his eyes in paperwork, told you to collect the package yourself from the parcels office."

"All the local people did it."

"How long were you in or near the station?"

"I didn't notice the time. A few minutes."

"The stationmaster has stated that it was some considerable time before he heard you start up your car."

"I wanted to make sure they'd sent exactly what I ordered. If there had been a mistake, it wouldn't have been the first time."

"So you undid the parcel?"

"Yes."

"In the truck?"

"Yes."

"Where you could not be seen by anyone. Another coincidence to add to the rest. When you arrived home, you left your purchases on the kitchen table. Your wife was in the garden, transferring the washing from the line to a basket. Did you go out to her? Did you kiss her good-by before you left?"

"We didn't go in for that sort of thing. It wasn't as if I was going on a journey. I called out from the porch: 'Expect me when you see me!' "

"You didn't tell her you'd got the jam?"

"Why should I? It was there on the table for her to see."

"Did you spend any time in the kitchen?"

"Just before I left, I noticed the percolator simmering on the hot plate, and I had a cup of coffee."

"That, if I'm not mistaken, is coincidence number five at least."

Why was Diem making such a point of this chain of coincidences? What, Tony wondered, was he expected to do about it? Protest? Fly into a rage? He was long past that stage, and answered the questions put to him with indifference. It was a dull, mild day, just like that day in February, February 17th, when the sky was a sheet of gray, the atmosphere leaden, the countryside seemingly deserted, with puddles here and there from a recent downpour.

"Why did you go through Triant?"

"Because it was on my way."

"There was no other reason?"

"I wanted to talk to my brother."

"To ask his advice? In spite of the fact that you were the elder brother, you did sometimes go to him for advice, did you not?"

"I often talked over matters of business with him. Besides, he was the only one who knew of my worries about Andrée."

"You don't deny that you did have worries?"

"Those letters bothered me."

"Isn't that putting it rather mildly, in view of what you said to Mani?"

"Let's say they frightened me."

"And you had come to some decision? Was that the subject of your discussion with Vincente? It appears, Monsieur Falcone, that all the time you and he were talking, your sister-in-law was out shopping, and Françoise was upstairs doing the rooms."

"It would have been just the same any other morning. When I went into the café, Vincente wasn't there either. I heard the clink of bottles in the cellar, and saw that the trap door behind the counter was open. My brother was getting his stock of wine for the day, and I waited till he came up from the cellar."

"You didn't let him know you were there?"

"I didn't want to disturb him. I wasn't in any hurry. I took a seat near the window, and thought over what I was going to say to Garcia."

"You had come to consult your brother with your mind already made up?"

"More or less."

"I don't understand."

"I knew Garcia wouldn't want to rush into anything. He was a cautious man, easily frightened off. It was a gamble, and I knew it."

"You were prepared to stake your future and your family's on a gamble?"

"Yes. If I could get Garcia to agree, I would sell. If he wasn't prepared to risk it, I would stay where I was."

"And where did your brother come into it?"

"I wanted to put him in the picture, that's all."

"And there were no witnesses, not even your sister-in-law, so that, apart from yourself and Vincente, there is no one who can tell us anything about this conversation. You and your brother are very close, are you not?"

Tony remembered the days when he used to take his brother to school along roads that were often clogged with mud or slippery with ice. They wore thick overcoats. In winter, they left home in the dark and came back in the dark. Vincente was often tired, and had to be dragged along, his hobnail boots scraping on the road. During recess, Tony watched over him from a distance, and when they got back to La Boisselle before their father, he fixed bread and butter for his brother.

But one did not talk of such things, everyday things that no one could know about who had not experienced them, as Judge Diem had not.

He had, undoubtedly, more in common with Vincente than with anyone else in the world, and Vincente was grateful to him for not behaving like an elder brother. The fact that they sometimes talked Italian to one another was a further tie, going back to the time when their mother, who knew no other language, was alive.

"If I stay on, I'm afraid I'll never have any peace."

"Didn't she say anything to you this morning?"

"There were other people in the shop. I expect in a day or two there'll be another letter, and God knows what will be in it this time!"

"How will you explain it to Gisèle?"

"I haven't had time to think about it. If I tell her that I want to expand but that the prospects are poor in this area, she'll take my word for it."

Facing one another across the bar counter, they had each had a vermouth. Then a delivery boy had arrived with some lemonade, and Tony had made for the door, which was standing open.

"It's in the lap of the gods!" Vincente had called after him.

Diem found it hard to credit that the two brothers had discussed such a critical problem in this matter-of-fact way, forgetting that they had been familiar with misfortune from childhood.

"Did he not try to dissuade you?"

"On the contrary, he seemed relieved. He disapproved of my affair with Andrée from the start."

"Let us go back to your movements that day."

"I spent no more than a few minutes at the Ambasse fair. It's only a small winter fair, and after I'd handed out a few prospectuses I went on to Bolin-sur-Sièvre to attend to the repair job."

"One moment. Did your wife know the farmer's name?"

"I don't remember mentioning it to her."

"On days when you were moving around a good deal, did you not, as a rule, let her know where you could be reached in an emergency?"

"Not always. With fairs, it was quite simple. I always went to the same cafés. As for farms, she usually had a rough idea of where I was going, and could leave a telephone message."

"You didn't tell her about Poitiers?"

"No."

"Why not?"

"Because nothing was settled, and there was no point in worrying her unnecessarily."

"Did it never cross your mind to tell her the truth straight out, and confess to your apprehensions about Andrée? If, as you say, the affair was over and done with, wouldn't this have been the best course? Did you never consider it?"

No. However foolish that might seem, it was the truth.

"The farmer at Bolin-sur-Sièvre, a fat fellow by the name of Dambois, gave me lunch, and at two o'clock, when I'd finished the job, I started out for Poitiers in plenty of time."

"How was the appointment with your friend Garcia arranged?"

"I had written to him the previous Saturday, suggesting that I should pick him up at the factory gate. Garcia was my foreman when I worked at head office there. He's ten years or so older than I am, and has three children, including a son at high school."

"Go on."

"I was far too early. I could have gone into the assembly shop, but that would have meant meeting all my old workmates, and I couldn't face it. The factory is on the Angoulême road, about two miles beyond the town. I stopped in Poitiers and went to a newsreel."

"What time did you come out?"

"Half-past four."

"What time was it when you left your brother?"

"Just before ten."

"In other words, we have the unprecedented situation whereby, from ten in the morning until half-past four in the afternoon, no one, neither your wife nor anyone else, knew where to get in touch with you."

"It never struck me."

"Supposing, let us say, that your daughter had met with a serious accident . . . Well, never mind! You went to meet Garcia at the factory gates."

"Yes. My letter had intrigued him. We thought of going into the café opposite, only it would have meant seeing a lot of people we knew. Garcia had his motor-bike with him, so we made our way separately to the Brasserie du Globe, in the town."

"No one knew you were to be found in the Brasserie du Globe either? Not even your brother?"

"No. Garcia and I exchanged family news, and then I put my proposition to him."

"Did you say anything about the reason why you wanted to leave Saint-Justin?"

"Only that it had to do with a woman. I knew that he had saved quite a bit, and he had often talked of setting up on his own. I had a well-established business to offer, along with the house, the storage shed, and all the equipment, not to mention the good will, which was growing into a very valuable asset."

"Was he interested?"

"He wouldn't commit himself. He asked for a week to think it over and, in particular, to discuss it with his wife and eldest son. The main snag, as far as he was concerned, was having to leave Poitiers and take his son away from the school where he was doing so well, and where all his friends were. I pointed out that there was a very good high school at Triant.

" 'With a twelve-mile journey each way, unless we made him a boarder!' was his reply."

"How long did your discussion last?"

"Around seven, Garcia suggested that I should go home with him. I told him my wife was waiting for me."

"In the event of Garcia's accepting your offer, what were your plans?"

"I would have asked the company to appoint me as their representative in the north or east—in Alsace, for instance—as far away from Saint-Justin as possible. They would have agreed. I know they think highly of my work. One day, I hoped, I might be able to start up again on my own."

"You would not have minded leaving your father by himself at La Boisselle?"

"Vincente isn't very far away."

"Would you care for a short break, Monsieur Falcone?"

"May I open the window?"

He had to have air. From the start of this session, ostensibly much like the others, he had felt stifled. These statements of fact had sinister, nightmarish overtones, because of their bearing on tragic events of which he had known nothing as he went about his business that day.

"Cigarette?"

He took one, and stood staring across the road at the windows opposite, at the wet rooftops. If only it could be got over now, once and for all! But even if Diem were not to come back to it at some future interview, it would all have to be gone through again at the Assizes.

Resigning himself to the inevitable, he sat down.

"We've almost come to the end, Falcone."

He nodded, with a sad smile for the Judge, in whose manner he detected a hint of compassion.

"You went straight back to Saint-Justin? You didn't stop anywhere on the way?"

"I felt suddenly that I must get home to my wife and child. I drove very fast, I think. As a rule, it takes about an hour and a half, and I did it in under an hour."

"Did you have drinks with Garcia?"

"He had a couple of apéritifs, but I only had one vermouth."

"As you did with your brother."

"Yes."

"You drove past his place. Did you not stop to let him know the result of your meeting with Garcia?"

"No. At that time of the evening, there are always a lot of people in the café, and I knew Vincente would be busy."

"It was dark. You must have seen the lights of Saint-Justin some way off. Did you notice anything unusual?"

"I saw lights on in every room in the house. We never had all the lights on at once. I was worried. I knew there must be something wrong."

"What did you think could be wrong?"

"I thought something must have happened to my daughter."

"Not to your wife?"

"With a child, there are so many things that can go wrong. It was Marianne I always thought of as vulnerable, as likely to have an accident."

"Instead of driving your truck around to the shed, you drew up about twenty yards from the house."

"Half the village was outside our gate, so that I was more certain than ever that something was wrong."

"You had to push your way through the crowd?"

"They made way to let me through, but they didn't look as though they were sorry for me. They looked angry, and I couldn't understand it. Fat old Didier, the blacksmith, in his leather apron, blocked my path. He stood there with his hands on his hips, and spat on my shoes.

"All the way across the lawn, I could hear muttered threats. I hadn't time to put my hand on the doorknob before it was opened by a policeman. I knew him by sight, because he was often about at the Triant market, and his first words to me were:

" 'This way!' and he pointed to the door of my office.

"I saw Sergeant Langre sitting at my desk. Instead of saying 'Hello, Tony,' in the usual way, he barked:

" 'Sit over there, you swine!'

"Then I shouted at him:

" 'Where's my wife? Where's my daughter?'

"He said: 'Your wife indeed! You know where she is as well as I do!' "

He choked on the words, and could say no more. He was not overwrought. If anything, he was unnaturally calm. Diem considerately refrained from prompting him, and the clerk stared at the tip of his pencil.

"I don't know, your Honor. It's all a blur. I remember Langre telling me that the Molard sisters had taken Marianne home with them, and after that I knew I didn't have to worry about her.

"He said: 'You might as well admit it! You didn't expect to find either of them alive! Stinking foreigner! Lousy scum!'

"He stood up and I could see he was just waiting for a chance to get his hands on me. I repeated:

" 'Where is my wife?'

" 'In Triant Hospital, as you very well know.'

"Then he looked at his watch:

" 'However, seeing what time it is, I very much doubt if she's still alive. We'll know soon enough. Where have you been all day? Hiding somewhere or other, I suppose. Of course, you wouldn't want to be on the scene, would you? Well, here you are at last, anyway. We thought you might have beat it.'

" 'What's wrong with Gisèle? Did she have an accident?'

" 'Accident, my foot! You've killed her, that's what. And very good care you took to be out of the way when it happened.' "

Soon after that a senior police officer had arrived by car.

"What does he say?" he had asked the Sergeant.

"He's all innocence, just as you'd expect. They're all a bunch of liars, these Italians. To listen to him, you'd think he hadn't a notion of what's been happening here."

The senior police officer was not much more sympathetically inclined than his subordinate, but his manner was at least correct and distant.

"Where have you come from?"

"Poitiers."

"What have you been doing since you left this morning? We've been trying all over the place to get hold of you."

"Since when?"

"Since half-past four this afternoon."

"What happened at half-past four?"

"We had a phone call from Doctor Riquet."

Tony felt suddenly desperate:

"Please tell me, officer, what exactly has happened? Has my wife had an accident?"

Here, Inspector Joris looked him full in the eyes:

"What are you playing at?"

"I swear to you on my child's life, I'm in deadly earnest. Tell me, for God's sake, how is my wife? Is she alive or dead?"

The Inspector too looked at his watch:

"She was still alive three quarters of an hour ago. I was at her bedside."

"She's dead!"

It was not possible. He could not believe it. The house

was full of unfamiliar noises. There were heavy footsteps overhead.

"What are those men doing in my house?"

"They're searching the rooms, though we have already found what we were looking for."

"I want to see my wife."

"You'll do as you're told. As from now, Antonio Falcone, you are under arrest."

"What am I charged with?"

"I'll ask the questions, if you don't mind."

Slumped in his chair, he sat with his head in his hands. Though no one had yet told him exactly what had happened, he was questioned in detail about his movements since early morning.

"You admit that it was you who brought home this pot of jam."

"Yes, of course I did."

"Did your wife ask you to get it?"

"No. She asked me to get sugar and soap powder. Andrée Despierre gave it to me. Gisèle ordered it a couple of weeks ago, it seems."

"Did you come straight home from the grocer's?"

The call at the railway station . . . the spare piston . . .

"You're sure this is the pot of jam you brought home?" They pushed it under his nose. It had been opened, and was half empty.

"I think so. The label is the same."

"Did you hand it over personally to your wife?"

"I left it on the kitchen table."

"Without saying anything about it?"

"I didn't see any need to. My wife was busy taking down the washing in the garden."

"When was the last time you went into your shed?"

"This morning just before eight, to get my truck out."

"Didn't you take anything else from the shed? Were you alone?"

"My little girl was waiting for me at the front of the house."

It was all so recent, and yet it seemed so long ago! The whole day—everywhere he had been since the morning, everything he had done—was beginning to seem unreal.

"Take a look at this, Falcone. Do you recognize it?"

He looked at the tin, which was familiar enough, since it had stood for four years on the top shelf in the shed.

"It must be mine, yes."

"What does this tin contain?"

"Poison."

"Do you know what poison?"

"Arsenic or strychnine, I'm not sure which. When we first moved in, the field where the shed is now was a dump. The butcher used to put his waste there, and even after I cleared the field, there were still rats, and Madame Despierre . . ."

"One moment. Which Madame Despierre, the old lady or the daughter-in-law?"

"The old lady. She sold me a tin of the stuff all the farmers used around here. I can't remember now whether . . ."

"It's strychnine. How much did you put in the jam?"

Tony did not go berserk. He did not even cry out, though he clenched his teeth with such force that he broke one.

"When did your wife usually eat jam?"

Somehow or other he managed to reply, feeling strangely remote from it all:

"At about ten in the morning."

Since they had come to live in the country, where the day starts earlier than in town, Gisèle had got into the habit of having a midmorning snack. Before Marianne started school, they had it together, as they still had afternoon tea together, when the child got back from school.

"You knew about it, then!"

"Knew about what?"

"About her habit of eating jam in the middle of the

morning. Do you know how much strychnine is a fatal dose? Four grains. Doubtless, you are aware that the poison begins to take effect within ten or fifteen minutes, at which time the first convulsions occur. Where were you at ten o'clock?"

"Just leaving my brother's place."

"And your wife was lying on the kitchen floor. She was to stay there, alone in the house, unable to call for help, until your daughter got home from school some time after four. Accordingly, she had to endure six hours of agony before anything could be done for her. Very efficiently planned, wasn't it?"

"But you said she was dead!"

"Yes, Falcone. And in my opinion, none of this is news to you. The likelihood is that, after the first attack, she felt relief for a time. That, at any rate, is what Doctor Riquet believes. I don't know why, at this stage, she didn't try to get help. Later, when the convulsions started again, there would be no further respite for her.

"When your daughter got home shortly after four, she saw her mother lying on the floor. I prefer not to dwell on the state in which she found her. She rushed out of the house in a hysterical condition, and pounded on the door of the Molard ladies. Mademoiselle Léonore came across to the house and telephoned for the doctor. Where were you at a quarter past four?"

"In a movie in Poitiers."

"Riquet diagnosed poisoning, and arranged for an ambulance to take her to hospital. She was beyond the help of a stomach pump. All that could be done for her was to administer sedatives.

"Riquet also telephoned me and drew my attention to the pot of jam. While waiting for the ambulance, he had a look around the kitchen. The loaf and bread knife, the remains of a cup of coffee, and a plate with traces of jam on it were still on the table. He tested the jam with the tip of his tongue."

"I want to see her! I want to see my child!"

"You can't see the child for the present. If we tried to get you to her, you'd be lynched by the mob. Léonore lost no time in spreading the news all over the village. When my men searched the shed and found this tin of strychnine, I got in touch with the Public Prosecutor at Poitiers.

"You will now accompany me to the Police Station, Falcone. There we shall proceed with the formal interrogation. Since it is unlikely that you will be setting foot in your house again for some considerable time, you would be well advised to pack all you require by way of clothing and personal effects into a suitcase. Let us go upstairs."

By dint of patient questioning, Diem led him to retell the whole story, to relive his departure from Saint-Justin-du-Loup, suitcase in hand, with police elbowing a way for him through the crowd of onlookers. He heard again the angry murmurs, saw again the fear in people's eyes, as though the discovery of a murderer in the village meant that they had all gone in danger of their lives.

"You are required by law to identify the body."

He had been kept waiting in a hospital corridor with the Inspector and a police guard. He was already in handcuffs and, because he was still unused to them, they cut into his wrists every time he made a sudden movement.

Diem, when he spoke next, studied Tony's expression intently.

"After they had finished laying out your wife's body, you were taken in to see her. You did not go up to her, but stopped a few steps from where she lay. You did not move, or speak a single word. Was this not the conduct of a guilty man, Monsieur Falcone?"

How could he make the Judge understand his feelings at that time, his inner conviction that he was indeed guilty? He could only allude to it obliquely:

"It was, after all, because of me that she died."

CHAPTER 7

That session was to be his last in the office of Examining Magistrate Diem. The Magistrate may have hoped to clear up one or two points in a subsequent interview, or to confront Tony once again with Andrée. But reports received by him on the prisoner's state of mind inclined him to leave well enough alone.

Two days later, Professor Bigot, visiting him in his cell, found him listless, inattentive, indifferent, taking scarcely more interest in life than if he were a vegetable.

His blood pressure had dropped sharply, and the psychiatrist had him transferred to the infirmary for observation. Here, in spite of intensive treatment, the prisoner showed little sign of rallying.

He ate, slept, and spoke when he was spoken to, but his voice was flat, lifeless, impersonal.

Even a visit from his brother had not roused him. Tony had stared at him in blank amazement, apparently unable to fit the Vincente he knew—looking just as he always did in his café in Triant—into the alien world of the infirmary.

"You've got to pull yourself together, Tony. There's your child to think of, remember, and we're with you all the way."

"What's the use?"

"Marianne has settled down very well with us. You know we sent her away to school for a bit at the start."

Listlessly, he asked:

"Has she been told?"

"You can't stop the other kids at school talking. One evening she asked me straight out:

" 'Is it really true that Pap killed *Maman?*'

"I comforted her, and assured her that it wasn't true.

" 'Is he a murderer, just the same?'

" 'Of course not. I told you he hasn't killed anyone.'

" 'Then, why has he got his picture in the paper?'

"So you see, Tony, she isn't unhappy—she doesn't really understand what it's all about."

Was this at the end of May or the beginning of June? He had lost count of time. Days, weeks, no longer meant anything to him, and when Maître Demarié told him that the Grand Jury had decided that he and Andrée were to stand trial for the murder of Nicolas and Gisèle, he seemed scarcely to take it in.

"They would not agree to separate trials, which puts an added burden on the defense."

His condition was unchanged, though he was back in his cell. Far from chafing at the monotony of prison life, he accepted it with surprising docility.

From one day to the next, his contacts with the outside world ceased. He even saw less of the prison guards. A vacuum was being created around him. The end of the law term coincided with the beginning of the nation's summer holiday, and hundreds of thousands of people were out on the roads, making for the sea, the mountain resorts, and secluded country retreats.

The newspapers were hinting at disagreement in the ranks of forensic medicine, and forecasting that this disagreement would dominate the trial.

Following the receipt of an anonymous letter by the authorities, and subsequent investigations in Triant which had confirmed the allegation that Tony and Andrée were lovers, Nicolas's body had been exhumed, and the preliminary tests had been carried out by a Poitiers specialist, Doctor Gendre, who had reported finding a massive deposit of strychnine in the stomach of the dead man. In consequence of this, some ten or twelve days after Tony's arrest, Andrée Despierre had been charged and taken into custody.

Maître Capade, the lawyer to whom she had entrusted her defense, had sought the opinion of a Paris specialist, Professor Schwartz, a man of world-wide reputation, who was outspokenly critical of his colleague's methods, and considered the evidence of poisoning far from conclusive.

In the space of three months, Nicolas's body had been exhumed twice, and there was talk of a third exhumation, to enable the forensic laboratory at Lyons to carry out such further tests as they deemed necessary.

There was press comment, too, on the sedative drug that the Saint-Justin grocer was in the habit of taking every night, whenever he felt an attack coming on. The druggist in Triant who sold it had been interviewed, and stated that the drug in question was dispensed in capsules, which opened like boxes, and could therefore easily be tampered with.

What did all this have to do with Tony? He no longer cared whether he was found guilty or not. He did not even ask himself what the sentence would be if the case went against him.

The people crowded together in the courtroom at the Assizes on October 14th, and the multitude of lawyers assembled there, were amazed at his indifference, and the newspapers described him as insensitive and callous.

He was forced to share a bench with Andrée. A police guard sat between them, and Andrée leaned across and said:

"Hello, Tony!"

He gave no sign of having heard her. He did not even turn his head.

The defense lawyers and their clerks, on a bench in the well of the court, were busy with their papers. In addition to Maître Capade, Andrée had engaged Maître Follier, a member of the Paris Bar, famous for his advocacy, who drew the crowds like a movie star.

The President of the Court had a fine head of silky gray hair; one of the Assessors was a very young man, and seemed ill at ease, the other spent his whole time doodling.

Tony was aware of the place and the people, but they seemed to have no connection with him, like places and people seen from a moving train. The jury fascinated him, and he subjected each of them in turn to a long scrutiny, so that, by the second day of the hearing, he knew every line in their faces.

Standing, with an air of respectful attention, he answered the questions put to him, readily and unhesitatingly, as he had done throughout the preliminary examination. After all, he had heard all the questions so often before that he knew the answers almost by heart.

The first witness was the old woman with a squint, La Louchote. She, it seemed, was the first person to have seen Andrée going into the Hôtel des Voyageurs by the back door, one day as she was coming out of the station at Triant.

As luck would have it, she was in the Rue Gambetta two hours later, just as Andrée was leaving the inn. After this, as her train to Saint-Justin was not due for some little time, La Louchote had gone into the café, and the first person she saw there was Tony.

This, then, was how all the rumors started, the rumors of which Falcone was to remain in ignorance until long afterwards. Painstaking Inspector Mani had cast his net wide, and he had found La Louchote at the end of a long trail.

Witness after witness was called to the stand, men and women known to him, many whom he called by their Christian names, some whom he had known at school. They were dressed in their Sunday clothes, and from time to time one or another of them provoked a burst of laughter in the court with some unintentionally comic remark or gesture.

Old Angelo was there in the second row, motionless and impassive, as he was to remain from beginning to end of the trial. Vincente, until his turn came to give evidence, was in the waiting room with the other witnesses, among whom were Françoise and old Madame Despierre. Afterwards, he sat beside his father.

"You are the brother of the accused, and, as such, you cannot give evidence on oath."

It was very hot in the courtroom, and there was a smell of unwashed bodies. A pretty young woman lawyer, a pupil of Maître Capade, kept handing peppermints to her Master. Once she turned around and offered one to Andrée, and then, with some hesitation, to Tony.

Tony had a kaleidoscopic impression of noses, eyes, smiles, yellowish teeth in gaping mouths, the incongruous brightness of a woman's red hat, and, interspersed with all this, words and phrases which might have meant something if he could have been bothered to put them together.

"You say that your brother Tony and the accused, the Despierre, met about once a month in room Number Three of your hotel, the room you call 'the blue room.' Did you make a habit of letting rooms for assignations of this kind?"

Poor Vincente, to be publicly insulted, when all he had ever done was to exhort his brother to make a clean break, the sooner the better!

And there was another thing too. During Tony's evidence, the President had remarked:

"You were so passionately in love with Andrée Despierre that you had no compunction in exploiting your brother and sister-in-law by using their home as a place for your illicit love-making."

Well, after all, it was a hotel, wasn't it? There were times when he could not help smiling, as though it were all happening to someone else. The President, striving after effect, never missed an opportunity for a sardonic or wounding comment, which he knew the newspapers would be only too eager to report.

Each time, the famous advocate from Paris, not to be outdone, got to his feet to counter with some barbed witticism of his own.

Maître Demarié had urged Tony to engage a second lawyer for the defense, as Andrée had done, but he did not wish it.

In his opinion, it was all a waste of time. For the benefit of the jury and the public, they were re-enacting the long-drawn-out drama previously rehearsed in Judge Diem's office.

The setting was more solemn, there were many more actors, not to mention the extras and the added glamour of ceremonial and rhetoric, but in essence it was unchanged.

They moved from one significant date to the next, with details of all the comings and goings, and when they got to the letters, there was pandemonium. Fierce argument broke out, not only between prosecution and defense, but between individual lawyers on either side. Every word was torn to shreds, and at one point Maître Follier brandished a volume of Littré's dictionary, to illustrate the diversity of meanings which could be read into words which people use every day of their lives.

Andrée, wearing black, followed the debate with more interest and attention than he could muster, and she leaned across to him from time to time, with a smile or a look which seemed to say: "What do you think about it?"

The battle of the forensic scientists was held over until the third day.

"Hitherto," said the President, "I have always believed that the sale of poisons was strictly controlled by law, and that they could not be procured without a doctor's prescription. But what do we find in this case?

"Kept in a shed, which is always unlocked in the daytime, an old cocoa tin containing more than six hundred grains of strychnine, a sufficient quantity, in fact, if the toxicologists are to be believed, to kill twenty people.

"In Despierre's grocery shop, in the storeroom at the back, next to the foodstuffs, we find five pounds—five pounds, do you hear—of the same poison, not to mention quite a large stock of arsenic."

"We all deplore it," retorted one of the experts, "but unfortunately that is how the law stands. While the sale of poisons by pharmacists is strictly controlled, highly poisonous pesticides can be bought freely at any farmers' co-operative, drugstore, or village general shop."

There they all were in their places, from morning to night, day after day, magistrates, members of the jury, lawyers, policemen, journalists. Even the spectators seemed to have reserved seats, and their numbers were swelled by the witnesses who joined them one by one as they left the witness box.

From time to time one of the crowd of lawyers near the little door would slip out to represent a client in another court, and during the adjournment the sound of people relaxing after long tension filled the room.

Each time the Court adjourned, Tony was taken to a dark room with one small window high above his head. Andrée, no doubt, was taken to a similar room somewhere in the building. Demarié brought him fizzy drinks. The magistrates, he supposed, had them too. In time, they were all summoned to their appointed places by a bell, as in a theater or movie house.

It was a dramatic moment when Madame Despierre, her chalk-white face even whiter than usual, took the stand. And with her, the President's manner was gentler, for she was, in a sense, one of the victims.

"I never approved of the marriage. I knew no good would come of it. Unfortunately, my son loved this woman, and I hadn't the heart to oppose his . . ."

Why was it that some things stuck in his mind more than others?

"Much as it grieves me to distress you, Madame, by reviving unhappy memories, I must ask you to recall the circumstances of your son's death."

"If she hadn't pushed me out of my own house, I would have been there to look after him, and no harm would have come to him. That girl never loved him, you see. She knew he hadn't long to live. When she took a lover . . ."

"You were aware, then, of her association with the accused, Falcone?"

"Everyone in Saint-Justin was, except my poor Nicolas."

"It appears, however, that in August of last year his suspicions were aroused."

"I was hoping he would catch them in the act, and throw her out. Instead of which she managed to get around him somehow."

"What was your reaction when you found your son dead?"

"I suspected at once that it was not due to one of his attacks, and that his wife had some hand in it."

"You had no proof, of course."

"I bided my time, waiting for them to do something about his wife."

She was pointing at Tony.

"I knew it was bound to come. And I've been proved right by events."

"Was it you who wrote an anonymous letter to the Public Prosecutor two days after Madame Falcone's death?"

"The experts were not able to identify the handwriting as mine. It could have been anyone."

"Let us turn to the jam, the jar bought by Monsieur Falcone. Who took delivery of the goods?"

"I did. The previous night. That is to say, Tuesday, February 16th."

"Did you open the parcel?"

"No. I could tell what it was from the label. I put it in the stock room."

Tony, for once, roused himself and listened with interest. He was not the only one to favor the witness with his marked attention. His lawyer got to his feet and moved a little closer, as though wishing to be sure of hearing every word. If he was hoping, by this means, to disconcert the witness, he was in for a disappointment.

It was Madame Despierre's evidence that would tip the scales one way or the other for Tony.

"What time did you go into the shop that morning?"

"The morning of the 17th? At seven o'clock as usual."

"Did you see the parcel?"

"It was still there, where I had left it."

"With the string intact and the strip of Scotch tape unbroken?"

"Yes."

"You were behind the counter until ten minutes to eight, when your daughter-in-law took over, and you went home for a bite to eat. Is that correct?"

"That is so."

"How many people were there in the shop when you left?"

"Four. I had just finished serving Marguerite Chauchois when I saw that man coming across the road toward the shop. I went home through the garden."

She was lying. And she gave Tony a look of open defiance. She could not help herself. If she had admitted having seen the parcel unwrapped that morning, as it must have been, or, better still, the night before, it would have proved that Andrée had had all the time she needed to poison the jam.

If, on the other hand, the parcel had been, as the old woman claimed, intact when she left, Andrée could not have done it in the time—barely two minutes—that she kept him waiting in the shop.

It was not enough for old Madame Despierre that Andrée should pay for Nicolas's death. Tony must pay for it too.

"If your Lordship pleases, I humbly submit . . ." objected Maître Demarié, above the murmur that had broken out at Madame Despierre's last words.

"You will have ample time to present your case to the jury when you address them in due course."

Tony was not looking at Andrée. According to the newspapers, she had smiled at this, smiled avidly, as one correspondent put it.

For the first time, Tony noticed the Molard sisters, sitting way at the back, wearing identical dresses and hats, with identical handbags in their laps, their faces more moonlike than ever under the milky courtroom lights.

Andrée had been called to the witness box before Tony, and in the course of her evidence she had stated with pride, or rather proclaimed to the Court and the public, as though it were a declaration of faith:

"I did not poison my husband, but I might have done so if he had lingered on too long. I loved Tony, and I love him still."

"How were you intending to get rid of Madame Falcone?"

"That was none of my business. I wrote to Tony. I said 'Over to you!' I only had to wait. I knew I could trust him."

"Wait for what?"

"Wait for him to get his freedom, as we had decided he would as soon as I was free myself."

"You did not foresee that he would kill her?"

Andrée, holding her head high, had said, her powerful, throaty voice ringing through the Court:

"We loved each other!"

The uproar was such that the President threatened to clear the Court.

The whole course of events had been determined from the first day. And that was not the day of Nicolas's death, nor the day of Gisèle's agony.

The first day was August 2nd of the previous year, when Tony stood naked in the sizzling heat of the blue room, feeling very pleased with himself, and looked at Andrée's reflection sliced in half by a beam of sunlight.

"Have I hurt you?"

"No."

"Are you angry with me?"

"No."

"Will your wife question you?"

"I don't think so."

"Doesn't she ever?"

Gisèle was still alive then, and soon after these words were spoken he was back home in their brand-new house with her and Marianne.

"You have a beautiful back. Do you love me, Tony?"

"I think so."

"Aren't you sure?"

Had he loved her? There was a policeman sitting between them, and from time to time she leaned across to look at him with the expression he had seen on her face in the room at Triant.

"Would you like to spend the rest of your life with me?"

"Of course!"

The words had ceased to have any meaning, yet this was what it was all about, this ludicrously solemn trial; about things that were lost in oblivion, about a man, for that matter, who was lost in oblivion.

The Public Prosecutor, his face running with sweat,

spoke for the whole of one afternoon, and concluded by demanding the death penalty for both the accused.

The whole of the next day was taken up with the closing speeches of the lawyers, and it was eight o'clock in the evening before the jury retired to consider their verdict.

"There's still hope," declared Maître Demarié, pacing up and down the little room. Tony was much the calmer of the two.

Did the lawyer believe in his innocence? Or was he undecided? It was of no importance. He never stopped looking at his watch. By half-past nine, the bell to recall them to the courtroom had not yet shrilled in the corridor.

"It's a good sign. As a rule, when the jury is out a long time, it means . . ."

There was half an hour longer to wait, then they all filed back into the courtroom and resumed their seats. One of the ceiling lights had blown a fuse.

"I must warn members of the public that I will not tolerate any disturbance."

The foreman of the jury got to his feet and read from a sheet of paper:

"Concerning Andrée Despierre, née Formier, the verdict of this jury is: on the first count, guilty; on the second count, guilty; on the third count, not guilty."

She had been found guilty of the premeditated murder of her husband, but not guilty of the murder of Gisèle.

"Concerning Antonio Falcone, the verdict of this jury is . . ."

He was acquitted on the charge of murdering Nicolas, but found guilty of the murder of Gisèle. In his case, too, premeditation was held to have been proved. The President of the Court bent down to talk in an undertone to one or another of his Assessors, and, as everyone waited, the tension in the silent courtroom was electric.

At length the President pronounced sentence. The death penalty for both the accused, commuted to a life sentence of hard labor on the jury's recommendation of mercy.

In the tumult that followed, with everyone milling about, shoving and colliding in the well of the Court, Andrée stood up and slowly turned toward Tony.

This time, he could not turn his head away, but fixed his eyes on her face, mesmerized. Never before, even in their most intimate embraces, had he seen her so beautiful, so radiant. Never before had he seen her voluptuous mouth curve in such a smile of love triumphant. Never before had she so completely taken possession of him as she did now with a single look.

And then her voice rang out:

"You see, Tony, we'll never be parted now!"

THE ACCOMPLICES

CHAPTER

I

It was brutal, instantaneous. And yet he was neither surprised nor resentful, as if he had always been expecting it. He realized in a flash, as soon as the horn started screaming behind him, that the catastrophe was inevitable and that it was his fault.

It was not an ordinary horn that was pursuing him with a kind of anger and terror, but a mournful, agonizing howl such as one hears in a port on a foggy night.

At the same time, he saw in his mirror the red and black bulk of a huge bus bearing down on him and the contracted face of a man with grizzled hair, and he realized that he himself was driving in the middle of the road.

It did not occur to him to free his hand which Edmonde continued to press between her thighs. He would not have had time.

He had almost reached the bottom of the Big Hill where the road took a ninety-degree turn to the right and seemed, from a distance, to be blocked by the wall surrounding the Château Roisin estate.

It had been raining for some minutes, just enough to cover the asphalt with a sticky film.

Oddly enough, at that moment he accepted everything, both the catastrophe and his guilt. He knew that his life was about to be cut in two, that perhaps it was going to be over, and, without believing in what he was doing, he did what had to be done. He made an effort with his free left hand to pull over to the right. But, as he expected, the car skidded and whipped around into a position athwart the road.

Nevertheless, the bus whizzed by miraculously, and Lambert thought he heard the oath that the terrified driver shrieked at him. Behind the glass, he caught sight of the heads of children who were not aware of anything. There was a shock, a tearing of sheet metal, and the mastodon, which had hit a tree, kept rolling, sideways, to the bottom of the slope.

His own car, which had almost stopped, picked up speed again, docilely, as if nothing had happened, whereas the bus crashed headlong with all its mass into the Château Roisin wall.

Lambert did not stop, did not think of stopping. He fled so as not to see and had the presence of mind not to follow the highway but to take the road to the right that led to La Galinière.

Edmonde had not screamed, had not moved. He had merely felt her body stiffen and draw back, and it seemed to him that she had shut her eyes.

He dared not look in the mirror to see what was happening behind him, but he could not help casting a quick glance before the first turn and seeing a blazing mass.

Never had he had such a ghastly sensation in all his being, not even when he had been buried by the bursting of a shell. It seemed impossible that he could keep driving, breathing, looking in front of him. Something was going to crack in his head, or in his chest, and he was in such a sweat that his hands slid on the wheel.

He thought of stopping, of turning around, but he simply couldn't. It was beyond his power. He didn't want to see. Panic drove him forward, an uncontrollable force on which he had no grip.

And yet he was able to think of details. At about a hundred yards from the turn, from the wall into which the bus had just crashed, was a gas station and snack bar run by Despujols and his wife. He knew them. He knew everyone within a radius of five miles from town. Old Madame Despujols was deaf, but her husband, who must have been working in the garden at that hour, had probably heard the crash. Did they have a phone? He couldn't remember. If not, Despujols would have to go to Saint-Marc, a hamlet a half-mile away, to give the alarm. He did not have a car. He would go by bicycle.

Lambert still did not dare look at Edmonde, who remained motionless. She must have pulled down her dress without his noticing, for he no longer saw the light color of her knees.

Something had to be done, he had to go somewhere, he did not yet know where. Now that he had taken the bend and was on the road to La Galinière, he had lost the right to turn around and go back. Nor did he dare show himself in the village, which was a half-mile away. He took the first dirt road, on the left, frightened at the thought that he might pass a peasant.

If he got to the Coudray highway, he would be safe. He could pretend to be coming from anywhere, not to know anything, not to have been on the Big Hill that day.

A farm loomed up at the right, but he saw no one. It was still raining, a late-summer slanting rain, almost an autumn rain. His heart kept pounding away. His damp hand continued to tremble on the wheel.

He was ashamed, and he felt miserable. Yet he was already forcing himself to think of everything, to foresee, and he heard himself say aloud:

"We'll stop at Tréfoux."

It was almost on the other side of town, around which wound the road to Coudray. He was familiar with all the roads, for he had construction jobs going on all over the region and he inspected the work almost every day. It so happened that he was on his way back from one of the jobs, at the Renondeau farm, where his men were putting up a metal barn.

He was also the builder of the milk co-operative in Tréfoux, which had a model cheese-dairy, and his men were now setting up, two hundred yards from the buildings, a large pig farm which would use the by-products.

He had worked hard, even harder than his father, harder than anyone else in town, and the labor of twenty-five years was now suddenly being threatened.

How many seconds had it taken? So few! Not even time enough for him to remove his right hand.

The driver must have blown his horn the first time about halfway up the hill. He wasn't sure. He hadn't been paying attention. Nevertheless, it came back to him as fragments of a dream come back. The driver had blown his horn to warn him. He had been going fast, driving children from a summer camp back to Paris or some city in the north.

Lambert finally reached the main road, and from then on it was as if he were returning to life. Cars and trucks were speeding along the smooth highway. Three hundred yards away was a red gas pump, and a little farther on was an inn with a terrace. He almost stopped there for a drink, perhaps to create an alibi by saying casually that he was coming from the Renondeau farm and was on his way to Tréfoux.

Wasn't that being too cautious? Wasn't there a danger of its being used against him? He often stopped at a country bar to drink a half-bottle of white wine, but never when his secretary was with him.

Edmonde seldom accompanied him. He could not have said why he had suddenly said to her this time, as he was about to leave for the farm:

"Take the blueprints with you, Mademoiselle Pampin, and wait for me in the car."

Marcel, his brother, who was in the office, had looked at him in that calm, exasperating way of his. What could Marcel have been thinking? Everyone lives in his own particular way. Marcel had chosen the life he wanted and seemed content with it. That was no reason for forcing his principles on others.

"Do you need the plans?"

Joseph Lambert had looked his brother in the eyes and answered, "I do."

This was not the first time they had affronted each other in that way, if it could be called affronting, since Marcel invariably backed down—which, be it added, is also a manner of speaking, for Marcel merely did not insist but simply looked at his brother with a smile that was as light as his blond, fluffy little mustache.

At that moment, it was not yet raining. The sun flooded the offices, which had been completely remodeled three years before and were separated, as in modern establishments, by glass walls. Joseph alone had an office in which he could isolate himself, in which it was even permissible, under the pretext that the sun was too bright, to lower the Venetian blinds. Therefore, nothing prevented him from calling in Mademoiselle Pampin as if he were going to dictate to her, or for some other work, for nobody, not even Marcel, would have taken the liberty of entering without knocking.

What had just happened was no doubt bound to happen. He had said, without thinking, without any precise desire:

"Take the blueprints with you, Mademoiselle Pampin, and wait for me in the car."

She was not unaware of what that meant.

They had driven about a mile south of town when suddenly they heard the fire siren.

Lambert knew it was too late. He had been in the war, he had seen tanks and trucks go up in flames and planes shot down.

He had to keep cool, to ignore the wail of the siren which reminded him of the desperate scream of the bus.

The dairy was lower down, on the bank of the same canal where his own plant was located, but the latter was on the edge of the town, just a stone's throw from a populous neighborhood. The men who worked on the new pig farm had just knocked off, and the only one around was the foreman, who was about to leave on his bicycle, carrying the knapsack in which he had brought his lunch. He put his hand to his cap.

"Good evening, Monsieur Joseph."

He had worked for Lambert senior for more than thirty years and had known his sons when they were youngsters. He called them Monsieur Marcel, Monsieur Joseph. He seldom had occasion to say Monsieur Fernand, since the third brother lived in Paris and hardly ever went back to his home town.

"Good evening, Nicolas. Everything all right?"

Edmonde had not got out of the car. For the first time since the Big Hill, Lambert ventured a glance at her. Would anyone have suspected, from looking at her, that she had just been involved in a catastrophe?

She was, of course, pale, but hardly more than usual. Her skin was naturally colorless, which was all the more surprising since she had the round face, full cheeks, and tall body of a healthy girl.

"Did you have time to prepare the girders?"

"A few minutes before the shower. Did you hear the siren? There must have been a fire somewhere."

"Must have been," repeated Lambert.

It bothered him to feel that Edmonde was staring at

him. What was she thinking? What did she think about what had happened? About what he had done? What was she thinking about him at that very moment? There was no way of telling. Never had he seen a face so indifferent as hers, and her body was as motionless as her features. One could have observed her for minutes on end without seeing a movement.

When he had hired her the year before, after the failure of Penjard, the hardware dealer, whose secretary she had been, the clerks were at first amused by her name and never missed an opportunity to repeat it and dwell on its syllables in a humorous way:

"Good morning, Mademoiselle Pampin!"

"Good-by, Mademoiselle Pampin!"

Among themselves they referred to her as *la Pampine,* and one day, through his open window, Lambert had heard a young mason say:

"That one's all animal!"

A man wearing corduroy breeches and leather leggings was walking toward them from the dairy, of which he was the manager. Lambert, who was standing near the car, put out his hand and the foreman again touched his cap.

"Hello, Bessières."

"Hello, Monsieur Lambert."

"Did you hear the sirens?" asked old Nicolas.

"Yes, and I immediately put in a call to town. It seems that a bus full of children crashed into the Château Roisin wall and caught fire."

He took out his handkerchief and wiped away the beads of sweat on his forehead. He had six children. They were playing in the yard of the dairy. And his wife was pregnant again.

This was the first serious test. Lambert, who had not been expecting it so soon, did not have time to decide what attitude to assume. Edmonde's presence disturbed him. He was surprised to hear himself say, in a natural tone:

"A summer camp?"

"Probably. There are no details."

Lambert also wiped his face, with what seemed to him a calm movement, and glanced at his hand to see whether it was trembling. It was better not to say that he had come from the Renondeau farm by the Coudray highway. He was always tempted to talk too much.

"I came to take a look," he murmured. "Nicolas was telling me that if we have a few sunny days the whole job will be finished by the end of the month."

"Will you come in and have a drink?"

"Thanks, but I still have work to do at the office."

He had behaved normally. It had gone off as usual between people who had known each other a long time and had occasion to meet often.

"Is everything all right at home?"

Instead of answering, Bessières muttered, "I wonder whether I oughtn't to drive out and take a look at what happened over there."

That was all. Lambert got in his car and drove back. In the suburbs and then in town there was already an atmosphere of abnormal excitement. Groups were standing in front of doorways. Men and boys were riding off on their bicycles, all in the same direction.

At Town Hall Square, where he had an appointment to play bridge at the Café Riche in a half-hour, he passed an ambulance, which looked empty, on its way to the hospital. That was the worst moment of all. He almost stopped at the curb, as if all the energy had drained out of him.

In the café he caught sight of Lescure, the insurance agent, in the company of Nédelec. They were already at their table.

"Aren't you going to stop at the office?" asked Edmonde, as he seemed undecided.

It was the first time she had opened her mouth since the Big Hill. Her tone of voice was indifferent. He nevertheless wondered whether her question was not a discreet reminder.

"Perhaps I ought to."

"It's half-past six," she added.

He did not understand what the time had to do with it.

"What of it?"

"I was wondering whether you wanted me to go with you to the Quai Colbert or whether it wouldn't be better for me to get out here."

She was right. The office closed at half-past six.

"You can get out."

"Shall I leave the papers with you?"

"Yes, do."

"Good-by, Monsieur Lambert."

"Good-by, Mademoiselle Pampin."

She shut the door and went off in the direction of the nearby Saint-Georges quarter, where she lived with her mother. On seeing her disappear, he felt both relieved and slightly bewildered. They hadn't agreed on anything. They had made no allusion to what had happened. He didn't know whether she would talk or not. Did he even know what kind of person she was?

"Are you coming?" asked Weisberg, the owner of a local department store, another one of the bridge players, just as Lambert was starting up his engine.

"Not immediately. I've got to drop in at the office."

"Have you just got into town?"

"This very minute."

"Have you heard the news?"

"I was told about it at the dairy."

"I went over to take a look, but I couldn't. It was so awful that I rushed home to make sure my kids were alive."

Lambert managed to ask, "Was anyone uninjured?"

"No one. To be more exact, one of the girls. There were boys and girls in the bus. But it'll be a miracle if they manage to save her. Benezech is out there. So are the gendarmes. They're expecting the Deputy Prefect any minute, and the Prefect said he'll come before dark."

Benezech, the local Chief of Police, was another one of the bridge players, a tall, redheaded man with a bushy mustache and long light hair on his hands.

"See you later."

"All right, see you later."

In an hour, in two hours, perhaps no one would be talking to him in that tone, and perhaps there would be no one left to shake his hand. He had driven off, and all along the road people's faces were more grave and grim than usual. Women were crying on the sidewalks and in the stores.

As far as he remembered, there had been no traffic on the road when he drove down the Big Hill. He was practically sure that there had been no cars coming in his direction, and he had not seen any truck parked in the middle of the hill, as often happened.

But weren't there any bicycles? Would he have noticed them?

And when he turned right in the direction of La Galinière, wasn't some member of the Despujols family on the doorstep? That was unlikely, but not impossible. His car was black, but there were lots of others like it in town and in the surrounding area. People rarely have the presence of mind to note the number on a license plate.

A peasant in his field, for example, might very well have recognized him as he drove by. He had a distinctive face, and he was one of the well-known men of the region.

From Château Roisin onward, he was practically sure of himself, for everything had automatically registered in his memory, including a reddish brown cow that had escaped from its pasture and was wandering along the edge of the road.

But higher up? The man with the goats, in particular, whose name he didn't know, an odd creature who owned a shanty on the national highway and who took his four or five nanny goats out to pasture along the road for hours on end?

People were so used to seeing his figure when they drove up or down the Big Hill that they paid no attention to it. At that moment, Lambert did not yet have any reason to be concerned about whom he passed. It now became important. Between the time of the accident and the arrival of help it had not rained enough to wash away the tracks of tires on the road. The gendarmes must have been interested in that. Likewise Benezech and his men.

Lambert had read in the newspapers about amazing reconstructions of accidents of which there had been no witness. It would be known immediately that the bus, which had been going downhill, had made a desperate maneuver to avoid another car which was in the middle of the road and which, instead of pulling over, had skidded even farther to the left.

It was inevitable that they look for that car.

Right in front of the plant, above which was a signboard with the words "J. Lambert & Sons," a canal boat was moored to the unloading dock. On its ropes hung linen which had been soaked by the rain. A little girl was pressing her face against one of the windows of the cabin. Her faded hair and flattened nose and the mist of her breath on the glass gave her a ghostly look.

The lamp was already lit inside, where it grew dark early. The man must have gone for a drink at the little café by the canal lock, three hundred yards downstream, while his wife was preparing the evening meal.

The office was closed and the employees had left. So had Marcel, who perhaps had rushed to the scene of the accident when he heard the siren. Being somewhat frail, he had been assigned to duty as a nurse during the war, and afterwards he had joined the Red Cross. He took his role seriously. He took all of life seriously, and he was proud, in particular, that his elder brother had been admitted to the Military School of Engineering and that his younger brother had been the most brilliant student in the lycée.

As for his daughter Monique, where would he have sent her to school if not to the Convent of Our Lady?

Lambert almost left the Renondeau documents in the car. He went back to get them, opened the office door with his key, and placed the folder on Mademoiselle Pampin's table.

Jouvion, the night watchman, was already in his hut, behind piles of beams, bricks, and bondstone, for smoke was rising from the stovepipe which projected above the tin roof.

Someone was walking on the first floor—Lambert's wife or the maid. So that things would be no different from what they were other days, he took the stairway leading to the apartment.

It had formerly been his parents' home, and he and his two brothers were born there, at a time when the plant was much smaller and less modern. He was at least seventeen when the first bathroom was installed.

If his mother and father could have returned to life, neither of them would have recognized the look of the rooms and the way they were furnished. His mother had been the first to go, ten years before; it was only three years since old Lambert had died. Not of old age or sickness, but as a result of a fall from an unbalanced beam sixty feet from the ground. To the very end, active work had been his pride and joy. He would wave the young men aside and say, in his throaty voice, "Let me do it, my boy!"

Lambert caught sight of Angèle, the maid, in the lighted kitchen. She must have known what had happened, for she was sniffling and her eyes were red.

"Isn't Madame home?"

"No, sir. She left as soon as she heard the news."

"Alone?"

"Monsieur Marcel took her in his car."

He suddenly felt overwhelmed, as if everything were being directed against him, as if an enemy clan were already in the process of formation.

"Didn't Monsieur go to have a look?"

"No."

"It seems that it's awful, one of the most horrible accidents there's been. All those poor darlings who were going back to their parents and who . . ."

He lit a cigarette feverishly, the first since the Big Hill.

"I wonder how many of them they'll be able to save. It was announced on the radio a little while ago that . . ."

He noticed merely that the little kitchen radio was on, though it was turned down.

He could not go to bed, could not say he was sick and shut the door on everyone as he felt like doing. He had to behave as he did other evenings, had to talk, to listen, to nod his head and sigh, he too.

"I'll be back at the usual time, Angèle."

That meant at about eight o'clock. He walked to the bathroom as usual, likewise so as not to change his routine, washed his hands, and ran a comb through his hair. As he soaped his hands, it seemed to him that they retained the odor of Edmonde.

He was tempted to drink a glass of brandy, the driest possible, in order to calm his nerves, but he had the courage not to. He liked to drink. It was almost part of his work. After a few glasses, he sometimes talked too much, with a certain pomposity, which he then took for sincerity. Sometimes, at the Café Riche, he would let himself go so far as to bang his fist on the table and roar:

"If only we weren't surrounded by that gang of jerks!"

Or else he would exclaim indignantly, referring to God knows whom, "The day everyone decides to stop being fooled by those bastards . . ."

It was agonizing to be walking in the empty apartment and then in the unlit office, which he went through as if he were fleeing. He envied the people on the barge who were about to sit down at the table, for they got up at five in the morning. He even envied old Jouvion, who was probably cooking potatoes on the cast-iron cover of his stove.

Tomorrow, the day after tomorrow, he would feel better, for he would know. If they were bound to arrest him, he would rather they did it right away. Tough luck! During the war, hadn't he been in danger of death almost every minute? Or of having a leg shot off? Or of becoming blind?

So?

He would not defend himself. He was in the wrong. Granted! No need to repeat it to him, since he had been the first to know it. As for the rest, that was his affair and no one else's. Everyone makes the best he can of his life, and he considered himself as decent a man as anyone he knew.

He drove off in his car and for a hundred yards forgot to turn on the lights. Though night had not yet fallen, the sun had set quite a while before.

The city looked more sinister in the lamplight, especially since the factories and offices were closed, for everybody was outside, on the sidewalk, in the cafés, discussing the accident, gesticulating, bewailing, with women crying and children whom they didn't know what to do with and in whose presence they suddenly grew silent.

At the Café Riche, however, four men were playing cards, as they did other evenings, at the table which Lambert had christened the "butcher's table" because Repellin the butcher was the life and soul of it, the one who took up the most room and spoke loudest.

Opposite them, Lescure and Nédelec were having their apéritif and conversing in low voices, but they had not laid out the green cloth or called for a deck of cards.

"Isn't Weisberg here?" asked Lambert in astonishment. "I met him a little while ago and he said . . ."

"His wife rang him up."

"Something wrong at home?"

"One of his friends who has a store in Paris heard the news over the radio, and since his son . . ."

"In the bus?" he asked.

"Yes. Most probably. They don't quite know. Two buses left at about the same time, each with half the campers. The second is still on the road somewhere, but they haven't been able to contact it yet, so there's no knowing which children were killed and which weren't. Town Hall's been flooded with phone calls. Since those people know Weisberg . . ."

"What will you have, Monsieur Lambert? As usual?"

"As usual" meant a pernod, and he nodded.

"I saw Benezech with the Lieutenant of the gendarmes. They both looked pretty sick. The hotels don't know what to do. Everyone's reserving rooms, the papers for their reporters and photographers, and the parents who still don't know . . . When the train arrives from Paris this evening . . ."

Nédelec, the grain merchant, interrupted the insurance agent.

"Two journalists, one of them from the radio, have already arrived by plane. They were almost killed landing in a field."

Lescure also had children, and even grandchildren, for his two daughters were married. Nédelec, who was a widower, lived with his only daughter, who was deaf and dumb.

They could hear the noise of traffic on the square. It was denser than on other evenings, and four or five policemen were stopping cars from going in the direction of the Big Hill.

Lambert, who had just sipped his apéritif, was himself surprised at being able to ask:

"Do they know how many there were?"

"Forty-eight, plus the driver, a middle-aged woman who they assume was the camp mother, and a girl who was a counselor."

He could see himself in the mirror opposite, among other faces, and also the reflection of the lighted lamps and of the smoke that drifted above their heads. Didn't they have anything else to tell him? Would he have to ask *all* the questions?

He emptied his glass and signaled to the waiter for another.

"Don't they know how it happened?"

"Some engineers have come to help the police and the gendarmes. As far as they know now, a car was zigzagging along the road and suddenly got in front of the bus, which tried to avoid a collision. The bus hit a tree and was literally thrown against the Château Roisin wall. For ten years there's been talk of demolishing that wall, which no longer serves any purpose, and of reshaping the curve. How many accidents have there been on that spot in the last ten years?"

"I don't know."

"Benezech was talking to me about it the other day. It's a matter that I've studied, too, from the point of view of insurance. Sixty-eight accidents, twelve of them mortal. This time, they're obviously going to do something about it."

The police office was directly opposite, on the left side of the Town Hall building, the windows of which were all lit up as on the evening of the big annual ball. Behind one of them could be seen the silhouette of Benezech, recognizable by his mustache, and that of a gendarme who had not removed his cap. Cars and motorcycles were constantly stopping at the foot of the stone stairway, where policemen were vainly trying to scatter the onlookers.

A black car on which was painted the name of a newspaper of a neighboring region stopped at the curb, and a tall young man in a raincoat rushed into the café.

"Can I telephone?"

Souriac, the proprietor, who was standing near the bar, merely pointed to the booth.

"Have you seen any other newspapermen?"

"Not yet."

The four belote players at the butcher's table were fingering their cards and chips, though they looked somewhat uncomfortable. But what else could they have done? They had merely muffled their voices.

"I trump! Ten of hearts, that does it, spades, that does it, and, last of all, this nice little seven of clubs which does me no good at all."

The butcher was proud of what he had done and looked at the others defiantly.

Capel, the history teacher at the lycée, who played bridge almost every evening, entered the café with his measured pace, slowly took off his hat and raincoat, hung them on their usual hook, and, turning to the table, asked with surprise, "Isn't anyone playing?"

CHAPTER

2

It was ten past eight when he parked his car along the curb. Looking up, he saw a light in the dining room. Without going through the office, he went up the main stairway. He heard the radio in the kitchen and found the dining room empty, with only one place set. He opened the bedroom door, mechanically, because the slightest change in his usual routine seemed to him dangerous that evening, and, looking into the darkness, asked, "Are you there?"

It was ridiculous. The bedroom was empty too. In the hallway, on his way to the kitchen, he almost bumped into Angèle.

"Hasn't Madame come back?"

"She phoned and asked that you call her at the home of Madame Jeanne."

"A long time ago?"

"About half-past seven. Shall I serve dinner?"

He was about to answer no, that he wasn't hungry or

that he would have dinner out, but from now on he had to be wary even of people as insignificant as the maid.

"I'll telephone Madame first."

When Nicole was out, he could always be sure that she had gone to see one of her three sisters, most often Jeanne. In their mother's lifetime, the four Fabre girls, who were all married, met in her house almost daily, as if it were their real home.

"Hello! . . . Who's speaking? . . . Is that you, Jeanne? . . . Raymonde?"

Raymonde's presence at the other end of the wire meant that the eldest daughter, whose husband, Barlet, was in the insurance business, like Lescure, was also dining at her sister's.

"I'll call Nicole, Joseph . . . It's frightful, isn't it? . . . It's made us all sick . . . Poor Jeanne . . ."

The telephone had to be taken from her hands. Nicole's voice replaced her sister's.

"Joseph? I phoned Angèle to tell her to give you dinner. I'm staying at Jeanne's. She had the most terrible shock a little while ago and she's not over it yet. She was returning from Bonnières with the children . . ."

Bonnières was a few miles from the Renondeau farm, and Lambert suddenly remembered that his sister-in-law, who had a small car, went there often to spend the afternoon with a friend.

"Did she come back by way of the Big Hill?"

"She did. Just imagine, she arrived at Château Roisin only a few minutes after the accident. Actually she was one of the first on the spot, while the bus was in flames. It was impossible to go near it. You can imagine what she went through, with her two children in the car. She returned in such a state that she had to be put to bed. . . ."

He found nothing to say. It frightened him to learn that his sister-in-law had been not more than a mile or two behind him and could have recognized his car from the top of the hill.

"I won't be home late, but there's no need to wait for me. Are you planning to go out?"

"I don't think so."

"See you later. Victor will drive me back."

Jeanne and her husband, who had a job at Town Hall, were the least affluent members of the family, the last to buy a car, a secondhand Renault, and this made them even more eager to use it.

Lambert sat down alone in the dining room, and Angèle immediately appeared with the soup tureen. He filled his plate absent-mindedly, without looking at the maid.

"Has Monsieur heard the latest news? The radio's been making a special announcement every half-hour."

He didn't realize that he was eating and that the warmth of the soup was doing him good.

"The catastrophe was the fault of a touring car which, according to the police, was being driven by a drunken driver. The car zigzagged along the road, and the bus driver, trying to avoid him . . ."

He looked up at her and wondered what her reaction would be if he declared:

"That was my touring car, and I wasn't drunk."

No doubt she would be all the more ready to condemn him in that the only feeling she had ever had for him was a kind of contemptuous pity. She despised men in general, regarding them as monsters, and him in particular, but a monster hardly responsible for his acts.

At the age of forty, she was without charm, without femininity. Had men ever looked at her? They must have, since she had had a child, a boy who was now about twelve and who was being brought up on a farm as far out of town as possible, more than twenty-five miles away.

She had never spoken about him, not even to Nicole, who had learned of his existence by pure chance, and Nicole had never mentioned him to Angèle either.

As a result of her experience, all men, especially men

like her employer, were a contemptible breed, and perhaps she felt no more kindly toward Nicole, for she also disliked those whom she called the rich.

The world, as she saw it, was filled with millions of sinners and only a few right-minded people, like herself, who inevitably were victims but who would have their revenge in another life.

"He didn't even stop to help those innocent babes, and he didn't even have the decency to give the alarm. Old Monsieur Despujols had to ride all the way to Saint-Marc before he could finally telephone to town. I wonder what ought to be done to people like that."

She spoke with such passion that he feared for a moment she might have a notion in the back of her mind. Had the radio mentioned a black Citroën?

"I'll bring in your cutlet."

He ate it as he had eaten his soup, observing the maid, who, when not addressing him, moved her lips silently, the way sanctimonious women often do. Wasn't this an undreamed-of opportunity for women like her to unbosom themselves? Weren't there hundreds of them in town and elsewhere for whom the Château Roisin catastrophe became a kind of outlet?

He was going to stay at home, as he had informed Nicole, and when he had finished eating he went into the living room, where he was about to put on the radio. In fact, he turned the knob. The light went on, but, not having the heart to listen, he immediately switched it off and plopped down into his usual chair.

He and his wife seldom went out. Except two evenings a week when they played bridge at the home of friends—Nicole, who did not play, took needlework with her—they remained alone together without exchanging a half-dozen remarks. She was almost always knitting for the poor, for she was involved in all the local welfare organizations. He would read newspapers and magazines, occasionally a book. At times, no longer able to bear it, he would suddenly stand up and go down to the dock for a quarter of an hour for a breath of air.

There had never been any real trouble between them nor any serious arguments. The vacuum had been created imperceptibly.

When he had married her, she had been, like her three sisters, a rather gay and pretty girl, and he had thought it would be pleasant to spend his life with her.

Her father, Doctor Fabre, was fond of good living, and their home was cheerful, always full of whispering and laughter.

He would have been unable to tell how it had happened. There had been no spark. Nicole had not become a Lambert wife. She had remained a Fabre girl.

He dared not ask the other sons-in-law how they put up with it. Barlet, the insurance man, did not seem unhappy, but he spent three weeks a month out of town. Soubise, who sold fertilizer, thought only of making money, and Nazereau, the husband of Jeanne, who was the youngest, had a job at Town Hall and seemed delighted, when he came home, to find one or two sisters-in-law there.

When Nicole's husband went out alone and returned late at night, she never reproached him. She was probably kept informed, if only by her sisters, of most of his escapades, but she never alluded to them.

One night, however, a few years earlier, after a rather scandalous affair with a girl, she had simply said to him, when he moved over into her bed, "No, Joseph, not that. No more of that."

She had not wept. He was certain that it had not made her suffer, that perhaps it had been a relief to her. They did not have separate bedrooms because of the nature of the apartment. They had twin beds, and when they went to sleep they undressed in front of each other in all simplicity. When he was sick, Nicole took care of him.

Should she have married his brother Marcel? As for himself, would Marcel's wife have been happier with him?

What was the point? In spite of everything, the fact that she wasn't there that evening made the house unbearable. He got up, took his hat, and went to the kitchen, where Angèle was cleaning up.

"If Madame gets back before me, tell her I've gone out for some air."

"Are you going over there? You won't be able to, because hundreds of cars are coming in from everywhere and they've had to block the road."

He did not take the car. All he really wanted was to breathe the night air and calm his nerves. He was thinking of too many things at once. His brain was racing, like an engine, and it was physically agonizing.

He stood for some time looking at the canal and noticed that a second barge had noiselessly moored itself to the first. Floating side by side on the still water, with no other light than a lantern on deck, they gave a strange impression of peace and comfort.

The women and children were in bed. Yet, in the silence of the night, Lambert could hear the murmur of voices, and when his eyes grew accustomed to the darkness he finally made out two men sitting near the helm. He could see their bright white shirt sleeves and the red tip of a cigarette.

Without quite making up his mind, he started walking toward the Rue de la Ferme, where radios were blaring from almost all the houses. At the corner of a blind alley was a small, dimly lit bar in which the only two customers were standing at the rail and chatting with the proprietor.

He would have liked to go in, to order anything, to join in their conversation, or merely to listen, for he suddenly felt a desire for human contact, any human contact. He knew what would happen if he let himself go. He would not be satisfied with one drink. He would have more in order to steady his nerves, and, instead, the liquor would excite him and make him talkative. He might be overcome by an irresistible need to confess.

It had happened in the case of trifles, things that most men don't worry about.

At the end of the almost deserted street, he found himself, after a bend, at the beginning of the narrow Rue du Vieux Marché, one of the oldest streets in town. It was full of little shops that were squeezed together. During the day it teemed with people, and even now it was far from empty. A small grocery and, farther on, a dimly lit herb shop were still open. One could feel there was life in the darkness of the alleys. Men and women were leaning against rails and talking from window to window.

As he walked by, he heard, in the characteristic tone of radio announcers, *"The police have good reason to think that they will shortly identify . . ."*

He did not stop to hear the rest of it. His first reaction was:

"So much the better!"

In that way, they would get it over with immediately. He wouldn't defend himself. He had made up his mind not to provide them with any explanation.

What could happen to him? Prison? Would he miss very much his evenings alone with Nicole? Even the late afternoon bridge games at the Café Riche disgusted him to some extent, and the proof was that every now and then he felt a need to lash out.

He wondered why he had fled. Panic had got the better of him, particularly of his flesh. His first and sharpest reaction, the one that determined all the rest, had been *not to see.* He would have been incapable of seeing. Precisely because of his feeling of guilt.

And now, to be really honest with himself, wasn't it fear that was making him almost sick? He could feel a wave of hatred rising up in town and no doubt all over France against the man who was still unnamed. If he denounced himself, would it be possible to stem the anger of the mob?

No one, he was sure of it, not even his friends at the Café Riche, would be clearheaded enough to examine his case fairly. Perhaps in a few days, when the feeling had subsided a little. He dared not look squarely at the people he passed in the street, though he listened eagerly for scraps of conversation. What he heard was not reassuring.

Feeling ran high, and the half-hourly radio bulletins keyed it up instead of dispelling it.

When he neared the quiet Rue Drouet, he felt a temptation to go and knock at Louise's door and perhaps tell her everything. Wasn't Louise capable of understanding? For twenty years she had been his father's friend, in fact his mistress. Everyone in town knew it. Had his father been luckier than he? Lambert was not judging his mother. He had never regarded her as anything but a mother and had no fault to find with her. She had worked all her life without complaining, keeping house, raising her children, attending to everything, the last to go to bed and the first to get up, nursing the others without accepting sickness for herself.

At the time of her marriage, she worked at the spinning mill and Joseph Lambert was a mason. Later, the firm and workyards were founded on the Quai Colbert. The business kept expanding and the workyards were now transformed; they now bore the name "J. Lambert & Sons" in tribute to the founder.

Why had old Lambert taken a mistress when he was about fifty, though his wife was still in her prime? His oldest son was the only member of the family who referred to the matter without shame or resentment. Marcel, for example, avoided all mention of Louise and had openly snubbed her at the funeral. The family pretended to think that she had acted only out of self-interest, though they knew quite well that this was untrue. When the father first met her, she was a typist in the office of Aubrun, the notary, and she remained there until the latter's death. She must have been about thirty at the time, twenty years younger than her lover, and in spite of her limp was an attractive woman. Her eyes in particular were beautiful, and her shoulders were so elegant that women would turn and look at her enviously.

"He nevertheless built a house for her," people said to his discredit.

It was true. After a few years, Lambert did build a little house for her on the Rue Drouet. Out of tenderness, or perhaps to amuse himself, he displayed such ingenuity that it resembled a toy.

When the father died, people thought that Louise would be remembered in his will. But she wasn't, and Louise, who was in her fifties, still worked in an attorney's office on the Rue Lepage, where she had been employed since the death of Monsieur Aubrun.

Whenever Lambert met her in the street, he greeted her. He had gone to see her, for the first time, shortly after the funeral in order to be sure that she was not in need, for he felt she had been treated unjustly. When he saw her in her own setting, he thought he understood his father's conduct and spoke of it the following day to Marcel, who interrupted him curtly:

"Please talk about something else."

Perhaps it was because Marcel took after his mother.

Joseph, on the other hand, had his father's sturdy, muscular build and thick, plebeian features, including a fleshy nose which tended to be shiny.

"What are you doing around here?"

He gave a start, as if caught red-handed, for he had not recognized the voice of Lescure, with whom he had nevertheless drunk an apéritif earlier in the evening.

"I'm not doing anything," he stammered. "I went out for a breath of air."

"I'm on my way home. I've just been at Town Hall Square. It's full of rubbernecks. I bet they'll spend the whole night there. Benezech is furious about the general hysteria. It interferes with the work of the police. Weisberg's friend . . ."

"Yes . . ."

"Everything's all right! He's wild with joy. He cried on the telephone and could hardly speak. His son was in the second bus, which arrived at Montargis and will be in Paris tomorrow."

Lescure lived nearby, in an old house with an inner court which dated from the seventeenth century and the portal of which was surmounted with a coat of arms.

"Are you going over there?" he asked.

"I'm not going anywhere."

"Don't you feel well?"

Lambert felt uneasy at his friend's noticing that he wasn't quite himself, and he was about to turn around and go home. He shook hands with his old schoolmate.

"Good night."

"Good night, old boy. See you tomorrow."

"Probably."

Even the word "tomorrow" took on a special meaning. How would things stand with him the following day? Had the man with the goats been wandering along the road at about half-past five, and had he recognized him as he drove by? The radio news bulletins implied that the police were on the trail of something. If they were after him, wouldn't they have already come and knocked on his door? And wouldn't Benezech have spoken about it to Lescure, who was a close friend of his?

In all likelihood, the highway engineers knew by now that the car was a Citroën, the tracks of which were different from those of other cars. There must have been at least fifty of them in the region. Had it been possible to find specific tire tracks despite the fact that it had continued to rain?

That worried him. He had changed his set of tires four months before, at the beginning of summer. He had bought a standard brand.

There were other possibilities, in fact so many that he had certainly not envisaged all of them. Could he have guessed, for example, that his sister-in-law Jeanne was behind him? It was about three miles from the bottom of the Big Hill to the crossroad nearest the Renondeau farm, and at the crossroad was a garage with four or five gas pumps.

Had a garage attendant seen him go by in the direction of Château Roisin a few minutes before the bus? He had been driving slowly, and it was for that very reason that he was not in control of the car when the emergency arose. Edmonde had not been talking at the time. Neither had he. He was now almost sure that when he had been about halfway down the hill a horn had blown some distance behind to warn him. The fact that he remembered it meant that it had registered, and yet he had paid no attention to it at the time. He had not kept to the right. His reflexes had not functioned, and that was how the accident had started. He had heard the horn as one hears a familiar sound which one no longer notices, just as he had passed the man with the goats dozens of times without seeing him.

He had not been drunk. Renondeau had insisted that he come and have a glass of white wine in his wine shed, but Lambert had refused a second glass. The fact is that he was capable of drinking two bottles, and even three, without feeling it and without its affecting his driving.

There was, of course, something else, but that was impossible to explain. People would recall certain escapades of his, particularly the one that had made Nicole refuse to allow him to get into bed with her. It had happened one night when he had really been drinking and had taken a girl to the Hôtel de l'Europe. He had known that she was just a tart, that she was one of the four or five streetwalkers who operated at night in the neighborhood of Town Hall.

She had gone too far, that was all. Either she had misjudged him or else someone had told her that when he was drunk he threw his money away. Humiliated at being taken for a sucker, he had lost his temper and thrown her into the corridor naked, after kicking her in the behind.

Benezech had fixed things up for him. But nevertheless it had been the talk of the town, and for weeks Marcel had looked at his brother with a bantering expression. What *didn't* people say about him? They had quite a choice. He made no secret of what he did. Often he showed off, on purpose, in order to shock people, "the horses' asses," as he would then call them.

Wouldn't people start saying that the fact that he had no children partly explained why he had driven away so heartlessly? Perhaps it was because Nicole and he had no children that they had never been a real couple. That was a subject it was better not to bring up when he was in a certain mood.

It was assumed, or people pretended to assume, that Nicole was barren. But her three sisters were mothers. Did that mean anything? Deep down, the question bothered him, and he often swore to himself that he would find out once and for all, that he would undergo certain medical tests.

At the last moment he would back out, because he was afraid. He would not admit it for anything. He had often wondered whether other people—his wife, for example—had had the same thought, and that was enough to make him sick or furious.

His brother Marcel had surely thought about it. Lambert remembered a day in the garden when he had stripped to the waist and was lifting heavy planks just for the fun of it. Marcel had looked at his hairy chest and, with an expression of false admiration, had whistled and said, "Quite a male!"

The fact is that it was in order to amuse Marcel's son that he had shown off that Sunday afternoon, since he had no children of his own to whom he could display his strength.

"Quite a male!"

The Town Hall clock, which looked like a brownish moon at the top of the dark tower, was ringing out half-past nine when he reached the square, which was as lively as on the evening of election day. The Café Riche was mobbed. There was not even a free seat on the terrace, the awning of which had been raised when the rain had stopped.

The air, which was still humid, was warmer than the night before. All the windows of Town Hall were still lit up. The crowd, which was moving slowly in couples or small groups, tended to congregate in front of the newspaper office, on the street window of which were already pasted a number of photographs of the bus after the accident. There were also some shots of the Deputy Prefect, the Prefect, a group of investigators in the middle of the road, and Police Chief Benezech in the company of the Lieutenant of the gendarmes.

On a bulletin board was a typewritten page containing the latest news:

"Dr. Poitrin and Dr. Julémont are still at the bedside of little Lucienne Gorre, whom they are trying to save. She has been given two blood transfusions. So many persons have gone to the hospital to offer blood that there has been a radio announcement requesting that they kindly refrain."

Another page, which was edged with a black ribbon so as to look like a funeral announcement, contained the names of the victims, with their ages and addresses. They all came from the Sixteenth Arrondissement of Paris, for the camp was connected with a school in that district.

By telephoto, announced a bulletin.

And below it were pasted other photos, grayish and all the more dismal, of parents massed in the schoolyard waiting for news. It had also rained in Paris, and some of them were holding umbrellas.

Lambert stood at the back of the crowd, fascinated by the gruesome exhibition and insensitive to the jostling of the passers-by. The newspaper had had time to enlarge a photograph for which it had also found a title:

Diagram of the Accident.

It showed simply the road on which the rain, by wetting the dust, had formed an almost plastic layer. One could see the tracks of the Citroën's tires and trace its path, and also follow the broader and deeper tracks of the bus as it headed for the tree, the damage to which was shown in another photo.

Thus, it was now known that when the driver of the automobile reached Château Roisin he did not continue on the main road but turned right in the direction of La Galinière. The gendarmes or the police had only to follow the track on the asphalt. How far did it lead them? The road to La Galinière was not covered with the same coating but with a granular substance. Had the rain washed away the marks of the tires before it had occurred to anyone to take prints?

There was no mention of this. But that meant nothing; in fact, perhaps something was being concealed.

Suddenly he opened his eyes wide at a sight which in itself was not extraordinary but which for him, at that moment, was nevertheless unexpected. As he stood on the edge of the sidewalk, facing the street windows of the newspaper, people kept passing between him and the backs of the other spectators.

He saw two women go by in that way, slowly, arm in arm, carried along by the stream of people, and glance at the display without stopping. One of them was Edmonde Pampin, pale as usual, but calm and relaxed, who was walking with her mother. They did not notice him. The mother, who was shorter than her daughter, was a heavy-set woman with broad hips. Both of them had gone out without a hat. Probably, as on Sundays, they were taking a walk around the square before going home and to bed.

He did not quite know why the sight of them upset him so. Perhaps it was Edmonde's serenity. She had merely cast a casual glance at the photographs. The mother and daughter were simply two ordinary persons in the crowd who had gone out for a bit of air on a very mild September evening.

He had a desire, for his own satisfaction, to give vent to

his feelings by blurting out an obscene word, any word, the most vulgar word that came to his lips. Was it possible that the girl who was walking so casually, with the face of a madonna, was not aware of anything? Or was she really as dumb as all that?

The words of the mason came back to him:

"An animal!"

And a wave of hatred welled up within him, choked him. He wheeled about and went off in the opposite direction.

He had just decided to drink, regardless of what might happen later, but he did not go to the Café Riche, which was too crowded and where there were too many of his friends. He kept walking until he got to the Rue Neuve, where he entered the first bar he saw.

There, too, it was more crowded than usual, but most of the customers were watching a boxing match on the television screen which was set up between the two rooms.

"What'll it be, Monsieur Lambert?"

The proprietor knew him. Lambert had often stayed on drinking until closing time, and it was there that he sometimes picked up a girl. The Hôtel de l'Europe, where he had been involved in the famous scandal, was just a few yards away.

"I'll have a marc!"

He ordered it because of its harshness and strong smell. He had a desire for something low, something that represented a kind of protest, a profession of faith. It was at such times that he would blurt out as he looked at the people around him:

"Gang of bastards!"

"How goes, Monsieur Lambert?"

"All right, Victor."

"Have you seen the excitement that the accident has whipped up in town?"

"I have."

"And it's not over, take my word for it."

Victor looked at the clock on the opposite wall.

"The train from Paris will be here in three-quarters of an hour with the families. It seems there are already more than five hundred rubbernecks waiting at the station to see them arrive."

"God damn it!"

"What?"

He had sworn between his teeth in a flash of anger, and he tossed the brandy down his throat with a furious gesture.

"Nothing. I'll have another!"

"I wouldn't want to be in the shoes of the guy with the Citroën. I bet that if he were tossed into the crowd on the square there'd be nothing left of him in ten minutes."

Perhaps Victor, who had been through the mill, was capable of understanding.

"Got to put yourself in the parents' place," he continued in a low voice. "As for me, I also put myself in the guy's place because I've witnessed quite a number of accidents in my life. What is there to prove that . . ."

"Shut up, Victor!"

Someone had snapped at the proprietor in a categorical tone and with a hard look.

"I'm only pointing out that certain people . . ."

"I said shut up! Do you hear me?"

And Victor remained silent, though looking at Lambert as if to say:

"What's the use?"

The man who had shut him up was one of the town's shady characters, a former boxer who made the rounds of the fairs in the region and was often in trouble with the police. The minute before, he had been following the boxing match on the television screen. The mere mention of the driver of the Citroën had been enough to make him fly off the handle.

Two whores at a table near the door were sitting and staring. Lambert knew them by sight, and they must have known who he was. One of them, who had a gold tooth, smiled at him when their eyes met.

He was tempted. Not that he felt any desire for her, but as a gesture of protest, as with the brandy. In view of how he felt, why not do something really low-down? They would then be able to go for him. His brother Marcel would be content, and Angèle and others like her would have good reason for despising him.

He imagined what the morning papers would say:

"The police searched the city all night long looking for Joseph Lambert, who was responsible for the catastrophe at Château Roisin, and finally arrested him in a hotel room where he was in bed with a streetwalker."

Wasn't that the kind of place where most criminals were picked up? He had never thought about it, but he began to understand why.

The woman with the gold tooth, who had perhaps noticed his hesitation, opened her bag and powdered her face without taking her eyes off him.

"I'll have another, Victor," he ordered.

From where she sat, the girl asked with a simper, "Me too?"

He shrugged. Let them drink as much as they liked, she and her friend, and all the women wandering around Town Hall as if they were at a fair!

"Should I?" asked Victor.

"Why not?"

His wife was at Jeanne's place, with her other sisters. All the Fabre girls were there with Nazereau, Jeanne's husband, a decent sort of moron, and, by God, all four of them were deeply moved! And all the high-minded folk in town were crying to their hearts' content. The photos weren't enough for them. They were all rushing to the station to watch the parade of the parents.

"Something wrong?"

That was the second time he had been asked the question, and coming from a man like Victor it was dangerous, for he was more subtle than Lescure.

"Why, I'm like everyone else!" he exclaimed.

"Off your feed, eh?"

There was a moment of silence.

"Did you have a look?"

"No."

"Lots of people did. Afterward, when everyone started going, they had to block the road. Those who saw the sight came back sick."

"Another!" he grunted.

Victor hesitated. He had, on other occasions, advised Lambert, in a friendly way, to stop. Why didn't he this time?

"You're not going . . . ?" he asked, without finishing his sentence, but with a glance at the two girls.

"Of course not!"

"Better not. Between you and me, I'm not sure they're clean."

He almost answered:

"Maybe it wouldn't be such a dumb thing to catch a dose!"

But he didn't. He paid immediately, feeling that things were going wrong, that he had to get home as fast as possible.

In the street, he kept repeating to himself in an undertone, "I've got to get home, I've got to get home . . ."

He was fed up with everything, with his wife, with his brother Marcel, with the girls in the bar and the bridge players, with the town, with the newspapermen and photographers, fed up with the radio, with the rubbernecks who wandered about with an innocent look, with the women who cried and with Victor who gave advice. He was fed up with himself, fed up with being a man.

CHAPTER

3

Just as Lambert arrived at the gate of the plant, a figure emerged from the shadow. Lambert was not startled. He reached into his pocket mechanically, took out his package of cigarettes, and handed it to Jouvion.

"Keep it."

"Thank you, Monsieur Lambert. Good night."

And the night watchman disappeared into his realm of bricks, beams, and trucks, at the back of which a small lamp was shining in his shack.

It was a tradition, when Lambert got back at night, to give him two or three cigarettes. The old man did not smoke them but made a quid of them and chewed it. With his shapeless hat and floppy jacket, he resembled the tramps on the quays of Paris and, like them, put old newspapers under his shirt in winter to keep warm when he made his rounds.

Perhaps he was a former tramp and had come to the plant in search of security. He shaved once a year, in the spring, the same day he had his hair cut. In all likelihood, he was the only person in town at that hour who knew nothing about the catastrophe.

The apartment was dark, except for a streak of light under the door of the kitchen, where Lambert found Angèle sitting upright in her chair, with her head bent forward and her hands crossed on her lap. With her eyes half closed, she was listening to a play on the radio.

She declared with a start, as if he were at fault, "Madame isn't home yet."

"Who the hell cares!" he answered.

He did not say good night to her. Without another word, he walked away, convinced that he had just given her great pleasure. She needed to feel that she was a victim of men's callousness. That was why she spent her evenings in the kitchen on an uncomfortable chair. Nobody asked her to wait up. Even if she thought it her duty to do so, she could have taken the radio to her room, where she had a very comfortable chair, or could have stretched out in bed.

He undressed, spent a moment in the bathroom, where he looked at himself sternly in the mirror, and then, with the taste of the brandy still in his mouth, fell into a deep sleep. Later, the light went on. He half opened his eyes and saw Nicole undressing, but when she turned her head toward him, he pretended to be sleeping so as not to have to talk to her. In fact, he fell asleep again before she got into bed, and he did not waken until six o'clock.

Like his father, he did not need an alarm clock, and he liked to be the first one up in the house. Noiselessly, without lighting a lamp, he put on a pair of trousers, a shirt, and an old jacket and went to the kitchen to make coffee. He did not have a hangover. He had never had one. There was only the aftertaste of the brandy, which disappeared when he had his coffee and smoked his first cigarette.

In the early days, Angèle had made a point of getting up to prepare his coffee. Had she continued, that would have been an additional reason for thinking she was being exploited. For weeks he had found her in the kitchen before he got there, and he had to lose his temper so that she would stop spoiling the best moment of his day.

The sky was gray, as it had been the day before, though a lighter gray, and people were already busy on the decks of the two barges.

Lambert went downstairs, his bare feet in slippers, without a tie, his hair uncombed, as he had seen his father do for so many years, and, before anyone else arrived, went to the office to consult the day's program.

Except in winter, they almost always had five or six projects going at once, some of them ten miles away. Certain jobs, such as unloading the barges, were done by two teams so that the boats would not be immobilized needlessly.

Twenty years before, the plant had occupied only the site of the first yard, the one on which the new offices looked out. They had had to purchase some lots, then buy out a blacksmith shop and later a little café where a few couples spent Sunday afternoons when the weather was good.

It was he, Joseph, who was responsible for the expansion. His mother had wanted him to be a doctor or a lawyer. She saw to it that he went to the lycée, where he remained until he was eighteen without passing his final examinations. After he had failed twice, she resigned herself to his working with his father. Like the latter, he had climbed up on scaffolds, handled a trowel, fastened beams.

After three or four years, he already had ideas of his own.

"If we stick to masonry," he said to the old man, "we'll never get any really big jobs."

Their chief clients were the farmers in the surrounding countryside for whom they began to build metal barns and silos.

This was a new branch of activity to be studied. New

work crews had to be trained. While they were at it, why not go in for heavy carpentry as well?

It was also he who had suggested that Marcel, who was five years younger, attend a good technical school, and the boy was sent to Saint-Etienne.

The two brothers had never had a professional disagreement. Each had his own work and responsibilities. Marcel was, in a sense, the brains of the business, and Joseph the live wire.

And when, after their father's death, Fernand, the youngest brother, who lived in Paris, asked for his share, they decided to borrow enough money from the bank to pay him a lump sum and thereby have complete control of the business.

They had equal power. As for what Fernand had done with his money, they were left in the dark. They had heard talk about his having opened a picture gallery somewhere near the Boulevard Saint-Germain. It was possible. With Fernand, anything was possible. He did not take after either of his parents. With his long face, light brown hair, and delicate movements, he had always been a kind of foreign element in the family.

Because of a threat of tuberculosis when he was eleven or twelve, he was taken out of school and for two years lived a hothouse existence at home, where he spent his days devouring books.

Then he was sent to a boarding school in Haute-Savoie, and when he returned he was so different from the others that they felt ill at ease in his presence.

At the age of seventeen, he left for Paris without a word to anyone, and eight or nine months went by without news of him. Later, he went home occasionally to see his parents. Every time he returned, he seemed more polished and refined, in fact so refined that Joseph often wondered whether he was a homosexual. He had been a member of an avant-garde theater group which was occasionally spoken of in the papers, and had worked in an obscure publishing house. And he had once written to their father from Capri asking for money.

How old was he now? Four years younger than Marcel. Hence, nine years younger than Joseph. In other words, thirty-eight. At their mother's funeral, he seemed to be the one who was hardest hit. He left for Paris the same evening, after which they did not see him again until the old man died.

Joseph had observed him very sharply that day, particularly at the cemetery, during the procession of friends and acquaintances. He had been struck by the ethereal quality of his younger brother. It was as if by virtue of a kind of grace Fernand had escaped from reality, from the cares of daily life, as if he were not subject to the law of gravity.

Joseph had spoken of his impression to Marcel the following day.

"Don't you have a feeling that Fernand takes drugs?"

Marcel had looked at him with his cold, mocking eyes, the eyes of a man who knows everything, and had shrugged his shoulders.

What good did it do to think about Fernand, or about Marcel, who was punctual and sure of himself and who at nine sharp would be in his office which was strewn with drawing boards?

Men started gathering on the dock. Most of them were North Africans, poor devils who were badly dressed and were still half asleep and cold. The office picked them up in the slums whenever there was a boat to unload. It was not regular work. Often, two weeks went by before a barge moored at the landing.

They stamped their feet in the cool morning air, trying to get warm, and some of them slapped their shoulder blades with broad puppetlike movements.

Finally, old Angelot, whom everyone called Oscar, slowly arrived on his bicycle.

Lambert met him in the yard.

"How goes, Monsieur Lambert?"

"All right, Oscar. Are your men there?"

"Not all of them. I'm sure we'll need a few more."

A local newspaper, edged with black, as on days of national mourning, stuck out of his pocket, but Lambert did not ask to see it.

Old Angelot went to the cloakroom to change his clothes, while Lambert crossed the roadway. He stood in front of the barges. The bargemen had already removed the hatches. The boats were each carrying a load of sleek pink bricks which little by little would pile up on the dock in neat columns as regular as houses.

The bargemen waved at him. There was a smell of coffee in the air near the cabin, and one could hear the voice of the little girl, who was being dressed by her mother and who could be seen through the porthole in her white underwear.

Another copy of the black-rimmed newspaper was lying on the deck. Old Angelot came back and blew his whistle. The men gathered around him to receive instructions while other workmen, the regular employees, were beginning to arrive on bicycles and motorcycles.

A quarter of an hour later, work was under way everywhere. Equipment and tools were being loaded on the trucks and vans that were to take the men to their places of work.

"Will you be dropping by to check the framework, Monsieur Joseph?"

"I'll be there at about ten. Is that all right?"

"That'll be fine. We'll get started on something else meanwhile."

He counted eleven newspapers sticking out of pockets and noticed that things were getting under way that morning less noisily than usual. The men did not call out to each other as cheerfully as they generally did, and there was very little joking.

It was the hour when Nicole got up and took her bath.

Breakfast would be served at eight, and then Lambert would also bathe.

To buy a paper, he would have had to walk about three hundred yards to the Rue de la Ferme, and he didn't want to go there in his slippers and with his hair uncombed.

He was both afraid and eager to know. His feverishness and excitement of the night before had given way to a mood as gloomy as the morning sky or, better, as his reflection in the dirty water of the canal. A bad taste lingered in his mouth, but it wasn't the taste of the brandy he had drunk in Victor's bar the night before, and he was ashamed of the way he had hesitated when he had looked at the girl with the gold tooth.

An expression flashed across his mind, an expression he had heard used only by the strange curate who had taught the boys their catechism: *the bitter aftertaste of a bad conscience.*

Since getting up, he had been walking, behaving, talking, and looking at people like a guilty man.

He had a feeling that everyone knew, that Benezech was merely waiting until it was a decent hour to come and arrest him. He prowled about in the carpentry shop, in the warehouses, and, as Oscar was still on the dock giving orders to the North Africans, he slipped into the cloakroom to take the newspaper from his pocket.

He did not open it until he was in his office and had shut the door.

The first page was almost entirely covered with the photos he had seen the night before in the display window on Town Hall Square. There were, however, two which were new to him. The first, which had been taken by an amateur, showed a little girl of about eight standing in a garden with her head bent to the side and her arms pressed stiffly against her body.

Beneath it was the following caption:

"Little Lucienne Gorre during vacation last year."

Next to it was a photo showing a hospital bed and a man in a white smock bending over a motionless body, the face of which was covered with bandages:

"Dr. Julémont is doing his utmost to save the child's life."

The photo also showed a rubber tube attached to the patient's arm.

A sub-headline in the middle of the page stated:

"A sixty per cent chance, according to the doctors."

It was only on the second page that there was any reference to himself:

"Wide-scale police operation to find the Citroën."

He almost stopped reading. He felt like reaching out for the telephone on his desk, calling up Benezech, and saying:

"Stop looking, my boy, it's me."

From where he sat he could see the Citroën that dozens of policemen and gendarmes were hunting for throughout the region. He could see it through the window, against the curb where it had spent the night. Had any of the workmen, when they arrived that morning, looked at it and wondered: "Maybe it's that one?"

Many of them knew that he had been to the Renondeau farm and had probably gone by way of the Big Hill.

In addition, Marcel knew that he had taken Edmonde along and knew why, for he had caught them together at least once, not in the car but in what was called the record office. Marcel, as was to be expected, had not said anything and had never alluded to what he had seen.

Joseph suddenly felt most afraid of his brother, not so much afraid that Marcel would denounce him as that Marcel knew. If that were so, wouldn't the simplest thing be to shoot himself? Lambert had a big army pistol which he had brought back from the war. He had kept it in his desk ever since the time there had been a wave of holdups in certain cities on payday.

Why not get it over with now, right away, without

bothering to go up and have breakfast, to take a bath, without having to talk to his wife and then later to face Edmonde?

The newspaper stated that carpenters had worked all night making coffins for the victims, while an attempt was being made, with the help of the parents who had already arrived, to identify them. By late morning, the main room of Town Hall would be transformed into a mortuary chapel and the crowd would be allowed to file by.

Would he have the strength to go through with it all?

The father of the little Gorre girl was a widower, though still quite young, with gentle eyes and the face of a weak man hounded by misfortune. He had been photographed in the corridor of the hospital, sitting on a bench like a husband in the waiting room of a maternity ward.

Suddenly the phone rang. Lambert hesitated to answer. He was sure it was Benezech or the Lieutenant of the gendarmes, or perhaps Marcel, who had just discovered the truth. He let it ring several times and finally picked up the receiver because the sound was unbearable.

"Hello!"

"Is that you, Monsieur Lambert?"

He relaxed so quickly that his whole body slackened. He had recognized the voice of Nicolas, the foreman in charge of the work at the pig farm.

"I was sure you'd still be in the office. I should have counted the bags of cement last night. I'm afraid we're a little short. In order not to lose time, perhaps you could send over twenty more."

Lambert's voice was completely natural. While carrying on the conversation with Nicolas, he skimmed the page of the paper that lay open before him. Suddenly his eye caught the following passage:

"The police have launched a veritable manhunt with the help of the entire population, which is boiling with indignation. . . ."

Still holding the receiver, he straightened up and squared his shoulders. His body grew hard again.

"I'll send over a truck in a few minutes. I may drop by later in the morning to look things over. . . . No! It won't rain. . . . You can go ahead. . . ."

When he hung up, he had forgotten about the pistol. He got up from his chair, leaving the newspaper spread out, like a challenge. Since a manhunt was going on and he was the one being hunted, it became another matter!

He gave instructions to the man in charge of the stock-room, then went upstairs.

"I'll have breakfast, Angèle!" he called out from the hall.

He sat down at his place in the dining room, where his wife joined him a few moments later. She was already dressed for the day, for she was not the kind of woman who goes around in a bathrobe or housedress.

"You came home early last night," she said.

He merely said yes, hardly looking at her.

"I stayed with Jeanne until half-past eleven. She was in such a state that we were thinking of calling the doctor."

"Poor Jeanne," he murmured, without apparent irony.

"I've just phoned her husband. She's up and about. It seems that the morning paper is so awful . . ." She broke off.

"Have you read it?" she asked.

"Yes."

"What does it say?"

"I'll go and get it for you."

That was easier.

"No, no, don't bother. . . ."

He went down anyway and returned with the black-rimmed paper. He put it down beside her.

"Did you go and have a look yesterday?"

"No."

She observed him more closely.

"Were you drinking?"

"I had a few glasses of marc."

Without asking why or where, she gave her attention to the photographs on the first page.

"If only they save the little girl!"

While eating his soft-boiled eggs, he watched his wife, but it would have been hard to tell what was going on in his mind. He had a grim, fixed expression, as when he was in a bar and felt there was going to be a fight or when he was about to start one.

"If Jeanne had got to Château Roisin two minutes earlier she would have seen the driver."

"Too bad she didn't!"

"I wonder how he had the heart, with all those children screaming in the flames, to . . ."

He managed to remain seated and even to finish his eggs, but if his wife had looked at him at that moment instead of being absorbed in her reading, she would have realized that he was trying not to vomit.

"When Marcel and I got to the scene of the accident, the fire was out, but the wreckage was still smoking. Marcel worked with the firemen until nine at night trying to . . ."

He stood up and, without haste, walked to the door.

"Excuse me. I'm expected in the office at nine."

He bathed and shaved, as he did every morning. As he was about to put on the suit he had worn the day before, he changed his mind. If anyone had seen a man in a dark blue suit driving a Citroën, it would be better that he wear a suit of another color for a few days. He picked a gray one, changed his tie, and even his hat.

They had announced a hunt, hadn't they? And he was the game.

"Do you need the car?" asked Nicole, at five to nine, just as he started down the stairs.

"Why?"

"If you're not using it, I'll take it. I have an appointment at Town Hall to help prepare the mortuary chapel, and I promised to go to the market first to get all the flowers I could find. We've divided the work. Renée Bishop is going to make the rounds of all the flower growers . . ."

He handed her the key without a word.

"Are you sure that you . . ."

"I'll take the small car."

He had almost smiled ironically when she made her request, for that was the very best thing that could have happened. He would not have thought of it himself.

She was going to use the Citroën for her committee work, and it wouldn't occur to anyone that there might be a connection with the car that was being looked for.

"Will you be back for lunch?" she added.

"Probably."

"I may be detained . . ."

He made a gesture meaning that it didn't matter, and went down the small stairway. He found most of the clerks and typists already at work. Through one of the glass walls, he saw Marcel, in shirt sleeves, working in the draftsmen's office.

They did not necessarily go to say good morning and sometimes did not greet each other until much later, when they happened to meet or when they had work to discuss.

He stopped to say a word to the stock clerk.

"I sent twenty bags of cement to Nicolas this morning," he informed him. "He was afraid he might be short."

"Very well, Monsieur Lambert."

For most of the staff, particularly the old-timers, he had become, since the death of his father, Monsieur Lambert instead of Monsieur Joseph, whereas his brother had remained Monsieur Marcel. It pleased him all the more in that it had happened by itself.

"Hasn't Mademoiselle Pampin come in yet?"

He was surprised not to see her in her place at nine-five, for she was punctual.

"She was here a moment ago. I don't know where she . . ."

The clerk looked about him. Lambert wondered, with a frown, whether she was waiting for him in his office. A moment later, he saw her come out of the ladies' room. She looked so much her usual self that he was taken aback.

"Good morning, Monsieur Lambert."

"Good morning," he muttered.

It was not his usual tone, but she showed no surprise. She sat down at her typing table, opened the drawer, and took out her pencils, erasers, and steno pad.

"Are you going to dictate now?"

If she wanted to be alone with him in order to talk to him, he would know at once.

"Yes."

He opened the door of his office, sat down in his swivel chair, and leaned back, as he generally did when he dictated.

"Come in. Let me have the folder of letters to be answered."

She put it down in front of him, moving noiselessly, without touching anything, and rolling her body in a way that was all her own. She sat down in her usual place, put her pad on the armrest, and waited. She did not raise her eyes until several minutes went by without his speaking.

He was so astounded by her calmness, by her inhuman indifference, which suddenly reminded him of his brother Fernand, that he almost attacked her. Fernand had the same way of handling objects, as if he were juggling them or as if they had no substance.

"Dear Sir . . ."

He broke off.

"It's to Bigois and Company in Lille."

"Very well."

"I regret to inform you that, in spite of our comments of . . . put in the dates of my last two letters."

"July 18th and August 23rd."

She said it quite simply, without vanity, without wanting to astonish him.

"Good. Let's continue . . . *our comments of July 18th and August 23rd, the packing cases continue to be defective, which involves a loss of almost twenty per cent. . . .*"

"Monsieur Bicard estimates the loss at twelve per cent."

Bicard, who was the chief bookkeeper of the firm, occupied, by himself, a glass cubbyhole crammed with account books.

"I said twenty per cent."

"Very well, sir."

"Please don't interrupt."

"Very well, sir."

He pulled his handkerchief from his pocket and wiped his face furiously. He was losing control.

"Where are we?"

"*. . . a loss of almost twenty per cent. . . .*"

"Add that, in view of this, we can't continue to do business with them and end with regretfully yours. . . . Do you have the Beauchet file?"

"I put it on your blotter."

"Take down the following: *Dear Beauchet, I am enclosing a copy of the estimate for which you asked and which, I think, you will find satisfactory. I wish to point out, however, that if the total cost is somewhat higher than earlier estimates, this is due to the new customs duty on wood from the north. I thought that . . .*"

He called out in a rage, "Come in!"

Someone had knocked at the door. The door opened. It was Marcel. He put his head in and seemed surprised at finding his brother and Mademoiselle Pampin at work. What had he expected?

"Am I disturbing you?"

"What do you want?"

Marcel looked particularly at Edmonde, somewhat the way Lambert had looked at her when she came out of the ladies' room.

"Has your wife left?"

"I don't know. Why?"

"Because if she hasn't, I'll ask her to go and pick up mine, who doesn't have a car. They're supposed to meet at Town Hall at ten o'clock and . . ."

"Go upstairs and see. All I know is that Nicole asked me for the car."

"Are you going out this morning?"

"I am. I promised to drop in at the Renondeau farm."

Marcel looked as if he were hesitating to leave, as if he had other questions on the tip of his tongue.

"Well? Will you let us work?"

"Excuse me."

Lambert was perhaps mistaken, but he would have sworn that his brother was disappointed, as if he had been expecting something. Did he really have a suspicion? Had he thought he was going to surprise Lambert and Edmonde whispering like two accomplices?

"Reread the last sentence."

"I thought that . . ."

He continued and in less than a quarter of an hour dictated about ten letters. When he finished, he was standing up, facing the window through which he could see the file of North Africans, like a long, sinuous caterpillar, going up and down the springy boards that linked the barge to the dock.

"If I'm not back by noon, have the letters signed by Monsieur Bicard."

Bicard also held power of attorney and for the past two years had received a share of the profits. He was a plump, jovial little man who could spend hours in his chair, bent over his accounts, without feeling the need to stretch his muscles. He was bald and had the pink face of a baby. The only trouble with him was that he had bad breath, and, knowing it, he always had a can of catechu within reach.

"That's all for the moment."

He was curious to see whether she would finally say

something, but she stood up without looking as if she had any intention of speaking, and walked to the door.

Whereupon it was he who felt a need to talk.

"I happened to see you last night with your mother on Town Hall Square."

She turned around with a look of surprise.

"Really? I didn't see you."

"Opposite the newspaper office."

"As a matter of fact, we went out for an hour to get some air. My mother stays at home almost all day long."

Someone had told Lambert that the mother made men's trousers.

Edmonde waited, looking as if she wondered whether he had anything else to say.

"That's all!" he exclaimed with repressed anger.

It was too much for him. It humiliated him. He was always irritated when he didn't understand things, and now, after a year of the most intimate relations possible between a man and woman, he still had no notion of what went on in the girl's head.

For a moment, as he watched her leave, he wondered whether she wasn't planning to blackmail him.

He had asked himself the same sort of question in the beginning. He tried to avoid having sexual relations with the girls who worked in the office, knowing that it almost always led to complications.

The day after his first experience with Edmonde, he had watched her carefully, expecting that she would take certain liberties, that she would become slack in her work.

The very opposite had happened, which had almost worried him. She had remained unchanged, so much so that he had wondered whether he hadn't been dreaming the day before. It was impossible to detect anything in her expression or behavior or tone of voice that recalled the female he had made groan with pleasure.

For several days he had hesitated to touch her lest she push him away.

That was a little more than a year ago, and she never called him anything but Monsieur Lambert. She never asked for the slightest favor.

No sooner was the orgasm over than she pulled down her skirt with a mechanical movement and in an instant was again the calm, efficient, quiet-looking secretary who had just stepped out of her office. Her nostrils remained dilated, like those of a person who feels sick, while her heart kept pounding behind her dress.

His eyes looked for the hat he had taken with him when he left the apartment. He put it on and walked slowly across the office. Edmonde, who had gone back to her place, did not look at him.

It was his turn to drop in on his brother, who was bent over plans for a garage.

"Did you see Nicole?"

"I did. She's going to pick up my wife."

It was the same with Marcel. One could never guess what he was thinking, and today in particular it drove Lambert wild, as if people were amusing themselves by playing cat-and-mouse with him.

Nevertheless, in the case of Marcel he at least knew what his smile expressed: a condescending irony. He was so intelligent, so sure of himself, so superior to that poor idiot Joseph who charged about like a bull!

Poor Joseph! He had made blunders. He would make others, since that was his nature. Luckily, he had at his side a brother who was level-headed, free from passion, and who set things right.

Damn it all, why hadn't Marcel married Nicole, since they went so well together! They could have spent their life in front of a mirror admiring the superior couple they formed. And the two of them might have had children!

"See you later."

"See you later."

When he got to the door, he turned around briskly to see whether his brother wasn't looking at him ironically, but Marcel was bent over his drawing board, and his cigarette was burning in the glass ashtray in front of him.

The only one who smiled as if he understood was a seventeen-year-old draftsman with long hair.

The idiot!

CHAPTER

4

Some reporter or other wrote that evening—again—that the sky had gone into mourning. The Lamberts used to call it "All Saints' Day weather." Yet the All Saints' Days of Joseph Lambert's childhood memories were marked by low clouds driven by blustering winds that tore the dead leaves from the trees, whirled them about, and finally dropped them, like toy boats, on the foamy water of the canal.

But today there was no wind. It was not raining. The whole sky was light gray, like a dome of frosted glass that deadens sound, and the people in the street seemed gloomier and more furtive than on other days, as if each were partly responsible for the tragedy of the day before.

Lambert, who had taken the small car, made a point of driving through the center of town. On Town Hall Square, he saw the black hangings with silver teardrops that had been draped around the portal. He had a choice of at least three ways of getting to the Renondeau farm but deliberately took the one he would have taken normally, that is, via the hamlet of Saint-Marc and the Big Hill.

Saint-Marc was only two miles out of town. After the kitchen gardens, which were separated from each other by barbed wire, one could see, standing alone, Despujols's little grocery-café with its tile-covered wall that faced west.

He drove slowly, making a deliberate effort to control his nerves. Madame Despujols, a round little woman dressed in black whose belly stuck out in the manner of country women, was standing near her gas pump filling up the tank of a car. He waved to her and saw her, in his mirror, trying to make out who it was, but he was unable to tell whether she had recognized him.

What was hardest of all was to take the turn at Château Roisin, where a barrier had been put up around the charred and twisted remains of the bus and where two gendarmes were on duty, while three or four civilians, who looked like experts, were rummaging in the debris.

According to the morning paper, the engineers had several different theories. Some of them assumed that the doors had been twisted by the shock and that it had been impossible to open them, others that the driver, whose name was Bertrand, had been killed instantly and that no one had been able to operate them. As for why the bus had immediately burst into flames, making help impossible, that was controversial, and the controversy was all the keener in that it involved important interests.

Although there had not yet been any talk of money, it had been announced that the company which insured the bus had sent its best agents to determine not only the exact cause of the accident but also why it had turned into a catastrophe.

The damages were said to come to tens of millions of francs and maybe more. If the owner of the Citroën was found and if his responsibility was established, it was *his* insurance company that would have to pay.

One of the gendarmes with whom Lambert had often been in touch recognized him as he drove by and waved to him. Interested spectators, most of whom had come by bicycle and of whom there were fewer than the radio announcements led one to believe, stood around patiently outside the barrier.

He started to drive up the hill. His face was red, the blood had rushed to his head. He had not gone more than a half-mile when he caught sight of the goats on the side of the road. Their owner was there too, a tall, lean man with exceptionally long arms and big hands that looked like those of some village idiot.

He stood holding a stick and watched the car as it drew near. Lambert had the impression that he paid no more attention to it than to any other car but that he had recognized it. He did not stop. Perhaps it was only his imagination. Was there really a sarcastic smile on the usually blank face of the man with the goats? Had the gendarmes already questioned him as they were questioning everyone who lived along the road within a radius of several miles?

Lambert almost turned around in order to go back and talk to him so as to be dead sure. He had had a hunch the day before that the danger would come from that man.

He had never heard his voice, he did not know whether the man was feeble-minded or not. People claimed that he ate crows and other repulsive creatures, like another old man who, when Lambert was a child, devoured everything the youngsters brought him for the fun of watching him, including field mice and slugs.

The hill seemed long, and he passed several motorcycle policemen, who gave the landscape a special tone.

There were two others, one of whom was standing in front of the garage at the first crossroad, near the gas pumps. He was holding a little notebook. The redheaded garage owner, whom Lambert knew and who had often filled his tank, was scratching his head as he was answering questions.

That was another test. He had to act natural. As he turned right in the direction of the Renondeau farm, he waved and called out, "Hello!" The young man waved back. The gendarmes did not even turn around. Lambert looked in his mirror to make sure the redhead wasn't following him with his eyes, that the sight of him didn't suddenly remind the man of something.

He would have to act that way for several days, with Renondeau too, who was waiting for him in the middle of the workyard where the rectangle of the future barn was outlined by the framework. The men were waiting for him before pouring the cement around the metal uprights that had already been set up. He got out of the car and shook hands with the farmer, then immediately went over to the foreman and inspected each of the forms. He seemed preoccupied and grumpy, as he usually did on a job. He looked up at the sky and saw a flock of starlings flying through the air.

"All right, boys, you can go ahead!"

Standing next to Renondeau, he watched the first caisson being filled. They were near the machine, which was making a deafening noise. It was useless for them to try to hear one another. After a moment or two, the farmer pointed to the house and the wine shed at the top of the sloping meadow, and Lambert could read an invitation on his lips.

"How about a glass of wine?"

He followed him to the cool shade where the casks were lined up. Renondeau rinsed two thick glasses in a vat of water.

"Here's to you, Monsieur Lambert."

"To you, Renondeau."

"Didn't you bring the young lady this morning?"

His question was accompanied by a lewd smile.

"No, not today."

"A good-looking gal, I'll say!"

"The main thing is that she's a good secretary."

The farmer took the empty glass from his hand to fill it again from the cask. Lambert accepted a second drink.

"I thought of you last night while listening to the radio. I thought to myself that if you'd only left a quarter of an hour later, you'd have been at Château Roisin the very moment the accident occurred."

It was not a trap, Lambert was sure of it. He knew peasants well enough to be able to tell when they were up to something. Renondeau's seemingly innocent remark opened up new horizons for him.

The day before, he had gone to the trouble of creating an alibi for himself by letting it be thought that he had not gone by way of the Big Hill but had taken the road to Coudray. But now the farmer, without realizing it, had just provided him with the best alibi possible. If he had driven at a normal speed and had not stopped on the way, he would have reached the Big Hill about a quarter of an hour before the bus went by.

"It must have been a pretty awful sight!" continued Renondeau. "I wonder whether I'd have had the heart to look. Oh well! . . . How about another?"

"Thanks."

"Do you still expect to finish the work before November?"

"November first at the latest."

"Then everything's coming along."

They shook hands. Renondeau walked off slowly in the direction of the barn, while Lambert returned to his car.

He had done the right thing in not repeating too often that he hadn't gone by way of the Big Hill. If it became absolutely necessary, there would always be Renondeau's testimony, if not to clear him at least to confuse the issue.

What he had to avoid above all was to imagine that they were thinking about him, for then he would be in danger of losing his self-possession.

He drove again in the direction of the crossroad, which was a little less than two and a half miles away. Very few people lived on the plateau. The occasional farmhouses were in the middle of the fields, far from the road. A good deal of the land belonged to Renondeau.

About a half-mile away, on the right, was a grove, and actually it was there that the tragedy had begun and not, as he had thought the day before, on the Big Hill when the bus driver had blown his horn the first time.

When he asked Edmonde to accompany him, he had, of course, an ulterior motive, but it was still vague. He did not know where or when it would happen; most likely, he thought, on the way back from the Tréfoux dairy farm, somewhere along the canal road, on which there was almost never any traffic and which he was planning to take.

Hadn't Edmonde wanted to wait? Had she acted with an ulterior motive? As they neared the grove, she had said quite simply, "Would you mind if I got out for a moment?"

She had no modesty with him. He suspected that she had none with anybody. She had pushed open the door, jumped over the ditch, and, with her dress up, had squatted five or six yards from the road. He had hesitated to join her. He probably would have done so if, a little way back, they had not passed a hay wagon that would have caught up with them before long.

"I'm sorry," she had murmured as she sat down again and closed the door.

He had smiled and put his hand on her thigh.

"Now?" he in turn had murmured.

What it would be impossible to make anyone believe was that they were not in love or that they were not lovers, that their relations were more like a game which had its own rules, symbols, and language.

She had looked at him without saying anything, and he had realized, from her motionless expression, that that was the moment.

They had heard behind them the clopping of the horses' hoofs and the sound of the big, iron-shod wheels of the wagon. He had driven off slowly, using only his left hand, and Edmonde had stiffened at his side.

That was how they had reached the Big Hill and started going down the slope. He was doing not more than twenty miles an hour, and his mind was not on his driving but on the secret quivering that followed a given rhythm.

Though they were not in love and had never acted as if they were, there was nevertheless an intimacy between them, an intimacy of another kind that bordered on complicity.

It was on that plane that their relations had been established the very first day, without their intending it, simply by the nature of things. It had all started a little more than a year before, at which time Edmonde had been working for him only three weeks.

At the time, he regarded her body as not that of a woman but as the insipid body of an enormous baby, and what surprised him was that, in spite of her vacant look, she proved to be such an efficient secretary. He was almost ready to agree with the young mason:

"An animal!"

One August afternoon, at about five o'clock, when a large part of the office staff was on vacation and the weather was hot and sultry, he had gone swimming in a pool he had built for a friend about ten miles out of town. He had been expecting a telephone call from Chalon-sur-Saône.

"Shall I wait till you get back?" she had asked as he was about to leave.

"Yes, it would be a good idea. I'll be back at about six-thirty."

He had not returned until ten to seven and, in order to take a short cut, had entered by what was called the draftsmen's door, which led directly from the yard to their glass-enclosed office.

There was complete silence in the glass-walled plant, and he thought at first that everyone had gone, until he came upon his secretary and received a shock.

Had she heard him coming? He was certain that she hadn't and, now that he knew her, he realized that even if she had, her behavior would have been no different.

Pushing away her adjustable typing chair, she had thrown back her head and, with her dress up to her stomach, had put her hand between her thighs.

Her eyes were half closed and her body was so still that he would have been alarmed had he not noticed that her fingers were moving almost imperceptibly.

The heat of the day had accumulated in the office, and no coolness entered through the open windows, only a fine dust which remained suspended in the air and shone in the sun.

For the first time, he had seen Edmonde's nostrils dilate, like those of a dead person. Her upper lip was drawn back, revealing the teeth in a painful grimace that in no way suggested a smile.

Then her body had grown tense, as if she were going through a painful childbirth, and had remained that way for some moments before suddenly sagging. At the same time, Lambert heard a faint moan issue from her throat.

The girl's head had dropped to the side, and when her eyes had opened she had seen him behind the glass wall. She had expressed no surprise, had had no reaction. She had not quite returned from the strange world into which she had just escaped, alone, in silence. Then, he had opened the door and entered the room. He had stood in front of her, looking at her from head to foot, from foot to head, and she had finally murmured, "Were you there?"

She did not try to excuse herself. She had no shame, she did not pull down her dress, and her hand was still between her thighs. Seeing her fingers move again, he muttered in a hoarse voice, "You want some more?"

Her upper lip started quivering again, and he had the impression that he could hear her heart pounding in her breast.

"Stand up!" he ordered.

She obeyed, docilely, and went to him without trying to struggle, without seeking his lips.

Ten minutes later she had already resumed her everyday manner and said, in a voice in which there was no trace of what had happened, "The telephone call came from Chalon."

It was he who was embarrassed, perhaps for the first time in his life. He did not know where to turn his gaze.

"The three trains were loaded this morning and should arrive Monday. And you'll receive the shipping statement in tomorrow's mail."

"Thank you."

"Do you need me any longer?"

She was not being ironic but had merely used a stock phrase without thinking.

"No, thank you."

"Good night, Monsieur Lambert."

He had to make an effort to answer in the same tone, "Good night, Mademoiselle Pampin."

She had also tidied his office and gone to the ladies' room to powder her face. A few minutes later, he looked through the window and saw her walking toward the Rue de la Ferme with her placid, undulating gait.

Later on, Marcel came upon them by surprise in the record room. Perhaps others did too but said nothing and merely exchanged winks behind their backs. He had taken her several times to the Hôtel de l'Europe, where she had followed him without protesting, but it had been a disappointment each time, as much for her as for him. She had not complained, had not tried to apologize. Never was there any mention of what was going on between them, and neither of them ever made any attempt to discuss it.

Apart from their work, they exchanged, at most, a few monosyllables which were passwords between them.

She had not changed in any way. Her life, her habits, her way of dressing, of behaving, were exactly what they had been before, and he had not made any change in his way of life either. He had had other adventures in the course of the year but they had given him no pleasure.

And Marcel thought he understood!

He was now on the same road he had taken the day before. Again he went down the Big Hill and again he thought that he caught a cruel and ironic expression on the face of the man with the goats.

What did Edmonde think about what had happened, about the way he had behaved? What did she think about him? Had it been anyone else, he would have asked. But her—he dared not.

Why?

Was it because what existed between them was on a plane different from that of ordinary life, of life as one conceives it, as one lives it, as one wants it to be?

It was somewhat as if, at a given moment, for no apparent reason, they exchanged a signal and then escaped.

He was not modest in her presence either. They entered a different realm, a realm which resembled that of childhood rather than that of evil.

Despite the years that had gone by, he still remembered very clearly a toothache he had had one summer when he was about nine. In those days, the linden tree still stood in the middle of the workyard. The dentist had given him two white pills, no doubt a sedative. After lunch, the pain came back. It was very acute, and he swallowed both pills.

"You ought to sit in the garden and rest," his mother advised him.

Under the tree were an iron table and three iron chairs. The child sat down in one of the chairs, with his legs crossed, while above his head the rays of the sun seeped through the foliage, which was buzzing with flies.

With his eyes half closed, he saw the water of the canal shimmering. Directly opposite him, on the other bank, an old pensioner, now dead, was sitting in a folding chair and fishing. He was wearing a panama hat and was smoking a long curved pipe which rested on his chest.

The boy would have been unable to describe what had taken place inside him, and though Lambert had often tried, even as an adult, to provoke the same phenomenon, he had never succeeded.

Was it the heat, the drowsiness one feels after lunch, or was it because of the pills? He continued to feel pain in his left cheek, but it no longer deserved to be called pain, it had been transformed into pleasure, a kind of sensual pleasure, the first such pleasure he had ever experienced.

From a specific, ultrasensitive point, perhaps the nerve of the bad tooth, waves radiated, as the clanging of bells radiates in the air. They spread to his entire cheek, his eye, his temple, and faded out at the back of his neck.

He could feel the waves coming and little by little learned how to provoke them, to direct them, as if they were music. The foliage above, with its light and shadow, the slight swaying of the branches, and the flight of the flies, took part in the symphony, as did the secret life of the canal, its breathing, the reflections which stretched slowly, the red float at the end of the fisherman's line, and the white patch of the straw hat in the shade.

In the blacksmith shop, which old Lambert had not yet bought out, the hammer struck the anvil in a lazy rhythm, and chickens were cackling in a nearby yard.

It was all taking place in a wonderful world that reminded him of something. He tried in vain to recall what it was, but his mother's voice suddenly tore him away.

"Joseph! You're right in the sun!"

The sun, continuing its course in the sky, had finally reached his retreat under the linden tree.

"You'd better come in now."

He stood up, numbed and bewildered, and was angry with his mother for a long time.

It was because of that experience, which he had never been able to repeat, that he did not judge his brother Fernand severely. What means of escape had Fernand found? He didn't know, but he was sure that Fernand had one and that he spent a large part of his time far from the earth.

He had never spoken about it to Edmonde. He suspected that she herself did not realize what she was doing. In any case, she did not think it was wrong, otherwise she would have reacted differently when he had come upon her by surprise and many other times later on.

It was he who sometimes had doubts and felt embarrassed, though he had never in his life passed up an opportunity to tumble a girl on a bed or in the grass.

With the others, he could laugh and even talk about what they were doing. With Edmonde, he did not dare; the idea did not occur to him. And yet, there was no communion between them. He did not seek it. Their relationship was rather one of unspoken complicity—until the moment when, the day before, he heard the frightened scream of the horn and saw in his mirror the huge machine that was rolling down the hill . . .

Was he really and truly convinced that he was guilty? He no longer knew. He had looked at Edmonde, who had not batted an eyelash and who, as she walked arm and arm with her mother that evening on the square, seemed as innocent as when she took dictation.

Was it she who was right? He was annoyed with her and envied her. Suddenly he decided to take exactly the same route he had taken the day before. He had enough presence of mind and was crafty enough to realize that when the peasants who might have recognized him were questioned in a day or two, they would get the dates wrong.

He drove to the dairy farm by way of the road to Coudray, found Nicolas busy, and spent a quarter of an hour with him, but did not see Bessières.

"He just left for Town Hall," Nicolas informed him. "He told me that the bodies are being taken to the station this afternoon at four. My wife and daughter-in-law are bound to be there. The government offices and the banks have given their employees the afternoon off."

"Do you want to go there too?"

"Not me, Monsieur Lambert. I've got trouble enough of my own!"

Town Hall Square was even more animated at noon than it had been the night before, and there was a long line of people on the sidewalk in front of the entrance to the mortuary chapel, but there were very few customers in the Café Riche and the other cafés of the neighborhood, as if people were ashamed to be seen drinking that day.

"Get your morning *Eclair!* . . . Special edition! . . ."

There was still a crowd in front of the newspaper office. Lambert stopped his car to buy one of the freshly printed sheets.

When he got home, the office was closed. Workers from the yard were sitting in the shade eating lunch. The North Africans were doing the same beneath the trees along the canal, and some of them were stretched out in the dust sleeping.

"Will you have lunch immediately?" asked Angèle. "Madame phoned to say that she wouldn't be home before five or six o'clock."

This meant that Nicole was accompanying the funeral procession to the station. Perhaps, after all, that too was a way of escaping. He had never really been hostile to her. She irritated him at times, even exasperated him, mainly because of the opinion she had of herself and because she failed to make allowances for others.

Was she as sure of herself as she tried to seem? Was Marcel really sure of himself?

He sometimes wondered. It might be a mask or, who knows, it might be modesty. Wasn't it true that when he entered a room with those broad shoulders, fleshy face, and thundering voice, with his air of being ready to smash everything, people imagined that he had a kind of aggressive self-confidence?

While eating, he looked through the paper that was spread out before him.

The order of the pages had been changed that morning in order to highlight the latest news.

"High hopes of saving Lucienne Gorre."

Lambert, too, hoped that the child would recover, and he thereby deserved more credit than the others because for him that could very well be the beginning of the end. It depended on where she had been sitting in the bus at the time of the accident. All he remembered was seeing the faces of boys and girls pressed against the windows.

It was unlikely that she had noted or even looked at the number on his license plate, but perhaps she had seen him and, even more important, perhaps she had seen Edmonde.

Thus far, there had been talk only of a Citroën supposedly driven by a drunken driver. The field of investigation was enormous. But if it ever came to be known that there had been another person in the front seat, a young woman, things would start getting really dangerous. Even Renondeau would not fail to see a connection.

"The police have drawn up a list of all Citroëns registered in the region and, in collaboration with the gendarmes, have begun to question inhabitants within an increasing radius."

He wondered anxiously why they specified *"in the region."* Did they have witnesses or information that was not being mentioned? Couldn't a car from any part of the country, from Paris or elsewhere, have been on the Big Hill at the time of the accident?

He found the explanation lower down.

"Yesterday afternoon, between three and six, a motorcycle patrol made a routine check of all vehicles on the road at the Boildieu turnpike, not far from Marpou Bridge, ten miles north of the Big Hill.

"The investigators have thus been able to estimate closely the number and make of the cars going in the direction of Château Roisin at the time of the catastrophe. However, there is no Citroën on the list. This indicates that the reckless driver was not coming from far away and

leads the investigators to assume that he lives in the region."

He stood up, feeling sick, for that was a direct threat, and he hoped that Renondeau did not read the article.

"Aren't you eating any more?"

He was about to answer that he wasn't hungry, but he didn't want to make matters worse by arousing suspicion in his own home.

"What is there for dessert?"

"Peaches and pears."

"I'll have them. You can bring in the coffee."

"I asked Madame for permission to go this afternoon to . . ."

He understood.

"Of course."

"Aren't you going?"

"I'll try to be there."

"The banks have given their employees the afternoon off."

"I know!" he replied impatiently.

It had been wrong of him to run away—granted. And now it was too late. No one would forgive him. Should he turn himself in, expose himself to the general fury, become from one minute to the next an object of hatred and contempt?

That would mean ruin, not only for himself but for all those who depended on him. Might as well shut up shop right away and declare the firm bankrupt.

He was sure that if he gave himself up even Marcel would blame him for being a coward, because it would mean ruin for him too.

And what about Nicole? He tried to imagine what Nicole would advise him to do, and he could hear her voice answering, *"Why don't you go to a father confessor and ask for advice—for example, Father Barbe?"*

Father Barbe was her own confessor. He was a Dominican who was also the spiritual director of the other three Fabre sisters and therefore probably knew something about him. The priest was a good-looking man, and his white gown emphasized his distinguished bearing. When he passed Lambert in the street, he never failed to greet him, and Lambert returned his greeting.

He had nothing against Father Barbe or against the religion in which he had been brought up, and he had been a choirboy for a long time. To put himself in the hands of the Dominican was nevertheless too easy a solution, just as it would have seemed to him, at the present time, cowardly to turn himself in.

Wasn't it harder to stick it out, to say nothing, without help, without external comfort, and to try to avoid the traps that were being set?

He was as fond of children as anyone, and he would be haunted all his life by the memory of the contracted features of the bus driver, by the carefree faces of the boys and girls behind the windows.

All his life, he would imagine that he could hear their screams in the blazing furnace, screams from which he had fled, but which the newspapers spoke of so blatantly, as did the high-minded people he met.

Tomorrow, this evening, things would be normal again in town. In a little while, the train would be taking the coffins to Paris. In a few days, the wreckage of the bus that had smashed the Château Roisin wall would be removed.

The police and gendarmes would continue their investigation. Little Lucienne Gorre, if she recovered, would return to Paris with her father.

Little by little, people would forget, but not he. The memory of two or three minutes, not even that, of a few seconds, would cloud his whole existence.

He did not even have the comfort of seeing his anguish reflected in the eyes of Edmonde, on whom the catastrophe seemed to have left no mark.

For the time being, he was not even able to fall back on drinking, lest he betray himself. He had to control his gestures, his voice, the look on his face. And if he expected to get out of it by pretending that he had to leave town on business, that would be the best way of arousing suspicion.

He flung himself on his bed, intending to take a nap, something he had not done since the vacation he had spent with his wife at Saint-Tropez. Contrary to what he expected, he fell asleep almost immediately and did not awaken until he heard the door open. He sat up in bed and was surprised to see his brother standing in front of him. Marcel seemed to be as surprised as he.

"I've been looking for you everywhere."

"What time is it?"

"A quarter past three."

"I saw your car down below, but not finding you anywhere I thought you'd walked to town."

"I took a nap."

"I wanted to consult you. I finally decided by myself to give the office staff the afternoon off. Most firms . . ."

"I know."

"It was impossible to let the workmen off at the last minute. . . ."

"Of course."

He had got out of bed feeling stiff all over and started walking to the bathroom in order to wash his face with cold water.

"I didn't see Angèle in the kitchen. . . ."

"She went too."

"Aren't you going?"

He did not answer.

"The procession is leaving Town Hall at four o'clock."

He wiped his face. Marcel still did not leave.

"Joseph!" he exclaimed after a moment's hesitation.

"Yes?"

He felt that this was the really big moment, and, unexpectedly, he felt strong enough to take care of himself. The immediate danger restored his calmness and self-control, perhaps because he was facing up to Marcel.

"Well, I'm listening."

"Look at me."
"All right."
He looked him in the face, still holding the bath towel.
"Is it you?"
"No."
He said it with such conviction and simplicity that he saw a change come over his brother's face. Marcel's features relaxed.
"You realize it's a serious matter, don't you?"
"It would be hard not to."
"Are you sure you're telling me the truth?"
"Absolutely sure. You can go and join the procession in peace."
"Aren't you coming?"
"No."
"Why?"
"Because I've had enough as it is."
Marcel stared at his brother once again, and, before going off, murmured, as if reluctantly, "I believe you."
At the door, he stopped and turned around.
"I hope you won't hold it against me for having thought that."
"Of course not."
Lambert had the audacity to add, "It could very well have happened to me."
He had never lied so well in his life, and never had it been so hard for him to lie. He heard his brother's footsteps on the stairs, the opening and closing of doors, and then the sound of a car getting under way.
He was alone in the building. The metal saw was buzzing at the back of the shop. Outside, the North Africans were still following each other in Indian file up and down the planks between the barge and the dock.
Edmonde must have left too, like the others. It was a good thing she had.
He remained for a long time with his forehead against the window, vaguely watching the dockers go up and down.

Then he put a cigarette between his lips. As he lit it, a kind of overflow rose to his throat from his chest, and he burst into tears, still standing with his arms dangling, and looking out at the canal which was distorted by the tears in his eyes.

He was alone and had no need to hide his face.

CHAPTER

5

When he entered the Café Riche at seven o'clock, the atmosphere was different. It was as if the crowd had exhausted its stock of emotion. After only twenty-four hours of almost continuous commiseration, above all after the solemnity of the ceremony at the station, people were exhausted and empty-headed and were in a hurry to be home and get back to their petty, everyday worries.

The streets and Town Hall Square, where the drapes had already been taken down, were almost empty. Five or six persons at most were standing in front of the newspaper office reading the latest bulletin about Lucienne Gorre, whose state continued to be satisfactory. In the café, most of the regular customers were in their usual places, though still somewhat hesitant, but Théo, without being asked, brought them the red cloths and the cards as if to mark the resumption of normal life.

A cloth had been placed on the first table, too, where Lescure, Nédelec the grain merchant, and Capel the history teacher had been waiting for Lambert to come and be a fourth.

"Were you there?" asked Lescure as he took his place on the seat against the wall.

He and Capel, who had gone to school together, were the only ones who used the familiar *tu*.

"No," said Capel.

"Neither was I. It seems that for once the town council did things right."

Weisberg was not present. He turned up less regularly than the others and at times arrived only toward the end to play a hand when someone had to leave.

"Shall we play?"

They cut for dealer. Capel was the kind of player who kept his mind on the game and was annoyed by any interruption. Being a bachelor, he lived in a boardinghouse, and he was always complaining about the food.

"I suppose," remarked Nédelec, "that it'll be some days before we can count on Benezech."

"Especially now that young Chevalier has arrived!" said Lescure, who was shuffling the cards.

The lamps were lit. At the butcher's table opposite them, the belote players were all on hand, plus, as always, a few spectators.

"It's true you don't know who Chevalier is. You have to be in the insurance business to know him because he's hardly ever mentioned in the papers."

"What does he do?"

"He's a kind of super-cop who graduated from lycée at fifteen and who has all kinds of degrees. He's an inspector for the company that insures the bus. I caught sight of him a little while ago as he was entering the Hôtel de France. People probably take him for a student, though he must be over thirty. He won't go to see Benezech, but Benezech certainly knows he's here. Chevalier makes a point of never contacting officials. He doesn't see experts either, but carries on his investigation alone, in his own way, whether it's a matter of a jewel robbery, a doubtful suicide, or an accident like yesterday's. It doesn't matter to him whether he spends weeks or months on a job, and it doesn't matter to the company either."

"One club."

"Pass."

"One spade."

"Pass."

"Two hearts."

"Pass."

"Three no trump."

Capel got the bid, and Lescure, who was dummy, continued:

"The company rang me up from Paris this morning in a panic. They've got the jitters, and I can understand it. They wanted to know the number of Citroëns I've insured in the region."

"How many?"

"Twenty-three, including Lambert's and Benezech's, but not counting taxis, which have a special policy."

Lambert had played his card without batting an eyelash despite Lescure's remark, which had struck him.

"What are they afraid of?" he asked.

"Don't you understand? If, tomorrow, they discover the guy who caused the accident and if he's one of our clients, it can cost us hundreds of millions of francs."

"Hundreds of millions!" exclaimed Nédelec.

"Only about two months ago, the court of Riom awarded damages of fifteen million to the widow of a gatekeeper who'd been killed by a truck as he was closing his grade crossing. Multiply that by forty-eight victims. Add the driver and the two women. That's enough to put the company out of business."

"Your play, Lambert," growled Capel. "There's a lot of gab this evening."

"Excuse me. What's been played?"

"Hearts."

They threw down a few cards in silence.

"That's why the others have sent Chevalier," resumed Lescure, in spite of himself. He was worried.

"In order to establish at the very beginning," ventured Lambert, "that the driver of the Citroën is responsible for the accident?"

"To try, in any case."

"So that if they find him, the two companies will fight it out?"

"Probably."

"And each of them will try to prove that the other party was responsible?"

It was so obvious to Lescure that he merely shrugged.

"And what if they don't find him?" continued Lambert.

"At any rate, the case will go to the courts and the thing will drag on for at least two years, maybe more."

"Gentlemen, don't you think that you're much more concerned with insurance than with bridge?"

Capel, who had missed his three no-trump by one trick, was in a bad humor.

"Whose deal?"

"Whoever wants it, as usual."

Lambert stayed in the game, but he was more concerned with Lescure's comments than with his cards. He had had to make an effort a few minutes before not to burst with indignation and blurt out, as he did periodically, a resounding: "Gang of bastards!"

For them it was no longer a matter of dead children, of a little girl who might be disabled for the rest of her life, but of how many millions of francs were involved. The question was not to determine responsibility in the name of justice, but to know who would pay.

An inspector, their high and mighty Chevalier, who was already on the spot, was careful not to get in touch with the officials so as to be free to work on his own.

Lambert had a burning question that he could not bring himself to ask.

"Well now," he felt like saying to Lescure, *"suppose the driver of the Citroën goes to see you and admits that he caused the accident out of negligence . . ."*

He was sure that Lescure was an honest man, but he had been working for the company for thirty years and depended on it.

"What happens in such a case? He's one of your clients, and if he goes to Benezech with his story, it may, as you've just said, cost you hundreds of millions . . ."

In all likelihood, the big shots of the company in Paris were also what were called honest people.

He suddenly smiled—which he had not done for twenty-four hours—with a smile that was both cruel and bitter. He was imagining Lescure's frantic telephone call to his bosses. Or rather, no—he would not phone, because the matter was too important to run the risk of an indiscretion.

He would probably beg the other person to say nothing for a day or two and would take the next train to Paris.

"Next?"

Lambert was in a state of mind in which he would have liked to try the experiment, out of curiosity.

"Spades, Lambert!"

"I'm sorry."

Would the company likewise ask him to say nothing, and would it go so far as to send one of its own inspectors, also a topnotcher, to get in Chevalier's way so as to confuse the issue?

Perhaps not. There was obviously no way of his knowing. Would they ask him not to mention his passenger and to say nothing about what they were doing when the accident occurred?

"Lescure, why did you put your king on my ace?"

Lescure's thoughts were elsewhere, and Capel was getting nervous. The butcher at the other table, who was on his fourth or fifth apéritif, was talking more and more loudly and rapping the table with his fist.

If Lambert had gone to the Café Riche, it was because

he had been unable to stay in the empty house any longer. At one point, he had poured himself a big glass of cognac and, after drinking it, had reached out for the bottle to have another. He had resisted only at the last moment.

Never had he felt such a desire to get drunk.

Nicole would be home late. Angèle, dressed all in black, including black gloves, and with a veil over her face, had returned at a quarter to six with the expression she usually wore on Sundays when she came back from Mass.

"You made a mistake in not going."

She had added, in a state of ecstasy, "It was so beautiful, so touching! With the children from the church clubs and the boy scouts who were lined up in front of the station . . ."

In a little while, he would go home and have dinner with his wife. Then, since it was not one of their nights out, they would spend the evening in the living room.

The prospect made him feel like drinking again, and he was furious at being unable to do so without talking too much. He had cautiously had only one apéritif at the Café Riche and was determined to have no more.

Sitting against the wall, he saw himself as a kind of exile, and he began to hate those more or less florid, more or less shapeless faces which were there in front of him every evening, those starched or soft collars, those voices whose loudness changed with the time of day. Capel in particular irritated him, for no reason at all, and he saw the teacher's face as that of a rat.

Customers went in and out. He knew most of them and waved to them or greeted them with a grunt. One of his clients came over and talked to him in a low voice about a roof that needed repairing, and, in order to rile the history teacher, who had nervous tics, Lambert dragged the conversation out as long as possible.

While he was talking, a young woman entered. The bridge players could smell her perfume as she went by. He knew her too. Her name was Léa. He was not the only one in the café who knew her intimately. The difference between him and the others was that they didn't admit it.

She had nothing in common with the girls one met in Victor's bar, like the one with the gold tooth, and even less with those who prowled around Town Hall at night. Nor was she like the hostesses at the Blue Mill, the night club with the moonlight atmosphere which had opened six months before and where there were never more than two or three shamefaced customers.

There had been others before her, a good dozen, if Lambert counted correctly, who had hung out in the Café Riche with the consent of the proprietor and the tacit permission of Benezech. They would spend a few weeks or months in town and suddenly disappear without anyone's knowing whether it was because they had gone off with some out-of-towner or because they did not make a living.

Léa had been holding out for a year. She was a plump, gay, appetizing girl whose clothes were discreetly suggestive. She gave the impression of being a kept woman rather than a professional.

Lambert had gone off with her two or three times—three, to be exact—the last two times in everyone's presence. He had sat down at her table after the bridge game, and they had left the café together. The others must have gone about it differently. They probably nodded to her on their way to the men's room and then joined her outside.

"Gentlemen, I ask you to be so kind as to keep your mind on the game," insisted poor Capel. "I said four no-trump."

He stared at Lescure, his partner, fearing he might not understand and obviously wanting to make a grand slam or a little one.

"Pass," sighed Lambert.

"Five clubs," mumbled the insurance agent, who probably did not have much of a hand.

"Pass."

"Five no-trump."

Lescure shrugged as if not knowing what to do.

"Six clubs," he finally sighed in resignation. "You asked for it."

Meanwhile, Lambert had made up his mind. He wasn't going to spend the evening watching his wife knit or listening to the radio or reading the papers, which were still full of the catastrophe. He would spend it with Léa, not that he had any desire to go to bed with her, but because he felt a need to be with someone like her, a partner who didn't matter, with whom he could relax.

"Are you playing?"

"Yes."

He often felt such a need, even with a streetwalker.

"I finesse, naturally. Jack of diamonds? In that case, I trump the ace of hearts, I play clubs, clubs again, and that does it!"

Capel laid down his hand and pushed back his chair a little so as to puff himself up, for he had not only made a little slam, but a grand slam too, and he now went for Lescure, who hadn't backed him up all the way.

It was Lambert's turn to be dummy. He got up and murmured, "Do you mind, gentlemen?"

He walked off, not toward the washrooms, but toward the table where Léa, who was drinking a glass of port, was smiling at him and already moving over to make room for him beside her.

"How goes it?" she asked, putting out her hand.

He shook it mechanically, sat down, and glanced at his friends, who were squinting in his direction.

"Are you free this evening?"

"You know very well that I'm always free."

"Good. Where would you like to have dinner?"

She hesitated a moment.

"How about the Gold Cask?" she suggested.

Though the restaurant of the Hôtel de France was the smartest in town, the Gold Cask, which was a kind of basement in an alley near the market, was the one where the food was best. It was also the most expensive.

"Fine! There aren't too many people there," he said. "Here's what I'd like you to do. I've got to be home for dinner. You eat there and I'll join you as soon as I can."

"You won't stand me up, will you?"

He shrugged.

"Doesn't your wife let you have dinner out?"

Her question almost made him give up the idea of being with her.

"Do what I say and don't worry about the rest."

Whereupon he got up and went back to his table.

"It's your deal," said Lescure, handing him the deck of cards. "Do you see the customer who just sat down at the table near the cashier?"

He turned around and saw a thin, arrogant-looking man, a kind of super-Marcel, who was giving the waiter his order.

"What about him?"

"That's Chevalier."

"So what?"

"Nothing. I'm pointing him out because I was talking about him earlier. He hasn't even been to Château Roisin to take a look. It doesn't interest him. But by tomorrow night he'll know the whole town as well as we do."

"I said no-trump," declared Capel, emphasizing each syllable and looking at them fiercely.

It went on that way until a quarter after eight. The teacher was the big winner. The four men shook hands like people who see each other often, and a little later Lambert drove off in his small car.

The inspector's presence in the Café Riche had finally got under his skin, and he had spoken loudly, feeling a need to show off, as if to attract attention. He promised himself to have more self-control and to avoid such childishness. It was essential.

His wife had come home and had left the Citroën outside. When he entered the living room, Nicole was already there, gathering up the magazines. She was tired and her face was drawn.

"Have I made you wait?"

"Dinner's been ready only a few minutes. Shall we eat now?"

She went to inform Angèle, then returned to the living room.

"Have you been playing bridge?"

"Yes."

"Are you going out this evening?"

Why did he look for an excuse? He usually did not account for what he said and did, and when he felt like going out he did so without saying where he was going.

"I have an appointment in town with a client."

She did not ask which one. She knew he was lying, but she didn't show it.

"How's your sister?" he asked.

"She's quite all right now. But her little girl seems to be coming down with the measles. She has no luck, just before the beginning of school. Jussieu is to see her this evening. If she has it, her brother will catch it. . . ."

Nicole said nothing about the mortuary chapel at Town Hall or the ceremony at the station. There were domains from which he was barred. She seemed to take it for granted that they wouldn't interest him or that he was unworthy of taking an interest. That was the case, for example, with her welfare activity, her committee work, and also, of course, whatever had to do with religious life.

"Marcel told me that you gave the staff the afternoon off."

What else had Marcel told her? Had he spoken to her about his suspicion and about their conversation in the bathroom?

Why did Lambert care about what people might or might not say? He was in a hurry to get out, to escape from the atmosphere of the house, where, at bottom, he had not felt at home ever since it had been altered, ever since it had stopped being the home of his parents. Everything was too slick, too bright, too clean, an aggressive cleanness that was not the good old cleanness of his mother. It was Nicole's home, Nicole's order and cleanness.

Was it true? Perhaps not. Hadn't he himself drawn up the plans of the apartment, and hadn't he always dreamed of that kind of home?

Perhaps it was simply that his wife took the thing too seriously, attached too much importance to it.

She herself, whenever she had an opportunity, escaped from it to steep herself in disorder in Jeanne's home, where everyone helped himself as he pleased and where they ate in the kitchen.

"Aren't you having dessert?"

"No."

"Will you be home late?"

"Probably. I don't know."

"Don't forget to put the car back in the garage."

Why did she add that? Did she have an ulterior motive? The day before, he had left the Citroën out all night, and it wasn't the first time.

Although he observed her, he was unable to tell whether she meant more than she had said.

"Good night."

"Good night, Joseph."

He always felt something protective about the way she pronounced his name, something that made him bristle. She was, in short, giving him her benediction, or rather her absolution—in advance, for she knew he was going to do something foolish, but she also knew that it was his nature to do so and that he couldn't help it.

That was what her unctuous "Good night, Joseph" actually meant.

He had a need to be at the wheel of his car and to drive

through several streets in the darkness before he could feel that he was himself again, a man, not a child, not a weak or sick creature whom a woman felt it her duty to protect.

He parked his car at the corner of the one-way alley where all one could see was the lights of the Gold Cask through red checked curtains. He opened the door and was immediately enveloped in a warm smell of cooking. Fred, the proprietor, who was wearing a white apron and chef's cap, went to meet him and shake his hand.

"What a nice surprise, Monsieur Lambert!"

Yet Fred knew from Léa that he was going to come. The only other diners in the low room were four blond Swiss, two men and two women who looked like brothers and sisters.

Léa had chosen a corner near the big fireplace, which was enframed with copper pots.

"Already!" she exclaimed, putting out her hand again. "Did you have time to have dinner?"

She was eating boiled beef with coarse salt, one of Fred's specialties. On the table was a bottle of Beaujolais.

"Will you have a little with me?"

"I'll have some wine. But no beef."

"Were you at the ceremony this afternoon?"

"No."

"Neither was I. That kind of thing makes me sick. Last night, after listening to the radio for a minute, I got into bed and read."

Perhaps he had made a mistake in not meeting her elsewhere. Perhaps he would have done better not to have made an appointment with her at all. Because of the elegant atmosphere, she thought she was obliged to speak differently from the way she usually did. It didn't become her. He looked at her with disappointment, wondering whether he wasn't going to put a bill on the table and leave.

And go where? Besides, she had realized her mistake.

"What's the matter with you this evening?"

"Nothing."

"Did your friends say anything to you before?"

"About what?"

That made her laugh.

"Because you calmly came up to me right in the Café Riche. Usually the only ones who act that way are out-of-towners. The others are too scared."

"Of what?"

"He asks what! He's terrific! Of their wives, of course! And also of what people will say."

The waiter had brought him a glass, and he poured himself some Beaujolais.

"Admit that something's bothering you."

"I don't admit anything."

"You were different the other times. I could tell you were in a good humor."

"And today?"

"Am I wrong?" she asked, looking at him with a smile that did not hide her seriousness. She must have felt she was on the wrong track again.

"Yes, I'm mistaken. I apologize. You're not like that, but I'm so used to those who have a desire to talk . . ."

"Only to talk?"

"The rest almost always comes later. But that's not the main thing. What they want most is to talk."

"Who, for example?"

"Would you like to know? At your table alone, a little earlier, there were two."

"Lescure?"

"Which one is he?"

"The tallest one, in the brown suit, with the rosette of the Legion of Honor."

"No. That one hasn't ever said a word to me, and I don't think he's ever been tempted to."

"Nédelec?"

"I don't remember their names, but if it's the little fat one who sells grain . . ."

"Has he been with you often?"

"Twice. The first time, thinking I'd understood, I left the café and walked slowly, stopping in front of all the shop windows. I had to keep going almost to the end of town before he made up his mind. He's pathetic. He's very unhappy."

"Because he lost his wife?"

"That too. He was fond of her. It's mainly because of his daughter."

"Did he talk to you about his daughter?"

"That was all he talked about. It ended by being a kind of consultation. I know that her name is Yvonne, that she's twenty-eight years old, that not only is she deaf and dumb, but that she's not like other women."

Lambert had often seen her in the street, in the company of her maid, but had never heard it said that she was feeble-minded. Wasn't that what Léa was insinuating?

Yvonne Nédelec was deformed, or rather unfinished, without anyone's being able to make out, at first sight, what was lacking.

"One day, when she was only about eight, her father caught her in the act of savagely undressing a boy younger than she, who was crying. Does that interest you?"

"Go on."

"Later, when she reached the age of puberty, she started going after men."

"Did she undress them too?" he asked ironically.

"Don't be silly! There's nothing to laugh about. She rubbed up against them and went so far that it became dangerous for her to be alone. There was an incident with the bill collector of the gas company, who was caught just when he was beginning to take advantage of her. The maid came in just in time . . ."

Nédelec had never mentioned the matter to him or to the others, and probably nobody in town knew anything about it, apart from Léa, and perhaps some doctors.

They sat there silently while the waiter cleared the table

and handed Léa a huge menu on which the specialties were written in red.

"Have you had dessert?"

"No."

"Would you like to have some crêpes suzette with me?"

"If you want me to."

When they were alone, she continued in a low voice:

"The poor man had to confide in someone, especially since the doctor recommended an operation to sterilize the girl. He was scared stiff. So I told him that I'd had two ovaries removed and that it didn't keep me from being as strong as an ox or from enjoying myself like everyone else."

He remembered the scar which he had noticed the first time she had undressed in his presence.

"Did he end by going to bed with you?" he asked, without apparent irony.

"Of course."

"Was it because you were afraid to have children that you had the operation?"

"It was altogether different. At the hospital, they didn't ask me for my opinion. I was deathly sick."

"Did you see him again?"

"Three months ago. He was as gay as a lark because the operation had taken place and had been a success. He said to me, 'At least that danger's out of the way.' Do you want me to tell you what occurred to me then?"

She had started to use the familiar *tu,* which she usually didn't do until she began to undress.

"Go on."

"You know, it's probably somewhat extreme, but not so dumb as it seems. If the poor old guy found a halfway decent boy, not to marry his daughter, because no one would want her, but to satisfy her from time to time so that she doesn't go after whoever comes along . . ."

He had understood.

"What do you think about it?"

"I don't think anything about it."

He pitied Nédelec, to whom, apart from their bridge games, he had never paid much attention. He thought of Edmonde and went on to think of other women and other men he had known, his brother Marcel too, and even Marcel's wife, who, as everyone in town knew, had fallen in love with a young, out-of-town pianist and who had been caught on the platform of the station when she was about to take the train with him.

They silently watched the pancakes blazing on the red copper stove. Fred was officiating in person. The Swiss turned around in order to follow the operation more closely.

"It's good!" said Léa, enjoying the first burning mouthful.

"Coffee, Monsieur Lambert?"

"Yes, two coffees."

Then, when Fred had left them, he asked, "What about the other one, the bridge player with the ratlike face?"

"Well, well! So you think he looks like a rat too! I've seen him only once and have no desire to see him again. He was barking up the wrong tree. To begin with, as soon as he got to my place he said that he was a very bad boy and that I ought to be very severe with him. Imagine, I was dumb enough not to realize immediately, I called out to him while undressing, 'You're kidding!' But he wasn't at all. He was embarrassed and very unhappy, and he tried to explain his case. He was afraid of putting it into words, he didn't know how to go about saying it. Then he mumbled that he needed to be punished physically, otherwise . . ."

"I get it!" said Lambert.

He was not disgusted, but he did not laugh either. He was sad. And suddenly he was almost angry with himself for having said that Capel had a ratlike face.

"In the end, he cried on my shoulder and told me about his childhood in some city in the north, I no longer remember which, Roubaix or Tourcoing, I think, and he begged me to be sympathetic. You know, it's not that I'm old or that I sleep around like mad, but I could tell you stories like that till tomorrow morning."

"Why did you think, when I got to the restaurant, that I felt like talking?"

"Because you suddenly seemed to me to have problems, you too. After all, everyone has problems. I have mine, and if I let myself go I might pity myself for hours."

"Don't you ever?"

"Who'd listen to me?"

"Don't you sometimes feel like doing it?"

"Let's drop the subject. If you don't mind. Let's talk about you, about the crêpes suzette, about anything you like. What are you planning to do after we have coffee?"

"Nothing."

"You see!"

He had drunk only two or three glasses of Beaujolais, and yet his chest was hot and the blood had gone to his head.

"Aren't you coming to my place?"

She lived in a smart little apartment, very modern and very feminine, of which she seemed as proud as a young bride. She had once shown him about, stark-naked, pointing out the tiniest details.

"Do you do your own cleaning?"

"Who else? I even cook. When you feel like having chicken in wine sauce such as you've never eaten in your life, all you have to do is give me a day's notice."

There was now a strain between them, and he felt that she was wondering how to put him at his ease. It irritated him. But Nicole was still up, and he didn't want to go home before she was asleep.

"But you're not complicated!" murmured Léa, as if to herself. "You're a decent sort of fellow who wants everyone to be happy. Isn't that so?"

He did not answer.

"You know who else is nice in this town? He's one of your friends with whom I've often seen you, Benezech, the

Chief of Police. You realize, don't you, that I more or less depend on him? All he has to do is lift a finger and I'd have to clear out of town. Lots of others in his position would take advantage, almost everyone. Not him. And yet, take my word for it, he'd really like to. Besides, I may as well admit it, I said to him, 'If it's because you're afraid I'd boast about it or that I'd blackmail you . . .' He almost gave in. Finally he said, 'All right, girlie, get going!' And he added jokingly, 'We'll see about it in a few years, when I retire.' Don't you think that's pretty nice? I wouldn't be surprised if he's never deceived his wife, because he's afraid of complications. What do you think?"

He was no longer thinking about Benezech but about himself and Edmonde, for it was true that he too had a problem, that he too had a question to ask, but after what she had just told him, he no longer dared.

"Would you care for an Armagnac brandy, Monsieur Lambert? And a Chartreuse for Mademoiselle?"

He nodded, waited for the drinks to be served, and, while Fred put on his glasses and prepared the bill at the desk, he ended by murmuring, as confused as Capel must have been, "Tell me . . ."

"Yes?"

"Do you ever play with yourself?"

"Good God! Why do you ask me that?"

"Because. Answer me."

"I've already answered. I do almost every day, in the morning, in bed, just as I used to when I was a little girl and didn't know what it was. Take it from me—most women do. But lots of them don't admit it."

She was not triumphant, though he had come round like the others.

"Who is it?"

"Nobody," he answered.

And he signaled to Fred to bring the bill.

Out of human decency he took her home. He had made up his mind to stay only a few minutes.

Two hours later, sitting on the edge of the bed on which she was lying with her hands clasped behind her neck, he had told her all about his relations with Edmonde, except, of course, the matter of the car.

CHAPTER

6

The following day, which was Saturday, was one of those days so neutral that we remember them only as a void and wonder later how we filled the time. Lambert must have got up at about six, as usual, gone through his morning routine, made his coffee, dropped in at the office, and then stepped outside to watch the North Africans, who were still unloading the barge, start their day's work.

At breakfast Nicole asked, "What do you think I should buy for Marcel?"

He looked at her as if he had been so far away that she could not help laughing.

"Have you forgotten that tomorrow is your brother's birthday?"

Not exactly the next day, but the following Tuesday. However, the family had fallen into the habit of celebrating all birthdays on a Sunday.

"How about a book?" he suggested.

That was the easiest and also the best way of giving him

pleasure. Whether genuinely or because it was fashionable, Marcel was interested in the history of art and had a collection of art books containing reproductions of paintings and sculptures and even of furniture.

"I'll drop in at Blanche's this morning," Nicole decided.

Old Monsieur Blanche ran the bookstore on the Rue du Pont. That was where Marcel bought his books, and consequently the old man knew which works he already had.

What had happened after that? Lambert had taken his bath and then gone down to the office, where, because of his intimate talk with Léa the night before, he avoided looking at Edmonde. Then, after shoving some documents into his pocket and signing some papers for Monsieur Bicard, the chief bookkeeper, who was to go to the bank for money and pay the workmen, he had driven off in his car.

He had taken not the small car but the Citroën, for he was going rather far, to Verdigny, where they had just finished the new school buildings and where he had an appointment with the architect. It was fifteen miles south of town. He crossed the canal and covered the distance with his mind completely blank.

He had decided the night before, on his way back from Léa's place, to stop plaguing himself, to stop having problems, as she had put it, and simply to let things happen.

Soubelet, the architect, was waiting for him at the school entrance in the company of the Mayor and two teachers. They spent an hour and a half examining the buildings in detail, testing the faucets, the flushes, and so on, and, as he had expected, he had to have lunch with them in a hotel for traveling salesmen where they had reserved the round table.

After that, the Mayor insisted on showing him his house and making him taste his plum brandy.

It was four o'clock when he drove back across the bridge over the canal. Since it was a Saturday, the offices and plant were closed. Without stopping on the Quai Colbert, he drove to the center of town and went to see a movie.

He then spent a half-hour at the Café Riche but did not play bridge, for Weisberg was there and they did not need him to be a fourth. He vaguely watched the cards being laid on the table, had only one drink, and returned home at eight o'clock.

It was the night for bridge at the home of Doctor Maindron, whom he had met through Nicole and most of whose guests were doctors. Doctor Julémont, who was present that evening, gave details about the condition of little Lucienne Gorre, whom he was now sure he would save.

Nothing else? That was all he remembered. He had spoken very little, had been rather uncommunicative all evening, and, when he drove home with his wife, had not opened his mouth.

In the fall, he would sometimes go hunting on Sunday. But this time he felt all the less like going since he would have had to be home early in order to dress and go to see Marcel. He decided to sleep and did not get up until Nicole had already left to attend High Mass.

He disliked Sundays. The offices and the plant were empty and he didn't know what to do with his time. And he cared even less for family celebrations of the kind he had to attend that afternoon.

The weather had cleared up. When he went to the kitchen to get his coffee, it seemed to him that Angèle's clothes—she had been to early Mass—still smelled of incense.

From his window, he saw a few men fishing along the canal. The bargemen were dressed in their Sunday best, and the little girl was wearing a pink dress and a big bow in her hair.

It was too late to eat. He took his coffee into the bathroom and then shaved. He was displeased with the face he saw in the mirror. It seemed to him ugly, vulgar. He was displeased with his eyes, which were baggier than usual. In short, he was displeased with everything, he felt uncomfortable in his body.

While bathing, he wondered whether Edmonde went to Mass. She probably did. Probably, too, she dressed differently on Sundays from the way she did on other days. He had never met her on a Sunday. He had no idea of what she did with her time. She lived with her mother, but perhaps she had uncles and aunts, or girl friends.

In any case, it was of no interest, and, if he thought about it, it was in order not to think about other things.

He was standing naked, drying himself in front of the open window, when suddenly he caught sight of the man with the goats. He frowned. His train of thought was broken. The man was also in his Sunday best. He was wearing a dark blue suit, which was too short and narrow and made him look even lankier than he was, a white shirt, a tie, and a cap.

He was sauntering along the unloading dock, occasionally stopping to stare at the barge with the same vacant expression as when he watched the cars go by on the Big Hill.

It was the first time Lambert had ever seen him without his goats. Never before had he seen him in town or on the Quai Colbert, and the man's presence now made him feel sure that his intuition the first day had not been wrong.

The man with the goats had evidently recognized him when he had driven by with Edmonde. Was he hanging around in order to talk to Lambert? The man walked to and fro, slowly. Then he sat down on a pile of planks, facing not the canal but the buildings on which were inscribed in black letters "J. Lambert & Sons."

Perhaps it was because he was not holding his stick that he seemed not to know what to do with his long arms, which he kept folding and unfolding. Then he sat for a long time with both hands flat on his knees. He had looked up at the windows of the apartment at least once and he must have caught sight of Lambert, who at that moment was combing his hair.

His face, as far as one could tell from a distance, was expressionless. He made no gesture, did not move.

Was he planning to propose a deal? If so, it was better to give him an opportunity to do so right away. Lambert dressed quickly, went downstairs, opened the door, and lit a cigarette as if he were merely stepping out for a breath of air.

They were only about ten yards from each other. Behind the man, the little girl was sitting on the deck of the barge dressing her doll. Her mother was shelling peas near the helm. There were five fishermen, one of them a boy, on the other bank. A slight breeze ruffled the surface of the water.

The man continued to sit there without moving, and Lambert began to get impatient. He walked a few steps along the pavement in order to tempt him. Since the man still could not make up his mind, Lambert crossed the street, and then, the moment he set foot on the dock, the man with the goats hastily stood up and strode off in the direction of the Rue de la Ferme.

Lambert could have sworn that the man had been afraid of being beaten. He quickened his pace and walked about a hundred yards before daring to turn around.

Lambert looked away for a moment and was surprised to see his wife, who had returned from Mass by the short cut, standing at the door. She was astonished to see him there and stood watching him.

"What are you doing here?" she asked.

"Nothing. I came out for some air."

She said nothing more. A quarter of an hour went by before he went back to the apartment, after buying cigarettes and drinking a glass of white wine.

Why had the man with the goats come to the Quai Colbert? Why had he got panicky? The simplest explanation was that he had been questioned by the police, that he had spoken about Lambert and the woman who had been with him, and that he had been prowling around that morning in the hope of witnessing his arrest.

But no one came to arrest him. Nothing happened. The sunny streets were almost empty, and the occasional noises that broke the silence sounded different from the way they did other days.

There was no newspaper to read. He had no desire to listen to the radio. And so he wandered from room to room, smoking cigarettes until it was time for lunch.

At three o'clock, he drove off with Nicole to the house that Marcel had built for himself on the hill, at the other end of town, in a new quarter which was becoming the most fashionable. It was rather a large villa, modern but not excessively so, surrounded by a sloping garden which was wonderfully cared for by old Hubert.

They were not the first to arrive. Marcel's parents-in-law must have had lunch at the villa and perhaps, too, one of Armande's sisters-in-law.

Armande was the daughter of the assistant director of the Banque du Commerce, a local bank that had been founded more than a century before, in which he had started as an office boy. The Motards had other children, three or four, all married, but only one of the daughters still lived in the region and it was she who was there with her husband and children.

It was a family tradition that when one arrived no mention was made of the occasion. The visitors were merely dropping in on Marcel and his wife, and, when they entered, they tried to hide their gifts behind their backs and then put them in a corner.

Motard was a rather solemn little man, and his son-in-law, Bénicort, who worked under him at the bank, pretended to hang on his lips, nodding, approving, and laughing heartily whenever the old man made a joke.

Marcel's two sons were there, Lucien, who was a student at the Military School of Engineering, and Armand, the bookish member of the family, and also their sister, who had already taken her girl cousins out to the garden.

Marcel's wife was a handsome woman who reminded

Joseph somewhat of Léa, though she was more full-blown, more striking-looking. At the age of forty, she was more desirable than ever, and she knew it. In her bearing and general manner she was less reserved than the girl who plied her trade at the Café Riche. In the presence of a man, any man, she always looked as if she wanted to be sure of the effect she was producing.

"How are you, Joseph?"

"And you, Monsieur Motard?"

Handshakes. Small talk. The women kissed. Everyone was all dressed up. There was a smell of perfume in the air. The coffee cups had not yet been removed from the table on the porch.

Marcel went from one to the other, very much the host. A car stopped at the door. Françoise, one of Nicole's sisters, stepped out of it with her husband and daughters.

It was odd that Nicole's family felt so at home in the house of Marcel, who was only her brother-in-law, and not in her husband's. Raymonde, Françoise, and Jeanne often spent Sunday afternoon there though they practically never set foot in the house on the Quai Colbert, as if they were afraid of Lambert or did not feel at ease there.

Only one of the Fabre girls was on hand that day—two, counting Nicole, of course. The latter apologized for Raymonde, the eldest, who had had to visit her husband's family in Moulins, and for Jeanne, who was taking care of her daughter, the one in bed with measles.

Little by little, the women gathered in one corner and the men in another, while the small children and the older ones remained outside not knowing quite what to do, for they were not the same age and there was no possible contact between the young ones and the older ones.

Before long, Lucien came in and joined the men's group, and his brother went off by himself to another room to play the phonograph.

What exactly did they talk about? Contrary to what

might have been expected, very little was said about the Château Roisin catastrophe and much more about jet planes and, for a half-hour, international politics.

Lambert sat there grousing, without taking part in the conversation, and wondering whether Marcel liked such gatherings any more than he did. In any case, Marcel kept up the conversation with his father-in-law, and it was he who said at one point, "By the way, I've made the acquaintance of an amazing fellow named Chevalier who has a very unusual kind of job. He works for an insurance company and carries out investigations the way the police do. Listen to this, Lucien . . . At the age of fifteen," he continued, turning to his son, "he graduated from the lycée and then, for his own pleasure, for the fun of it, just to see what would happen, he took the entrance exams of the Naval Academy, the Military Academy, and the Ecole Normale. . . ."

"Which did he finally pick?"

"The Ecole Normale. And, at the same time, he studied chemistry and God knows what else. He's loaded with degrees and he's only about thirty."

"What's he here for?"

"The bus that was destroyed at Château Roisin was insured by his company, and he's trying to find out who was responsible."

"Have you met him?"

"At the Bergerets'. I don't know how he knows them. Perhaps through their son, who was also at the Ecole Normale and who's just about his age."

Guillaume Bergeret was a presiding magistrate. The important people in town and those who lived in the nearby châteaux met at his handsome mansion on the Rue de l'Ecuyer.

"Has he been able to reach any conclusions?" asked Motard.

If Chevalier had expressed any opinion about the accident, they did not learn what it was, for, in keeping with the tradition, Armande came in and announced, "Gentlemen, tea is served."

The women had disappeared a while before. When the men entered the dining room, they found the women and children sitting around the table, in the middle of which was a huge cake with burning candles.

"Happy birthday, Marcel!"

Every year he pretended to be surprised and confused, and kissed everybody, merely grazing the cheeks of the men, as in ceremonies when decorations are awarded. He was given his presents and put them down on an end table because before unwrapping them he had to blow out the candles and cut the first slice of cake.

Was Lambert a monster? There were times, such as then, when he wondered. He looked at them all, one after the other, and found them grotesque. He thought there was something false about that well-ordered scene.

"Joseph, would you uncork the bottles?"

The bottles of champagne and the glasses were on the table. Armande added, with a lilt in her voice, "You're used to that, aren't you?"

Later, the children who were present and the nephews and nieces who weren't there that day would regard him as the black sheep of the family, the uncle of whom one is a little ashamed but whom one secretly envies. Armand, the schoolboy, who must have seen him go by in the street with women, devoured him with his eyes. His sister always avoided kissing her uncle as if she were afraid of him or of catching some contagious disease, though she kissed all the others.

He filled the glasses, assisted by Motard, who burst out laughing each time a cork popped.

"Happy birthday, Marcel! And may you have many more!"

Was Marcel really happy with a wife whom he had had

to catch at the station and who was excited by every male she saw?

Perhaps Motard was happy, people thought he was, and perhaps too that other idiot of a son-in-law who hung on his lips in the hope of someday succeeding him at the bank.

The storm that was gathering within him was probably visible on his face, for he saw the almost imploring look of Nicole, who seemed to be saying:

"Above all, don't make a scene!"

He did not, but silently amused himself watching them, listening to what they were saying, and no one noticed—nor did he, for that matter—that he was emptying one glass of champagne after the other.

Armande's gift to her husband was a fawn-colored leather golf bag, for Marcel had taken up golf three years before, which obliged him to drive a distance of more than thirty-five miles on weekends. The surprising thing was that by dint of will he had become a good player and the year before had won a rather important tournament.

Nicole, following the advice of Monsieur Blanche, the bookseller, had chosen an album of Egyptian sculpture.

"Who wants more cake?"

It was hot in the room, but in order not to upset his wife Lambert kept his jacket on, though he would have taken it off any other Sunday.

Several people were talking at once. The children had all gone off to the garden or elsewhere, for they were no longer around, except Raymonde's youngest boy, an eight-year-old who for some mysterious reason was weeping bitterly.

"What's the matter, Jean-Paul? Tell Mamma what's wrong."

Lambert had been frightened that morning when he saw the man with the goats. He had been living in a state of fear for three days, and that afternoon, when Chevalier's name had been mentioned, a cold shiver had gone down his back.

What if they came and arrested him today or tomorrow, or any time? What would he lose? This? The cackle that was going on around him? The kind of life he was living? The bridge games at the Café Riche with Lescure, poor Nédelec, and the rat-faced fogy?

What had kept him from putting a bullet through his head as he had thought of doing? What was there to prevent him?

He hated the evenings with Nicole. In the office, he spent most of his time grousing. Occasionally he would go on a spree, like a soldier or sailor, and would come home all droopy and haggard-looking.

"I maintain," little Motard was saying sententiously, "that if modern education is to have any effect, it must reckon with . . ."

With what? Another jackass who had an answer to every question. Didn't he ever feel the need, he too, to unbosom himself to a Léa?

"Be careful, Joseph."

This time his wife had not confined herself to a look. She had gone over to him discreetly and whispered a warning in his ear.

"Of what?"

"Sh! You know very well."

His eyes were starting to gleam. There was no need for him to look in the mirror to know it. And his ears were becoming crimson. His nose was shining. It wasn't his fault if he had old Lambert's nose! It was *he* who was now old Lambert!

"You'd make everyone feel awful!"

It had happened once, years before, when Marcel's children were little. The family had been together for the same occasion, not in that house, but a more modest one in which his brother had lived at the time, near the railway. Before leaving, he had had several drinks, he had forgotten why, probably because that day, too, he had felt ill at ease in his body. Monsieur Motard had been holding him by a button of his jacket and delivering an endless speech on political economy.

"You see, my young friend . . ."

He called everyone "my friend" or "my young friend."

What had happened after that? He had never been able to remember, for, while pretending to listen to the old man, he had emptied every glass within reach. Finally, he had cried out, "Ladies and gentlemen, what a lousy party! I'm getting the hell out of here, and please accept my very best wishes!"

Marcel had held it against him for a long time. So had Nicole. Armande was the only one who had burst out laughing, but her laughter stuck in her throat when her husband looked at her.

Marcel had a hold on her because she had no money of her own. Otherwise he probably would not have been able to bring her back from the station.

Lescure had not been entirely wrong the day before in claiming that Chevalier was a remarkable young man. He had not gone poking about in the debris of the bus at the foot of the Big Hill, but had made it his business, as soon as he arrived in town, to be invited to the home of Georges Bergeret, with the result that he already knew all the gossip.

The men followed Marcel into his book-lined study. Lambert went along, but not before draining the few glasses on the table that were full or half full. His sister-in-law, who saw what he was doing, smiled at him. She was a real female, and probably he had only to make a gesture . . .

Cigars were handed out. Marcel did not smoke them, but Lambert took one. The smell of the cigars, added to that of the champagne, thickened the atmosphere of family celebration. Albums were opened on the desk. The men bent over them admiringly. Joseph went to the window, and, looking out, saw his brother's daughter lying on her stomach in the sun. She was fourteen and was already very well developed, for she resembled her mother. Perhaps it was better not to say so to Marcel, to whom it gave no pleasure.

Whereupon he thought of Edmonde and wondered, as he had done that morning, where she was at the present moment. At some movie with her mother? Or likewise at a family gathering? Or else out with a boy friend?

He knew nothing about her. He had never asked her whether she had a lover. All he knew was that she was not a virgin when he took her the first time.

Was he going to start being jealous?

"What do you think about them, Joseph?"

"About what?"

"The Egyptians."

His head was already beginning to swim, a feeling that was all too familiar, and his scowl and grim expression were equally revealing. He looked around and spotted on a sideboard a decanter of liqueur surrounded by crystal glasses, an earlier birthday gift. As everyone's back was turned, he poured himself a drink. He tossed it down stealthily, but just then Marcel looked up and saw him.

Marcel said nothing. It was not the moment. Lambert felt ashamed at being caught, and since he loathed being ashamed he left the room abruptly and walked out of the villa. He was fed up. Nicole had asked him not to make a scene, and if he stayed any longer he was bound to. He did not meet anyone. The women must have gone upstairs to Armande's room to powder their faces and would probably spend part of the afternoon there.

He slammed the door of his car and started the engine. The sound was enough to draw Nicole to the window.

The hell with it! Someone in the family would drive her home. They were now all by themselves and were probably glad to get rid of him. The bad uncle, the brute whose behavior was unpredictable, had left.

He hadn't the slightest idea where he was going. Suddenly a wild thought occurred to him, and for a moment or two it seemed to him almost reasonable. What was to prevent him from driving to the Big Hill and seeing the man with the goats so as to have it out with him and know once and for all what he was up to?

The man had come prowling around the dock that morning. Lambert would return the visit, except that he would go straight up to him and ask him what was what.

Either he *had* seen something or he *hadn't.*

Either he had spoken to the police or he had kept his mouth shut.

It was clear, it was definite. There was no other alternative. If he hadn't spoken to the police, who had surely questioned him as they had questioned everyone along the highway, he must have had a reason for not talking.

Clear as could be, wasn't it? Lambert wasn't drunk. He'd been drinking, but his mind was clear.

Where was he? Oh yes, if the man with the goats hadn't said anything that meant he had a plan. And if he had a plan, there was no reason to wait.

Clear as day!

He would stand up to him, would look him in the eyes, like a man:

"What exactly do you want?"

He was sure that the idiot would start trembling. People like that were cowards, always ready to take advantage, but as soon as you looked at them in a certain way, they backed out.

Money?

If necessary, he'd give him some, so as to have peace.

How much?

No! It was unwise to give him money. He'd start spending it. Everyone knew that all he had was his goats and his shanty and they'd begin to wonder. The gendarmes would hear about it in no time, or else Chevalier, who already knew the town and before long would know the countryside.

He wouldn't give him anything at all. He'd shut him up some other way. How? He didn't know yet. That was precisely what he had to find out, how to shut him up. It required thought. It was absolutely essential. *Ab-so-lute-ly!*

He was thirsty and suddenly wondered what he was doing near the gasworks, where there were only workers' houses and not a single bar. He turned the car around so brutally that the wheels screeched, and then he tore off toward the center of town with the thought of stopping at Victor's. He was in no mood to sit down at the Café Riche. He was completely fed up with people who resembled the ladies and gentlemen at his brother's place.

Victor was shrewd. He did not ask him, as he usually did, "How goes it, Monsieur Lambert?"

He simply shook hands with him, without a word, with just a questioning look.

"Sorry, Victor. Just been with the family celebrating my very dear brother's birthday and it's made me thirsty. Do I look it?"

While talking, he glanced at his reflection in the mirror behind the bottles and felt an even greater dislike for himself than he had that morning while shaving.

"Let me have something very dry so I can get rid of the bad taste of the family. But no marc. Applejack, that's it. A big glass."

His voice resounded strangely, and he understood why when he realized that the bar was empty. At that hour on a Sunday afternoon, Victor hardly ever had a customer, and he had the television on for his own pleasure.

"Do you know someone named Chevalier?"

"No."

"A tall fair guy with a poker face who looks even more intelligent than my brother Marcel. If he comes to see you and asks you about me, tell him I said he can go to hell."

"Who is he?"

He stopped in time. He was playing with fire, perhaps because he was really beginning to be scared.

"Nobody," he answered in a tone of indifference. "Forget it."

Victor did not press the point, and Lambert explained:

"Pay no attention. The damned family's been getting under my skin. Do *you* like family gatherings?"

"I don't know, Monsieur Lambert. I was brought up by the Foundling Society."

"In Paris?"

"At first, and then, when I was twelve, on a farm in Corrèze."

"Were you unhappy?"

"I never asked myself."

"Would you do it again?"

"I don't know. I suppose so."

"Well, as for me . . ."

But it wasn't true. It was better to keep quiet. He was about to say that he himself would refuse to live his life over again. He sometimes thought so and then two days later would go to see the doctor about a vague discomfort in his chest or simply a heavy feeling in his stomach.

At bottom, he was afraid of dying, just as he was afraid of no longer being Joseph Lambert, contractor, Quai Colbert.

"Hilarious!"

"What?"

"Nothing. I'm talking to myself and I know what I mean. Have a drink on me."

Victor poured himself a bit of mint-flavored syrup and a lot of water.

"Here's to your health, Monsieur Lambert."

"Here's to yours. . . . Tell me, just between you and me, have you ever been in prison?"

The barman remained silent for a moment.

"Funny question," he finally murmured.

"Would you rather not answer?"

"You'd find out anyway by asking Benezech."

"For long?"

"Once for six months and once for a year. The second time, it was unjust. I paid for others."

It had been wrong of Lambert to ask. He was drunk, but not enough not to realize it. Why, when he got started in that way, was he unable to stop?

"What do I owe you?"

He had better leave. Besides, the Sunday atmosphere of the bar depressed him.

"So long, Victor!"

"Good-by, Monsieur Lambert."

He forgot that he had left his car on the square, and walked down the Rue du Vieux Marché, thinking at one and the same time of Victor, the man with the goats, and his brother. Perhaps it was dangerous, especially on a Sunday, in broad daylight, to go looking for the man on the Big Hill. Perhaps in the evening, when it was dark, when he had gone back to his hut.

Why not more simply go and ring Lescure's bell and announce the bad news to him?

"You remember what you were telling us yesterday at the Café Riche, the hundreds of millions that your company would have to shell out and all that? Well, my boy! That's how it is! The guy in the Citroën is me, and somewhere around there's a kind of village idiot who recognized me. Do what you have to. It no longer concerns me. I may go to jail, but Victor's been there and he's none the worse for it. But for you guys it's a question of millions. . . ."

He turned around and walked in the opposite direction. The thought of the Citroën had reminded him that he had just left it on Town Hall Square, opposite the Café Riche. His friends did not play cards there on Sundays. The tables were occupied by families that had been out for a walk and were now waiting until it was time for dinner.

Chevalier was there, alone, at the same table as the evening before, near the cash register, and Lambert felt sure that the man was watching him get into his car.

Had anyone spoken about him to Chevalier? He was not a member of Judge Bergeret's circle, as his brother was. He knew the Judge's guests only by name or sight. A traffic policeman motioned to him to keep going. He was perfectly willing to obey. But where should he go? Not home, in any case. He was sick and tired of roaming about the empty apartment alone, with that mousy Angèle in the kitchen.

"Well, what are you waiting for?"

The car shot forward, then he turned left because it was the easiest thing to do, and since the street led to Léa's apartment, he decided to ring her bell. She didn't work on Sundays either, since it was a family day.

He rang once, twice, listening for a sound in the apartment, but he heard nothing. Then he rang without letting up and finally he heard footsteps. A voice called out:

"Who is it?"

"It's me, Lambert."

"Just a moment."

It was Léa's voice, but it was as grumpy as his own. She came back in a few moments, turned the key in the lock, and drew the bolt.

"It's you!" she murmured, as if she had not recognized his name a few seconds before.

And she looked at him exactly as Victor had, with a frown. She had understood. She resigned herself.

"Come in."

"Do you at least have something to drink?"

"I do, don't worry."

"Were you sleeping?"

"Come in!"

"Does it bother you to see me?"

"Of course not."

"Admit that it bothers you."

"It doesn't. Please don't stand there on the landing. I'm not completely awake yet."

"A problem!" he mumbled, as if the word explained everything.

"Eh?"

"I said a problem. Doesn't that remind you of something? The ones who come for a good time and those who come with their problem?"

The apartment was tidy, except that the bed was unmade and that a novel had fallen on the rug.

"What have you come for?" she asked. "I don't go out on Sundays. I take advantage of the morning to do my house cleaning, and I sleep in the afternoon."

"Maybe I'll sleep too."

"Do you mean that seriously?"

He was already starting to undress. Why not? That or something else! He wouldn't be alone there and would have the advantage of not seeing his wife return home with a sad, indulgent look on her face. It wasn't indulgence that he wanted.

"But first you've got to give me something to drink."

"All I have is vermouth."

"Bring in the vermouth."

She went to the dining room to get the bottle and returned with only one glass. The bottle was three-quarters full.

"Promise me you won't make a rumpus."

"Have I ever misbehaved in your apartment?"

"No, not in my apartment."

"Are you afraid?"

"I'm afraid of the landlord. He wouldn't give up the opportunity to kick me out."

It was odd: without make-up she looked like a nice wife and mother, even a country mother. He took long swallows of the vermouth, and she stood there watching him. He was sitting on the edge of the bed in his underpants, still wearing his shoes and socks.

"You're a nice girl," he declared with conviction.

It was not quite what he had meant to say. But he knew what he meant. As he saw it, it was a magnificent compliment, something very delicate. She did not try to stop him when he poured another drink, then a third, and finally finished the bottle. He kept looking at her tenderly and nodding his head without her being able to tell what he was actually seeing.

"A very nice girl . . . Wait! . . . That's it—you're a real sister!"

It relieved him to find the right word, and his eyes filled with tears. He drank the last of the vermouth, while she kneeled on the floor in front of him and removed his shoes and socks.

He remembered neither her undressing him nor his having gone to bed. He did not even remember having gone to the bathroom two hours later to vomit and having bumped into all the walls because he had thought he was on the Quai Colbert and did not know his way around.

Nor did he remember having called her Nicole.

CHAPTER

7

He was not quite asleep, he was not quite awake. He was deliberately maintaining his balance between sleep and waking. It was a familiar trick of his, one which he often used, especially when he had been drinking the night before. And probably it was the liquor, too, that made his flesh more sensitive, that gave his desires a particular form and edge.

He had begun by regaining consciousness at the same time as other mornings and had realized at once, without having to open his eyes, that he was not in his own bed and that the warm, naked thigh beneath his hand was Léa's. He was beginning to remember. Not everything. It was an over-all impression, with a few details here and there. For example, he was able to recall the emotion he had felt the night before as he looked at Léa and thought of her as a "sister." He did not smile at this. Nor was he ashamed of it.

He had opened his eyes just enough to get his bearings, to make out a cream-colored curtain behind which dawn was coming up, and he had dropped back into his torpor, somewhat as he had done under the linden tree in the garden the day he had had his toothache. He felt within him a refusal to return to ordinary life, and he plunged almost fiercely into a universe where all that mattered was the quivering of his senses.

It was, as a matter of fact, what Edmonde was able to do wide awake, in broad daylight, anywhere, when the click occurred, and when he was with her he could do it too. Perhaps she could even produce the click at will.

The universe then drifted away until it was only a kind of unimportant nebula. Objects lost their weight, human beings were merely tiny or grotesque puppets, and everything to which one usually attached value became ridiculous. All that remained in a shrunken, warm, enveloping, and kindly world was the pounding of the blood in their arteries, a symphony which at first was vague and diffuse, then gradually became sharper, and finally concentrated in their sex organs.

They were unashamed that their existence was focused for a moment in that area of their bodies, unashamed of exhausting the possibilities of pleasure.

He was eager to see Edmonde, to make a sign to her, to read the answer in her eyes, and to plunge with her into that universe.

Today it was essential that it last a long time, that he see her with her nostrils dilated and upper lip drawn back above her teeth, as if she were a corpse. He would go at her again without letting her come to her senses, he would invent new caresses that would make her beg for mercy. They would both go very far, farther than ever, to the very edge of the precipice, until they shuddered with fear that they might never come back.

He tingled with desire from head to foot, as if he had been skinned alive. Even the feel of the sheets was voluptuous. Yet he did not dream of satisfying himself with Léa, whom his hand continued to caress. On the contrary, he wanted to be even more excited and strove to imagine in minute detail what would happen later. Not in the office or elsewhere in the plant on the Quai Colbert where they had had earlier experiences.

The weather promised to be warm. The bright sun gilded the cream-colored curtain, and because he remembered the linden tree with the buzzing flies his thoughts drifted to a field in the countryside or a glade near which he would stop the car.

Was it a reaction against his fears of the day before? He was hungry for Edmonde, hungry for her body and the mysterious stages of her pleasure.

He no longer cared about the man with the goats or Benezech or his brother Marcel or young Chevalier. He still had what no one could take from him.

It would not be the first time that he stopped at the edge of a meadow. And each time, when he stood up, it was as if he were drunk with the smell of the damp earth and the odor of Edmonde. Once they had heard a sound behind a hedge, very near them, but she had dug her nails into his flesh and prevented him from moving. Never before had she been in such a frenzy.

He had to be at the Renondeau farm in the morning to check on the setting of the cement. Should he take her with him then or later, in the afternoon, for example?

He lay there half dreaming. He created the setting, conceived images that made his desire painful, and, as he continued to stroke Léa, she turned over, half asleep, spread her legs, and murmured in a distant voice, "Come."

He said no, and in order not to succumb, he got up. She watched him with an expression of surprise, but she was not sufficiently awake to feel like questioning him. It was not until he stood up that he realized he had a headache and was empty, but he didn't care, it didn't bother him, he knew that the sickly feeling would soon wear off and that his desire would remain.

He put on his shirt and trousers, then went to the

kitchen, where he lit the small stove, looked for the coffee among the white cans on a shelf, found it, and poured a few measures into the coffee mill that was nailed to the wall.

As he was pouring water into the pot, Léa silently appeared in the doorway, naked. The folds of the sheets had covered her smooth skin with pink lines.

"What are you doing?"

"Making coffee."

"What time is it?"

He looked at the alarm clock on the mantle.

"Twenty after six."

"Are you leaving already?"

He said he was, and, as her head began to clear, she again looked at him as she had done the night before. It was as if she were seeing something inside him that worried her, a kind of sign, as if she were reluctant to let him go.

"Your wife?"

"No."

"Doesn't she say anything?"

"No."

"You're lucky."

There was no point in explaining to her that she was wrong, that, quite the contrary, he had no luck at all.

"Business?"

It was not business either that was making him leave. It was not absolutely necessary that he go to the Renondeau farm that morning.

"The girl you told me about?"

He nodded. What was the good of lying at that point of the game!

"Was that why you didn't want me this morning?"

She felt no resentment, but seemed even more worried.

"All right, let me have a cup of coffee, too. It won't keep me from going back to sleep. Do you remember that you were sick?"

"No."

"It doesn't matter. I don't hold it against you. The hardest part of all was getting you back into bed. You're pretty heavy!"

"Did you have to carry me?"

"I had to hoist you up and pull you and push you as best I could."

"I apologize."

"Don't be silly!"

She sat down in a white chair. It was odd to see her drinking coffee in the kitchen without a stitch on her body.

"Are you going to take a bath before leaving?"

"I'll take one at home."

"As you like. How about some aspirin?"

"All right."

She went to the bathroom to get him two tablets. While she was there she brushed her teeth. He drank two cups of coffee and was able to light a cigarette without feeling nauseous.

"I'm going to finish dressing," he said.

"Do you always get up so early?"

"At six. Sometimes five-thirty."

She followed him to the bedroom and watched him dress, with the same thoughtful look on her face. Then she accompanied him to the door, pulled the bolt, and kissed him on both cheeks.

"Thanks," he said as he was about to leave.

He returned her kisses.

"Watch out for yourself," she said.

The remark did not strike him until he was in the street, where he looked around for his car. Since she wasn't aware of anything, why had she said that in such an earnest tone?

There were already a few North Africans on the Quai Colbert. A barge with a red and white triangle painted on the bow was gliding up the canal. The bargemen, who were standing on deck, waved a greeting to the men on the boat that was being unloaded and called out the name of a canal lock where they were probably to meet.

He went straight to the office and, with a certain embarrassment, furtively ran his hand over Edmonde's table as he walked by. He did not want his desire to peter out. The images he had conjured up in Léa's bed were already losing some of their plausibility in the harsher light of day. The scenes he had imagined, the gestures, the words he had planned to say, were becoming less real.

All the same, he would take her to the country, anywhere, and he would enjoy her savagely. He needed to. He needed, above all, to prove to himself that it was they who were right, that they were justified, that there was nothing dirty or guilty in the pleasure they gave each other.

When all was said and done, wasn't that what tormented him even more than fear and all the rest of it? The only moments of real joy he had ever known had been defiled. The moments with Edmonde and those he had experienced when he had had the toothache under the linden tree. It was the same thing, the same flight, the same leap into another world.

What he had once attained with two tablets of a drug, with torpor and the filtered rays of the sun and the sound of the flies, Edmonde and he attained with their two bodies.

So of what were they guilty? And if they weren't, why had he so often felt a veiled anxiety ever since he knew her?

Why, when the bus had let out its deathly shriek . . .

He refused to think about it, refused to remember it. On no condition would he relive the three days he had just been through. He went up the steps three at a time and opened the kitchen door. Angèle gave a start and looked at him as if he were a ghost.

"Make me a cup of coffee."

Didn't she regard him as the devil in person?

"Madame isn't up yet and hasn't left me any instructions," she grumbled as he walked down the hall.

"I don't care."

That gave him time to take a cold shower and to dress. He was ready when the door of Nicole's bedroom opened. She merely said, "You're there?"

He did not look for an excuse and gave no explanation. There was now no point in it. Nor did he make any mention of what had happened at Marcel's.

"Do you feel well?"

"Very well."

"Do you want breakfast?"

"I don't think I'll eat."

His stomach wasn't settled enough for that. Work was already under way on the dock and in the plant. He could hear the buzzing of the mechanical saw and the regular dropping of planks. His headache had already gone, but there persisted a certain vague feeling in his whole body and a heightened sensitivity.

For more than half an hour he stood around among the trucks and piles of material, talking with the foremen and workmen. Then he went to the dock to be sure that the unloading would be finished by the afternoon of the following day. The planks, which had still been horizontal on Saturday, were now sloping steeply, for as the boat emptied it rose on the water and exposed its grayish sides, which the bargeman was already coating with Norwegian tar.

At nine o'clock, when the employees arrived, he was in his office. He saw Edmonde walking up the quai and, for the first time, received a kind of shock. He grew feverish, and time seemed to drag until he opened the connecting door.

"Mademoiselle Pampin, would you come in for a moment?"

"With my pad?"

"There's no need."

Did she understand? Did she think it was for right away? He was not smiling, was not gay, in fact, he was rather grim and vaguely anxious. She closed the door and remained standing. He now wondered whether, after what had happened on the Big Hill, she would again be willing and whether the click would occur.

He paced up and down the office, putting off the moment when he would have to look at her. She stood there motionless, upright, with her hands clasped in front of her.

"I merely wanted to tell you . . ."

He finally looked up at her and had the impression that she was repressing a furtive smile.

"I'll probably ask you to come with me today . . ."

"This morning?"

He was watching her. He was sure she had already recognized his look. What he would have liked to know was whether there would be a click.

"This morning or this afternoon. I don't know yet."

He added in a less natural tone, "We'll be going rather far."

"Very well, Monsieur Lambert."

He had to turn his eyes away because he was looking at her with an almost pleading expression and did not want to be pathetic.

"Do you understand?"

"Yes."

He again observed her.

"Glad?"

She said nothing, but her eyelids fluttered, and he was almost sure she had turned paler. That was the sign.

"See you later."

He had just become himself again. He was suddenly happy and felt a need to go to Marcel's office, for he was surprised that his brother had not yet come in to see him. Three draftsmen were bent over their boards, and Marcel was working in shirt sleeves.

"I apologize," mumbled Lambert, "for leaving yesterday afternoon without saying good-by."

"It was a good thing you did, and it would have been better if you hadn't come at all."

It was the first time he had ever spoken in that curt,

contemptuous tone. Lambert felt the blood rush to his head. He clenched his fist and was about to grab Marcel by the shoulders and shake him. But he controlled himself, and his anger subsided almost instantly. He merely muttered, loudly enough for the employees to hear, "Little snot-nose!"

Nobody was going to teach him a lesson, least of all his brother! He went off to see Monsieur Bicard, who always needed him on Monday mornings for his signature, and then went back to his office with the intention of leaving for the Renondeau farm immediately. As for Edmonde, it was better to wait until the afternoon and go with her to Orville Forest.

At that moment, as he was about to take his hat from the rack, there was a sudden uproar on the dock. Turning his head, he saw one of the North Africans who was struggling in the grip of two others free himself and run like mad in the direction of the alley that Nicole had taken the day before on her way back from Mass and which was referred to in the plant as the short cut.

A body was lying on the ground among the scattered bricks. At first, all Lambert could see was the long legs. He opened the window and yelled out, "What's going on?"

Oscar motioned to him from the dock to come down. When the man had got away, there had been cries and comments in Arabic, but now there was complete silence. It was as if every man had stopped dead in his tracks at a given signal.

The noise had been heard in the other offices too, and Lambert found himself crossing the street at the same time as his brother, who went straight to the man on the ground and bent over him. His shirt was stained with blood. His eyes were staring upward. He did not utter a single moan.

"What happened, Oscar?"

"It happened so fast that I hardly saw anything. They were on the planks, one behind the other, each carrying his load, and the one in front was talking in a low voice. I noticed it. They didn't seem to be arguing. It looked instead as if the first one were saying a prayer. The picture changed in a flash, and I didn't have time to move. The one in back dropped his load of bricks on the dock, pulled out a knife from under his shirt, threw himself on the other one, and stabbed him in the back."

Marcel, who was still kneeling beside the wounded man, was giving orders to one of the clerks who had followed him. Other employees stepped out of the office hesitantly. The typists were standing at the windows.

"That's about all. Two of the men grabbed the guy with the knife and all the others started talking at the same time in their lingo. I think they were ordering them to let go. If they tried to hold him back, they didn't try very hard, and in order to catch him now . . ."

"Who is he?"

"Mohammed something-or-other. I've got the name on my list."

The clerk came back with a first-aid kit, which was often needed in the plant. Marcel was in his element. He was calm and meticulous and kept giving brief instructions to his assistant in the manner of a surgeon.

"Serious?"

"I don't think so."

The Arab was watching them as tranquilly as if he had nothing to do with what was going on, and the others remained standing in a silent circle.

"Has anyone sent for the police?" asked Lambert.

"I've contacted Benezech," replied Marcel.

The siren of the commissioner's car pierced the air, and a few moments later Benezech arrived.

"A fight?" he asked as he shook Lambert's hand.

"We don't know. They were unloading bricks when the man who was behind this one suddenly went for him and stabbed him."

"Is he an Arab too?"

"Yes."

"Did they let him get away?"

"Two of them tried to hold him back, but . . ."

"Hell!"

Benezech turned to Oscar.

"Do you have their names and addresses?"

"I've got the list in the plant."

"Go get it."

The Police Chief stood looking at the man who was stretched out on the gravel.

"I suppose you don't have anything to say?"

The North African's face remained motionless. He merely stared at Benezech with expressionless eyes.

"You don't know anything, do you? Neither why he stabbed you nor . . ."

He shrugged and turned to an inspector.

"Send for an ambulance and have him taken to the hospital."

He stepped aside to talk to Oscar, who had brought the list. Edmonde was also at a window. Her black dress made her skin seem whiter. But she was not facing the group on the dock. Following the direction of her gaze, Lambert caught sight of the man with the goats who was standing near a tree, about twenty yards away.

Some cars had stopped and a few passers-by had gathered, with the result that Lambert had not seen him.

He was not dressed up as he had been the day before, but was wearing his everyday clothes. He stood there, tall and gaunt, leaning against the trunk of the tree and idly plucking the leaves of a small branch he had picked up from the ground. He was not interested in the wounded Arab, but in Lambert, who thought he could see the glee in the man's pale gray eyes.

Now that he had come back, it was no longer possible to think that his stroll along the quai the day before was merely a matter of chance, and now, because of Benezech's presence, the menace was more definite than ever. The Chief of Police, who was still in conversation with Oscar and taking notes, had his back to the man, but a minute or two later, when the siren of the ambulance was heard, he turned around.

Then—Lambert was sure of it—Benezech's gaze, which had not been fixed on anything in particular, spotted the unexpected figure of the man with the goats, returned to it a second later, this time with a quizzical expression, and lingered on it for some moments.

It was more subtle than that, swifter. Lambert nonetheless caught the look of surprise that flashed across Benezech's face. The commissioner knew the man and did not expect to find him on the Quai Colbert.

It was almost over. Benezech was talking to the attendants, who had brought a stretcher. Marcel, who was now standing up, was informing them of what he had just been doing for the victim, while Oscar was trying to gather his men in order to send them back to work.

The faces were no longer at the windows. Slowly, with animallike movements, as if not to attract attention, the man with the goats moved off between the lines of perspective of the trees, but Lambert had time to catch his eye before he disappeared.

One of the attendants shut the doors of the ambulance, and the vehicle drove off. Marcel, Benezech, and an inspector formed a group in the sunlight in front of one of the pyramids of bricks. Lambert spotted the little girl from the barge, who had been on deck all the time watching what was going on.

"We'll find him," Benezech was saying. "We'll get our hands on him sooner or later. But in spite of what we do we won't learn a thing, and it'll be a devil of a job getting any of the others to testify against him. The victim himself won't say anything."

Was it an illusion or was he now really looking at Lambert somewhat the way he had looked at the man with the goats a few minutes before, as if a thought had just occurred to him?

"Which of you saw the incident?"

"Oscar."

"Did you, Lambert?"

"I ran to the window as soon as I heard the noise, but the victim was already on the ground and the other fellow broke away and started running."

"And you?"

It was Marcel's turn.

"I saw even less than that. A man running, a man on the ground, and the others watching."

The man with the goats, like the fugitive, must have gone through the alley, which was formed by garden walls on one side and a fence on the other and which led to the Rue des Capucines. It was one of the quietest and most deserted spots in town. The foliage of the trees overflowed the walls of the monastery, and there was only one small door which nobody ever used.

"I'm obliged to send for all these fellows in order to question them. Do you need them long?"

"The unloading should be over tomorrow afternoon."

"Then I'll have them come Wednesday morning."

He shook hands with Marcel and then with Lambert.

"Bridge this evening?"

"Probably."

Did he look at him differently from the way he usually did, quizzically, with a puzzled expression?

Lambert crossed the street again and went through the big office where he passed Edmonde, who was filing letters. When he was alone, he was seized with anguish and almost called her. What he was now afraid of was not the threat, which was still indefinite, that hung over him, but the possibility of being refused the joy he had promised himself that morning.

In his voluptuous torpor, lying against Léa's warm, soft body, he had envisaged the scene down to the most minute details, some of which were impossible. In broad daylight he had had to give up some of his dreams.

There was nothing to prevent him from calling her right away and shutting the door, or from driving off with her anywhere.

What kept him from doing it? He didn't know. It seemed to him that the time wasn't ripe. He wanted it to be so extraordinary this time that he had a kind of stage fright and put it off till later. Besides, hadn't he given her to understand earlier that it would be in the afternoon?

He wanted to brood over his desire, to make it so acute, so painful, that the appeasing of it would send him out of this world.

The telephone rang as he was about to leave. It was Nicole, who was calling from the apartment, where she was probably tidying up.

"Has there been a fight?" she asked.

"A stabbing."

"Anyone killed?"

"No. Marcel thinks it's not a serious wound."

"Are you going out?"

"I'm going to the Renondeau farm."

"Watch out."

He was struck by the words. It was the second time that day that he had been given a kind of warning, as if there were a fateful sign on his forehead. Léa had said to him dreamily, as she stood naked in the doorway, *"Watch out for yourself."*

His wife had merely said, *"Watch out."*

It was vaguer. It could mean drive carefully. She knew he had been drinking the night before and probably supposed that he wasn't quite himself.

"See you later," he answered.

And the next moment, as he walked across the big office, he looked at Edmonde with such intensity that the expression on his face must have been dramatic.

Neither of them said anything. She seemed to him even more inscrutable than usual, but he felt sure that there was a promise in her eyes.

Neither of them was cheerful. They were never cheerful. Wasn't there now something of the outcast about them? Nevertheless, Lambert was convinced of their own innocence. He would have liked to proclaim it to the world, but without hope of being heard.

By Benezech less than anyone else. Benezech, who, according to what Léa had told him, had trembled with desire in the girl's presence and who, when she had offered herself, had resisted coyly and consoled himself with a poor joke.

"Maybe in a few years, when I retire . . ."

Léa had admired him! Léa was fond of him, she respected him.

She had said to Lambert, without knowing anything, *"Watch out for yourself."*

He was on his way down the short stairway leading to the yard when he heard his brother's voice behind him:

"One moment, Joseph!"

He waited. Marcel arrived. His lips were quivering.

"I have just one thing to say. When you're back in your normal state, I'd like you to apologize in front of my clerks. There are limits. That's all."

He shot back:

"My answer is no."

Marcel was standing a step above Joseph. They stared at each other, then turned their backs without another word.

He would not apologize, either to Marcel or anyone else, because he owed no apologies to anyone, because he wasn't guilty of anything, whatever he might have thought earlier. He was sure he wasn't and he felt more and more convinced every minute.

It was so true, in fact, that he had no particular feeling about taking the road to Château Roisin and even felt completely indifferent when, a short way before the Despujols' grocery-café, he passed the man with the goats who was striding along the road. His goats, which were higher up along the Big Hill, in a tiny meadow surrounded by barbed wire, were bleating for him because they were troubled by his absence.

Renondeau was in the midst of gathering the second crop.

"Did you meet them?" he asked, wiping his face with his sleeve and putting out his calloused hand.

"The gendarmes. Not ours, those from Marpou. They must have gone farther up to see old Jouanneau. It's at least the third time I've been asked the same questions. They're doing the same thing at every farm. First the gendarmes from here, who are friends, then the men from police headquarters, now the gendarmes from Marpou: 'What were you doing on Wednesday between five and six o'clock, where were you standing, could you see the cars on the road, did you notice a Citroën?' "

"What did you answer?"

"The truth, of course!"

Had Renondeau informed them that Lambert had left his farm and driven in the direction of the Big Hill twenty minutes before the accident and that there had been a woman in his car?

He dared not ask.

"Well, what about the concrete?" asked the farmer. "Shall we take a look?"

They went to see the foreman. Before leaving, Lambert was invited to have the traditional glass of white wine in the shed.

"You're a hell of a lucky man, Monsieur Lambert."

"Why?"

"In the first place, because you make money hand over fist without having to pitch in. And then, because you're always driving around all over the region and because you have every possible opportunity. I, for one, would give a lot to say a word or two to the young lady who was with you the other day. . . ."

It was odd that he felt that way about Edmonde. In the office, for example, she was far from being appreciated by the men. Could it be that the farmer had caught on just by looking at her?

"Here's to your health and hers!"

"Here's to yours, Renondeau."

"Just between the two of us, when you're in the meadow down below, don't feel shy!"

He winked. One day in June when Lambert had stopped with Edmonde behind a hedge, he had not realized that he was on Renondeau's land. It was not the time when they heard a noise, but, as he now saw, the peasant nevertheless had his eyes open.

"No harm done, I hope?"

"None at all."

It was the farmer who blushed.

"A terrific female!" he sighed.

When Lambert got into his car, he regretted not having taken her along. There was no wagon on the road that day, nobody in sight, and he glanced anxiously at the spot where she had jumped across the ditch the last time.

It was too late to go and get her. The whistle would be blowing at the plant in a few minutes, and the employees would all be knocking off for lunch.

He had made up his mind that he would question her afterward, when his waking dream was fulfilled.

Would she answer? Did she realize how far they had both gone? They were not lovers like other people, they were not lovers at all, they were and had always been two accomplices.

What he wanted to know, and he would make her tell him, was whether she felt guilty. He was sure she didn't. If she had felt guilty, she wouldn't have been what she was. But he felt the need to hear it from her own mouth. He would do anything for that, he would hurt her until she spoke.

Because he had been content merely to follow her, to find in her what he had been groping for all his life.

The others didn't count. With them, even with Léa, he

had merely performed obscene movements that left no trace.

The revelation he had had of their power to flee . . .

Two gendarmes who were standing near a small black car signaled to him to stop. One of them put his hand to his cap and went to him.

"Are you from the region?"

They must have been from Marpou, for he didn't know them and they didn't know him either.

"Joseph Lambert," he said, "the contractor on the Quai Colbert."

He handed them his driver's license and owner's card, and the gendarme took notes in his little book.

"I wasn't driving too fast, was I?"

"No. We have orders to stop all Citroëns. Do you have business around here?"

"I'm doing a job at the Renondeau farm."

"Do you go there often?"

"Almost every day at the present time, to check on how the work is going."

"Were you there Wednesday afternoon?"

"I was."

"Around what time?"

"I must have got there around four-thirty and left at about five. I didn't look at my watch."

"Did you go by way of the Big Hill?"

He hesitated, his mouth was dry.

"I did."

"Before the accident?"

"I suppose so, since I didn't see anything."

"Did you go straight back to town?"

"I stopped at the Tréfoux dairy farm, where I have another job going."

It was already over. The gendarme handed back his papers and again touched his cap.

"You're the tenth one this morning," he said, as if to comfort him.

Lambert returned his salute. The gendarme was not aware of anything, but the information would sooner or later end up somewhere, perhaps on Benezech's desk, where it would be examined in the light of other facts.

"Watch out for yourself," Léa had advised him.

"Watch out," Nicole had said to him on the telephone.

Edmonde had merely looked into his eyes with an expression that had meaning only for him and her.

The man with the goats was beginning to walk up the Big Hill with his usual long strides and recognized him. Their gazes met. Again there was that look of diabolical joy in the man's eyes.

CHAPTER

8

His only fear, in the beginning, was that they might come for him before Edmonde got back. As for the rest of it, he had stopped hoping. Actually, he had known from the very first day that his life would never be the same again, that the Château Roisin accident had cut it in two. If he had struggled, it was because his nature forced him to fight against men and fate.

It was now only a question of hours or minutes. All that mattered was the appointment he had made with himself as much as, and perhaps more than, with Edmonde.

As for the rest, he no longer cared. At lunch, alone with Nicole, he looked at the apartment around him as if it were a strange setting and at his wife as if she were someone who had nothing in common with him. Their years together had left no mark. Nothing remained between them, not even, for example, the familiarity that exists between men who have shared the same barrack room.

It was as if she knew, as if she had been warned by some instinct, she who was so mistrustful of instincts. She spoke in a more subdued, more neutral tone, with a certain softness in her manner, as one speaks to a sick person or to someone who is going away forever.

He was not excited, but simply anxious. He was thinking not about Nicole, but about Edmonde, about the minutes separating him from her return.

The other fear did not come over him until later, when he went downstairs and strolled about, first in the offices and then in the plant and stockrooms where work had started again, and this fear was even less rational than the first.

What if Edmonde didn't come? What if there were a hitch? What if someone, for some unforeseeable reason, detained her elsewhere? That had never happened. She was punctual. In over a year, she had never taken sick leave. He seemed to be trying to find reasons for torturing himself. Every time he looked at his wrist watch, his impatience increased. At ten minutes to two, he was already standing on the sidewalk near the Citroën.

Marcel arrived and got out of his car. He looked at his brother with a scowl but did not say a word.

Lambert no longer cared what anyone might think of him, particularly Marcel. He no longer had time to bother about others. He had something to do, and it had become an obsession, an obsession that was now emptied of all he had put into it that morning as he lay half awake.

Even if it was to be only a kind of symbol, it was essential that it exist. The rest had receded into the background, had faded away. The employees were returning from lunch, and he looked at them as if he had never seen them before.

When she rounded the corner of the Rue de la Ferme in her black dress and white hat, he opened the door much too soon and stood there motionless, no doubt absurd-looking, waiting for her. He motioned to her not to go to the office but to join him.

Somewhat confused, she obeyed and sat down in the front seat, with her handbag, which was as white as her hat, on her knees.

He kept himself from sighing "At last."

Without looking at her, as if he were escaping with booty, he brutally started the engine and threw in the clutch, and he drove off so noisily that two or three faces appeared at the windows.

"I was afraid," he said, unable to refrain from admitting it.

"Of what?"

The time for self-respect was over.

"That you weren't coming."

He still did not look at her and did not see her reaction. She said nothing. Was she surprised? Did she understand him? Or was his image of Edmonde a figment of his imagination?

Could it be, as the young mason had crudely put it, that she was only an *animal*?

He drove fast, cut corners. When he reached the open road, he looked in the mirror to make sure that no car was following him.

He had won! He was proud, happy, as if he had just gained a major victory. On the highway he stepped on the gas in order to relax and at the same time blew his horn. It sounded like a cry of triumph. He drove through villages, along broad stretches of flat meadows. Edmonde was as motionless as ever. She looked straight ahead. He could not yet tell whether she was in unison with him, whether she realized that today it had to be ten times, a hundred times more wonderful than ever before. He turned left at a crossroad and shot forward. Orville Forest, where he had a permit to hunt and where he went from time to time, was not far off, beyond a former forester's lodge which had been transformed into an inn that was frequented by hunters. About a half-mile away was a road that cut through the forest. He was planning to leave the car at the side of the road and go off with Edmonde to the woods.

"What's the matter?"

He had just sworn angrily at the sight of two men carrying rifles who were leaving the restaurant followed by their dogs. He knew both of them. One was Weisberg, the other Jean Rupert, who ran a candy shop on the Rue Saint-Martin. He hadn't realized that it was a Monday, that most of the stores in town were closed, and that it was the shopkeepers' day off. Weisberg, who had recognized him, waved at him.

It was now impossible to take the road he had planned to take because the two hunters would be coming along soon. The whole forest was closed to him, for others were probably out hunting too.

He had frowned, his eyes had grown hard. At the next crossing, he took the sunken road that went downhill. He was forced to change his plans, to improvise. At the foot of the hill was a pond, known as Notre Dame Pond, which was surrounded by a few trees. It was too muddy for fishing and the shore was usually deserted.

Edmonde sat quietly while he drove, glancing at him occasionally with a puzzled expression. She must have sensed his tension, which had been heightened by the obstacles. She was not anxious but only surprised.

With a menacing look, he stopped the car at the side of the road, in the mud.

"Get out," he ordered and then slammed the door.

They had only a hundred yards to walk along the path in order to reach the water, but they did not go to the end of it, for they suddenly heard the yells of children and then saw a half-dozen local boys bathing nude in the pond.

He was grateful to her for not smiling, for awaiting his decision without looking him in the face. The very excessiveness of his disappointment restored his calm.

"Come! I apologize."

The other places which he knew were not in that direction but on the other side of town, along the canal or on the way to the Renondeau farm. He didn't want to run the risk of showing his face in the streets, and so the only thing left was to look around for some deserted spot.

He was clinging to his desire. As he stepped into the car, he feverishly lit a cigarette and muttered, "It's idiotic!"

He was aware of the absurdity of the situation but was unable to laugh at it. On the contrary, for him it was the threat of a deathblow, of a grotesque end. It brought to mind the silent laughter of the man with the goats, and he was sorry he hadn't gone to see him the night before and got the thing over with, as he had thought of doing for a moment.

He avoided looking at Edmonde lest he realize that the girl at his side was an ordinary typist who wanted to get back to the peaceful, reassuring setting of the office as quickly as possible.

It wasn't true! He recalled ineffable details which would probably have meant little to anyone else but which meant a lot to him—for example, the time when she was lying on her back and staring, as if fascinated, at the sturdy trunk of an oak tree. He had understood that fascination because of the way she had just reacted. For her, the mighty tree was another principle of life, like the male organ that she was caressing, and when she saw sap flowing from the wound of a pine tree she naturally thought of a man's sap. In her mind, everything merged, everything that swells with life, everything that reproduces, everything that tends obscurely toward natural fullness.

He had stopped once again at the side of the road and now sat at the wheel with a vacant expression. She looked at him in surprise.

He merely tossed away his half-smoked cigarette.

"Let's go!" he sighed.

He had just wavered. His faith was now less firm. He doubted. He had been at the point of suddenly turning around and going back to town without trying the experiment. He drove slowly, almost relaxed, as if it were now less important, looking at the roads that came into view, in search of a lonely spot as if they were stupid Sunday lovers.

Two or three times, he thought he had found one, but there was a jinx on him. Each time, at the last moment, he caught sight of a peasant in his field, an old woman looking after her cow, a nearby house that he hadn't seen at first.

He no longer knew where he was, for he had kept away from the highways and had been going around in circles. He ended by following, without much hope, a bumpy road that suddenly ended in the middle of nowhere. Two fences opened out on meadows where black and white cows were grazing. Nearby were thorny hedges where the grass was thick and dark green. The damp ground was shaded by three big elms.

Realizing that this was the place, she got out of the car with him. For the first time, each was as embarrassed as the other. He would have liked to talk before they went any further. Earlier, while waiting for her on the sidewalk of the Quai Colbert, he had planned to talk about himself and had even prepared whole sentences. Like his dreams that morning, they were no longer in keeping with reality. They had become meaningless, they would have rung false.

He walked to the second fence and saw that there were cows in both meadows. At the far end of the one on the right, above the line of the horizon, he made out the red roof of a farm.

"Lie down," he said in a hoarse tone.

She hesitated a moment, then sat down in the grass, ten feet away from the muddy car.

"Lie down!" he repeated, kneeling beside her.

He had to. He had promised himself. It was a test. He owed it to himself to go through with it.

"Lift up your dress."

He stared at her face, which was turned upward. He wanted it to be as it had been the other times, better than the others, and suddenly, with a rough movement, he uncovered her belly and threw himself on it in a fury.

She had not moved. She was not afraid. But the pupils of her eyes, which were still gazing upward, had become more set, and her mouth had quivered with pain.

"Do you understand?" he growled, mindless of what he was saying, for there was no relationship between his thoughts and words.

He was relentless, almost fierce, and watched her face cruelly.

"Tell me, do you understand? You've got to understand. Do you hear? I've got to know . . ."

Three times he hoped. Three times he thought he was going to triumph, for her nostrils dilated and her upper lip began to draw back with the expression that haunted him, that he had to see again at any cost because it was the sign.

It was essential that it happen again, for it would prove that he was right, that it was on the Big Hill, when the bus had screamed, that he had been wrong.

"Do you understand, tell me? Do you understand?"

Then, just as he was about to reach the goal, her features lost their tension, a salty teardrop oozed from her eyelid, only one, and she dropped her limp arms and moaned in a low voice, "I can't. Forgive me."

His body slackened, and he stood up. He avoided looking at her while she in turn got to her feet and arranged her dress. He heard her walk to the car, where she remained standing in front of the door, waiting for him with her head bowed.

When he finally went to the car, he was himself again, or seemed to be, but his features were drawn and his eyes had a vacant look.

"Are you angry with me?" she murmured.

He shook his head, took his seat, and started the engine.

She must have believed him, must have thought it didn't matter, for her face had taken on the serene expression it had in the office.

They had nothing to say to each other. Since he was unable to turn the car around, he drove in reverse. After two bends in the road, he was back on the highway. He hadn't realized it was so near.

What she would probably never suspect was that a few minutes before, when she had been looking up at the white clouds in the sky, he had resisted a desire to destroy her.

It was over. He was now so calm that she was surprised

and from time to time stole a glance at him. He seemed to be smiling. Perhaps he really was. The grimace of the man with the goats was also a smile. It no longer mattered. Nothing mattered now. If he had been mistaken, that concerned no one but him, and it didn't mean he was entirely wrong.

Could it be that when the tear of impotence had flowed from her eye she was thinking of the bus that had screamed with fear behind them, or of the still joyful faces of the children who were going to burn?

He had thought of them, too.

What about it? Did that prove they were guilty? Had she felt guilty, had she felt ashamed?

That too was of no importance. The girl sitting beside him was Mademoiselle Pampin, and he had nothing in common with Mademoiselle Pampin, apart from dictating letters and other office routine. No letters today. Nor was there any need to take her to any of the plants.

He was almost embarrassed by her presence, the presence he had longed for so eagerly. She had become even more foreign to him than Nicole. The image of her and her mother, arm in arm, walking on Town Hall Square, flashed across his mind and seemed grotesque.

He was really smiling, but she wasn't the kind of person who could have interpreted that smile. Perhaps the man with the goats?

As they neared town, the setting became more familiar. He looked without seeing at villages, at châteaux, at a bridge over a river, sights on which his eyes had rested thousands of times.

There was now no reason to hurry, nor was there any need, as when he drove down the Big Hill, to go slowly.

What sign had Nicole and Léa seen on his face? It puzzled him. He was sure that something was eluding him.

"Watch out for yourself," Léa had said, she who, a moment before, had so nicely spread her thighs and whom he had disdained.

"Watch out," his wife had cautioned him on the telephone.

He crossed the bridge over the canal where, as a child, he had caught his first fish with a stick, a piece of string, and a bent pin. In front of him, on the white wall, he could see the words:

"J. Lambert & Sons."

The North Africans were still walking up the springy planks to the barge and coming down in Indian file laden with bricks.

He stopped the car at the curb and opened the door for Edmonde, who, without waiting for him, walked toward the office.

The last thing he looked at on the dock was the pink bow in the hair of the little girl from the barge.

Then he in turn went up the six stairs and opened the door. Mademoiselle Berthe, one of the clerks who acted as telephone operator, a chubby little woman with a dimpled chin, said to him, "Monsieur Benezech telephoned. He asked that you call him as soon as you get back."

"I know," he replied absently.

"Shall I put the call through?"

"In a little while."

Edmonde, who was already seated at her varnished table, was taking out her pencils and erasers. Marcel was watching him through the glass wall of the draftsmen's office.

Lambert turned around to look at Monsieur Bicard in his cubbyhole. The yellow can of catechu was next to the big account book.

He opened the door of his office, hesitated, then closed it behind him. The windows were open, and the smell of pitch reached him from the barge.

Because of the bricks which the men had been unloading for three days, specks of pink dust were dancing in the sunlight. He sat down at his desk, calmly. As he opened the pad to take a sheet of paper, he thought of his brother Fernand, whom he knew so little. There was no time to waste, for anyone might drop in and he hadn't wanted to bolt the door.

With the blue pencil that he used for annotating documents, he printed the words:

"I am not guilty."

He laid the sheet on the blotter, opened the right-hand drawer, and pulled out the army revolver that he had brought back from the war. No longer remembering whether it was loaded, he had to make sure.

He granted himself another moment to look out of the window. His eyes sought the pink ribbon in the hair of the little girl.

He did not see her. It was four o'clock and she had probably gone to the cabin for her afternoon snack.

He glanced at the ceiling, wondering whether his wife was upstairs. Then, very quickly, he had a vision of what would happen in a few moments, the coming and going, the panic, the phone calls, the sudden stopping of work in the office and the plant.

He also thought of the burial, of the family group, including little Motard and his son-in-law, of the other groups, the office staff, his friends, his cronies at the Café Riche, the hunt club, the clients, the suppliers, the anonymous crowd.

Last, he thought of Léa, but he refused to think of Edmonde.

He started to raise the barrel of the revolver to his mouth, knowing that the thing to do was to fire into the mouth, upward, but he paused and laid the weapon on the desk. His eyes were staring at the sheet of paper.

He again picked up the big blue pencil, then hesitated, pensively, as to whether to cross out what he had written or correct it. Finally, changing his mind again, he crumpled the sheet in his hand and threw it into the wastebasket.

What was the use? Was it for him to decide?

He had the impression that footsteps were approaching, that someone was going to knock at the door, and, shutting his eyes, he hurriedly fired.

ONE O'CLOCK JUMP

ALSO BY LISE McCLENDON

The Bluejay Shaman

Painted Truth

Nordic Nights

ONE O'CLOCK JUMP

Lise McClendon

THOMAS DUNNE BOOKS
St. Martin's Minotaur
New York

THOMAS DUNNE BOOKS.
An imprint of St. Martin's Press.

www.minotaurbooks.com

Design by Tim Hall

Library of Congress Cataloging-in-Publication Data

McClendon, Lise.
One o'clock jump / Lise McClendon—1st ed.
p. cm.
ISBN 0-312-25195-5
1. Women private investigators—Missouri—Kansas City—Fiction. 2. World War, 1939–1945—Missouri—Kansas City—Fiction. 3. Kansas City (Mo.)—Fiction. I. Title.

PS3573.E19595 O54 2001
813'.54—dc21

00-045776
CIP

First Edition: March 2001

10 9 8 7 6 5 4 3 2 1

To the children of the Depression:
Keep dancing and never forget.

ACKNOWLEDGMENTS

MANY THANKS to the folks at the Kansas City Jazz Museum at 18th and Vine, the *Kansas City Star,* the Kansas State Library, and the Kansas City Public Library; and to Denise Morrison, archivist at the Kansas City Museum. Historical errors are completely my own. Apologies to all literalists; I am one myself except when it doesn't serve my purposes.

Thanks to Angie and Bob Brickson; Ken Mueller, M.D., for the pathological advice; Robin Edmiston, Bob Snider, Pat Murtagh, and Virginia Tranel, for their critical eyes and kind encouragement; Sue Grafton; Bill Moody; Karin Slaughter, for one good line; Barry Neville; and Laura Blake Peterson. And thanks to all the musicians, especially William "Count" Basie and Jelly Roll Morton, who accompanied and inspired me.

ONE O'CLOCK JUMP

ONE

1939

INSIDE THE PLATE-GLASS WINDOW of the Hot Cha Cha Club, the bar girl was taking off her apron. Soon she'd be out the door. Dorie Lennox stubbed out her Lucky under her shoe and got ready to move.

The evening had been quiet, the sky softened with clouds. On the corner, a clatter cut the silence as two rummies stumbled out of a smoky joint. Lennox shrank back into the shadows. They saw her. The bandy-legged one stuck his face up to her. "How's about a little hootchie-cootchie?"

"Beat it." She fingered her knife, deep in the pocket of her trousers. The warm ivory handle was reassuring. The drunk smelled like the river, oily and overripe, the wicked smell of the Missouri. The shiver that had woken her up melted into disgust.

The taller fellow grabbed his arm. "Look at 'er—she's no quiff—"

"The hell." Shorty straightened his greasy lapels. "Not good 'nough fer ya, zat it?"

His breath knocked her back. "That's right, I got standards."

"Give us some sugar, eh, toots." The gee lurched right, blind with liquor.

"Scram, I said."

The tall one dragged Shorty down to the alley, where he sang overtures to a garbage can, then stumbled off. Lennox shook out the tension in her shoulders.

The bright hair flashed under the streetlamp as the bar girl came through the door onto the sidewalk. Lennox looked down. Her knife was in her hand, blade ready. When had she done that? She wouldn't have really hurt that harmless old lush. Just looking for love, wasn't he. In this world full of hate and war, who could blame him? The blade's point twinkled in the streetlight. Still, he shouldn't have called her "toots."

She closed the switchblade and dropped it back in her pocket. The blade was a necessary evil. It reminded her of the sharp edge between rage and mercy. Why she still needed reminders, she had no idea. Why she needed the knife was easier.

Across the street, Iris Jackson was in no hurry. The bar girl buttoned her gabardine jacket, checked her seams. The sheet of platinum hair fell against her cheek. Her eyes, Lennox knew, were a deep blue, the color of a storm rising at sea. Clutching a small handbag, the bar girl turned and walked toward the corner.

Lennox climbed into her Packard, turned the key. The radio came on, more war news. If only it was the Andrews Sisters with the "Beer Barrel Polka," we could all forget about Hitler, the Poles, the whole bloody mess. Follow cheating bottle blondes, do our duty that way.

If only. She eased the Packard down the street. The taillights of Iris's sedan, a slate blue rattletrap of a Nash, headed around the corner. Lennox gunned the big car, slowing to keep the bald tires from squealing. At least the old engine still had its getaway guts. With the streets deserted, keeping Iris in sight was easy work.

She wasn't in a hurry, and she wasn't headed home. Going north, more or less, jogging east, then west, but mainly north. Iris paused at Wyandotte and Eighth, as if she was lost. Lennox looked up to her office windows in the Boston Building, then followed Iris up Broadway. It looked like she was headed across the river, when she made an abrupt right turn onto Fifth.

The car stopped under a streetlamp. This was Lennox's

neighborhood. She knew all the flophouses and corn brokers and the warm-hop stench of the brewery by heart. Her shoulders tensed. The questions. Why they thought the hotcha bar girl was stepping out on her boyfriend. Nobody ever gave her reasons. Not the cold-eyed boyfriend, Georgie Terraciano, certainly not the tight-lipped lawyer, old Dutch Vanvleet. Not even Amos. He only speculated that Iris might find a little slap and tickle tonight. As if he remembered his slap from his tickle, the old jasper.

But the silence was jake. Reasons only made you think, conjure up wild scenarios. Better to smoke Luckies and watch the door. That was what she was getting paid for.

A U-turn, then a roll by Fifth. The Nash was parked opposite dim light from the small windows of a bar. THE CHATTERBOX, the pink neon said. Girls from the boardinghouse sometimes went there to play pool on Tuesday nights, when the tables were reserved for female customers. But it was Friday: The Day the War Began, that was how she would remember today. Iris Jackson climbed slowly out of the car, straightened her jacket, patted her hair, then slammed the door shut.

Gunning the beast south, Lennox turned onto Sixth and over to Central, whipped around the block in time to see Iris disappearing into the Chatterbox. A Studebaker rounded the corner and flashed its headlights in her eyes. She parked the Packard, put the camera on the dash to steady it, and, focusing on the Chatterbox's neon sign, snapped off a shot. The rest of the block was boarded-up shops, a warehouse for mattresses and springs, several garages, a warehouse for wholesale liquor, its sign bearing crooked letters: BEEWARE VISHUS DOG.

Lennox scribbled the time and address in the black-and-white notebook. The boyfriend, "Gorgeous Georgie," Amos called him, was keen on details, reports. He had a deep streak of suspicion, no doubt from the company he kept.

The Lucky pack was empty. She rolled down the window, catching a stink from the packinghouses that reeked of beef offal. Funny, wasn't it, how she'd lost her taste for beef. What had she expected from Kansas City—romance, glamour, fortune? No, she'd gone that route, only to get temporarily lost. Now she just wanted to be one of the girls, shoot pool on Tuesdays, go to the pictures, laugh, dance, share secrets. A humble plan. But those boardinghouse girls, poor but decent, they didn't need to carry a switchblade around to remember the gentler virtues. No amount of laughter or peach cobbler or dollar-an-hour jitterbug lessons would change that.

Thick air trapped the city's smoke and stink from factories and cattle yards and kitchens. The city had rescued her from Atchison. She should be grateful. Goddamn, she *was* grateful. But after five long nights on the same shadowy streets, left to her meandering thoughts, Lennox felt itchy and restless. At least Iris had changed her pattern tonight, not gone straight home to her Penn Valley Park apartment.

The news from Europe made it hard to concentrate. Kraków bombed, dire consequences predicted. Half a world away, a drumbeat of doom. Talk of war had been brewing for ages. Inevitable for us, too? Some said yes.

Suddenly, in the gloom, Lennox saw herself high in the air in a blue uniform, flying an airplane. Air in her face, hands on the controls. Going places, doing things. Like her hometown girl, Amelia Earhart, only for country, justice, democracy, glory. Then she remembered her bad knee and the vision melted.

Following the bar girl to work, then home: not much glory there. Not much excitement. But excitement got her into trouble the first time: the Charleston, Luckies, speakeasies, hooch. She looked at her cigarette packet.

Well, she wasn't completely rehabilitated.

The waiting was killing in this job. But she couldn't teach the shag at Arthur Murray and she couldn't balance books. Lucky, that's what she was, to have this job. She'd frittered away her short time in college. Another humble plan shot to bits. Do something right for once, she told herself in the dark.

Music. She twisted the dial. Count Basie was in New York. WDAF had a big band on; she wasn't sure who, maybe Artie Shaw. Or maybe, from the sound of the trumpet solo, just some local schmoes. You'd think in Kansas City on a Friday night a person could get a little swing.

She settled back into the wide seat. *Do something right.* Hadn't she been on the straight and narrow since Verna died? Played by the rules? And look where it had gotten her. She shook out her hands, tried to relax. She'd begged Amos to let her work alone. She was ready; the run-in with the rummy proved that. Switching her knife without realizing it, that bothered her. But better switching it out than being too afraid to switch it at all.

The thought that Iris Jackson might slip out the back made her move. She was halfway to the saloon when the woman stepped out of the Chatterbox, her hair blushed with neon. Iris paused before stepping away, alone, toward Broadway, not toward her car. Meeting the other boyfriend at last?

The bright hair disappeared around the corner. Lennox ran back to the car, grabbed the camera, skipped up to the Chatterbox. The place was quiet except for the clack of billiard balls. She walked by the windows and paused at the corner.

Iris Jackson was a block away already, walking purposefully toward the bridge, her hair neat and shiny under the streetlights. She walked steadily on the high platform shoes, backside in action, a girl with experience. She skipped up the ramp to the bridge, skirting the tollbooth, and melted into the shadows.

Lennox broke into a hobbly run. The knee complained with each step, the switchblade thumping against her thigh. The upper level of the bridge was reserved for automobiles, and the occasional pedestrian. The tollbooth operator hollered something ornery as she passed. Below, the shine of the train level's rails was muted by mist.

She slowed, breathing hard, cursing her stiff new leather oxfords. Torturous, vain purchase. The walkway stretched into the night. On the riverbank below, rail lines snaked along the bottoms to the east; then willows and rushes filled in the swampy banks. Tar-paper hovels with kerosene lanterns flickering were tucked into the reeds. Downriver, several barges were tied up at the wharf, one empty and two piled high with cargo. A ghostly white steamboat rocked on the current, its tall smokestacks dissolving into a cloud. The tinkle of piano music faded in and out. The night darkened and the boat's glow dimmed to hazy yellow points in the mist.

High above the river's edge, she paused. Where were the cars? The quiet made her shiver, as if a pause before—what? Darkness stretched across the wide Missouri. A car rushed behind her and away, its headlights streaking down the platform, taillights bleeding dots. Across the river, a light from the airport tower blinked its eye in the night.

She squeezed the clammy steel railings of the bridge. Only a bridge, over an ordinary river. The tiny voice came suddenly to life in her head: *I'll sing you one oh, green grow the rushes oh, what is your one-oh, one is one and all alone and evermore shall be so.*

Lennox shook her head. No, little sister, not now. *I'll sing you two-oh.* She squeezed the steel harder, listened to her ragged breathing. Rest now, Tillie Mae. Finally, the sweet voice was gone. From railing to upright, she tiptoed down the edge, fingering the knife in her pocket. She had wanted excitement. Well, here you are. She pulled the knife out, held it closed in her hand. It was warm, solid, even if a person had to get too close to use it.

She'd cut a girl once, at Beloit. Lucille, who called Dorie a dyke in the yard at the girl's school. Said she'd been playing pussy with her friend Irene. Lennox had a tough hide, she could take names, but Irene, a bad-luck girl with a tender heart, her face burned up and she started to cry. Lennox cut Lucille across the palm.

She peered into the blackness now, trying not to think about that blood, to focus on Iris. Where was she? The camera dug into Lennox's chest, the strap cutting the back of her neck. Her breathing slowed, only to be replaced by the thumping in her chest. Maybe she should go back for the car. Maybe Iris would get away for sure then.

It wasn't possible to get through life without hurting people. Life had conspired to teach Lennox that much. With another weapon, a gun, you'd be farther from the blood, removed from the necessary damage you inflict. Times like these, she debated the benefits of other weapons. But the knife, well, she and the blade went way back. She'd tried giving it up after Beloit, but that was a piss-poor experiment in gentility. Most damage, the most cruel kind, was invisible anyway.

A truck motored up from the North KC side, slow and smelly. She pressed into the space behind a girder as it passed. Her back felt damp now, and a chill set in.

A nervous laugh escaped her. She claimed to hate the blood, but she knew herself. The rush of the fight, the release of the rage, was too sweet. It had its own life.

Far below, the river smelled alive. Snakes and fish with huge snouts and hairy jaws and mighty teeth lived in it. It moved silently along, oblivious. She'd made wishes to the river, in Atchison, back when things like that mattered. Beloit, and all that followed, had cured a lot of bad habits.

High above the river, she felt suspended, weightless. As if the past had never happened, or the future would never come. She opened her eyes wide to see better in the deep shadows. No sign of movement down the narrow walk. Had someone picked Iris up on the bridge? If so, they must have been waiting for her, stopped, then gone north. No other cars had come this way.

Damn, the truck. Was Iris giving her the slip? Had she crossed over and jumped into the slow-moving truck?

Lennox walked faster, still keeping in the shadows. The oxfords made a soft, rhythmic clang. Iris must have seen her. But what was she hiding? Who the hell was she to jump into a truck and make her getaway—just a meat packer's girlfriend? The lack of moonlight shadowed everything. A glint of city light off the water kept up a little glow from underneath. Where could she be? The truck, it had to be the truck.

Lennox muttered softly, hauling herself over the coals for blowing the tail. The sound of an approaching train filled the night. With a squeal of metal on metal and a crunch of gears, the train turned onto the bridge, shaking it down to its tall rock piers. She held on to a girder. The vibrations increased, the clickety-clack echoing off the water. Leaning out over the water, she watched the cars go by. Two engines pulled a short string of passenger and Pullman cars, a longer line of rust-colored boxcars, perforated cattle and horse cars, oil tankers, grain cars, north to Chicago and points east.

A blast of the whistle pulsated through her ears. She closed her eyes. The full effect of the train's weight, bending and rattling the metal of the old bridge, moved through her hands and into her shoulders. The bridge throbbed. Finally, it faded away. As the clackety-clack conjured old memories of midnight train rides, she opened her eyes.

Mist swirled in the train's wake. Lennox peered after the green caboose. A pale figure flickered in the corner of her eye. Down on the rail level, less than ten feet to the left, there was Iris Jackson. Was she standing on the railing or leaning over it? The blue shirtwaist floated out on the wind. Her head was bowed as if in prayer. For a second, she was there; then she fell.

Dorie held her breath. Shining like the friar's lantern, the figure twisted into the air, too small for a human, too light, too insubstantial. The dress pressed against her legs, then billowed up over her face. Silver hair flying, streaming, down into the muddy river. She hung, growing smaller and smaller, caught in the moist, chill air.

Then the river swallowed her up. The river, whose open arms were always ready for those with nothing left to lose.

A small, distant, liquid slap. Then silence.

Lennox shuddered, gripping the camera. She followed the pale figure with her eyes, floating now, arms splayed. Toward the dimly lit riverboat, down the river.

"Damn it to hell."

Lennox rested the camera on the railing and clicked off three shots in rapid succession. The figure of Iris was nothing more than a small rise in the wide brown-black surface of the river, a chalky smudge in the dirt. Then she was gone.

Kicking the nearest girder, Lennox hurt her toes, cursed harder. The vibrations made a eerie whisper up and down the steel, like voices.

"Damn you, Iris Jackson!"

Down the long bridge, the white head of the tollbooth operator popped out of the ramshackle building. Lennox took a breath, looked up at the cottony sky and down at the muddy, catfish-laced water. It looked like the Iris Jackson job was over. She was alone, again.

Yes, little sister, we are all one-oh, and ever more to be so.

TWO

WHAT'S THE HOLLERING ABOUT, THEN?"

The rheumy eyes of the old man in the tollbooth protruded, alarmed. Lennox marched up to him, holding the camera behind her leg. A couple of cars came from the north now, business as usual.

"You have a telephone?" She could see very well that he did not, his solitaire game strung out across the dirty green felt of his podium desk. He shook his white head.

"Well, the cops might be out." She took a step back, reconsidered. "You saw the woman, the one before me?"

"The blonde? Uh-huh."

"Did you see anyone else?"

The man wiped his dry lips with blunt fingers. "Darker'n inside a cow's stomach. City thinks we don't need no lights after midnight. What'd the damn city ever know?"

"You work here every night?" He said yes. "Ever see that woman before?"

"Can't say as I have. Not many on foot, neither. You two were the most we've had in three weeks, since that steamboat got snagged upriver and people come to waggle."

Lennox backed away.

"So what happened, then? Where is she?"

"Jumped."

"Pretty gal like that?" He shook his head. "Shame."

An overcoat of guilt hung on her as Lennox drove back downtown to police headquarters. She had failed. She'd let the woman get away, and kill herself. At the tall desk in the wood-paneled lobby a desk sergeant was talking to a man in a gray suit. Lawyer or reporter, too happy otherwise. She waited for them to quit laughing. She didn't feel like joining. Finally, the sergeant looked up.

"Help you, miss?"

"A jumper. Going into the river."

"A brodie, huh?" The policeman sighed. Red-faced Irish, the name Bannon on his desk plate, he eyed the gray suit. A "Get lost" look, but the man held his ground, one elbow on the wooden counter. The cop ignored him then and picked up his pen.

"All right, your name, miss."

She thought about using a different name. Georgie Terraciano probably didn't want cops involved. But to use another name, that caused problems. They would think she was hiding something. All she wanted really was for them to look for the body. Iris deserved that.

"Doria Lennox."

Something in the way she said her name made them both frown at her. They stared as if only a second before she'd been a mere slip of a girl but now she was more.

"And what did you see, Miss Doria Lennox?"

The cop was being overly polite, no doubt because of the suit. Was he some reform lawyer working overtime? Their expressions were cool, calculating.

"A woman jumped off the Hannibal Bridge. About fifteen minutes ago. I was driving across and saw it." A plausible reason to be walking across the Missouri River in the wee hours of the morning didn't come on short notice.

"About one o'clock?"

"I wasn't watching the clock."

The cop scribbled on his ledger. "And you were just driving across the bridge. Don't know the woman?"

"No, sir." Amazing how the "sirs" just came out around uniforms, how the old habits came back.

"See her enough for a description, then?"

"Bleach blonde. Curves, you know, so I guess she wasn't too old."

"What was she wearing?"

"Blue dress, a gabardine jacket."

"You see her face?"

"No, sir."

"All right. Your address, then, Miss Lennox."

She gave it to him, the boardinghouse on Charlotte Street, then said, "You know Herb Warren?"

"Captain Warren?"

"He's my uncle, that's all. He's not on shift now, is he?"

The cop straightened, as if the captain were watching. "No, miss, I don't believe he is. But I'll leave him a message you was in, and reported the jumper."

"That's okay."

But the cop wouldn't wait, not with an opportunity to look good to Captain Warren, now when half the cops in Kansas City had been found dirty and fired. Uncle Herb wouldn't be one of them; he had taken her in after Beloit, and there was nobody squarer. Kansas City was desperate for the honest man. Amos had lost two operatives to the new police chief. Roger and Willard were fighting crime the newfangled way, with a badge, so she got her first solo tail. Iris Jackson, a woman who went almost nowhere but work—what could be easier? She'd been so proud, and now this. She felt hollow, like somehow she had run the woman off the bridge. That her clumsy oxfords and the twenty-five dollar Packard had made the woman desperate.

She was just outside the door when the suit caught up with her. "Miss Lennox?"

He was younger than she'd thought, not thirty, pale, with dark hair. His suit fit badly, with cuffs too short and pants too big. His white shirt was dirty and spots decorated his maroon tie.

"Talbot's my name. I'm at the *Star*."

"My condolences."

He stuck out his hand, but she headed down the steps. She had nothing against the *Kansas City Star*. They'd helped bring down the Pendergast machine. Putting Boss Tom behind bars had changed everything for the city, even, if you counted Roger's and Willard's departure from gumshoeing, led up to her losing Iris Jackson off the Hannibal Bridge.

"Can you give me some more details about that jumper? Because, see, I got this idea. Now don't laugh. It'll sell some papers. You say she jumped at about one o'clock. So how about 'One O'clock Jump.' Like the Count Basie tune."

"They pay you for these flashes of brilliance?" She walked around to the driver's side of the Packard. Talbot was at her side before she could open the door.

He put his hand over hers on the door handle. "Aw, come on. Give me something. You were just driving across? Where were you going? Do you live on the other side?"

The sudden touch made her flinch. "You heard where I live. I told the cop everything. I'm tired and I want to go home. If you don't mind."

Talbot threw up his hands and grinned. "You know," he said as she closed the door, "you're pretty when you're mad."

Lennox tried not to smile. Her eyes felt scratched raw. He stood there in that ridiculous suit.

"Then I must be goddamn Jean Harlow."

She climbed the stairs of the boardinghouse to the third floor, the worn flowered runner muffling her footsteps. The old house was solid and plump, a kerosene lamp burning on the hall table. Her room was warm, full of the smell of cauliflower from the evening meal she'd missed.

On the edge of the bed, in the dark, she tried to reconstruct what had gone wrong. She pulled the bottle of gin from behind the dresser and poured a glass. She smelled the wild juniper, cracked the window to let the odors escape.

The little book Amos had given her, the one she'd read through almost three times and still couldn't make a dent in, sat under the pleated shade of the bedside lamp. She riffled through the pages to a postcard that held her place. From Arlette, comrade in crime. In Chicago now. News from Arlette was vague but regular. Just hearing that Arlette was alive and kicking made the week.

Out the back window, a light shone in the brown boardinghouse across the alley, its tidy vegetable beds surrounded by looping wire. Someone was playing the piano. The sound of the music rose and fell on the humid night air, a jumping song. Reminded her of a record her father had sent, years ago, before he quit her for good. She listened for a minute to the boogie-woogie syncopation; then the hollow feeling returned, and she turned away, drinking the gin.

She licked the rim of the glass, thinking about a second. But there was no sense tempting fate. What had happened to Verna could happen to her. She put the bottle back in its hidey-hole and washed out the glass at the sink.

Over the bed, next to the photograph of Amelia Earhart on the wing of her Electra, the framed photograph of the last race hung askew. She put it right. The clipping was faded now, encased in its simple wood frame. In the starting crouch, Dorie Lennox, sprinting champion: hair pulled back, tendons in her neck taut, a slingshot ready to shoot.

The old house creaked and shuddered, settling in the night air. She lit a cigarette from a pack in the back of the cupboard, then paced. The music from outside was saccharine; it grated on her, pulling her out of the thing that held her together, the will to forget. She pulled a hard drag off the cig. Something was creeping onto her memory plane, something from Verna's old diaries. Lennox used to read them every night, trying to figure out what had made her mother tick, until they made her crazy and Uncle Herb made her put it all away.

A name. Myrna? She paced, two steps to the door, turn. Melva. That was it. She sucked on the fag until it burned her fingers; then she stubbed it out in the sink. She debated for half a second, then sunk to the ratty throw rug, pulled out the box from under the bed, blew off the dust.

It took three tries to find the right book. Nineteen thirteen, an unlucky year for Melva. Sixteen, in trouble with a man who wouldn't marry her, Verna's cousin had found no comforting shoulder, no kindly friend, so ended it all off the Atchison bridge.

Her mother had told her every gruesome detail. If there was something Verna had wanted to teach you, you learned through brutal repetition of the facts. Thank you, Verna. The lesson stuck, despite a strong tendency to forgetting. Also lessons about bridges, rivers, snakes, men. And especially kindness.

She slammed the diary shut and pushed the lot back into the dusty cave. Reading Verna's acid thoughts made her too alive. She was gone, never recovering from Lennox's fall from grace and Tillie's death, drinking herself into oblivion. The end was mercifully swift, in a car on a dark road.

Lennox lay back down, took a deep breath to exorcize Verna. Had Iris found the world as unforgiving a place as Melva had, a place where no one cared? Was she so low, so afraid of living?

Lennox tried to feel an inkling of release for Iris. Desperation must have overwhelmed her—no. It felt so wrong. It was cowardice, weakness, to throw it all away. These vices were always there, inside of everyone. But not to act on high on bridges. Only to give a nod to late at night, with gin and piano notes floating in your head.

She climbed into bed and closed her eyes. Imagine that final moment when the earth slipped away, when nothing held you up but your own decisions. How sharp the focus would be just then. How clear the world would be. She knew the tug of the end of pain. The end of complicated problems. It was a drug that could turn you inside out. She let the black tingle of relief settle into her bones, her toes, fingers, chest, neck, until she drifted into sleep.

By the sound of it, the banging had been going on for some time. Lennox opened her eyes, looked at her wristwatch: 10:00 A.M. The sun streamed through the window facing the street, a yellow spear of light. She closed her eyes again, felt the black hollowness of the dream. Something about talking, struggling on a bridge, over a river.

"M-m-miss Lennox! Are you sick? Miss Lennox."

On her feet, tucking in her wrinkled blouse, she braced herself for the police. She opened the door. Luther stood there, half-frantic, his jittery eyes trying to focus on her.

"M-m-miss, you're not sick, are you?"

"Just tired, Luther." There were no cops behind him. Maybe they waited in parlors now that Pendergast was gone.

Luther stuttered and spit. Someone here to see her? Why Mrs. F. had sent him up to her was a mystery. The poor man lived off the kindness of Mrs. Ferazzi and others. His tattered red brocade smoking jacket had a mock elegance but smelled.

"M-m-m-man. In the, in the, in the—"

"Parlor?"

Luther nodded. "M-m-miz F. said you missed breakfast. Said to see if you was around at all."

"All right. Come in a minute and I'll see if I have a cookie for you."

"Oh, n-n-no, miss. Can't come in, no sir, no sir." His eyes widened in panic. She found three crackers in waxed paper. He took them, then stood staring over her shoulder.

"What is it?"

"You read books? I used to read b-b-books. All the, all the—"

He stared at the volume of Kafka by the bed. "You want to borrow it?" She crossed, returning to place it in his hand.

Luther looked stunned, then gave her a toothy smile as he pressed the crackers and book to his chest and ran down the stairs. It would serve Amos right if a man who'd lost his mind could fathom that book.

She shut the door and went to the small mirror. She combed her dark brown waves, arranged the three blond streaks that crowned them, clipped them into a barrette, washed her face. Changing into a clean blouse, she put on lipstick and went downstairs.

As her foot hit the front hall's scuffed oak, she heard the hacking cough from the parlor. Amos Haddam stood hunched by the velvet-draped window, newspaper under his arm, bent over in a fit. From the back, dark hair graying, shoulders thin and wasted, he could be an old man. His pasty complexion was what you'd expect from an Englishman who'd taken the brunt of a canister of mustard gas and was too stubborn to die.

Smothering his cough, Haddam turned to see the girl silhouetted in the doorway. The plainness to her features was a plus in their line of work, and although her pale cheeks often looked unhealthy, he was not one to lecture on pallor. In her light hazel eyes was a quick anger. And sorrow he knew he looked too hard for. It was a curse.

Because sadness always led to Eugenia. He'd been thinking about her too much lately, a bad habit. Very unhealthy. Her memory fed on him, his grief the last of her. It must be the worsening cough. Eugenia's memory made being ill somehow romantic, as truly pathetic as that truth was.

Lennox had done something new with her hair. Her ever-present trousers looked slept in. But where had she gotten those ridiculous shoes? Bloody hell, he thought, she's gone fashion plate.

She moved toward him, edgy but confident, her gait favoring the right knee. She held that half smile, as if she wasn't particularly happy about your presence.

Then he remembered the newspaper under his arm and his irritation returned. She saw it on his face, he understood. A last thought of Eugenia, her own watery death like this one. He pushed aside the vision of Eugenia's innocent face and slapped the paper against his palm.

"Sleeping Beauty arises at last. Were you going to tell me about this?"

She opened the newspaper he held out for her, the morning *Star*. A huge headline about the fighting in Poland blared across the top. But down at the bottom, a headline read MYSTERY LADY TAKES ONE O'CLOCK JUMP. The woman had not been identified yet, but she had been witnessed by one Doria Lennox, of the city, as "a bleach blonde with curves." Damn him. He'd put her in it. She should have been more polite. There was a recap of the decade's history of jumpers, some forty-two. A bad decade.

She folded the newspaper and handed it back. Amos's face was lined and pale, but his dark, hot eyes fixed on her. The high patrician forehead topped with thick, loose hair made him look like a duke who'd lost his shirt. What she'd gone through last night had left her strangely calm this morning.

"She jumped off the bridge."

"I can bloody read that much, ducks."

Lennox stared him down, then steered him into a chair by the window. In the dining room, a small group huddled around the radio, listening to war news.

"All right. Let's have it," he said.

"There's not much to tell. After work, she went to a late-night place called the Chatterbox, over on Fifth. She wasn't in there more than ten minutes. She came out, walked straight to the bridge, and took a leap."

"Just like that? No phone calls, no messages in bottles?"

"I don't know what went on inside the Chatterbox."

Amos rubbed his forehead. "And then you called the paper?"

"I reported it to the cops. I thought about calling you, but it was late. I figured you'd tell me to report it, too. You being so straight-out."

His frown relaxed. "Just ask any of the famous KC coppers. You didn't mention Vanvleet, or that you were working on a case?"

"Of course not."

"But Herbert'll know."

"He'll find out."

"Well, hell, you did nothing wrong."

Lennox looked at her plain nails. She supposed this was his apology for jumping all over her. "What will Vanvleet say?"

"What can he say? Oh, he'll blow hot air, but you did your job—you followed her. That's what they wanted, not some hero's antics." Amos stuffed his handkerchief in his pocket. "I just wish they were flat-footed with us."

"About Iris?"

He looked out the window. The parlor felt crusty and neglected. The upright piano sat silent, a maroon fringed scarf draped over the closed lid. A portrait of an iron-haired lady dressed in black silk frowned down on them.

"This is no bloody girlfriend watch," Amos said. "Not with Vanvleet involved."

"Isn't he on the level?"

"He's represented these Italians, and plenty of other gangsters, charged with all sundry crimes against the Volstead Act. Or gambling or girls. Not a one went to prison, while plenty o' poor ol' mothers with ten children got locked away for making a bathtub full o' hooch."

"Georgie was a bootlegger?"

"Doesn't matter anymore. But since Pendergast got locked away, things've changed. Maybe Georgie's feeling the heat. He's got his hand in all kinds o' tills, legal and not." He gave a little cough and cleared his throat. His face went crimson. "You got water around here?"

Lennox hurried to the kitchen, nodded a good morning to Poppy and her daughter Frankie, who were working on the dishes, then grabbed a clean glass off the drain board. She sloshed a little water on the carpet as she returned. Amos was still red, holding off the fit. He gulped it down.

"Worst water I ever tasted," he said finally.

"Kaw water. Straight out of the river." Both Iris and the dream clung to her. On a bridge, over a river. She shook herself. "What now?"

"Now we go meet with Vanvleet and Georgie to explain how Blondie did her brolly hop."

She looked at her hands again. If she'd been closer to Iris, she could have prevented it. Been brave, leaned out, jumped down, saved her. But she hadn't; she'd been afraid of the river, afraid of being alone on the bridge in the dark. And there was no changing that, in a dream or here in the light of day.

The radio clicked off in the dining room; the listeners drifted away, heads down, silent. In their faces was the gloom of the beginning of the promised war. From the kitchen came the slap of a pan hitting the dishwater. So like the distant, final plunk of a body against hard water.

Amos stood up. "Let's get it over with."

On her way back upstairs to get her handbag, she ran into Betty Kimble telling Ilo Gobbs a joke. "What did Scarlett Polsky say when the Nazis came to town? 'War, war, war. I'll think about that tomorrow!' "

Betty's smile was contagious. Sometimes, Lennox wished she was more like her. Betty nudged her. "You know. Like *Gone With the Wind*."

"She's read it four times," Ilo said.

"Five," Betty corrected. "I can't wait to see Clark Gable as Rhett. I saw *The Wizard of Oz* last night at the Palace. Luther hadn't seen it, so I said, 'Dang, son, I'll take you.' They didn't want to let him in, accounta they said no coloreds, until I gave them the what-for. Told that white trash I'd be asking her granny for documents of who she rolled in the hay with. He wore the funniest old coat that smelled like last week's sauerkraut. Oh, golly, do you s'pose we won't eat sauerkraut no more?"

Betty bubbled off down the stairs, regaling Ilo with tales of naughty dance moves at the jitterbug contest at Municipal Auditorium. When she'd first moved into the boardinghouse, Lennox had tried to keep up with Betty. Now a joke on the stairs was about all she had the energy for. At the top of the stairs, the twins, Norma and Nell Crybacker, smiled a good morning.

"Off to slay a few dragons before breakfast?" Norma—or was it Nell?—asked. Gray-haired and identical in neat navy blue suits and heavy black shoes, the two schoolteachers had romantic notions about detective work.

"Have to get my sword."

"Look at her, Nell." Norma tugged on her sister's elbow. "Isn't she energetic and smart and everything a young woman should be?"

"Oh, to be sure. But you're embarrassing her, Norma."

Lennox felt herself blush. She smiled at the ladies and let herself into her room. She found her handbag on the dresser. It felt heavy; she found the switchblade inside. She always kept it in her pocket, handy. Last night had shaken her more than she'd thought.

Amos said little on the drive downtown. He had taken the streetcar to the boardinghouse, for some reason he kept to himself. It was Labor Day weekend, and an air of holiday was in the streets despite the war news, with children jumping rope and squirting themselves with hoses as the heat rose in waves from the pavement.

The law offices were on the fourth floor of the grand old New York Life Building at Ninth and Baltimore. Its arches crowned a bronze eagle on its nest, meaning, Lennox supposed, that the company was guarding your nest egg. Not much comfort, since the ten-story building, as tall as it could go in 1890, now sat half-empty.

The marble stairs were the only option, with the elevator cage locked and dark. Thick Oriental rugs covered the polished oak floor of the hushed reception area. Amos had mounted the stairs at a snail's pace, paused now, rasping, then began to walk down the hallway unescorted, a sin on a weekday, when the man himself stepped out of his office.

Vanvleet glared at them, tall, stout, mouthing an unlit cigar. As they stepped to the door of the corner office, Georgie Terraciano stood up and Vanvleet sat down. Georgie gave the lawyer a dark look and sat again in the leather chair. His gray silk shirt billowed over a trim torso; fancy wool slacks led to patent-leather loafers that had seen neither dirt nor pavement. Amos and Dorie sat in well-worn red velvet wingback chairs.

The sun through the east windows lit up the law cases filled with leather-bound books, dark file cabinets of carved oak, brass lion's heads for pulls. The old man's desk was spotless, gleaming cherry. The room smelled of lemon oil and tobacco.

The cigar rotated in Vanvleet's stained teeth. With his freckled, hairless scalp and double chin, the name Warbucks came to mind. He carried his weight well behind impeccable pinstriped clothes, but his chair groaned as he leaned back.

No one spoke. Amos appeared serene. Georgie played with his large gold and diamond ring. Lennox shifted on the chair and let the men play out their games. Finally, Vanvleet threw his soggy cigar butt in a brass wastebasket with a ringing thud.

"So, you lost her," he said.

"Aye, sir, we all have lost her," Amos said in a scratchy voice. "A sad, sad thing."

Georgie's face was set in a mix of anger and menace. Handsome in a hard way, deep lines ran from his nostrils to the corners of too-red lips. His black hair was slicked back from a thick brow.

"That it is," Vanvleet said.

"I'm so sorry, Mr. Terraciano," Lennox said a little too loudly. The three men looked at her. "For your loss."

Still no reaction from the stone-hearted Georgie. This was no girlfriend tail. Anger seeped up in her. She felt used by these men who didn't know her but wanted her to do their dirty work. She tried to tell herself that's what she was getting paid for, but the anger didn't hear.

"All right, all right." Vanvleet stood up suddenly and turned to the window, hands clasped behind him. "The question is, What happens now. What do you want to do, Georgie?"

"Do the cops know who she was?" Georgie said, his voice gravelly.

"Not yet," Amos said. "But don't count on them not finding it out."

"Since somebody went and sang to them," Georgie said, his eyes hot on Lennox.

"Mr. Terraciano, my operative did exactly as I would have done," Amos said. "We operate within the law."

Georgie squinted. "Hey, whaddya—"

Vanvleet turned. "Forget it, Georgie."

Terraciano eased back into his chair, as if he really intended to fight for his honor.

Lennox suppressed a smile. "I was only thinking that they might look for her body if I reported it. Otherwise, they might drag her out in St. Louis and drop her in a pauper's grave. I'm sure you don't want that for *your girl*."

Georgie chewed his tongue. Amos cleared his throat and looked for somewhere to spit.

"This really doesn't change anything," Vanvleet said. "Georgie wants you to continue to work on the case."

"That's right," said Georgie. "Keep on the case."

"And what, exactly, would that be?" Amos croaked.

"You don't need to know nothing about it, Haddam," the Italian said, sneering.

"If you want us to work on it, I need to know what it is we're to do."

Vanvleet sat down at the desk. "It's simple. Instead of tailing Miss Jackson—"

A loud explosion burst from Amos. He bent over, coughing hard, then stumbled to the door. The other three listened as he hacked down the hall, into a room. A door shut.

"He'll be all right in a minute. He's got a cold," Lennox said.

"We're well aware of Mr. Haddam's condition." Vanvleet tapped his fingers on the desktop. "And it's you we're interested in taking on this case anyway, Miss Lennox. We were impressed with your diligence this week."

Lennox couldn't look at the old man's face. His kind words almost wounded her. "I didn't stop her."

"I don't blame you for that. And neither does Georgie."

The Italian had cemented on a scowl unchanged by Vanvleet's prompting.

The old man continued. "I understand there are some photographs."

"Not developed yet."

"Then I can expect them tomorrow."

"Tomorrow's Sunday. But sure, I can have them tomorrow."

"That's what I like about you, Miss Lennox. You're don't give me excuses; you just do the job. Bring them by my house and we'll take a look at them."

She nodded, the anger and guilt about Iris tempered by his praise. She looked past him, at the view of the ASB Bridge and the river snaking away east, golden, serene, the trees along the boulevards heavy with summer's green. People going off to the country to boat and picnic, to camp in the Ozarks and the Flint Hills. She remembered the gold rocks of the Flint Hills, with her father, on horseback, some holiday. The horse's mane, her father's breath on her back, his arms around her, the rush of adventure, and something else, the loss of all of it.

The office was silent. When was Amos coming back?

"Ah, Weston, you working today?" Suddenly, Vanvleet was up again, smiling. "Come in here. I want you to meet somebody."

A man appeared in the doorway. Tallish, a junior partner by the look of his haircut, dressed in golf clothes, with a jaunty striped collar on his knit shirt.

"Just picking up some briefs to review over the weekend," Junior Partner said.

"You know Mr. Terraciano, don't you?" Vanvleet said. "We do all his company's legal work." The Italian turned a cynical eye on the plaid golf slacks. Vanvleet turned to Lennox then and she rose.

"This is one of Amos Haddam's operatives. Miss Lennox. You may have some business for her over the coming years, right, Weston?" Vanvleet clapped his back.

Not junior partner. Golden boy being groomed for partnership. Weston held out his hand and she shook it. When she looked up into his face, a chill ran through her. He seemed to feel it.

"We've met before, haven't we?" Weston said. "Where did you go to school?"

"Weston's a Yale man," Vanvleet puffed. "You didn't go to Yale, did you, Miss Lennox?" The old man's caustic chuckles were joined by Georgie's.

"No, it's Atchison, isn't it?" Weston said.

"Yes," she said. "Atchison."

Always Atchison. Whenever something bad happened, Atchison was involved. She wiped her hand on her slacks and tried to stay calm. Did this mean something bad was coming? He didn't remember her after all. Just the face.

"You know each other already. Wonderful." Vanvleet

grasped both their shoulders as if he were a preacher joining them. "I like my people to feel comfortable together. So whenever you need a little digging, Weston, give Miss Lennox a call."

Vanvleet put his arm around the young lawyer's shoulders and guided him out the door. Weston glanced back, but she looked away, sat down. She and Georgie listened to Vanvleet yakking down the hall, lining up a golf game for Labor Day. It was only when Vanvleet sent him down the stairs and shut up that she could hear Amos still hacking in a room somewhere.

When the lawyer returned, she stood up again. "I need to see about Amos. He's been gone too long."

"Of course. And you'll want to get started right away on Miss Jackson's effects."

"Her effects?"

"Yes, we want you to look into all aspects of her life. Her apartment, where she worked, friends, enemies, family, everything. Take pictures, names, the usual. It should be a little more interesting than just tailing her."

Except for last night. That had been interesting.

Georgie put a finger to his chin, a smirk on his liver-colored lips. Vanvleet leaned back, satisfied. Iris's death was just a wrinkle to be ironed out by some shoe leather. Amos was quiet, wherever he was. She thought about coming up here, reporting daily, seeing Weston. It went against her code to forget. She went to the door.

"I would need more information about her. Where she's from, her family, that sort of thing." She doubted they had that information to offer, but it bought a little time.

"There was something about a little sister, wasn't there, Georgie?"

Georgie gave the lawyer a strange look. "Right. Younger sister, needs help or a leg up in business or somethin'."

She looked between them. "She has a hard-up sister—that's all you know?"

Amos began to cough again. A sliver of panic sliced through

her and she wanted to wash her hands of all of them. "I don't think I can help you. Maybe Mr. Haddam can work on it."

The lawyer hardened his stare. "Miss Lennox, you and I know Mr. Haddam is a sick man. We're counting on you."

"I'm sorry," she said, backing out the door. She listened for Amos, but all was silent again.

Georgie drew up his silky five-foot-eight frame. "Look, toots. This job is not done, and you will continue to do it until it is finished."

"She's dead. That is as finished as anything gets. I am so sorry, again, for your pain."

"Miss Lennox—" Vanvleet began.

"And don't"—she leaned close to Georgie's swarthy face—"call me *toots.*"

She turned into the hall, then began opening doors and calling for Amos. A bumping noise came from past the reception area. She ran across the oak and rugs to a door stenciled in gold: GENTLEMEN.

"Amos, are you all right?"

Through the door: "I'm afraid not."

She opened it a crack. "Can I come in?" She could see the porcelain tile walls and the fancy pedestal sink. Reflected in the large gilt-framed mirror was an awful lot of blood. She threw the door open.

Amos sat on the white tile floor, leaning one cheek on the wooden lid of the toilet, eyes closed. His lids fluttered briefly as she called his name.

"What happened? Amos, are you all right?"

"I thought you'd never come," he croaked, eyes closed.

"I'll call an ambulance." She stood up, thought how much that might cost, then kneeled beside him again. "Can you walk?"

"Hate ambulances." He lifted his head, his face colorless, blue veins in his forehead like roads on a map. On his lips was a crust of dried blood. "Help me up."

She threw his arm around her neck and wrestled him to his feet. Despite his emaciated condition, he was a good six inches taller and an unwieldy package. He rested his head heavily against hers. Dragging him out the door of the bathroom, she found his feet were pretty useless.

"See the sofa? Lie here and I'll get help." She managed to flop his limp body onto the brocade divan and arrange his arms and legs. "I'll get Georgie to help."

"Righty-o. Georgie's a pal."

Back at Vanvleet's office, she threw open the door. They were gone. She called for them, couldn't believe they would just waltz away. In the reception area, Amos's eyes were shut and he was breathing through his teeth.

"I have to go down to the lobby. Maybe there's a guard or a doorman," she muttered. She leaned over him. "I'll pay for the ambulance, Amos."

"Goddamn caisson hacks tried to kill me, they did. They tried; they had their chance with ol' Haddie. Never again."

Lennox patted his shoulder. "Okay, okay. I'm going downstairs to find somebody to help. I'll be right back. You stay here."

"I might want to dance," he said. She glanced back at him. His eyes were closed. "She looks so pretty tonight. What is it they're playing?"

THREE

LENNOX BURST OUT OF THE STAIRWELL into the high-ceilinged marble lobby. She looked for a doorman, a guard, but the space was deserted. She had parked down at the corner, not too far, but a Himalayan trek for a man in Amos's condition. She could at least move the car, maybe find someone on the street.

She pushed out the double doors, scrounging for her car keys in her handbag. As she turned on the sidewalk, she ran right into Weston's chest.

"Whoa there. What's the rush? I thought we could—"

"Get out of my way. Amos is dying up there and I have to get him to the hospital. Please, let go—"

"Let me help." Weston had ahold of her arm. "Dorie, please. You see? I remembered your first name. Where is he? Let me help."

Up close, he looked older, but then, so was she. Same blue eyes and honey gold hair, though. She hadn't wondered often how he'd turned out. He had money, connections, and more good looks than was legal; whatever he did, it would be eggs in the coffee.

She didn't have time to argue. "Come on."

They ran up the four flights, breathing too hard for conversation.

"Amos," she cried. "I'm back. We'll take you to the hospital."

He didn't answer.

Lennox felt his pulse; then tears stung when she felt the slow, unsteady drumming of his heartbeat on her fingertips. "He's unconscious."

"I'll carry him," Weston said. He began to gather Amos into his arms.

"He's too heavy."

"Get the elevator."

"It's locked. We'll carry him together," Lennox said. Weston lowered Amos to the sofa again. He took the shoulders, she the legs, and they carried him like a rag doll down the stairs. In the lobby, Weston gathered up the limp body again, carried him to the street, and deposited him in the Packard.

Her hands shook as she put her key in the ignition. No, he couldn't help anymore. But thanks. And she screeched away to the hospital.

A nurse nudged her shoulder. "Dorie. He wants to see you."

She straightened up, blinking. The waiting room was empty, although she remembered listening to Tommy Dorsey on the radio with an old man and his granddaughter. She felt the grit on her teeth.

"He's awake. Not feeling too chipper yet, but he wants to see you for a minute."

Lennox had spent the afternoon trying to make herself useful to the nurses, which included hearing about boyfriends, mothers-in-law, and landlords. This nurse, Helen, had boyfriend problems. The details were fuzzy now. Helen was very short, and the starched cap perched on her head like a topsy crown. "Come on," she said, holding out her hand.

They stopped at the door to room 322 in the shadowy hallway. A janitor washed the floors with a bucket and string mop. A kitchen worker was picking up trays.

"I'll be back in fifteen minutes. Don't tire him out."

Lennox eased into the room, passing a white-haired man

with a bandaged face. On the other side of the curtain, an oxygen tent enveloped the pale figure. He looked so small inside. She wrung her hands on the iron bed railing.

"If it isn't the oomph girl." His voice sounded weak and strange through the transparent sheeting of the tent. Below his shoulders, the tent's raw canvas was tucked into his bedclothes. His face was blurred, but he wiggled his fingers, pointing to a chair. "Sit down."

She sat, unable to think of what to say.

"Don't give me that creepy look, kid," Amos said. "This isn't the first time, and it won't be the last." He gasped a little air. "Used to happen every couple years; then it slowed down. It's been five now, but I knew it was coming."

"You might have warned me."

"Would it have made any difference?" He tried to sit up against the pillows. "So, you called the ambulance? After I said I hated the beasts. Well, I don't blame you."

"I drove you myself."

"Last thing I remember, I was on that sofa."

"We carried you to the car."

"We?"

"At the law firm. A lawyer. He's"—Amos wiggled his eyebrows, waiting—"from Atchison."

"Old swain?"

She'd never told him what had happened, although he knew she'd stolen the car and gone to the girl's school in Beloit for it. She wouldn't be following Roger and Willard into uniform. No chance of that.

"No."

"You sure about that?"

"How are you feeling?"

"Like hell. But a familiar hell. Three pints of blood and some forced air, and bingo. Back to normal. But I don't want to talk about it."

That she understood. She relaxed a little. She would have

to tell him about Vanvleet's request, and her refusal. Maybe it could wait.

"So who is this lawyer? What's the story?"

"Just somebody from Atchison."

She felt his eyes examining her face and wished he didn't always do that.

"Well, I'll listen to my wheezing and try to wheedle a sponge bath out of that pixie nurse. But wait. Is it a sob story? Because if it is, I'll ring for extra Kleenex."

She sat back, smiling at his efforts. "No, it's not a sob story."

She hadn't told anybody about Weston, about what had happened in Atchison, and she wasn't going to start now. She jutted her chin then tried to pretend she hadn't.

Amos watched her face, difficult through the haze of the oxygen tent. There was that sad purple shadow creeping in around her eyes, and its quick quenching.

"So, does this swell lawyer have a name?"

"Louie Weston. The old man seems very keen on him."

"Does he? What else did the little Hitler say?"

She opened her hazel eyes wide. "They say on the radio that France and England are going to declare war."

He lay very still under the tent. He felt the sinking dive of that last survey flight, the wind in his ears. He saw the soft blue flowers of his mother's garden, heard the whistling whine of the bombs, felt the stiff, fragrant paper of Eugenia's last letter in his hands.

"I knew it. I knew it."

"They say they're going to start moving the children out of London. They're afraid it'll be bombed."

"They'll bomb it. Of course they will. Blasted sons o' bitches."

"Amos, please. Breathe easy." She patted his arm. "I shouldn't have said anything."

"Can't keep a bloody war a secret." He resettled himself on

the pillow. "You don't know how it is, you don't want to know. It's hell." He stopped, tried to clear out the jumble of bad memories. He'd had practice; he could do it. "Never mind. What happened with Vanvleet?"

"The nurse said not to stay too long."

"She's not back. Tell me what the old man said."

"Can't we talk about it tomorrow?"

He glared at her.

"All right. He wants me to keep looking into Iris. Check out her apartment, the bar where she worked, things like that."

"So you start tomorrow."

"There's no point. She's dead."

"If Vanvleet says there's a point, there's a point. If he says the sky is down and the land is up, you say, 'Yes, Mr. Vanvleet.' He's the one puts food on the table. He's the one paid my hospital bills three times. *Three times,* and it was over two hundred dollars every time."

"You said yourself that they aren't on the level. Did you see an ounce of regret in that back-stabber? Georgie never cared a tinker's damn about her. It's all some game for them."

"I know that, you know that, they know that. So we're square. Clients never give you the full bill. If they were upstanding citizens, they'd be checking out their own dames. Or meeting a better class of women." He took a breath or two. "Look, they want some distance between them and Iris Jackson. You are the distance."

"I know you feel some loyalty to him, but for me, I just don't see how I can do it."

"I'll tell you how. You go around to her apartment, talk to the landlady, pick through her knickers. That's what we do. It ain't pretty and sometimes it ain't nice."

He hadn't meant to speak so harshly to her, but the war news had provoked him. How dare they send soldiers out again? Hadn't he come over here, where only the occasional old blighter without a leg reminded him of all of it? Where his daily hacking could be passed off as a simple lung condition? Where he could cough in peace, letting each day of agony pay his penance to Eugenia?

Lennox turned back to the window. She felt uneasy around Amos suddenly, guilty she couldn't tell him about Louie Weston. He was usually so breezy, so quick to joke, or to give easy instructions and tips. She had never seen him so angry. And so loyal to Vanvleet. For three years, she'd been wanting to be a full partner, and now, almost overnight, Amos had no one else.

He looked so helpless under the tent. "He paid your bills?"

"Without my knowing. Okay, he's mixed up in shady deals, no doubt about that. With clients like Gorgeous Georgie, you know he is. But for the last ten years, he's been the butter on my bread. Hell, he's been the bread on my bread. You think anybody else'd hire an old warhorse barking up his lungs?"

The sound of oxygen whizzing through nozzles and gauges filled the room. Behind the curtain, the white-haired man began to snore.

"Look, lass, haven't you ever lost somebody and you didn't know why? Sometimes, there aren't reasons, it's just life. But sometimes, you just have to find out." He closed his eyes, sighed. "Iris is one of those."

She thought of Melva, who had jumped into the Big Muddy because nobody cared. And of Tillie and her sweet voice. Just life, losing Tillie. Those old imagining games—what would Tillie have looked like at eight, twelve, fifteen? What would she have read? How would she fix her hair? Her palms itched with questions.

Lennox shook her head to clear out the memories. This business seemed so personal to Amos. "I didn't know," she said. "About the hospital bills."

But Louie Weston. She didn't want to talk to him. Didn't want to be reminded every time she saw his face that she had stolen the car as much for him as for Arlette that night. Dear

Arlette, still grateful. She thought stealing the car was all for her, only to get her to Kansas City for the abortion. She owed Dorie her life, her future. How many times had Lennox had to smile and nod and take the credit?

But she had stolen the car, driven to the back-alley butcher with his filthy hands and greasy breath, for Arlette *and* for Louie. It had seemed so important then that he have his clean, prosperous life. And he had, hadn't he? Yale, law school, money, country clubs. His life was cake. The crush she had on him at fourteen. She had grown up on the spot, helping Arlette survive the bleeding. More growing up in the shame and trouble she'd brought on Verna, in the soul-starving Beloit girl's school—then losing Tillie. It was all too connected.

Amos cleared his throat. "Not this old boyfriend, then, is it? Seeing him around Vanvleet's won't be a problem."

"He's not—he's not an old boyfriend. Anyway, that was years ago."

How Amos read her mind scared her; it was uncanny. She had to work harder, stay calm, not think about the past.

"So you'll take the job. Just sniff around a wee bit. Shouldn't be more than a day or two. Then I'll be out of here and fit as a fiddle."

She saw his eyelids dip, then struggle open again.

"Of course I'll do it, Amos," she said, standing. She thought then of all the things he had taught her, the chances he'd given her, and felt ashamed she'd argued. "I'll get Helen. You get some sleep."

"Righty-o. Get a wiggle on home."

Another humid night had descended, trapping the fetid city air. Saturday night, and she didn't have to work. Free, white, and twenty-one, as the boardinghouse girls said. Tonight, she could do anything, see *The Wizard of Oz,* do the Lindy at Sni-A-Bar Gardens, drink whiskey neat in a jazz club over the strains of a plaintive saxophone.

In the car, she felt aches all over her body. Reliving the bad old days of Louie and Arlette, seeing Amos in pain, she felt worn down. She drove back to the boardinghouse, climbed the shadowed stairs. A cool bath and early to bed. She hoped the piano player was as tired as she was tonight.

On the third floor, outside her door, the hair on her neck prickled. The lock had been jimmied; the door stood ajar. She looked around the dark hallway, then stepped to the wall and pushed the door open.

The light by her bed was on, casting a yellow glow at the mess of bedding, mattress askew, cupboard doors gaping, books and clothes strewn on the floor. Lennox pulled out her blade, switched it open silently.

"Who's there?" she said loudly. She took a step into the room, looked around, and dropped her arm. Whoever had tossed her room had taken a powder.

She reached back to close the door, when it came at her in a rush, smashing into her forehead and sending her backward to the floor. A foot kicked her in the ribs. She groaned. A heel caught her back as she rolled into a ball.

The blade was still in her hand. She swung wildly, pulling her legs around. The attacker kicked her hand, the pain loosening her grasp. She heard the blade clatter to the wooden floor and felt the boot against her jawbone, pressing her face into the floor. She tried to grab something, but just trying to breathe with her windpipe crushed against the wood made black spots appear in front of her eyes.

The laugh was high-pitched. "Watch your step, Miss Snooper. Because I'll be watching you. Everywhere you go." The voice, surprisingly, a throaty female one.

"Who—" The boot cut her off. Blood pushed against her eyeballs.

"I'm talking." The familiar sound of her switchblade closing, then opening again. "What is this—your nail file? You are so far out of your league, kitten. Now listen. Tell the limey to stay away from Edna. Savvy? You can't stop me, so don't even try."

Another swift kick to the kidneys shot pain up Lennox's back. She closed her eyes. Footsteps clattered in the hallway and down the stairs.

Lennox rose to her hands and knees, gasping for air. The blade was stuck into the floor beside her. She staggered to the head of the stairs. Taking them two at a time, she swung around on the railings at the landing on the second floor. At the bottom, Lennox hit the oak floor of the front hall and slid. Her knee collapsed under her. She fell in a clumsy heap. It didn't matter. The figure was gone, out the door into the night.

She lay on the floor, cursing, as Mrs. Ferazzi came out of her room under the stairs in a pink robe. "What is it, Miss Lennox?"

"Damn, Mrs. F. A woman."

Mrs. Ferazzi dusted her off. Lennox felt the knot on her forehead and gingerly tried putting weight on the knee. Mrs. F. was fussing, asking questions. She patted Lennox's shoulder and offered to help her back upstairs.

"I'm all right, really." Lennox's voice sounded scratchy. She'd made it to the first step, hanging on to the railing.

"You shouldn't try to be so brave all the time, dear. Running after a burglar like that, you coulda been killed."

"Don't worry about me," Lennox muttered, struggling up another step.

"Oh, but I do, dear, I worry about all my boarders. My family, that's how I think of y'all."

On the third step, Lennox winced from the pain in her ribs. If I could just lie down, she thought, then remembered all the stairs between her and her bed. She'd be damned if she'd let Mrs. Ferazzi tuck her in. Another mother was the last thing she needed.

"Stay there now, young jouster!"

The twins bustled down the stairs side by side, wearing identical green chenille robes and fuzzy slippers. Their gray hair was down, in single braids to their waists. Three mothers—how could she fight it? They took each side of Lennox and piloted her up the stairs. They gasped at the switchblade stuck in the floorboard. Lennox leaned off the bed, pulled it out, closed it, and tucked it under the pillow.

After settling her on the bed, one said excitedly, "We saw the whole thing."

"No, we didn't, sister. We only saw that person run out of your door, and you run after him, Dorie."

"Did you get a look at her?"

"Her?" they said in unison.

Lennox lay back against her pillows. "Did you see her come up?"

Norma and Nell shook their heads. "We went to bed early."

"And read Miss Christie."

"Never heard a thing?"

"We wish we had. We could have helped you, Dorie. Does your leg hurt awfully?"

"I'm glad you didn't come out. If you see somebody around my room again, stay behind your door."

The twins made ominous faces at each other. Norma volunteered to get an ice bag. Nell sat on the bed and talked about the Agatha Christie story, about a village parson and a stranger and an odd smell in the tea. A few minutes later, ice bag in place, Lennox shooed them off.

The room was a mess, clothes dumped out of drawers, books from under the bed strewn across the floor. What had the woman been looking for? Lennox glanced at the open cupboards, saw the coffee can where she kept her extra money, when there was some, and saw it tipped, empty. Two dollars and seventy-five cents, up in smoke.

Setting the lamp upright, she perched it on the nightstand and kicked off her shoes. The knee had been worse. All she'd really done was to twist it. She felt the ice numbing it and eased down on her sore back. She lay listening to talk on the street below, laughter, mumbling. She got up after a minute, found aspirin, hopped to the sink for a glass of water.

She put a record on the Victrola, Lester Young with Billie Holiday, and lay in bed smoking Luckies. Her hands shook. The woman had taken her blade in nothing flat. But who was she? A burglar out for two dollars and change? Not likely. Did she work for Georgie? He didn't trust her any more than she trusted him. But would he actually break into her room—and for what?

She lit another cigarette and sat on the edge of the bed, rearranging the ice. The woman had come to give her a message, that was it. But who was Edna? Somebody the so-called limey was investigating? Why not give Amos the message himself? She cringed, thinking she was the easier target, easier than a decrepit old soldier in an oxygen tent.

If the woman had broken in to give her this message about this Edna person, why had she tossed the place? Was this message business a false trail, something to take her attention away from what was missing in the room, whatever the intruder wanted so much that she'd baldly tromped up the stairs and broken into a room in a public hallway?

The photographs? The film was at the office; she'd taken the roll there during a bratwurst run for the nurses. But the thief didn't know that. Oh hell, the pictures weren't going to show anything anyway.

She lay back again. The more she thought about the attacker, the angrier she got. The words the woman had said, her sneering tone, put a chill in her. "You are so far out of your league, kitten." Lennox ground her teeth. She'd show her, whoever she was. Out of my league, my eye.

A cold shiver passed through her. Enough. She turned her mind to Iris Jackson. A little sister. There was a hot tip. It made her sad to think about Iris, but she had to. She'd promised Amos.

That night at the Muehlebach, all dressed up. Iris, with her hair like Jean Harlow, now dead like Jean. Lennox and Amos had watched her work the room like a quiff, then laugh at the men's whispered suggestions. A satin dress, gold earrings, shimmering hair. Vanvleet swore she wasn't a hooker, that George had too much class. Georgie and class, that was a good one.

She turned out the light, pulled up the covers, and listened to Lady and Lester sing about things that shouldn't have happened.

FOUR

LENNOX RANG THE BELL at the house on Janssen Place. The porch, bigger than her room in the boardinghouse, was stuffed with wicker furniture and yellow begonias. A headache from last night's thumps had been eased by aspirin, but her knee and back still ached when she moved. She fingered the envelope with the eight-by-ten prints. Her hands smelled like chemicals from the darkroom.

The Vanvleet mansion was one of only four houses that hadn't been converted to apartments on this once-proud street. The manses butted up to Hyde Park's trees and green swards, flanked with stone gates and fountains on the short but elegant street. The Vanvleet's three-story brick pile had been built before automobiles, with a carriage house and covered side entrance. To Lennox's eye, it was a guise, a pretense of respectability as corrupt as the old man who lived there. Cynical thoughts from an ungrateful girl, she thought, shaking her head on the porch.

A Negro maid opened the door, her uniform a crisp gray, with starched white collar and cuffs. Very proper, down to white gloves and a silly cap. She was light-skinned, the kind of Negro Arlette called "pe-ola."

Lennox announced herself. "Got some pictures for Mr. Vanvleet."

"What kinda pictures?"

"Photographs. He wanted them today. I work for Amos Haddam."

The magic word. The maid let her in through a dark hallway with oak paneling, then into a large library. Lennox had been here once before with Amos.

A grandfather clock announced the hour. One o'clock. It had taken some time to find someone to develop the film. That had been Willard's job. She could enlarge and develop the prints herself. And had, finally.

She scanned the dusty leather-bound books. Homer, Greek classics, forgotten Victorians, Dickens, Scott. The heavy odor of cigars clung to the leather furniture.

She was fingering the brocade drapes when the door opened. The lawyer was dressed in a velvet-collared purple satin smoking jacket with starched shirt and paisley ascot. The tie belt on the jacket accentuated his girth.

"Miss Lennox. The photographs already? I'm impressed." He crossed to the fireplace. She handed the envelope over.

Vanvleet peered over bifocals. "You satisfied with them?"

"Shooting at night is hard under the best conditions. You remember the Wobbly pictures." On one of his final assignments, Willard took night shots of union sympathizers for a Vanvleet client. None of them were good enough to make positive identifications.

"These are as bad?"

"See for yourself."

He untwisted the string and pulled them out, adjusting his glasses. "I thought you weren't working for us anymore, Miss Lennox. I'm glad to see you had a change of heart."

She grit her teeth.

"Some clients are a little more challenging than others," he said, eyeing the shots. "It pays to leave your delicate sense of morality at home, in your hope chest, with your other girlish things. Not that I don't admire you for it; I do."

Girlish things? Was that how he saw her, as a girl? "I don't have a hope chest, sir." He squinted at the photos. She said, "Someone broke into my room last night."

"Looking for these?"

"Could be. Although why, I don't know. She told me to stay out of her way. But she neglected to say who she was or where the hell she was going."

Vanvleet didn't seem interested. He moved behind an oak desk the size of a small barge, laying the photographs out. There were eight in all, of the three different locations: the Hot Cha Cha Club, the Chatterbox, the bridge. In one at the Hot Cha Cha, taken early in the evening, Iris was visible, leaning over a table, holding four beer mugs.

"This one's good," Vanvleet said, pointing at the shot. "But we knew she was there."

"It shows some of the men, regulars."

The lawyer rubbed his chin, leaning down to eyeball the river shots without his cheaters. "What is this?"

"The river. From the bridge." Lennox pointed to a white smudge. "Here. That's her."

"You don't say." He stacked them up again. "No shots of her on the bridge."

"It was dark. The lights were out."

"But you saw her. Jumping off."

"Yes."

The lawyer slipped the prints back into the envelope and handed them to her. "I don't think Mr. Terraciano needs to see them. But keep them handy." He leaned his knuckles on the desktop.

Lennox was halfway to the door when she turned. "Will he be having a memorial service for her?"

"You want to attend, get some leads there?"

"Can't you be straight with me, Vanvleet?" She had never addressed him like that. He was old, but, damn, that wasn't her fault.

He smiled. "What is it you want to know?"

"Why he wants to follow her, for starters. What he knows about her."

"I've told you all I know, Miss Lennox. She's—she *was* his . . . well, his girl."

"In a pig's eye."

"Miss Lennox—" Vanvleet was serene, unperturbed by her questions. That made her madder.

"How can I do my job if you all clam up? Who is she? Who *was* she?"

Vanvleet gave her a steady look. "Iris Jackson. Barmaid. Girlfriend. Sister. That should be enough to begin."

"You have a name or address on the sister? Where's she from?"

"*Do* your job, Miss Lennox." He checked the time on the grandfather clock. "Now if you'll excuse me, it's time for dinner with my family. I'll see you tonight at the country club. At the awards dinner for the Brookside Flyers."

Dorie blinked, caught unawares. "Oh, I hadn't thought—"

"As track coach for the children, you are expected to give out the medals. Two of your little runners are getting awards."

Their eager little faces flashed through her mind. So like Tillie, she thought. "It's tonight?"

"At five. Just mention my name to the doorman."

"Right." She didn't even know country clubs had doormen.

"When you see Mr. Haddam, tell him we're all hoping he recovers soon. Very soon."

She turned back. The man knew everything and shared nothing. Why was he paying Amos's medical bills? What did they know about Iris? She stumbled through the carved door into the hallway. A statuesque old woman in a flowing red dress stepped down the stairs. Her gray hair was piled on her head in a way that had gone out of style twenty years before. A younger man, with her pointed chin and cold eyes, held her elbow.

"Reggie. Who is this?"

Reggie gave Lennox the once-over as Vanvleet came to the

doorway behind her. She recognized the younger man's name from the law firm. The wayward son, the one who'd had to pay someone to take his bar exam.

The old woman tipped her head, her voice going sticky sweet. "Ah, pumpkin, is this a new friend? You didn't tell her we dress for dinner. Naughty boy."

Lennox smoothed her gray slacks. She should have kept walking, out the door, but the heavy perfume on the old woman seemed too thick to move in. Across the hallway, the double doors to the parlor were open. Two teenage girls dressed in organza pouted on the frayed Empire sofa. The coffee-skinned maid stepped in from the dining room, ready to announce the meal.

"I was just leaving," Lennox mumbled.

"Don't make her go, pumpkin," the old woman screeched. "The rules aren't so rigid that we can't make an exception." She frowned at Lennox's trousers. "She isn't *family,* after all. We made an exception for Dick's friend that time, before the war."

"This is Miss Lennox, Mae." Vanvleet caught Lennox's arm, swinging her to face the group. Reggie had the suave, blank look of the dutiful son, and, in his tie and tails, ludicrous. "My wife, Miss Lennox. And you know my son, Reg, of course."

"We've never met," Reggie said with a nod, "but I've heard of your work, of course."

Lennox blinked at the strange ensemble. Her work?

The old lady held out her gloved hand. "I can see you are from the countryside, miss. Sit at my right side, so I can advise you on proper attire. Come along."

She oozed away on Reggie's arm, toward parlor and granddaughters.

"Don't mind her," Vanvleet said in a low voice.

"Nice of her to include me."

"No, it wasn't." The old man opened the heavy leaded-glass

door. Outside, birds were singing. In here, time had stopped some years back. She wasn't sure if she should be insulted or relieved that Vanvleet had dismissed her. The smells of the roast turkey were at least tempting.

"I appreciate the speed on the photographs, Miss Lennox. I'm sure all your work will be just as timely. Reports every day now. Do not disappoint me."

The door shut in her face. She was relieved, she decided, to be outside instead of in the stuffy dining room with pinkies at the proper angle, discussing the grandeur of life before the war. She had been more right about the mansion harboring delusions than she could have guessed.

At the bottom of the porch steps, she straightened her shoulders and felt the warmth of the afternoon sun on her head as she passed beyond the iron fence and the oak tree. Inside the hot Packard, she looked at the photographs again. They were thoroughly dry now, and curling at the corners. The shot through the saloon window was a good one; the old man had been right about that. In profile, the bar lamps lighting her from behind, Iris with her flowing hair caught behind her ear. She had a grim smile for the customers, who made no bones about ogling her tits. And nice ones they were, especially from this angle, with a close-fitting dress left open three buttons at the neck.

She was pretty, but how old? Not thirty, although she looked it in the harsh light of the ladies' rest room at the Muehlebach. Indoor skin, pale, nice hands, manicured. Even in the photograph you could see her dark nail polish. She wasn't a barmaid for long. No, she'd done something else, office work, or sales, something where the hands are important. But something had aged her just the same. There'd been a hardness in her stormy eyes at the Muehlebach, as if the world had wronged her.

It probably had. The world had a way of doing that.

Sugar Moon Investigations smelled like the chemicals she hadn't taken time to dump before rushing off to Vanvleet's. She opened the windows, one on the south, one on the west, and listened to the sounds of the streetcars on the avenues below. Amos liked this location, on intersecting streetcar lines, but from Lennox's point of view, the building did nothing for their reputation.

A four-story brick building, the Boston Building was home to shady lawyers, bookies, a rummy dentist, a get-rich-quick outfit, and competing beauty parlors. The only decent office was occupied by a real estate company with a reputation for hustling farmers. The rest—all of the fourth floor and half of the third—sat empty, waiting for tenants who had moved farther from the clang of the railroad yards and the mingled stench of swamp and manure that seeped up the cliffs from the bottoms.

At least they had a nice corner on the second floor, where she now spread out the photographs on her desk. She and Willard and Roger had once shared the battered metal surface. There were two small offices and a reception area with a threadbare Oriental rug, a hard wooden chair for clients, and one dead plant. On weekday afternoons, Shirley Mullins came in to chew gum.

The darkroom occupied a large closet in her office. She pulled the string on the light, dumping the dead fixer and developer into a bucket. Trotting down the hall to the women's rest room, she poured the chemicals down the sink, rinsed the developing pans, and dried them with towels, all the while thinking about the phone calls she would make. She made a mental list of every place or person associated with Iris. It took five or six seconds.

Back in the office, she looked up Iris's address in the reverse directory and dialed the main number.

"Mrs. Faron?" Lennox explained she was Iris's sister Florence. "I've been trying to call her all weekend. Have you seen her?"

"Eh? Who?"

Deaf as a post, but so very good of her to answer the phone.

"Iris. Upstairs. Have you seen her?" Loud, and slow.

"Never see her. Works nights, my husband tells me. He keeps an eye on her."

Just bet he did. But Bud Faron knew no more than his deaf wife. He was pleasantly ignorant of all of Iris's activities, although he did say he hadn't seen her car since Friday. Didn't know if she'd been home. Didn't know if she had any friends. Knew exactly nothing.

Lennox hung up the receiver and leaned back, fingers laced behind her head. Shirley should know about Amos. Reaching one of the receptionist's grown sons, Lennox left the message that Amos was at City Hospital, then hung up.

She chewed on her fingernails and decided she could make one more phone call. The bartender at the Hot Cha Cha sounded irritated, and he got more so when the topic of Iris was brought up.

"Hey, I know she's your sister and everything," he said, "but tell her she's fired. She doesn't show up Saturday night, that's our busiest night."

"She didn't show? I've been trying to get her since Friday."

"She was here Friday. I remember. It was late, but she drove off. I saw her myself. Then nothing. Not a phone call or a note, just disappears."

"That's not like her. Is it?"

"Hell if I know. I got beer to tap."

"Did she mention anyone she might be visiting? A friend, a boyfriend?"

"She mentions nobody. One cold doll. Wouldn't take lip from any customer." His tone changed. "You look like her? Where you calling from?"

"Here in the city. I'm here on business."

"Oh, yeah, what business you in?" Suddenly he's friendly.

"Carpet. Wall-to-wall."

"Huh." Suddenly he's not friendly. Wrong business.

"You interested in any wall-to-wall?"

"Hey, you pay for that, buddy?—So long, toots."

She hung up the phone and said to no one, "Yeah, yeah—toots."

The afternoon had reached the temperature where motion ceased. Hot, moist air pushed down all desire for movement, purposeful or not. Lennox drove past a fountain of water escaping through the sidewalk from a water main. Children and dogs splashed and played. The rest of the city was taking a nap.

On Charlotte, the shadows of the buildings created spots of relief. On the far corner, the lady doomsdayer had set up her placards in the shade, proclaiming the end of the world. Who knew, this time she might be right. In another shadow near the boardinghouse was Luther. He was stripped to a sleeveless undershirt and torn gray pants, and barefoot. On his head, he wore a derby with a hole in it. Lennox started to pass him, but his speech caught her.

"I always wanted to snatch at the world with twenty hands, and not for a very laudable motive, either," he said, voice vibrant and dignified. "That was wrong, and am I to show now that not even a year's trial has taught me anything? Am I to leave this world as a man who has no common sense?"

She blinked at him. He was quoting the book she'd given him. She recognized the speech, near the book's end. Luther was eloquent, his bearing straight, hands gesturing. Now and again, he'd take off the derby to make a point.

He finished, doffed the derby, and bowed. Lennox stood rooted to the pavement. Impossible that any book could remake Luther into a proud, confident man. A poor choice of literature perhaps. Should she have given him her copy of *Gone With the Wind*? At least Scarlett would have charmed him with la-di-das.

The sound of clapping came from the curb. A man in shirtsleeves and dusty black slacks came forward, applauding. Luther took another bow.

"Humdinger!"

Lennox turned at the voice. The man smiled at her, still clapping. Luther took a step backward, derby at his chest, panic back on his face.

"Yes, Luther. Amazing. Wonderful." Lennox tried to touch his arm, but he pulled away. He shook his head, muttering.

"I never expected sidewalk theater in your neighborhood, Miss Lennox," the man said.

She stared at him, the lanky dark, hair. "Do I know you?"

"I'm crushed. What we had was fleeting, yes, but oh so sweet."

Lennox glanced at Luther. The would-be actor squinted and continued shuffling away, bent again with life's burdens. She looked from one to the other. Had the heat turned everyone loony?

"Harvey Talbot, at your service."

From Friday night, at police headquarters. "Oh, yes, the scribbler."

"Ouch. Headlines are my game. Did you like it?"

She walked after Luther, toward the front steps of the boardinghouse. A flowerpot with its contents dried to a crisp lay broken in the dirt. Talbot trotted along next to her. Again.

"Did you at least see it?"

"Oh, yes. Thanks for mentioning me in the article."

"No sweat." He laughed, fanning his face. "Well, today there's sweat. Listen, I want to do a follow-up."

Lennox could smell him, damp cotton and aftershave and hair oil that wasn't doing its job. "I can't help you."

Talbot mopped his face on a handkerchief and leaned into the pillar of the shady stoop. "That's where you're wrong."

"Let me put it this way, Talbot. I don't *want* to help you."

"Call me Harvey." He looked up at the hulking boardinghouse, its clapboard a deep oyster gray peeling to reveal a sickly yellow, and, in a few places, an innocent pink. "Nice place. You live here alone or with your husband?"

"Look—"

"Wait. Don't tell me. Divorced. I can spot a divorcée a mile away."

"I'll bet." She started up the steps, and damned if he didn't follow her to the door. "You're annoying me. Go away."

He put his hand over hers on the doorknob. "Not until you hear what I know about that jumper."

She slipped her hand away. "What do you know?"

"I know where she is." He grinned at her. "See? You *are* interested."

Across the street, Luther was setting up his crate of apples and sad little sign in front of the Czmanski's garage, ready for business. Down on the corner under the green awning at Steiner's grocery, Anna Steiner made short work of the sidewalk with a broom.

"Okay, I'll bite."

He took her elbow, but she refused to budge. "Come on. I'll show you."

"Where is she?"

"You're a hard case, aren't you? Well, I'll tell you. But you have to agree to go with me."

"Go *where*?" She felt her blood pressure rising. Why did he have to keep touching her?

He threw up his hands, as he had on Friday night. "Oh, I guess you got a date or something," Talbot said, nonchalant now. "I s'pose I could go see her by myself."

"You're right, Talbot. I don't have all day. So spill it."

"Call me Harvey."

She gave him her level look. "Don't fuck with me, Harvey."

He laughed. "That's good. Trashy but good." He skipped down the steps. "My car's right here. She's waiting for us. Cool as a cucumber, and divinely peaceful."

Vanvleet's question: Had she seen Iris jump? The image in her mind was so fleeting. She could hear the distant slap against the river, see the blue dress sailing out behind her.

But was Iris really dead?

FIVE

AND THE PRETTY GIRLS ARE KEEPING A WATCH ON ME, just in case a little pneumonia should creep in, like that time in Detroit."

Amos peered through the tent at the blurred outline of Helen, tongue at her lip, bent over the pad of paper. "You can spell *pneumonia*? My mother was a teacher; she doesn't tolerate poor writing."

Helen frowned. "Are you sure you want to worry her about that?"

"You don't know my mother. Here's the picture: London, war is breaking out. All down the streets of Mum's neighborhood, families fleeing to the countryside. Little tykes are sent off to grandma, even to strangers."

"Because of the bombing?"

"Righty-o. The kiddies have to get the hell out. But not my mum. No, she will stay, like she stayed before, through thick and thin and bloody Nazi bombs."

"Is it safe?"

"Course not. It's the principle. She would never run away from danger."

"That seems foolish."

"That it does." *Pigheaded* was the word. "So while the bombs are raining down on her, she'll have me to worry about, not herself."

"I don't get it."

"She can't worry about herself. If she did, she'd run away to the country like everybody with a brain in their head. So I'm giving her something else to worry about so she can be brave. It's like a gift, love."

"Wouldn't it be better *not* to give her anything, so she'd leave?"

"Doesn't work that way. Believe me, I've tried."

Helen sighed. "Mothers. Is that the end?"

"Tell her we've had decent rain, that the corn and wheat crops are expected to be good. Looks like the Dust Bowl is over for good. She loves hearin' about crops, for some reason. And the bleeding weather."

"It makes her feel like the world is the same over here. That's what my mother says."

"And where does she live, love?"

"Joplin."

"Clear across the state? Aren't you the adventurer."

Helen grinned. She had a straight set of white teeth that would have pleased his mother. Always thoughts of Mother when he was laid up. Helen made a more-than-adequate replacement. He always fell in love with his nurses, a feeling that faded as soon as he recovered.

"Look in my jacket, will you, ducks? There's a small notebook. Not the blue one. That little black one."

Helen handed it to him. "It looks old."

"Plenty. If this notebook could talk." He tried to laugh, then thought better of it. His chest felt like a ton of bricks sat on it.

Helen went back to the letter. He opened the cracked leather cover, worn thin over the years. He'd started carrying it again about a month before, as he had off and on for the last ten years, and he was glad now, because he had the time to read it again.

Notes on Miss Eugenia McAughey. 1898–1918.

He thumbed forward to midway, where he'd copied out the short newspaper report of her death. Its cold, factual tone was reassuring, perhaps because it said so little.

Niece of Dover Shipping Magnate Lost at Sea

When the freight and passenger ship the *Mantiquaine* was sunk in the Irish Sea yesterday, one of the passengers lost was Miss Eugenia McAughey, 19. Known in Dover as the frequent visitor of her devoted aunt and uncle, Horace and Marcella Conwyn, Miss McAughey was a summer member of the White Cliffs Natural History Society and graduate of London College of the Arts. She had an exhibition of her watercolor paintings at the Quex House in Margate last summer.

Miss McAughey was the daughter of Mrs. Conwyn's sister, Henrietta McAughey, and the late Sir Lowell McAughey of Corsham.

Arrangements through Williams and Wright, Bath.

So little, and yet what more was there to say? One girl lost, when hundreds of others were rescued. Why had she been found in the water, when there was room in the lifeboats? Why had no one helped her? Had she lost hope when the false reports of his death reached her?

None of the questions mattered. Time had passed.

And yet. Damn, even after more than twenty years, he couldn't let her go.

Helen continued scribbling on the pad as the shadow of the man crossed her hands.

"Reg?" Amos leaned forward inside the oxygen tent, straining to look at the tall, dark-haired man in a severe but perfectly cut suit, who was fingering his brown hat. When he gave his Clark Gable smirk, Amos was sure it was Vanvleet's son.

"Hello, Haddam," the boy said. They were the same age, more or less, but still Reg was the boy.

Helen stood up. "Do you want to sign this now?"

"Let's wait till morning. I might think of more thrilling news."

The nurse backed out of the room, leaving them alone. The roommate with the snore had been sprung that morning.

"Good of you to come out on this dreadful evening. Is it dreadful out?" Amos said, pointing to a chair.

"Not particularly." Reggie sat on the edge of the straight-back chair and looked around. He had an aquiline profile and girlish lips. "My father says to tell you not to worry about anything while you're in here. He's taking care of everything."

"Give him my sincere thanks."

Reggie squinted. "And he wants to know what came of the search for that girl."

"The long-lost chippie?" Amos's throat hurt from all the talking to Helen. It was impossible for him to keep quiet. The hospital stays were full of boredom. Tormenting visitors was the only diversion. "I ran down the leads he gave me. Name of Edna something, right? Last known address, they never heard of her. It's been seven, eight years. Last known employer—Big Lolly—died two years ago."

"What about the other girls at the hook shop?"

"Good idea, Reg. Only they're dead or scattered to the four winds. Girls die after two or three years in that business. If they manage to survive and get out, they change their names, addresses, hair color, everything, to erase that life. Can't really blame them."

"So you gave up? You want me to tell the old man that?"

"Put it however you want. I couldn't find the chippie."

Reggie gave an irritated sigh and stood up.

Amos's throat burned. "Hand me that water glass, would you?"

Reggie slipped the glass under the tent. "I don't know why my father keeps a decrepit old boondoggler like you on the payroll."

Amos felt the water cool his throat. “When he has such a debonair gallant as yourself?”

Reggie walked toward the door. Pretending not to hear was one of the boy’s chief preoccupations. Like when folks around the law firm snickered when he flunked the bar five times. Rumor was he’d finally passed, with outside help. The old man kept him on because he was the son, the only one left, for better or for worse. The word was that his days as the golden boy might be limited. One of the secretaries had hinted he’d overstepped his privilege once too often.

In a second, Reg was back.

“I almost forgot. He says you don’t need to do anything more on Palmer Eustace. The client lost interest. Or something.”

Amos saw the boy’s eyes flick away, toward the window; then he straightened and brought them back.

“Lost interest in the racetrack?”

“He said the auditor was done. Forget it.”

“ ‘Forget it’? Those were his words?”

“Yeah, Haddam. Clear?” And then Reggie was gone for good.

Clear as mud. It was clear that Vanvleet had let the boy extemporize. The old man must have been seriously distracted to let that happen. Palmer Eustace was a partner in a racetrack built last year in Blue Valley. Vanvleet said Eustace suspected the partner, one Floyd Wilson, of keeping a double set of books and cheating him out of the profits. Amos had gone along with the auditor and leaned on Wilson.

Forget about profits? Unlikely, in such a lucrative business as horse racing. So maybe Eustace had changed lawyers. But who else in the city had more clout than Vanvleet? Had Vanvleet loused up?

Impossible. Amos lay back on the pillows, feeling the bricks settle back into position on his chest. He tucked the old leather notebook into his pajamas.

He had to get up to use the bathroom, and he hoped Helen was still on shift, so he could smell the orange shampoo she used. It reminded him of the fruit trees in the glassed conservatory in Eugenia's aunt's country house, before the war. And of Eugenia. He reached over to push the call button and collapsed back on the bed.

He'd never met Palmer Eustace. Maybe it was time. But first he had to get out of this sick ward. Damn the Jerries. They hadn't learned a damn thing. Would there be trenches and gas again? No. Tanks and bombs. Get the job done quickly. What was modern war if not efficient in the killing department?

Helen rushed into the room.

"A mission to the loo, ducks."

She pulled back the oxygen tent and got him to his feet, her arm around his bony waist. As they shuffled forward, toward the door and bathroom down the hall, with the heady clean smell of her hair in his nostrils, Amos began to cough.

SIX

THE CLAPPING OF HEELS on the marble steps rang out in the silence. The wooden handrail leading down to the basement felt warm, safe, but the hallway beyond was cold and silent. The building was just a few years old, built with WPA dollars and Pendergast cement, but it already looked ancient.

The cool air would have been soothing on this hot afternoon, but for the smell of formaldehyde and the stench of bodily fluids. A cloying dampness hung in the contaminated air. Each breath made Lennox feel less human, and somehow more so.

Talbot seemed to know everyone at police headquarters. He said he'd been a reporter at the *Star* for two years, and before that for the sister paper, the *Times*. And he laid his charm on every cop, secretary, clerk, and assistant. The morgue's door was open and a large, disheveled woman smiled when she saw Talbot.

"Eloise! How's the body business?"

With her gray hair cut in a blunt flapper's cap, the woman blushed a deep scarlet. "You shouldna sent those flowers. The boss thinks I've got a secret boyfriend," she said. She wore a wrinkled pink-and-white-striped dress with shoes run down at the heels.

"Well, don't you, old girl?" Talbot moved around her desk and gave her shoulders a little squeeze. Over her head he gave Lennox a cross-eyed look.

"Oh, stop that, you." Eloise wiggled out of his grasp. "What is it today, then?"

"My friend here wants to see a body. Oh, excuse me. Mrs. Eloise Perkins, this is Miss Doria Lennox."

"Do you have one in mind, miss, or are you just a ghoul like your friend?"

Talbot gave her a mock frown. "A particular body, of course, Eloise. You're a jealous woman, trying to make me look bad in front of my friends."

Eloise gave Lennox a hard look. A bit possessive of a boy young enough to be her grandson, wasn't she? Despite all the bad smells, Lennox was starving. Her stomach was telling her to quit skipping meals. Talbot was wearing her out with his charm.

"The jumper," Lennox said. "The woman they fished out of the river."

"What for?"

Talbot said, "She might know the woman. Identification purposes, Eloise. You know me. I wouldn't have any indecent interests."

Eloise snorted. "Right. Well, ain't nobody else taking any interest in the poor thing."

They followed her through the wooden door behind her desk, into another dim hallway, one that led back into the bowels of the morgue. The rooms were shadowed and quiet.

"Nobody blipped off today," Talbot whispered. "Some days, this is the busiest department in the building."

They passed an examination room, an enameled porcelain table gleaming in the dim light. A closed door labeled MICROSCOPY. Mrs. Perkins stopped, opened an unmarked door, and flicked on overhead lights.

Brown metal drawers with chrome handles were stacked on the wall like file drawers. The clerk shuffled to the end of the row and put her hand on a drawer at knee level.

"Jane Doe, that's what they're calling her."

"Hmm. One O'clock Jane?"

The woman turned to Lennox. "He has to make a joke out of everything." Then to Talbot: "Have a little respect."

He bowed solemnly. Eloise pulled out the drawer, revealing a body covered with a sheet. She paused as she picked up the corner of the white sheet, by the head.

"You've seen a body before, miss? I mean, just after?"

Lennox pictured her mother's body in Atchison after the wreck, when blood streaked across her still-downy cheeks. Crystallized tears hung in her eyes, her lips bruised and dark. This couldn't be as bad as that.

"Yes. It's all right," she said.

Talbot stood at Eloise's left shoulder, his boyish face eager. Lennox stood opposite them, not quite as eager. He had probably seen many dead bodies: sharpers, diamond-cuff dealers, innocent bystanders caught in cross fire. Maybe the two cops killed last year in the raid or the ones gunned down by Pretty Boy Floyd. What was one more?

Eloise pulled back the drape. The white-gold hair was full of sand, tangled and dirty. Then the face. Lennox stared at it, trying to understand why small chunks of flesh were gone from the nose, the chin, one eyelid. The skin was gray, with a tinge of green, dirty with mud and sand, not even washed for the morgue drawer.

Talbot was lifting up the other end of the sheet, at her feet. "One leg broken. Helluva fall from that bridge. Plenty of bruises."

Lennox saw the long blue bruise down the neck, and the odd angle of it, as if it was broken. But her eyes kept going back to the face, the missing flesh. The river had done this to her, with its carnivorous devils.

"Where did they find her?" she asked.

"Up against the wharf. Wedged between the steamboat and the pier. A dock worker was getting a barge ready and spotted her hair in the water."

"When?"

"Early this morning. Can't you still smell the river on her? Poor thing." Eloise frowned at Iris's face. "So young. Seen enough, then?"

Lennox fought an urge to smooth out her hair, to soothe the look of chaos on the dead woman's face. "Did they take her clothes?"

"Oh, yes, miss. The department strips 'em before we see them down here. All the jewelry and clothes and personal effects."

"Will there be an autopsy?"

Eloise ruffled her lips. "Waste of money. Unless you know her, miss."

Lennox tipped her head to look again into the disfigured face crowned by the corn-silk hair.

Anxiety made her step back. "No, no. I don't know her."

"Right. So, thanks a million, Eloise." Talbot gave the old woman another shoulder squeeze and walked quickly around the drawer. He took Lennox's arm and pulled her out of the room, down the hallway, and into the outer hall. They were halfway to the stairwell when Lennox pulled away.

"Christ, Talbot, I can walk."

"You're not going to be sick?"

"Of course not."

He peered at her face. "You got the look back there, a little green around the gills. I've seen it before. Even happened to me once." He headed toward the stairs. "Let's get out of here."

They ordered coffee at the hash house around the corner, the one with a view of both monuments to corrupt progress, City Hall and the County Courthouse. Lennox ordered a hot turkey sandwich and Talbot decided lemon pie would hit the spot. They ate in silence. As Lennox finished her sandwich and her head cleared, she felt awkward and itched to go. If she hadn't been so hungry, and yes, face it, a little shook-up from seeing the stiff, she would have gone home. She lit up a Lucky.

"Bum a butt from you?"

She tapped out one for him and they smoked for a minute. He was half-done with his cigarette when he set it on the glass ashtray and squinted at her through the smoke.

"You weren't going to be sick, were you? No, it was something else," he said, scrutinizing her in a way that made her uncomfortable. It was the same way she sized people up.

"Yeah, I was gaga on the fish nibbles."

"That was nothing." He took a drag. "You know something about her, don't you? You know who she is."

"I only saw her jump."

"That's right. You saw her jump."

A short, sweaty man in black suspenders paused in front of the booth, eyeing Lennox, then Talbot. Harvey looked up as the man smiled, showing black-edged teeth.

"What are you doing here, Russell?"

"Same as you, Tal-butt. Eating when the deadline looms, like a vulture. Aren't you going to introduce me to your girlie?"

Lennox stubbed out her cigarette. Talbot's eyes darkened.

"Dangle, Raunch."

"She's not your usual broad, all skirt and pout. She looks like she might know how to count to twenty." Russell showed her the full complement of bad teeth. His white shirt was thin enough to see his undershirt and matted chest hair, not to mention several days' worth of stains under his arms.

"Don't you have socks to wash?"

"Whaddya know, Harve. I got some hot juice on that Blue Valley track. They're taking a lot of the Pendergast lettuce." Russell leaned down to her conspiratorially. "I know who really owns it," he whispered, nodding. He had a powerful stink.

"Who?" Talbot asked.

"You won't believe it. I had to slip some silk stockings to a certain secretary I know. I got a good supplier for silk stockings, if you're interested, girlie." Russell looked around the café. "A dinge," he whispered.

"A colored owner? Who gave you that flimflam?"

"Impeccable source, Harve. Impeccable." But his lips began to quiver.

"You better get some more sources before you run that one by Big Ed." Talbot looked at Lennox as if he'd forgotten she was there. "Now scram, hombre."

Russell waddled away. Talbot flicked back the rogue lock of hair that tickled his eyebrow. "Where were we?"

"Is that right? The Blue Valley track is owned by a Negro? I thought it was some Chicago goons."

"Probably is. Russell's a blowhard."

Amos had been working on something about the track last week. She would ask him tonight, also about the mysterious Edna.

"Now, where were we?" He squinted at her hard. "Oh, yeah, you saw her jump from the bridge. But why?"

"Why what?"

"Why were you there? I don't believe in coincidence."

"That's your problem, Talbot." This had gone on long enough. "Where's that waitress?"

"Why? That's what I was asking myself. So I did a little checking up on you."

"I'm going to get her." Lennox slid to the edge of the booth.

"You're a snoop. A peeper. You were tailing her that night."

Lennox glanced at him, affecting nonchalance, as she'd seen Amos do a hundred times. He, and she, hated to be made. It changed all the rules.

"How'd you get that bump on your noggin? Playing rough?"

"I like to play rough."

He grinned. "So do I. Where and when?"

"On the job, ace. Keep your pants on." She let him squirm for a moment, but he seemed to be enjoying it. "Somebody jumped me in my room last night. Told me to stay out of her way. But as I see it, she was on my turf."

Talbot examined her face with his eyes. "I hope she looks worse than you do."

"Doesn't everybody?"

He laughed. "You talk a good game, sister."

She stood with a buck in her hand. "Leave the tip."

At the cash register, Talbot slapped down two quarters for the pie and grinned at her. "Big-time reporters have expense accounts."

Outside, the metal siding on the diner reflected the hot sun, making the concrete a bake oven. Lennox walked toward his car, a green Chrysler, big as a boat. She was faster than he was, and she sat on the front seat, letting the heat turn her to mush, as he climbed in.

He put the key in the ignition but didn't turn it.

"All right," Talbot said, smiling still, but his words were not. "Let's have it. You were following her. I don't need to know why. I've got where and how and when. I just need to know who she was."

Downtown was deserted. Sunday afternoon, the last weekend of summer vacation, war jitters breaking out in a heat rash. Lennox watched a thin, mangy dog wander by a garbage can, sniff, dump it over, paw through the rotten detritus and smelly wreckage of the modern American city. She felt a kinship to that dog.

"I can't tell you anything, Talbot."

"I thought you were going to call me Harvey."

Always the smoothy. "Don't you ever turn that off?"

"Turn what off?"

She sighed. "Look, *Harvey*. Just take me back to the boardinghouse. I'm turning into a fritter here."

Talbot started to say something, changed his mind, turned the key. The boiler roared to life. He put the pedal down, careering around corners so fast that Lennox had to hold on to the door handle to stay on the seat. In minutes, he was idling the Chrysler on Charlotte Street. Here the shadows reached deep across the narrow street and the atmosphere was cooling.

"So, who's the bum?"

Luther had fallen asleep at his apple stand, stretched out on the cool pavement, the old derby over his eyes. His unshaven chin, open mouth, and filthy bare feet made him look like a true stewbum. She felt a flash of shame for him.

"Just can't stop asking questions, can you? His name's Luther. He lost everything in the crash."

"Including his mind?"

She nodded, biting her lip. What had gotten into him? His performance was so out of character.

"Was he an actor?"

"I don't know what he was." She climbed out of the car. leaning down, she said, "Thanks for the trip to the morgue. It was . . . historic."

The door slammed. She found him at her elbow as she climbed the concrete steps. "Look, maybe I can help you," he said. "I'm pretty good at tracking people down. If you told me her name—"

"It would be in your rag, front page."

He dropped his hand, defeat on his face for an instant. "What if I promised not to write anything until your job's over?"

"It's over now. She's dead."

"Then what's the problem? Come on, Miss Lennox, you gotta help me out."

"If you're so red-hot at tracking people down, track her down."

"Okay, sure." He opened the door for her. Christ, was he going to follow her inside? "But if your job's done, why can't you tell me?"

He *did* follow her, into the front hall. Smells of chicken soup and yeast rolls. In the dining room, Frankie was setting out plates and spoons. She gave Lennox a surprised smile.

"Talbot, go home," Lennox whispered. "Somebody's going to make off with your bus."

He moved closer. When she tried to step back, he put his

hand on her elbow. She really wished he wouldn't keep touching her.

"What about that girl's family?" He leaned closer, his breath lemon and cigarettes. "Don't they have a right to know? Maybe her mama's home crying right now. Wondering what's become of her baby girl. Looking at pictures in the album. Did you think about that?"

"Worry about your own mama. She's probably waiting supper for you right now."

He looked in her eyes. "I was right. You are a hard case. Nut-hard, through and through."

"That's right," Lennox said as he backed away. "And don't forget it. Now breeze off home to mama."

Frankie had disappeared by the time Talbot stepped back outside. Lennox watched him through the screen door. He climbed into the car, slammed the door. The car jerked away. He was a dog with a bone. With reporters, there was always something to lose—information, privacy, self-respect, reputation. She would have to be more careful. The thought of his colleague—if the term was appropriate for someone as oily as Russell—made her more resolved.

As Dorie turned to go up the stairs, Mrs. Ferazzi popped out from her rooms under the stairs, eyeing the door for a glimpse at the departing male. Mrs. F. had the widow's love of household intrigue.

"Miss Lennox! I spoke to the policeman down on the corner about the woman in your room. I just wanted you to know I don't forget things like that. He said he'd look into it."

"Thank you, Mrs. F."

"I asked everyone if they saw that woman. And nobody saw a thing."

"Well, the police will look into it." If the sun didn't rise tomorrow.

"Three messages for you." The landlady extracted three slips of paper from the pockets of her faded flowered apron. Her plump fingers were pink and well scrubbed. She smoothed back the graying wings of her thick black hair. "This heat is jus' awful. Is your room suffocating up there?"

"I haven't been up since morning," Lennox said. "And I have that fan you lent me."

"Oh, keep it as long as you want. You need to use my telephone?"

Given how jealously Mrs. F. guarded her personal telephone line, the offer surprised Lennox. Tenants had to use the pay phone on the second-floor landing. Mrs. F. must be feeling guilty about the intruder.

Lennox stared at the notes. One from the nurse, Helen, at the hospital. Another from her uncle, inviting her to Sunday dinner at two, which she had missed. And the last from Louie Weston. No number, no message.

"I could make a quick call." She followed the landlady into her tiny parlor, which was crawling with doilies and china figurines. Perched on the velvet telephone bench, Lennox dialed City Hospital.

Helen came on the line, her voice cautious. "He's had a bit of a setback. Could you come down? It's not urgent. He's all right; he's comfortable. Just sometime this evening."

"What's wrong?"

"A cough set in again. The doctor wants to keep him down for a while longer."

Lennox set down the receiver. Mrs. Ferazzi stood in the door to her bedroom.

"Someone in the hospital?"

"My boss."

"The lunger?"

Everyone assumed TB. "Mustard gas."

The landlady touched her neck. "Will you be at supper, then?"

Lennox checked her watch. The Brookside Flyers reception. If Vanvleet hadn't reminded her, she wouldn't have gone. "Not tonight, Mrs. F. But thanks for the telephone."

The bathroom was deserted for once. With five other people on her floor, weekend baths were a problem. The sound of the rattling fan she'd set in the window of her stifling room faded away. The cool water eased into her ears, her hair, and made her feel human again.

To feel human. Odd that would be good.

She rubbed soap on her arms and chest and thought again of Iris's gray-green body, battered by water, spoiled by the river and its creatures. Why had she done it? Did she have a mother somewhere distraught with worry? Could that brittle bar girl inspire that kind of attachment? Had there been a warm heart inside that cool, glossy exterior, the pearly skin, the flawless silk dress? Who was Iris Jackson?

Lennox dunked her head, trying to decipher the Iris enigma. Iris Jackson, the bar girl with angel hair, pinup girl legs and a broken heart.

She slathered on shampoo, dunked again. Underwater, the feeling of being trapped under the intruder's boot returned: "You're out of your league, kitten." She was beginning to hate the woman, not for messing up her room or kicking her or taking away her knife, but for those words.

Winkie Lambert knocked on the door. Lennox drained and rinsed the tub for Winkie, a fastidious secretary whose twice-daily baths drove Mrs. F. mad. In her room, toweling her hair, Lennox stared at her reflection in the mirror, not really seeing the wet ringlets, the hazel eyes, the pale cheeks, the bluish lump by her hairline.

Her mind was at the Chatterbox, on Twelfth Street on a dark night, high on a bridge, deep in the slippery soft mud of the dark, unforgiving river.

SEVEN

THE DOORMAN AT THE KANSAS CITY COUNTRY CLUB sneered at the Packard as if he had something against cars with bullet holes. He waved Lennox toward a shrub-lined parking lot, where she nearly turned her ankle on the gravel.

The cocktail party was in full swing when she arrived, and she let one of the lawyers from the firm press a Coke into her hand. They considered her too pure for alcohol. As if she were in training for the Olympics.

She wandered through the crowd, trying to get the eye of enough people to give the impression she'd been there. The head coach was here, and the trainer, a chiropractor. She said hello to both. A group of kids were corralled outside by a pack of mothers, but their screaming could be heard over the clinking of cocktail ice.

Louie Weston was across the room. She turned the other way and ran into one of the original partners, old Mr. Wintraub. The law firm sponsored the Flyers, and he'd twisted her arm to get her to help coach. Not that it needed much twisting. The kids were mostly cheerful and full of energy. The only problem was the little girl whose blue eyes looked like Tillie's.

A quick chat with Wintraub and she escaped to the large brick patio under the tall elms. It was cooler out here, a fountain-filled haven away from the smoky room and the crowd. The kids filed inside as she came out. Several called to her: Hi, Miss Lennox. School starts in two days, Miss Lennox.

Over the brick wall, on the lush greens, men were hitting little white balls into holes with sticks. They seemed to be enjoying it. The evening was sticky, and she pulled her hair up off her neck. She stood there a minute, hoping for a breeze, but there wasn't one. She let it go at a tap on her shoulder. Reggie Vanvleet stood there in a sports costume—madras pants, pink shirt, sport coat.

"Mr. Vanvleet. We meet again." She sipped her Coke.

"Call me Reg. I was wondering when that momentous occasion would happen. Been trying to manage it for weeks. Just didn't think it'd be in the old man's foyer." He put his hands in his pockets. He smelled like liquor.

"Momentous occasion?"

"When two dynamic lights meet." He leered at her, licking his lips. She found it amusing for a moment, then looked for a diversion. Seeing none, she steeled herself to his company.

"You and me?"

"That's right, sister. The two of us could turn that law firm inside out." He leaned in. "On its can."

Reggie threw back his head as if to laugh, but nothing came out. Odd, like a vaudeville skit gone wrong. Maybe he would need that chiropractor, inside drinking martinis with the coach.

"You got inside dope on some fancy-pants lawyers?"

His smirk drooped. "I am a lawyer, Miss Lennox." He swayed. Seemed a bit early in the day to go over the edge with the rams.

Looking beyond Reg, she saw his old man walk across the patio with Louie Weston and old Wintraub. They clotted into a tight circle, heads together as if hatching something big. Best to keep the boy talking, she thought.

"And a very good one, I hear."

Reggie squinted. "Yes, well, we could work together on the, um, Terraciano matter."

"Oh?"

"I have contacts in that sphere who could help you. I know many, many people. Give me a call." He reached into his jacket and handed her a business card. As she plucked it from the boy's hand, old man Vanvleet bellowed with laughter. Reggie turned, stumbled left, caught a chair.

The old man was clapping Weston on the shoulder. Louie and Wintraub were smiling. Reggie stared at them blackly and pulled a metal flask from his back pocket.

"Let's go get something to eat, Reg." Lennox touched his arm, but he pulled it away angrily.

Vanvleet and Louie Weston looked up to see Reggie advancing on them. The old man dropped his hand off Louie's shoulder, smiled a tight smile at his son. Old Wintraub, with his speckled head and sunken cheeks, stepped up suddenly, as if he was going to stop Reggie from speaking his piece.

"All right, there, Reginald, son," Wintraub began. Reggie brushed him aside like a feather. Dutch Vanvleet wasn't so easy to dismiss. He put both of his hands on Reggie's shoulders. His voice was low, calming. Behind the old man, Louie Weston looked a little chagrined, and smug, watching the crowd watching them.

Reggie stomped around, shouting about rights and family and honor. The old man brought Louie forward, made Reggie talk to him, as if his son were an eight-year-old on the playground.

Lennox lowered her eyes, humiliated for Reggie and fed up with plaid pants. She should wait for the awards. She really should.

Inside, she searched for her kids. A six-year-old boy had won the fifty-yard dash at the city meet and a girl, ten, took third in her age group. Lennox found them behind the ice sculpture, licking the mermaid's tail. She explained she had to visit a friend in the hospital. They shrugged their shoulders and returned to the best Popsicle they'd ever had.

Uncle Herb showed up at the hospital just as Lennox was leaving. She and Shirley Mullins had wrung hankies for an hour in Amos's new room, watching his tortured chest rise and fall.

They'd moved him, Helen said, to keep a better eye on him. He was not doing well; that much was clear. He had a fever, was mildly delirious, and went through bouts of coughing that left all of them weak.

"We missed you at dinner," Herb said. Her uncle was a raw-boned old bull, with little hair and hard, bright blue eyes, the only part of him that recalled his dead sister. "Your aunt says hello. She'll be up in the morning to check on Haddie."

They stood awkwardly by the nurses' station. Herb Warren had the unmistakable weight of the law on him. He made people uncomfortable, but not Lennox; she'd seen him in swim trunks, sitting in a kiddie pool, giving his dog a bath. He wasn't her father, but he was the best she had, and that wasn't bad.

"I didn't get the message until too late. Sorry."

He set his limp hat on the counter. "I see we found your jumper."

"Not *my* jumper."

"Oh?"

Lennox looked over her shoulder at Amos in his oxygen tent. Then back at her uncle. "I was tailing her that night. I guess I can't lie to you."

"I guess you better not," Herb said. "Have you identified her?"

"No one's asked." Talbot didn't count.

"All right, I'm asking."

Amos never shut Herb out, if there was any way. And what did it matter now to Iris? It would be better to be dead with a name, not a Jane Doe in a drawer.

"The girlfriend of a client," she said.

"With a name?"

"Iris Jackson. She lived over on Mercier, and worked at a joint downtown."

"Name of?"

"The Hot Cha Cha. Where the old Tenderloin was."

He nodded, put his notebook away. "That all you know about her?"

"Unfortunately."

"Except the name of the client," he said.

Lennox pleaded with him with her eyes. He picked up his hat. "That'll do for now." He squeezed her hand. "Call your aunt. She worries about you."

He lumbered over to the door to the patient's room, stepped to one side to let Shirley Mullins go by, speaking to her in a low voice and giving her hands a squeeze, too.

"Oh, Dorie, what are we going to do?" Shirley whispered. Her small face, usually a smiling Irish mug that brightened the office when she told ribald tales about her six sons, was blotched below the reddish bangs. "I have such a raw feeling, I do."

Lennox held her for a moment. "He'll pull through. You'll see."

They parted at the bottom of the stairs, Shirley going to the main entrance to wait for her son Sean, Lennox heading to the ambulance entrance. The unmedicated air past the hospital doors cleared her head. She couldn't let worry about Amos drag her senseless. She'd promised him she'd work on Iris.

The Packard was running rough. Maybe she could get it into Czmanski's garage this week, maybe it would take only a minute to fix, if Joe kept his mind on it. She squeezed the steering wheel, steered around the corners, heading vaguely toward the tall stick of the Liberty Memorial looming up on the hill above Union Station, then turning along the park, south down Main, wandering. She knew where she was going—it wasn't far—but forward movement through the night air was necessary for a few minutes more.

Past Linwood Boulevard. She should turn now. She kept checking her rearview mirror, but there had never been a sign of a tail. The smart-talking intruder must have been bluffing. On the corner of Armour Boulevard was the six-story apartment building made famous by the gangster's murder five years before. Thugs with tommy guns had cut down John Lazia right there in the circle drive, while his wife watched.

Reggie Vanvleet's drunken intimacies bothered her. Did he really have information? She doubted it. What was he up to, then? Should she report his interest in Georgie to his father? Maybe he was just trying to insinuate himself into the old man's good graces. He'd been doing a bang-up job today.

She turned right, made her way back up through the hilly streets, up Summit, then over to Mercier. She parked under a spreading oak tree, turned off the rattling engine. Lights burned on the first floor of the brick house. Now that she'd told Herb who Iris was, this was her last chance. The cops would be here tomorrow.

The old man answered her knock. Stoop-shouldered but bright-eyed, he might have been waiting just behind the door. Lennox went with the sister Florence story.

He took in her flowered summer skirt and plain white blouse, the anklets and slippers that made her look like a track coach who drank Coke or a girl who sold wall-to-wall carpet. The deaf wife was out of sight.

He led her toward the back, crashing through the bushes. "There's a path from the driveway. She always parks over there." He gestured left. "Quiet girl. Never gives us a lick o' trouble. Girls these days are plenty wild, had us one who took up flying, and roller-skating and bicycle racing, too. Always coming and going in short pants that scared my missus half to death."

He unlocked the door at the top of a long flight of wooden stairs up the back of the house. The old man stood panting at the door, holding it open for her.

A hot, musty smell, a space closed up on these scorching summer days. The old man flicked the switch to an overhead fixture with a harsh bulb. The apartment was spare, small, with a single room for eating and sitting, an alcove bath. Lennox walked to the only door, pushed it open. A single bed with an iron frame, neat and tidy, covers taut against the thin mattress.

"You talked to her recently?" the old man said behind her.

"Last week, I guess." Lennox walked to the bathroom sink, opened the cabinet. Hairbrush, peroxide, cold cream, used-up bottles of makeup. She shut it and fingered the yellow bowl on the sink, dried residue clung to the edges. Turning to the kitchen, a single linoleum-topped counter in pebbly gray, she ran her hand along the edge, wishing she could open cupboards. The wooden table by the window was bare except for an empty blue vase. Iris had arranged things. The apartment felt dead. One apartment, one bridge, one corpse.

"And you?" she asked.

"Middle of the week. She was supposed to bring by the rent check on Friday, but she never showed. I came up Saturday morning and knocked. Her car never was here." He glanced around. "All her things, though. She wouldn't just take a powder without her things."

Lennox took in the room, walls covered in faded cabbage roses, a sprung brown upholstered chair, two dog-eared magazines on the rickety table, a framed picture of mountains next to a tottering lamp, a rug with a hole. All *what* things?

"Is this a furnished apartment?"

"Oh, yes," the man said. "Me and the missus keep it nice for the girls."

"So nothing's gone, nothing's missing?"

The old man opened his mouth to answer when a shriek came from downstairs. After the third shriek it was apparent the wife was summoning him. Before he clomped back down the stairs, he gave Lennox a shrug and told her to stay as long she wanted.

Lennox went to the cupboards then, finding green glass plates and bowls, the kind they gave away free at the pictures. Two of each, and a well-used saucepan. A little cheap flatware. A scorched pot holder, can opener, rusty potato peeler.

In the squatty old refrigerator, a jar of mayonnaise, a butcher's wrap of bologna, sweet pickles, a hunk of hardened yellow cheese, half a loaf of white bread, a bottle of Muehlebach's. And a moldy smell.

Downstairs, the old woman was shouting at her husband, requesting something. Lennox moved to the sitting area, checked the magazines and the cushions, under the chair, behind the picture frame.

On the table, an ashtray held three dead butts with red lipstick. She pulled out the table's drawer, found matches, a pack of Camels with one left, a white linen handkerchief, and a torn envelope. She pulled out the envelope and turned it over in her hands. Addressed to Iris Jackson, here on Mercier, postmarked August 3, Kansas City. No return address. Why keep an empty envelope? Still, it proved she lived here.

Lennox put the envelope back for the cops and flicked the switch in the bedroom. Behind the door was a plain pine dresser with four drawers. Lennox slid them open one by one, feeling through lingerie, brassieres, panties, and girdles. Amos would be proud of her now, picking through the knickers. What we do best.

The undies were fancy, the kind of frilly stuff a rich woman might wear, or a rich man gives his girl, to compensate for living in a dump. Most from Emery-Bird-Thayer, with the department store's house tag. But shabby, long since worn-out, elastic stretched and rippled, lace torn and frayed.

In the next drawer, a couple blouses, a pair of shorts that would give Mrs. Faron apoplexy. Then, farther down, winter pajamas of a style inconsistent with the lingerie. In the bottom drawer, three pairs of white socks, balled.

She turned to the bed and saw the envelope propped on the pillow. Large, plain, white. Downstairs, the old man was telling the wife about the radio program. "It's Mr. Roosevelt," he hollered. Time for the fireside chat, to reassure the nervous populace that he wanted to stay out of the war, despite his wish to send many tanks, guns, and planes to England.

She picked up the blank envelope, turned it over. It was

sealed. Outside, the streetlight shone through the oak tree, freckling the window glass and the wool blanket on the bed.

She broke open the seal with her thumbnail, took out the paper. It was folded in thirds on cheap paper, written in a childish but careful hand. Signed at the bottom. Above, Iris explained that her life was meaningless and she meant to end it. She blamed no one, and had no one. She was estranged, she said, from everyone she loved and had no wish to go on living.

In a last paragraph, she wrote to someone in particular.

Wherever you are, my lost lamb, there will be stars burning.
And one of them, twinkling high above your head, is me—
my love that sputters and flares but never goes out.
Steady, love.
Take care, my lamb, and we'll be together soon.

A chill went through the stuffy room. It was what Lennox had been looking for, without knowing it. A confirmation that what had happened on the bridge was fate, what no one had any right to stop. Not her, not anyone. That Iris wanted to end her life, and had taken full responsibility.

She put the letter back in the envelope, smoothed the flap, set it back on the pillow. The red wool blanket pulled snug against the bed looked too cheery. And too hot for summer. But maybe Iris put on her best linens, knowing that her room would be searched. Suicides had the strangest ideas.

Switching off the lights, Lennox went back downstairs. Old man Faron came to the door, Mr. Roosevelt's sonorous voice booming in the room behind him.

"I was wondering," she said, "how long my, um, my sister lived here."

Mr. Faron scrunched his eyebrows. "Since the Fourth of July."

Lennox made a sad smile. It was something she was good

at. “We haven’t been too close these last few years. I was hoping things would change.”

Mr. Roosevelt sounded strong and apologetic and wise. She could only do apologetic. “The Fourth, you say?”

The old man nodded, worry on his face. “She went away for the weekend, is that it?”

EIGHT

TWO YOUNG BUCKS with cigarettes hanging from their lips played a lazy game of eight ball in the back of the Chatterbox. Along the long wooden bar, a line of empty stools gathered dust. The lights were too bright, illuminating the dull wax of the bar.

A middle-aged woman washed glasses in soapy water behind the bar, chatting with a weathered old man hunched over a beer. Lennox took a stool halfway down the bar. She wished she wasn't wearing the coed clothes. The billiard players made cooing noises in her direction.

The barkeep wiped her hands on a dirty towel pinned to her dress as an apron and made her way to Lennox. "Drink, miss?"

She ordered a draft. It arrived lukewarm. She let the bartender go back to the old man for a while, sipped the piss they called beer, then caught her eye.

Lennox slid her card across the bar. The woman squinted at it. She looked tired, her dark hair going gray. A wariness on her once-pretty features.

"Were you here on Friday night?"

The bartender nodded.

"Do you remember a woman who came in around twelve-thirty? Pretty, twenty-five, maybe thirty, with platinum hair."

"Twelve-thirty? I went home. Most of the crowd is gone."

"Somebody else, then?"

"He's not here tonight." The woman shouted down the bar. "Alfie! You here late on Friday?"

The old fella startled, sloshed some piss on the bar. "Friday, yah, sure."

Lennox slid down. "A girl came in late, about twelve-thirty. A bleach blonde." The man wore a black sailor's cap and a once-white waiter's jacket, his face wrinkled and dark but his eyes bright.

"Blonde, like Sylvia?"

"Wouldn't be her," the barkeep said. "A customer, Alfie."

He continued shaking his head.

"Maybe I could talk to the bartender who was working late that night."

"That'd be my Davy. Gave him today off. Had to run somebody down."

Lennox said she'd return the next day to talk to Davy. She laid a buck on the bar and stepped back out into the pink glow of the neon sign, ignoring the cat calls.

Halfway to her ride, she spotted the Nash. Just where it was on Friday, directly across the street from the Chatterbox. If it'd been a snake, it would have bitten her. Crossing Fifth, dodging a carful of picnickers, she approached the rusty jalopy. Behind her, in the liquor warehouse, the dog began a rhythmic howl.

The car looked empty. She flipped the door handles on the sidewalk side. Moving to the back, she opened the trunk. It creaked, revealing a bald spare, a tire iron, a pair of greasy towels. Shutting it, she tried the streetside handles, also locked.

Back at the Packard, she pulled the thin metal strip from under the seat. She tucked it in the folds of her skirt and walked back to the Nash, giving the tool the quick wrist movement that had begun her career. The door unlocked.

Inside, she ducked to feel under the seat, found a sticky Coke bottle. In the glove compartment were a set of keys, sunglasses, a gooey chocolate bar, two receipts from a grocery store on Main. She put everything back. The keys tempted her; what did they open? She put them in her pocket, knowing they would probably be a heartbreaker.

She took a last look at the blue Nash as it turned purple in the neon wash. How long till the local boys beat in the windows, took a joyride? Around here, it should've been yesterday.

Louie Weston leaned against a baby blue Oldsmobile under the streetlight in front of the boardinghouse. He was smoking a cigarette, looking at his shoes. Lennox saw him from the corner, a wave of heat flushing through her. She cursed under her breath.

He looked up and dropped his cigarette in the gutter. He wore a loose open-necked patterned shirt and brown pants, his hair less neat than at the office. He smiled, waited for her to approach.

"Take a wrong turn?" she said. The car was brand-new, chrome shining in the streetlamp. He pushed himself off it.

"Didn't even get lost," he said. "This your place?"

She glanced up at the lighted windows. "What are you doing here, Louie?"

He grinned. "So you remembered my name, too. I like that."

She stepped back. "It's late."

"How is your boss?"

"He'll survive." He damn well better.

Louie nodded. "Listen. Tomorrow morning, I'm going flying. I rent a little Luscombe. Why don't you come with me."

She stared at him. Was he teasing her? Wouldn't put it past him. What did he want? Was it his old weakness for the female—or was this about Vanvleet?

Louie cocked his head. "I'm good. You'll be safe. I got my license last month."

She examined the dimple in his chin. Christ Almighty, he was good-looking. But she didn't trust him as far as she could throw him. It would be foolish to go up with him.

"How come?"

"Just for fun. I love to fly, to see—"

"No. Why me?"

He smiled. "This is dumb, but after we met I was thinking about you and the old days. I remember a skit you did in fifth or sixth grade, about Amelia Earhart. You made big cardboard wings and strapped them on your arms."

She looked at the purple streaks in the darkening sky, glad of the shadows. "You remember that?"

"You said you wanted to fly around the world."

"Didn't work for Amelia, either."

"You been up?"

"Sure, a couple times. Barnstormers, that sort."

"Not in a long time, right?" He tugged her sleeve, made her look at him, and she knew her answer. "Come on."

Her worst decision, ever. In the Luscombe, high above the city, the rivers, the fields and hills, the hum of the engine hard in her ears, she didn't even think about him. About what he might want in return. No, the sky overtook her. Now she would dream about taking control of her own plane, of flying up here where the air was still and calm and filled with a rosy light.

A horrible idea. She grinned and couldn't stop grinning, so she clasped her hand over her mouth.

To the east, the view was hazy against the sun. To the west, the rolling prairie glowed gold with finished crops. Olathe and Lawrence were postcard towns, tiny streets crisscrossing, railroad tracks like strings of bailing wire. Up here, things were free, trackless, beyond the mentality of here to there, east to west, north to south, above the petty concerns of just getting somewhere. No grid, no one way only, no traffic at all.

Amelia's words came back—that the love of flying was the love of beauty. That the sky up here, the view of the earth, were more beautiful than anything she'd known. How did you know about beauty if you were from Atchison? But up here it was all so clear, so perfect. Up here, there was a plan—and it was a magnificent plan. Down there the plan might stink. But up here, it glowed.

Lennox felt her heart fill and wondered if she could ever see the world the same way again. It was so beautiful, so ordered. Everything was so large, so heavy, down there.

His touchdown was a little bumpy but fine. They climbed out of the plane. Her feet felt like bricks, no longer wild and free in the air. Louie started lessons, he said, just before Congress started the new civilian pilot program, so he got to take the rest of his lessons for next to nothing.

"For men only," she said.

"But that makes sense," Louie said, driving the Oldsmobile up on the Hannibal Bridge. "They need pilots, or will if we go to war."

"And women can't be pilots."

"Not combat pilots."

She looked at his profile against the morning sun. "Why not?"

"Because women can't be in combat. They can't kill. It's against their biology."

A couple of girls at Beloit would be surprised to hear that. "You mean to enlist?"

His grip tightened against the steering wheel. "I do. If we go to war."

"You're not running off to Canada?"

"I don't have that great a need to fly."

A need to fly. What were the signs of that? If you never piloted your own plane, how could you know? She closed her eyes for a second and was airborne again. All the problems of the present, all the wounds of the past were just tiny specks far below, hardly even noticeable in the sweet golden light that held up the shiny metal wings.

Louie was saying, "You should take lessons. It's not expensive. About three hundred dollars over six months. And you pay it little by little, every week."

She squinted at him and felt such a sudden lurch, she put her hand on the dash. But it wasn't the car. She'd just been grounded.

"Three hundred?"

They stopped at the streetlight at the end of the bridge. He looked at her for a moment and she felt his eyes graze her white duck trousers, red blouse, bare arms. She glanced at him and he looked away. *Atchison.* She could almost hear the word in the car. As if he'd just remembered who she was, who he was.

What was she doing here, with *him*? What would Arlette think? She felt a flash of shame. She was on the ground, not in some dreamer cloud where everything turned out well and true and fair. Hadn't she found that out after Beloit? She clenched her jaw. She couldn't trust anyone. Men hurt women; they take advantage wherever they can. No, no, that was Verna talking. *I'm not like Verna.* She shivered. Atchison was over. As long as she didn't have to see Louie Weston, she could forget it.

At Charlotte Street, Lennox jumped out of the car. He nodded when she said to say hello to the old man at golf. She watched the car drive away and let out a breath of relief. In Steiner's grocery, she bought a *Star,* a pack of Luckies, and a prune *kolache.* It was good to be back in the neighborhood, with its dirty gutters and bums and *kolaches.* She'd been blinded by a Luscombe and a nice haircut, but now her eyes were clear.

"A terrible thing, this war," Lennox said to Mrs. Steiner.

Anna Steiner gave a wan smile. Her English was good after five years in this country, but she didn't share much.

"You have family still back there?"

Anna's eyes widened. "No, no family. All is gone."

"They're over here, then. Good."

The woman frowned. The bell on the door tinkled as Lennox left. The doomsdayer had set up under the awning.

"Got a smoke?" Jenny asked.

Lennox opened the foil and shook out two cigarettes for

her. Jenny's ragged dress and shawl smelled like the swamp and sweat. Anna stuck her head out the door. "Go on, old woman. Don't bother the customers."

The old woman hissed at Mrs. Steiner, then picked up her sandwich board. "Don't own the sidewalk, does she?"

Jenny grabbed her board and shuffled across the cobblestoned street. On the boardinghouse steps, eating the prune pastrys, Lennox read the *Star*. More about Poland, bombs, tanks, war. And an article—Russell's?—inside the first section.

Blue Valley Track Denies Pendergast Tie

Owners of KC's newest horse track are quick to disavow rumors of Pendergast backing, the *Star* has learned.

Talk about the Blue Valley Racetrack has been building since it was revealed by *Star* reporters that a colored man was listed on corporation papers as one of the owners. Floyd Wilson and Palmer Eustace, corporate owners, deny that this is true. They also deny ties to the Democratic Party boss.

When asked about finances for the facility, they are mum. Last year, Jackson County floated $250,000 in industrial revenue bonds for the racetrack.

The *Star* has determined the first-year profit on the racetrack tops half a million dollars. The new track competes with Pendergast's own North KC park, said to be suffering with the Boss's incarceration this July, in the Federal Penitentiary in Leavenworth, Kansas.

Lennox hadn't gotten a chance to tell Amos about the track last night; he was too sick. She wondered again what he'd been looking into there. Next, she read a summary of Roosevelt's radio talk—"let partisanship and selfishness be adjourned." He offered "assurance that every effort of our government will be directed to keeping out of this war." Why didn't she feel reassured?

She read another story about mob boss Freddie "The Mink" Salvatore, indicted for attempted bribery, gambling, and tax evasion. She looked up, over the paper. Two men sat in the shadows across the street near Czmanski's garage. Luther, sitting on his apple crate, and another man.

She shielded her eyes from the sun. What was Harvey Talbot doing here? She squinted at him as a big black car glided to a stop in front of the boardinghouse, disgorging one burly gentleman, then another. They moved fast for big fellas. She felt her pockets for the switchblade. Then remembered it sat, useless, on her dresser.

Lennox stood up and stood her ground on the top step. Better to keep this—whatever it was—outside. She'd caused enough grief for Mrs. F. this week. The goons had heavy, round shoulders, long arms, and sturdy legs, obvious under the ill-fitting gray suit on the older one and the sleeker blue suit on the college-boy blond.

"Good morning, gents," Lennox said, tucking her paper under her arm. "Looking for someone?"

The older one, with a boxer's twisted nose, looked over his shoulder at someone in the black car. Then he said, "You Doria Lennox?"

Lennox squinted at the car. "Who wants to know?"

"Come on." The blond caught her arm. "Somebody wants to talk to you."

She tried to shake the hand, but he had clamped his mitt on hard. The other thug took her left arm. "Hey!"

"Let's go," the blond said as she kicked him hard in the kneecap. She wrenched her arm free as he bent with pain, then socked the older one in the chin. The pain shot up her arm to her shoulder and the thug blinked, surprised.

"Nice try, toots." He grabbed her free arm. She brought up her knee and caught him in the groin. As he let out an "Oof," the blond grabbed her from the back, pinning her arms, picked her up, and carried her kicking and screaming to the car. The door opened and she was tossed inside.

Lennox righted herself and went for the door handle. Locked. Next to her on the red velveteen seat, a woman watched her silently, dressed in a black hat with a veil, a powder blue dress, and gloves.

Lennox straightened her blouse, put her shoe right. The presence of the woman compressed her rage. She hated being thrown around. But a woman won't hurt me, she thought, even as a memory of Lucille at Beloit told her to be careful.

The car pulled away. Talbot and Luther stood stock-still on the sidewalk, dumb shock on their faces. She leaned forward, watching them as if she'd never see them again, until the car sped to the corner.

The woman began to talk.

NINE

"You know who I am."

Lennox crossed her arms. She felt like herself again, despite missing her blade and the rough treatment. "Someone whose manners could use a good brushing up." She had handled ol' Lucille back then; she could handle this plump broad.

They had turned down Broadway and were crossing the bridge. Again. The woman rolled down her window. The wind caught the black veil and she raised it, her eyes squinting against the glare off the water, the air in her face.

"I am sorry about that. But I had no way of knowing, of being sure that . . ."

The woman reached into her bag for a handkerchief to dab her nose. She looked married; full-figured, with short, wavy black hair that looked fake. Heavy makeup made it hard to pin her age, anywhere from twenty-five to forty. "You'd think I'd know about things like this. But . . . well, he's always been good."

Lennox examined her. Rock of a diamond ring, the smell of expensive perfume, tasteful powder blue sheath with matching jacket and shoes. "Your husband?"

She nodded. "You know who we're talking about? We don't have to get—"

"Personal?"

"Exactly."

"I don't know you, ma'am. I take it kinda personal when I

get tossed into cars. And I've got a telephone; most people make appointments."

The woman teared up again.

"But I'm willing to make an exception, because I can see that you had some kind of urgent matter on your mind."

"Yes, and I am sorry, again." She dabbed her nose. "Let's start over." She offered a white-gloved hand. "Marilyn Terraciano. Mrs. George Terraciano."

Lennox gave her hand a quick shake, suppressed a smile of interest. "Pleased to meet you, Mrs.—"

"Please, call me Marilyn. It's such a long name. My maiden name was Smith, and even after all these years, the married name is still too long for me." She looked up. "I suppose that sounds hateful."

"Not at all. It *is* long." And then there was the man himself. Who had somehow never mentioned a wife.

"You know my husband. He's your client."

Lennox crossed her arms.

"You don't have to answer. I know he is. I overheard him on the phone last week, and I've been so upset ever since. I can't sleep. I forget to kiss my children good night. I have no appetite. It's just—" She began to cry in earnest.

The two goons in the front seat muttered between themselves. They were now off the bridge, into North Kansas City, and caught in a stream of traffic heading for the Pendergast track. The trafficway was the best in town, four lanes of Pendergast cement, spanking new five years ago, and still far too special for a drive to see the ponies run. Low green junipers and cottonwoods dotted the dun-colored hills to the north, silhouetted against the hard prairie sky.

Marilyn Terraciano collected herself. "Please, Miss Lennox, you can't tell Georgie you saw me, or that we talked. Please."

"I don't speak to Georgie very often," she said.

"I can count on you?"

Lennox watched the woman. Something was battering the inside of her heart. "You can count on me."

"Okay." Marilyn took a deep breath. When she spoke again, she kept her voice low. "I don't need to go into details of what I heard. But the important part is, I know about *her*."

Lennox waited, unwilling to help the woman, as vulnerable and hurt as she seemed to be.

"Please, Miss Lennox."

"What is it you want from me?"

She rolled her bloodshot blue eyes. "Can't you see?" she hissed. "I know my husband has a girl on the side. I found out last week. I also found out you've been following her. You know all about her. You must . . . *you must* tell me everything." She batted her damp lashes. "I'll pay you, of course."

She began to open her purse. Lennox put out a hand. "Please, Mrs.—Marilyn. Don't." The woman looked up. "I can't tell you anything. Even if I knew anything, which I don't."

"But you've been following her—you must know."

Lennox shook her head. "Only the very basics. And I can't tell you because, you know, it wouldn't be right."

"It's certainly not right that he's . . . he's catting around!"

"That's not my business."

"It seems like it is. You follow them on their . . . their clandestine adventures, see how they dance, how they hold each other." She was making herself sick.

"I never saw them together. It was only a week."

Marilyn put her hankie to her forehead now, squeezing her eyes shut. "But he went out almost every night. And then she . . . she called last night."

A crowd in a ragtop drove up next to them, a bottle of wine passed around, laughing, music on the radio, hair in the wind.

"She called?"

"Her voice sounded so familiar, so smooth, the way she said his name, I knew it was her. He was out. God knows where." Mrs. Terraciano looked up at Lennox, squinting again.

"Did she say who she was?"

"Well, she made up a name, I could tell it wasn't hers. Said something like, 'Miss Jackson from Armour Packing.' "

"Jackson?"

"No girlfriend uses her real name when she calls up at home. This may never have happened to me before, Miss Lennox, but I know about these things."

They came to the gate of the large unpaved parking lot by the racetrack, pulled through, and parked in a spot near a dozen other dusty cars. The wind was blustery out here in the country, blowing dirt in five directions. The ragtop they'd passed on the trafficway pulled in next to them, full of squeals and laughter.

"Did you tell Georgie?"

"I couldn't. I was so upset. To think she had the nerve, the gall to call up the family home. Where his children eat and sleep." Marilyn clenched her fists and threw herself back against the seat. "That man! What am I going to do? You have to help me, Miss Lennox. What is her name? Where does she live? I have to know."

"This call was last night?"

"Yes. Sometime after seven. That's when he went out." Marilyn leaned forward again, touching Lennox on the knee with a gloved finger. "I'll hire you. You find out all you can about her. What's your daily rate? Ten dollars a day? Twelve? Make it fifteen a day for the rest of the week. Report to me on Friday."

She would have made a swell general. But these troops weren't going to fight. But if Lennox wouldn't hop to, some detective would. As the woman wronged, she would find somebody. She was what they called "a motivated client." Keeping her dangling might be what Georgie wanted.

"I'll think about it, Marilyn. I know how you feel and—"

The car door Lennox was leaning on opened suddenly, letting in a rush of wind and grit. She caught herself with the strap on the back of the driver's seat. Harvey Talbot stood in the open door, grabbing for her. His eyes were frantic, his face red.

"Talbot!"

"Come on, before these goons get into the act." He had one foot against the driver's door, and Luther was pressing the other side door closed with both hands.

"It's all right. My business is done." She tugged back her arm. "I'll see what I can do, Marilyn. No promises." She climbed out of the car and gave a merry wave to the thugs in the front. She smoothed her blouse. "Nice to see you, too, Talbot."

"Go, Luther!"

Harvey clasped Lennox's arm and dragged her around the car, down the aisle of autos, between a school bus and a Buick and two Plymouths, by an open-topped Willys, and down the next aisle. He threw her into his green Chrysler. *Thrown into another car. Just my luck. But the look of triumph on Harvey's face made it worthwhile. My hero.*

"Lock the doors! Quick!" Harvey spat as Luther hurdled inside. He turned to Lennox. "What's so funny?"

"Nothing." She tried to collect herself. The fear, then the rage, were still bottled up inside her, making her hysterical. "You looked so hell-bent." She put her hand over her mouth, forced her face serious. "Thank you for rescuing me, Harvey. Luther, thank you."

"We followed you all the way from t-t-town," Luther said. "Like in the p-p-pictures."

"Must have been thrilling," Lennox said. A chuckle exploded out of her.

Talbot turned back to the steering wheel, a black look on his face. Lennox leaned forward. "You must have thought the worst when you saw me get thrown into that car. I did, too, until I saw the lady."

"Lady?"

"Wife of a client. Wanted to know all. But, you know me, I didn't squawk."

Talbot's nostrils flared. He peered up at the stands of the racetrack, the white-painted boards bright in the noontime sun.

Outside, the wind died down and the sounds from passersby were muffled. He said, "Anybody want to place a bet?"

Lennox looked back to where Marilyn's car had been. A dark red sedan was pulling into the spot. What did the call to Georgie mean? Was someone playing a prank? How sly had Georgie been? Sly enough that his wife had just found out. Was someone blackmailing him? Had Iris been his girlfriend? Amos didn't think so, and, judging from Georgie's reaction to her death, neither did Lennox. Iris was dead, so who called for Georgie using her name?

The two men were staring at her when she looked up.

"What?"

Luther said, "The races."

"What about them?"

"Do you want to go?" Harvey said. He'd slumped low in the seat.

"I don't know. Do you?"

"No money," Luther said.

A stream of women dressed in summer halter dresses and sun hats, accompanied by men in seersucker suits and straw hats, walked behind the car toward the track. Harvey started the car, pulled out, spun gravel, and turned toward the city.

Lennox was quiet—they all were—as they headed back to the bridge and the city. Did Marilyn know Iris was dead? Obviously not; the threat was still real to her. What had Georgie wanted with Iris? What connected them? The first question, and now the last. She smiled to herself. Probably not her very last question.

"This is a very nice car, Harve," Luther said in the silence.

"Thanks, fella," Talbot replied, then jerked his head to look at the unshaven face. Lennox looked at him, too. His voice was calm, smooth, like his street recital.

Lennox wanted to hear him talk. "Luther, did you like that book I lent you?"

"Some of it," he said. He turned in the seat to face her,

dirty fingers over the seat back. "It was sad, Miss Lennox. Very sad."

"Yes, I guess it was. I'm sorry it made you sad," she said.

"Sad and happy don't mean that much to me anymore. Maybe they did once." He smiled a toothy, melancholy smile. "The book reminded me of a man I knew once. I'd forgotten about him, but reading that book, it was like he was back."

Harvey looked at her, then said to the bum: "It's a great-looking day, isn't it? So sunny and clear."

They turned onto the Hannibal Bridge, its girders flashing shadows across the windows, light/dark, light/dark. Luther looked up at the sky. "A perfect day for a picnic at the beach."

Talbot caught her eye again. "Yes, isn't it, Miss Lennox?"

The river below them shimmered, full of antediluvian life. The number from Talbot's article tolled: forty-two jumpers. Yet the muddy water could be as thrilling as counting ants at a Labor Day picnic.

A plan was hatched to take a basket of fruit and cold cuts down to a sandy bank of the Missouri. Lennox talked about apples as if she'd only heard their taste described in fairy tales. Luther mentioned a creamy golden cheese he'd eaten once. Talbot waxed musical about ice-cold bottles of beer.

Then the spell broke, a spun-sugar dream. As soon as the Chrysler stopped on Charlotte Street, the hobo looked at them as if they'd kidnapped him, then jumped from the car and ran around the corner, out of sight.

Harvey sat with both hands on the steering wheel, staring after him. Finally, he said, "What was that?"

"How did the two of you get—"

He put his forehead against the wheel. "I thought he was an interesting character. I thought maybe if he opened up to me, I could write a piece on him."

"He certainly opened up."

"Not really."

"Well, something happened in this car." Lennox climbed

out of the backseat. She looked at the reporter, who was still holding his forehead against the big steering wheel, as if it contained the answers to life's questions.

"I can give you her name now."

He turned his head. "Huh?"

"The jumper," Lennox said. "I can give you her name. The cops should be checking out her place today."

His mood changed, right there on his face, and he jumped from the car. "Okay, shoot," he said, drawing out his notebook and pencil. His transformation was almost as complete as Luther's.

"You just want her name?"

"Anything you can give me, Miss Lennox. That'd be swell." His eagerness was impossible to hate. So hopeful, so childlike.

"Since we're not going on that picnic, I've got somewhere else in mind. No apples or cheese."

Lennox had given him Iris's name and address by the time they drove the short distance to the Hot Cha Cha Club. He took a moment to scribble them down before looking at the street, nearly deserted on a holiday afternoon. He followed her down the cracked sidewalk, around the dried-up orange peels and rusted bean cans, by the alley with garbage bins and trash and heaps of rags. More pleasant with nighttime shadows. The odor of rotten fruit followed them from the alley.

"Ever been here before?" she asked at the door.

Talbot squinted at the faded storefront, scummy plate glass, tattered mat. "Haven't had the pleasure."

Lennox opened the door. The front of the saloon was a jumble of mismatched wooden tables and chairs, empty at this hour. Renovation here consisted of sledgehammer and broom. A wall had been torn down, the one that separated the phony butcher shop front from the speakeasy, and now a wide ragged line ran down both walls and across the ceiling. The same scuffed wood floor continued through the back portion, where exposed brick, pressed tin, and mouse droppings dominated the decorating theme.

They paused in the blue-green light struggling through the plate glass, reluctant to venture into the back of the joint, where shadowy figures hunched around tables.

"Now it all makes sense," Talbot muttered. "Do we dare have a beer?"

They were served two cold drafts, a significant improvement over the Chatterbox's refrigeration methods, at a scarred table. Lennox had glimpsed the bartender through the window: red-haired, stout, smiling. Whether he was the one she'd talked to on the phone, she wasn't sure.

The cold beer perked Talbot up. "So," he said, leaning in, "what are we doing here? Checking her background?"

"Drink your beer, ace."

Their eyes adjusted to the dim room. Afternoon revelers sat morosely over glasses of brew. They wore the uniforms of barges, trains, and streetcars, grimy with the grit of the hot, windy day. The air had the ripe quality of sweat, grease, and hops. Lennox took a sip, pushed back her chair, walked to the bar.

"Say," she said, smiling to the barkeep, "my friend Iris works here. Is she around today?"

The bartender's face flattened. "No, and don't expect her."

"She quit?"

"Disappeared. Took a powder."

"Just like that?"

He hiked his shoulders. "Left a pile of stuff, too. But managed to pick up her check before she took off."

Lennox turned to survey the bar, put her elbows up behind her. "This happen a lot, girls just taking off?"

"Infernal cheek. She my girl, she'd get a whipping." He wiped the bar near her elbows. She lifted them and turned back. "I never trusted that one. She was the type to rob the till while your back was turned."

"Did she?"

He shook his head. "I keep my eyeballs peeled. But you could tell something was always whirling inside her head. She's not stupid." He slapped the rag into his hand. "I saw her at the end of the bar one night, just standing there like the Queen of Sheba. Like she was going to rule some grand kingdom and it was only a matter of time."

"Sounds a little scary."

"She didn't scare me. And you know what? I'm glad she quit." He screwed up his eyes, then looked at the ceiling. "Don't ever want to see that witch's face again."

The way his eyes sagged as he said it, the way his voice lost its piqued edge—he was hurt by her disappearance, and at least half in love with cold, pretty Iris.

"Good old Iris. She must have brightened up the place a little. You got another girl now?"

The bartender swung his head from side to side. Lennox went on: "I could take that stuff she left off your hands. Haul it over to her place."

He shook himself. "Why not."

Lennox followed him into the back, to a green bathroom with a rust-ringed toilet and a small closet where the girls changed clothes. In the bottom sat an old muslin feed bag, which the bartender pulled out and handed to her. Extra shoes, he said, and turned off the light as they left.

Lennox found Talbot chatting up a table of streetcar drivers, their jackets unbuttoned and hats on the table. He had them laughing, beating hands on the table at some joke. She looked at the reporter and nodded toward the door. On the sidewalk, she showed him the bag.

"Some of her stuff, a pair of shoes and a blouse, it looks like. Not much."

Harvey led her to the car. "Those streetcar hacks are regulars; they remember her. A customer grabbed her one night. She said she'd let some chump do that to her once, but never again. Then she coldcocked him."

"My kinda gal." Lennox flexed her right hand. Her knuckles were swollen. It felt good having somebody to talk to about Iris. Maybe too good. Soon she'd be telling him about Atchison, about Beloit, all the sorry details. She told herself to trot as she slipped into the Chrysler. "Did they say anything else?"

Talbot flopped into the driver's seat and drummed his fingers along the steering wheel. "She liked tips. She would fawn over a guy she thought had money." He looked at her. "We going to do this together? 'Cause if we are, we have to tell each other everything."

Lennox looked out the side window. He took hold of her wrist, pulled her toward him. "Hey," she said, startled.

"Why can't we help each other? You don't have to tell me who you were tailing her for. Tell me what it was like. Were you on the bridge with her?"

The image of Iris on the bridge, the swaying of the rails below, the smell of the water, the mist rising from it—it was all too clear. Then, suddenly, the dream mixed into it, and Lennox was on the bridge herself, struggling with someone. But who—Iris?

He touched her cheek.

She pulled away. "I can't tell you, Talbot. I have clients."

"You want to find out what happened to her, don't you? Isn't that why you're still snooping around?"

"We know what happened to her."

"But why did she do it? She wasn't just another despondent jumper. She was a girl who slugged fellas when they got fresh, who had plans for the future, who wanted to be rich, comfortable."

"How do you know that?" Lennox squinted at him. His dark hair had draped over his forehead again.

"I know people. That's my business. Don't you see? She wanted something; this dive was only a stepping-stone. But something happened."

"No kiddin'."

"I mean something happened in here." He tapped his chest. "She lost that drive, that oomph, whatever it was."

An old Model A, rattling like crazy, passed on the street. "She left a note."

"You read it?"

She nodded.

"Well? What did it say?"

"Didn't want to live. Estranged from everyone she loved. She wrote somebody a little ditty. Something like, 'Wherever you are, my lost lamb, there will be stars burning. We'll be together soon.' "

"Poetic. Wonder who he was."

It was poetic. Romantic, too. And so out of character it made the mystery of Iris even murkier. "Nobody knows about a boyfriend. At least nobody I've talked to." Unless you counted Georgie, and she wasn't.

" 'We'll be together soon.' That sounds like he's already dead."

She hadn't thought of that. Together in heaven, or hell.

Talbot sighed. "Dead boyfriends aren't much help. Maybe she was in love with a lamb. We could interview him. Baaaaa."

"I wish I knew more about her. She's a blank slate."

"Didn't she go anywhere when you followed her?"

"Straight home from work. Oh, the first night, Amos went with me. She went to this dance at the Muehlebach. By herself."

"But not for long, I bet."

"There were a few wolves after her. One looked like you."

"I wasn't there, honest." He threw up both hands. It was getting to be his personal salute. "I was home taking a bath at the time, your honor."

"She was different that night. Wore a green satin dress, very classy. Gold earrings. That hair, it was like a siren. Like Jean Harlow in *Bombshell.*"

"Sounds like she was her own bombshell." He leaned back in the seat and turned his head to her. "Who was that woman in the black car? You can tell me, off the record."

"Off the record? That's a joke."

"Did it have to do with Iris Jackson?"

"Listen." Now she took his wrist, just to see what it did to his face. "Could we get something to eat? I'm starved."

He looked at her fingers, then took her hand in both of his.

"You always seem to be hungry, Miss Lennox. All right. On one condition. You have to like barbecue." He moved her finger to his mouth as if it were a spicy rib. Her body felt like the heat was searing it, a flash of fire. She snatched her hand away.

"Course I like barbecue." She took a breath, ran her damp palms down her slacks. "I live in Kansas City, don't I?"

TEN

AMOS HADDAM read the *Kansas City Star* inside his oxygen tent and felt worse with each story: 650,000 children evacuated from London alone. Dry-eyed soldiers in Warsaw and Paris and Berlin, quietly accepting a fate long foreseen. The previous war's costs—the First World War they were calling it now—tallied up with disgust: 8.5 million lives lost, $338 billion down the warlord drain. A peace that never lived up to that cost—starvation, inflation, depression, more starvation. Not to mention a simmering legacy of hate and fear.

The worst thing in the paper, though, was the sinking of the *Athenia*. He stared at the photo of the listing ship, going down in the Atlantic halfway to Iceland from the Hebrides, full of American refugees fleeing the fighting. He read about the rescues, how methodically it had gone while the ship hung, fatally injured. How the able seamen had calmed the hysterical women, loaded the lifeboats, saved them all. No panicked girls jumping into the icy sea, not this time.

He read the details, down to the end. WHITE HOUSE HORRIFIED . . . STEAMER CARRIED NO MUNITIONS. The only casualties were "some persons killed by explosion of the torpedo . . . all others picked up by rescue vessels." A miracle, all saved. No girls lost, no panic, no drowning.

He rattled the pages until he could stand it no longer. The newspaper collapsed under his hands, a paper lump now, wrinkled in his sickened grip.

Throwing the crushed newsprint on the floor, he listened to the sounds of the ward. The squeak of nurse's shoes was hard to detect, but it seemed there were few patients in the hospital. All who could had gone home. And why, by God, was he still here?

He took a deep breath and tested his lungs. They had been worse. They had been better, too. A cough was mildly productive. His fever was better; his forehead felt cool enough. He lay still, counting to ten, then swung his legs to the floor, pushed aside the oxygen tent, and sat up. Next to his bed was his supper, congealed goo, gelled rubber mystery meat, withered fruit. Desertion had its blessings. He thought about a bratwurst from a street vendor and his mouth watered.

He found his clothes hanging on the back of the door and he slipped into the water closet. This private room had its own facilities, which was handy now that he was springing himself. Dressed in the blood-spattered shirt and suit, he struggled to put on his shoes and socks, then wet down his hair. The clerk in Emergency was kind enough to call him a cab.

Like a schoolboy playing hooky, he escaped. The acrid chemical smell of the office greeted him. He fell into his comfortable old chair, swiveled a little for old times' sake, then surveyed the views. Out the west window a slice of the river between a warehouse and an office building, a shimmering twinkle in the dingy city. To the south, the streetcars clanged. Two cars were parked across the street, a blue Nash and a farm truck loaded with chickens. He sat still in an effort to calm his breathing after climbing the stairs.

He stared at the telephone. Only work would take his mind, and his nerves, off the war news. So, to work. He'd never had a telephone number for Palmer Eustace. Vanvleet sent and received all information. He rang Herb's number and told him he'd been sprung from the croaker bin.

"You're okay, then?" Herb asked.

"Couldn't be better. I have a favor to ask. Could you call

your pal Willie O'Brian in detectives and have him run some sheets for me?"

"Forget about work. Maureen made a peach pie."

"Sounds good. But, Herbert, old boy, call O'Brian for me. Need a poop sheet on two sharpers, names Palmer Eustace and Floyd Wilson."

Herb agreed, reluctantly, and Amos said to save him a piece of pie, although he would have to take a cab. They were too far from the streetcar line and he didn't feel safe driving, in his condition. He might black out and kill somebody. He checked his pocket watch, leaned back in the chair, and propped his feet up on the desk.

His eyelids felt weak. He'd give O'Brian an hour.

Almost three hours later—his eyelids were weaker than he thought—Amos Haddam heaved himself up to the second floor of police headquarters, making use of all handrailings, and cursing the Jerries again. He hadn't been so anti-German for at least a decade, when the crash had left him and everybody else with bigger worries. Not that he hadn't tried to forget about the trenches and the gas and all of it. But the news of the weekend brought back the old feelings. It sapped his strength, he once thought, to hate so much, but now it felt good, a purging of poisons from a toxic vessel.

The detectives' room was at the far end of the hall, behind wood-paneled walls, frosted glass, and a sea of desks. Because of the holiday, a skeleton crew manned the phones. The first detective Amos encountered told him O'Brian was boating today.

"But Captain Warren gave me the details." The young detective in rolled-up shirtsleeves and braces picked up a sheet of paper from his report-strewn desk. Like half the cops in the city, this one was new at the job. Amos remembered him on a beat downtown a few months before.

"Palmer Eustace. That the name? No such person in Kansas

City. I checked all the outlying areas, Johnson County, Independence, KCK. Nobody."

"You got the spelling right?"

"Tried it five different ways. Zilch, old man."

"All right. Word is, he's an owner of the Blue Valley Racetrack. That means he's not a local man like that reporter in the *Star* said today."

The detective pushed his brown felt hat back on his head. "Don't believe everything you read in the papers."

"Thanks for the tip, kid. What about Floyd Wilson?"

"Got six of 'em for you." The dick slid over the sheet of paper with addresses hand-lettered. "Tell me which one you want and I can go from there."

Amos had met Wilson on two occasions, once at the track and the other time with the auditor at the accounting office. He was sixtyish, a sharp dresser, and didn't miss a trick. Banking family, he knew, old money. But Amos hadn't gotten a home address—or a middle initial—damn! Haddam's brain felt stuffed with cotton. Did he have Wilson's number? Had Shirley given it to him? He was getting too decrepit for this legwork.

"Can I keep this?"

The cop smiled. "Be my guest."

Amos turned to go, then had a new thought. "Can you run me the corporation papers for the track?"

The detective lost his grin. "I ain't your lackey, chum."

A surge of energy snapped him to attention. "You coppers still taking bribes from the so-called locals?"

The young dick turned scarlet. "You got no call—"

"I'll just tell Herbert you were too damn sweet with the Blue Valley boys to question their sincerity." He sat on the edge of the detective's desk. "What's your name? For when I get back to Herbert."

The dick threw back his chair and stomped out of the room. Amos let his hero's posture relax and coughed to clear his throat. The energy was gone now. He felt light-headed and feverish. Wheezing, he mopped his wet brow. In ten minutes, the detective resurfaced.

"All in order, mac." The young cop tossed him the corporation documents for Blue Valley Racing, Incorporated. President was Floyd Wilson (no middle initial—a phony name?) vice president, Palmer Eustace. Wilson's address was the Blue Valley Racetrack itself, a rural box on the Ridgeway. Very helpful. An address for Eustace was given, on Tracy Avenue.

Amos looked up at the detective, thought about pointing out the address. But it was probably a vacant lot. Anyway, he'd find out, and the cop didn't need to care one way or the other. Besides, he didn't have the energy to fight about it.

He scribbled down the information in his blue notebook, snuggling it next to Eugenia's slim book in his jacket pocket. On his way down the stairs, black spots began to swim before his eyes. He had to stop twice and put his head down low by his knees.

When the late-afternoon sun hit him on the front steps of police headquarters, it felt like the devil's own blast furnace. Good God Almighty. Haddam swayed, grabbed the railing, and made it down a few steps. His guts felt ready to explode, his head a ripe watermelon.

Through the buzz in his ears and the glare off his eyeballs, he saw the woman waving. She stood by a car—that blue Nash again? A vision in a red dress. She'd cut her beautiful dark hair, but it was her, wasn't it? She was older, but then, Eugenia would be older, wouldn't she?

He toppled down four stairs, bent over the railing. His head swam. Besides the black spots, twinkling lights sparkled in his vision, dancing on the heat waves.

He called to her. Would she come? *Eugenia! Darling!*

The railing slipped from his fingers. He felt a wild euphoria. She had come back to him, his Eugenia. And he could tell her there had never been another. He had been true. All these years, he'd been true.

He was smiling as his head hit the granite stair with a clunk. The pain was nothing. Nothing mattered but Eugenia.

She'd come back.

ELEVEN

WHAT IS IT?"

Lennox turned in Talbot's Chrysler to get a better look at the Nash as they passed City Hall. "Her car, I think."

Talbot slammed on the brakes. "Where?" The tires slid. The Chrysler came to a stop on the corner north of police headquarters. Lennox pointed out the blue jalopy.

"They must have towed it over. Or some toughs got caught in it." She sat back in the seat. "Anyway, I already rifled through it and found nothing." Except those damn keys. Where could they fit? Lennox followed his gaze to the police HQ stairs, where a small crowd had formed.

"Must be a fight," he said. "There've been a few there." He put the car in gear and eased off. "Wife turning in husband for beating her, have another row just to prove it. Thug shoots his buddy, who is about to rat on him, adding a murder charge for good measure."

"Damn hot day for a fight." Lennox sat in the blast of heated air coming through the window. The barbecue feed at Bryant's had been an animal frenzy, a gnawing and gnarling and baring of teeth. She licked her still-sticky fingers, the sweet-hot sauce more pleasant than she deserved. She thought suddenly of Louie Weston, duffing around the golf course with the old man. Louie Weston would never take her for barbecue. He was nothing but bad luck, for herself, for her friend, for everyone. She tried to hold on to that thought, but it was too hot for heavy thoughts.

"Well, we won't fight then, will we?" he said, smiling. He turned around a corner, making a sudden decision. "What if you were so hot, you could just melt?"

"I've been that way about seventy-five times this summer. I survived."

"But if you could do something about it, where would you go? To the river?"

"No. Not the river."

"Take some cold beers, lie in the sand, dangle your toes in the current. . . ."

"Not the river." She glanced at him. Sweat dripped down his temple. "I was kidding about the picnic. I knew Luther wouldn't really go." She stuck her head out the window.

"Okay, I get ya. No rivers. I always go upstream from the packing plants, but I know what you mean."

He was staring at her as he drove. She felt like a ninny.

"Listen, Talbot. I changed my mind. Head down to the city wharf, will you?"

They bumped over the railroad tracks that crisscrossed over Delaware Street, until there was no farther to go. Front Street ran up to the wharf where the steamboat she'd seen Friday floated on the muddy water. The barges had gone, but a small tugboat was tied up behind the steamboat.

"This is where they found her, isn't it?" Talbot climbed out of the parked car and squinted into the sun.

He followed Lennox down the thick wood planks to where two stevedores lounged against a piling. They straightened as the two approached.

"Hey, fellas," Lennox said. They nodded. Talbot reached out a hand and they shook it.

"Harvey Talbot, *Kansas City Star*. This is my assistant, Doria Lennox."

She tripped on a piece of the dock and glared at him.

"We heard you fellas found a body down here yesterday."

The fatter stevedore, dressed in huge overalls, shook his

head. The thinner one said, "That was Manny." He was muscled from hauling freight but sported a very bad haircut. He had a thick Slav or Romany accent. "Not work Sunday."

"Manny." Talbot got out his notebook and pencil. "Got a last name for Manny?"

The thin stevedore frowned and shook his head.

"When does Manny work next?"

Another shake and frown and blank. Talbot asked them their names and they clammed up completely.

"Come on, Talbot," Lennox said. "Thanks, fellas."

They turned back toward the street. The water lapped against the sides of the wharf. From the steamboat came the sounds of laughter. Business was brisk, the holiday mood in the air. Overhead, seagulls swooped, an incongruous sight so far inland.

"That was productive," Talbot said, walking at her side. "Did you think Manny's buddy was going to tell you what he stole off the body?"

Lennox turned to him. "What was that taking over back there?"

"You could have asked the questions. Nobody was stopping you."

"And suddenly I'm your assistant?" But she turned away. He was right, of course, but it didn't stop her from being angry with him.

What had she been thinking, bringing him in? She worked alone, or with Amos, not some scribbler. She would go home, check out the bag of Iris's clothes, make some solid progress. She reached the Chrysler and was about to open the door, when the bridge caught her eye. High and wide, with its tall stone piers plunging into the Missouri, the Hannibal Bridge swept across the wide expanse of the river. She spotted the place Iris must have jumped from; a tiny ladder led from the auto level down to the train level.

Her eye followed the line Iris would have made, into the

water. A long way down, a long way to contemplate death. Better not to stare death in the face. What you didn't think about couldn't hurt you: Lennox's credo of forgetfulness. If death caught you with your pants down, you were just as dead.

Standing on the Chrysler's bumper, she could see the cluster of fishing shacks on the marshy banks along the river. Railroad tracks curled along the edge of the marsh, then cattails and other reeds. Red-winged blackbirds sat perched above the stagnant pools. What's down there? she wondered. A fisherman in rubber boots and battered hat emerged onto the sidewalk on Woodswether, carrying a string of small fish. Scales flashed in the sunlight. His boots were covered with mud and green slime. He turned away from them and disappeared down the hill. No, she wouldn't go down to the river. Even to find some clue to Iris's demise.

Talbot stopped at a stop sign on Independence Boulevard and turned, putting his arm across the back of the seat. "What if there was another way to cool off, one that didn't involve rivers? What would you say to that?"

She looked at him, unable to revive the anger of minutes before. In a strange way, she felt grateful for the company. He must have friends, family, a picnic to attend, a baseball game to pitch. It was Labor Day. The streets were deserted; everyone was playing, boating, swimming, canoeing, having fun. She could go back and sit in her stuffy, hot room, which smelled like cauliflower, play her father's old jazz records on the gramophone, make herself sick in front of Mrs. Ferazzi's fan.

"I'd say you were damn persistent."

He fingered her damp hair. "A swimming pool," he whispered. "Cool, clean water."

She closed her eyes for a second, feeling the heat on every inch of skin, the sweat rolling down her chest between her breasts, damp pants stuck to the seat, her armpits sticky, her ears—even her ears were sweating!

"I don't have a suit," she heard herself say. "I'd have to go home."

The house was enormous, a mansion by Loose Park, sitting regally with white trim and tidy hedges, a sheltering overhang of eaves and dark purple brick. Through the shrubs and a wooden fence, the swimming pool glimmered, still and inviting.

His managing editor's place, Talbot said. Away for the weekend. He was keeping an eye on things. Feeding the cat.

Lennox changed in the small bathhouse, white tile cool against her toes, and slipped over the side of the cement edge into the blue coolness. She didn't care whose house it was, whose pool, but God bless. Liquid heaven, seeping into her ears, over her head, into her scalp and hair. She let herself drop to the bottom and bob up.

"Watch this." Talbot did a cannonball off the board. The splash rocked her. She had no great notions for showing off; just lolling in the coolness was all too luscious.

She closed her eyes and hooked the back of her neck over the gutter, letting her legs float up. Talbot's hand pressed against her back, pushing her to the surface.

"You're smiling, Miss Lennox."

She opened one eye. "Getting the barbecue sauce washed off at last."

"I told you I'd help you with that," he said, licking her chin, her cheeks. He paused, but she kept smiling. Then he licked her lips. Her mouth, kissing her. When she put her arms around his neck and kissed him back, she tried not to think. On a day when the weather takes over your body, your mind simply follows.

They fell back in the shallow end. She pressed him against the wall of the pool, a water animal cornering its prey. He tasted like salt, and cigarettes, and cinnamon. She pulled his hair with her hands until he moaned under her mouth.

"Sorry," she said, and dunked him. He gulped to the surface

and dunked her. She twisted away and came up five feet away, laughing. "Is this what you mean by working together?"

He put on a mock frown, water dripping across his cheek from the hank of disobedient hair. "No." He grabbed her hand, pulled her toward him. "We need to have a much closer working relationship. Don't we, Miss Lennox?"

"Is that what you want, Mr. Talbot?"

He slipped his hands inside the back of her suit and moved her into the shady corner of the pool.

"Call me Harvey."

"What do you want, Harvey?"

"No—what the fuck do you want, Harvey?"

"Oh, what the fuck, Talbot."

They kneeled on the gritty concrete bottom of the pool and he cupped her breasts in his warm hands.

A quiver of fear went through her, unbidden, there in the shade. He was kissing her neck. The face of that man, the one back in Atchison who wrestled her into his car, came back to her. That man, who gave her back her love of her blade. That man, who made Verna send her away. She gasped, and Harvey stopped what he was doing and looked in her eyes.

Her mother would have liked Harvey Talbot. Verna liked 'em short and tall, skinny and fat, rich or poor. She didn't discriminate. She always said she just liked men, liked the way they made her feel, that special, wanted feeling she could get nowhere else. Even if you couldn't trust them, even if they hurt you, she liked men. Verna was like that.

Lennox reached up and smoothed Talbot's haphazard black eyebrows. She wasn't Verna, but she felt that need. But she didn't want to be lost. She had been lost and knew how that felt. She squeezed her eyes shut. She was thinking too much.

He leaned close to her ear, pressed his rough cheek against hers. "It's all right," he whispered.

She examined his face again, as if the future were hidden there, tea leaves to be read in the flecks of his irises. He had the most beautiful mouth.

Was it all right? Who was he? A reporter who had been pumping her for information, a man, yes, but first a reporter.

She pushed roughly out of his arms, backed up to the side of the pool. "Is this—is this about Iris? For information about Iris?"

Talbot flipped back his hair. The gesture somehow confirmed her worst fears. "Is that what you think?"

She hoisted herself out of the pool, pulled her knees to her chest. "Tell me you weren't thinking about Iris just now. Tell me."

He said nothing, just looked at her as if she'd lost her mind. Maybe she had. But something had snapped inside her and she couldn't change it. Not now.

She went toward the bathhouse and picked up her towel. Talbot climbed out of the pool, his long limbs tanned and strong. He looked smug, standing with his hands on his hips, dripping under the elm tree.

"Tell me, Talbot."

"I wasn't thinking about Iris. I was thinking about you. Would that be so strange?"

She shook her head. "I don't believe you."

"Dorie," he said, taking a step toward her.

She stepped back, holding the towel over her chest. His hair was dripping across his forehead, falling into his eyes. She couldn't look at his eyes now. She felt too open, too ready to believe him. He would use her, use that feeling against her.

She wiped the water off her face with the towel. Why couldn't she be like Verna, just have the moment and move on? People had called Verna a whore and a slut, but she'd been happy, hadn't she? But Dorie had never wanted to be like Verna. And now perhaps she was doomed to be the opposite.

Lennox felt dizzy, as if the world was spinning too fast, as if she'd forgotten to eat, to drink, to sleep, forgotten how to live, how she *had* lived, every day. It had to stop.

"I have to go," she said.

TWELVE

THE HEAVY SWEETNESS OF TWILIGHT descended on Janssen Place. The air was punctuated with shouts of children playing in the street and down along Hyde Park's sloping lawns. The yellow begonias on the Vanvleets' porch hung dully from shiny leaves.

Lennox parked in front and headed up the walk, trying to frame the words for her lack of progress. The old man was unlikely to let it slide; he would have words, recommendations, recriminations. There was a reason for his daily reports, even on weekends and holidays. He expected progress, round the clock.

Diligent, that was his word, but she had been anything but diligent today. Reckless, indulging in fantasies, from flying in airplanes to— A wave of shame washed over her. Why was she being so touchy? She felt bile rise in her stomach.

The voice from the shadows of the porch startled her. "The country girl, am I right? Come to take tea with us this evening?"

The old woman flounced on the porch swing. She pushed out a toe and made her seat rock, chain creaking. Lennox turned toward her. "Ma'am."

"A fine evening, my dear. Please sit down."

Mrs. Vanvleet wore a simpler dress this evening, but one that had seen better years, a pleated white-and-blue cotton print with a wide white collar that framed her proud head and the upswept hair. A WCTU ax-wielder with that glint of madness in her eyes. Lennox's hair was still damp from the pool. The ride back to the boardinghouse with Talbot had been agonizing and silent. She eased into a white wicker chair with a dusty blue cushion.

"Such a pleasant summer evening," the old woman murmured. "One of the last, I suppose. I have such a morbid feeling this evening, as if we won't be allowed to enjoy evenings anymore. As if taking the air will be unpatriotic."

The old woman rang a small bell on the table in front of her and called for someone named Totty. In a moment, iced tea with lemon was being served by the maid.

The old woman sipped her tea and said, "You *have* heard about the Germans, my dear."

"Yes, ma'am."

"Quite distressing, don't you think?" Although her words were appropriate, the old woman kept her tone breezy. She sipped her tea, rocking in the porch swing.

"Very." Lennox put down her tea. "Is Mr. Vanvleet in tonight?"

"My boy Dick fought the Germans. He died there. So many boys killed. It doesn't make much sense to me to take fine, healthy boys and put guns in their hands. I suppose we have no choice. Dick was my oldest, a fine, fine boy, in law school when he enlisted."

"I'm sorry, ma'am."

Mrs. Vanvleet gazed at the twilight hanging over the street. "And the Polish! No one really cares very much about the Polish as a people—it's not as if they've really contributed to the world's literature or art or great thinkers—but it is the principle of the thing. One cannot simply drop bombs on other people, can one? With no good reason?"

Good God. "No, ma'am." Where was the old man?

"So glad you came properly dressed today, my dear."

Lennox tried to smile, smoothing her green cotton skirt.

"The world is becoming such a place, such an awful place,

that certain customs are so very necessary. So, so very . . ." Her voice faded off as her eyes wandered the yard, from bush to flower and back.

"Excuse me, ma'am. Is Mr. Van—"

The old woman jumped to her feet. "Stop that, you wicked children! Stop it this instant!" She shook a finger at three children running down the sidewalk. They hit each and every upright in the iron fence with sticks, making a tommy-gun prattle.

The children shrieked and kept running, lost in the purple light. Mrs. Vanvleet eased back into the porch swing, causing the chain to groan. She put her hand across her forehead and eyes for a moment, a long-fingered, freckled, jeweled hand. Then came up smiling again.

"Where were we? Is your tea sweet enough? Can Totty get you some crackers?" She tinkled the bell again. "Totty! Cheese and crackers!"

Lennox sat forward on her chair. "Mrs. Vanvleet, I need to speak to your husband. Is he at home, ma'am?"

Totty arrived with a tray. Lennox picked up the thread, afraid it was hopelessly lost: "Is he home?"

The old woman arched her neck. "Well. No. He has gone to watch horse racing. Not that I dislike the sport so much. The horses can be so beautiful, so wickedly strong and healthy. You must know what I mean, young country miss."

The lewd glint in her eye embarrassed Lennox. She looked away, ate a cracker and a slice of cheddar. The woman was batty. And Vanvleet wasn't here. She felt a keen disappointment to miss the old man tonight. Strange, that disappointment, because he surely would have upbraided her for doing nothing today. Work, the case, that was what she needed.

"But the men and women who congregate at the races," the old woman continued, "that is another matter. If Punky feels it is necessary to be there for business reasons, then, well, of course he must go. But to drive there with that odious Italian? I ask you, is it necessary for the neighbors to see that man in my driveway, that hideous automobile? Who drives a red car? I ask you. Not a businessman, no, and that Italian is no businessman."

Lennox ate another cracker.

"The Italians are in cahoots with the Germans, for heaven's sake. Just another reason that he should not be seen at my home. We can't afford scandal. No, I told Punky at supper, no scandal should come down on our children and grandchildren. No, never."

"They've gone off to the Pendergast track, then?"

"Good heavens, no. The Blue Valley track has lights, don't you know? Well, you are from the country. There is no night racing at the Pendergast track, child."

For a woman who hated racing, she certainly knew a lot about it.

"Then they went for the eight o'clock run?"

Mrs. Vanvleet blinked at her. "Silly thing. The run starts at nine."

Four heats had run by the time Lennox drove east, through the Blue Valley industrial district, then around the Mount Washington cemetery and south along Blue Ridge Boulevard. The sun had set over this no-man's-land between the city and the small towns to the east, over the fields and pastures, the clumps of houses. There was still enough country here, with whitewashed barns, cows and ducks, creeks and cottonwoods rippling their leaves in the evening breeze. Enough to lure people out of the smelly city, for a picnic, a little white cottage, a day at the track.

The Blue Valley track sat back from the highway, with a huge lighted sign of a speeding horse at its entrance. Impossible to miss, coming from any direction. Hundreds of cars filled the gravel lot, not much different from Pendergast's—same cars, same bettors, here to cover losses.

The stands were crowded with revelers hunched over racing forms, talking behind their hands, drinking beer in the evening heat. A buzz of conversation swirled like a cloud as she made her way to the top, near the betting windows. The floor was littered with discarded tickets. Jostled by the crowd intent on the pursuit of free money, Lennox felt her energy flagging. She would never find the old man in the crowd. But the track—she had been curious with all the news, and Amos's inquiry.

The announcer came on, blaring the information that betting was closing on the fifth race. Urgency drove the bettors into a fury. This might be the race. The one.

Lennox scanned the boxes for Vanvleet's bald pate, but that area was too far away, too crowded. Odious Georgie would be dressed in something flashy. But flash wasn't in short supply. Hot and tired, she wanted to leave. But if she stayed a little longer, she could say she had made a good effort to talk to Vanvleet. Tomorrow, he would smile his benign little smile, and she would be forgiven.

The fifth race was fast and furious. A grumble of disillusionment followed it, winners glared at by losers. A long wait for the sixth race. Lennox walked the betting floor, back and forth, going to the ladies' room, buying a soda, searching faces.

The sixth race was announced. Final odds were posted, Angel Blue, the favorite at three to one, Toby's Girl at seven to one, Twinkle Toes at fifteen to one, Silver Sensation at seventeen to one, and the long shot, Smitty's Dream, at thirty-five to one.

The windows closed and a hush of anticipation fell on the crowd. The horses and jockeys rattled in the metal gates. With a gunshot, the horses plunged forward, the crowd jeering, stamping feet. Angel Blue, dark and sleek, was an early lead rounding the first turn; then Silver Sensation, gray, with a black mane, took over. At the middle of the last turn, the long shot, Smitty's Dream, a dappled brown-and-white that looked about as much like a beer wagon dray horse as a thoroughbred, nosed into the lead. The crowd held its breath. By the time the horses crossed the finish line, Smitty's Dream had won by a length.

A poof of epithets crossed the air. Paper flew. A young man jumped to his feet, waving a ticket, then his hat, and scrambled to the aisle. Down in the front boxes, a woman in a yellow-plumed hat rose slowly. She made her way past the others in her box, clutching a ticket. Lennox strained to see her face, but it was shadowed by the hat.

With a clatter, the windows reopened and the winners lined up. Not many, since the long shot had won. Wouldn't it be a kick, Lennox thought, to have put a load on that horse? Like God came down and tapped you on the head.

Her feet hurt. It was 10:30 P.M. and she wanted to go home. There were two more races to go. She stretched, trying to relieve the ache in her back. It had been a long time since the flight with Louie Weston.

The winning horses were led around the track by trainers and owners, patted and fed and encouraged. Backslapping was rife. Smitty's Dream's jockey held a blue ribbon, its gold lettering flashing under the strong lights. A dark-haired man had his face next to the horse's neck, holding the bridle.

Lennox straightened. The man patted the neck of the horse, took the ribbon. Then he turned. It was Georgie Terraciano.

She moved down the aisles for a closer look. In a small clutch behind Georgie, one man stood above the others, on the edge of the group, watching. Tall, slicked-back hair: Reggie Vanvleet. Had he bet on the horse? Why wasn't he in line? No sign of the old man.

Thirty-five to one. A man could make a small fortune on a win like that. She ran up and scanned the lines at the betting windows again. The woman in the yellow hat was gone. In a baggy summer suit, shuffling his feet, was a large man with graying hair. He kept his face toward the window, pushed his ticket under the glass. There was a pause while the attendant called a man to her side. The supervisor nodded, squinted at the bettor, nodded again. The attendant counted out stacks of bills, pushed them under the glass in bundles.

Stashing wads of money in all his pockets, the man walked away quickly. He kept his face down. Lennox moved around a group of beer drinkers to follow him. When he rounded the corner to go down the stairs, he looked over his shoulder. The boxer's mug. Marilyn's thug, the driver.

Marilyn Terraciano, whose maiden name was Smith.

Charlotte Street was deserted. Inside the boardinghouse, only the kerosene lantern lit the hallway. Lennox tried to remember if she had any food stashed in her room. She tiptoed through the dining room and into the kitchen. The door creaked on its hinges. A small intake of air told her she wasn't alone.

At the kitchen table, her round shoulders hunched under a small light, sat Frankie with a book, reading.

"You scared me, child. Thought you was Mrs. F., catch me in here using her electricity."

"What are you doing reading this late?"

Frankie's dark fingers were pressed against the pages of the book propped on the table. Poppy's daughter liked food, and she had gotten into a few scrapes with Mrs. F. over eating the leftovers. In a plain blue sack dress, Frankie fingered her ear under stumpy braids.

"Might be asking you the same thing, sneaking around in the kitchen so late."

"I'm starving. I missed supper."

"Wasn't nothing worth writin' home about. There's some cold ham; I'll get it."

"I'll get it myself."

With a slab of ham and a mound of mustard, Lennox sat at the table across from the girl. She cut up the ham, dabbed it with mustard. Frankie's bright eyes watched her.

"You look different tonight, Miss Dorie. Flushed. The day too warm for you?"

"It was hot, Frankie." Lennox paused. "Do I look different?"

"Like something real excitin' happened to you today."

She chewed. The airplane ride with Louie Weston? Tarnished by Louie himself. But Talbot, he lingered on her like an essential oil. She swallowed and tried to smile. "What's going on, then—what're you reading?"

Frankie rolled her eyes. "Don't tell my ma, will ya? It's for this course I'm taking, and she don't know nothing about it."

"How do you take a course without her knowing?"

"I send things off to this professor."

"Oh, a correspondence course. What on?"

"Books. Literature. I gotta come over here at night so my ma don't see my light on."

"I'm glad to see you improving yourself, Frankie. I studied English in college."

Frankie's eyes rounded. "English? You?"

"What? I don't look like the brainy type?"

Frankie shook her braids and laughed. "Well." She wagged a plump finger. "Mrs. F. told me you was a runner. She says you was very, very fast. Like the wind."

Lennox sat back in the chair. "I had to take classes, too; that's kind of a rule they have at the university." She looked at Frankie's book. "When I was little, I lived at the library. Sort of a second home."

"Mrs. F. says you had to quit running 'cause you tore up your knee." She eyed Lennox. "You quit books, too?"

Majoring in English was just turning her back on the knuckle-headed pragmatism that had gotten her mother and everyone else she knew exactly nowhere. But it ended up at nowhere, too. What did the enjoyment of books have to do with the living and dying that made your life? Were the trials of the imaginary more keen, more true? Or was it just a way to forget? If that worked, she would read more.

"No, I didn't quit books. It's just not the same. What is this, then?"

She picked up Frankie's book by the spine. Kafka again. Christ, was the whole world reading him as an initiation rite to another glorious and incomprehensible war?

"Did you read it, Miss Dorie?"

"Don't call me *miss,* Frankie. Makes me feel like I'm living at Tara." She stuffed her mouth angrily and chewed. She didn't like to think about college, and all that might have been. Frankie was rubbing her arms self-consciously. Lennox swallowed. "I'm sorry. I didn't mean that. Yes, I read the book."

"Then you can tell me what it's about."

"Wish I could. I never took on a course with it."

"You quit college?"

"No running, no scholarship. No scholarship, no college." She finished the ham and took her plate to the sink. When she sat down again, she wanted to change the subject. "Look, you know Luther. Do you know where he's from, what he did?"

Frankie's fingers fidgeted with the paper edges. She put her scrap of paper into the crease and shut the book. "Don't know nothing."

Lennox watched her. Her braids twitched, one loosening from a red barrette. She fumbled, getting it clipped.

"What's his last name?"

"I got no idea, Miss D—uh. I got no idea who he is, where he come from, nothing. He just always been around on this street, on our street, too. He's jus' always there, his hand out for something."

Her voice inched up the scale, like that phony darkey thing the movies played up. Frankie never talked like that. She knew something. *I don't know nothin' about birthin' babies, Miss Scarlett.* Back at Tara again.

Frankie looked up. "You won't tell Mrs. F. I was here so late, will you?"

"Don't worry. And if you figure out what the book means, let me know."

The young woman smoothed her dress, then put her book

in one of its large pockets. When she opened the back door, the tinkling sound of piano music floated in.

"I'll do that, Miss—I'll do that."

Lennox woke at dawn, when the birds began to chirp outside in the big tree. Lying on the bed, she wondered if she'd insulted Frankie. She hoped not. She didn't have enough friends to lose even one. Had she made and lost two yesterday—Harvey and Louie? What a day. She sat up in bed and remembered what she should have done yesterday. The bartender.

Understandable, considering everything else that had happened. But unforgivable. She cursed loudly. She had been distracted and forgotten to do her job. Lennox covered her eyes with her hand and could still smell the racetrack on her skin, the earthy, horsey scent.

She had been dreaming again. This time, the bridge was gone. It was just her and a stranger. At the edge of the river, waves lapping at her feet. She felt cold, damp, alone. The way she'd felt when Verna died.

Lennox pulled her hand off her face. Damn, she'd forgotten Amos, too. She would call first thing, after she got hold of Vanvleet.

She rolled over in bed, buried her face in the pillow. What about Talbot? She had accused him of pumping her for information. She moaned and put the pillow over her head. Where had he gone last night after he took her home? Probably to visit one of his other "skirts." No doubt he had plenty of them. Wouldn't he, with hands like that?

She sat bolt upright again and slapped herself on the cheek, hard enough to get the job done. She let out a long breath and put her feet on the floor.

Then whispered in her best James Cagney: "Knock it off, sweetheart."

THIRTEEN

SOMETHING LOOKED WRONG on Fifth Street. For midmorning, it was too busy, the wrong kind of busyness, with pedestrians rooted to the sidewalk, arms folded, huddled. Lennox parked the Packard next to the mattress warehouse and sat for a minute.

She hadn't been able to reach Amos or his nurse Helen this morning at City Hospital. Today was the day he'd said he might get out, but he would have called her for a ride. He wouldn't have taken the streetcar home, would he? And he wasn't at home or the office, either.

Her last view of the Chatterbox that night, with Iris stepping out into the rosy light: What was it that nagged at her? No, she thought, not here, but at the Hot Cha Cha. The slow, deliberate way Iris Jackson had buttoned up her jacket. Like she was waiting for someone, something. Had she waited for Lennox, till the rummies moved on?

Lennox picked up the compact on the seat. Down the street, two uniformed cops appeared on the sidewalk, heads down, talking. She took another look at the Chatterbox, but its small dark windows showed nothing.

The powder was caked hard inside the compact. When she'd found it at the bottom of the bag of clothes the bartender had given her, it hadn't seemed significant. A scratched gold-colored shell-shaped compact with old face powder and a flattened, oily puff inside. On the lid, under the scratches of use and abuse, was an inscription, initials: Something, then R. H. A? N? M? C?

Had Iris Jackson stolen it? Bought it at a pawnshop? Was it her mother's? Had it been left in the bar by Miss Howard, Miss Huckbert, Miss Alice Ruth Hottentot?

Lennox snapped it open, looked in the mirror at herself. A little sunburn on the nose, no lipstick on the teeth. She snapped it shut. She had Verna's old compact with ancient powder inside, tucked away with the journals under her bed. Somehow, Iris didn't seem like the sentimental type.

She palmed it, rubbed it between her hands, commanded it to yield up its secrets. The genie was silent. Lennox opened her small handbag and dropped it in. Down at the bottom were the keys from the Nash. She'd put them and the compact in her bag this morning, hoping their presence would work on her, make her smarter. Four keys. Two big, one medium, one small. She rubbed them and sighed, then chucked them back in her handbag. A heartbreaker, those keys. She was right about that.

She got out of the car into the morning air, warm already with the smell of burned hops from the brewery. A towheaded girl ran around the corner, as if someone was chasing her. An old woman and two men, standing across from the Chatterbox, startled as she bumped them.

Lennox watched the girl come closer. Her heart skipped. The girl was a dead ringer for Tillie. Her leather soles clapped the sidewalk cement, her hair flying in messy braids. So that's how she'd do her hair at eight.

When Lennox turned back to the Chatterbox, the cops stood at the door, talking to a woman. The bartender she had spoken to on Sunday. Her hair was in disarray, her dress wrinkled and dirty. As Lennox stepped up on the curb, she saw the woman's face was blotchy and swollen.

"I don't know, I don't know," the barkeep was saying, shaking her head. "Everybody liked him. Everybody. I just can't think—I can't—of anybody."

Lennox stopped on the sidewalk. The cop spoke to the bartender.

"No, no, don't know 'im, never heard of 'im," she said, putting her hand up to her forehead. "Can I go make some phone calls now? I have to call Joey. Joey needs to come."

The two policemen followed the bartender into the saloon. Someone was playing pool inside. The stench of stale beer wafted out the door. Lennox scuffed the pavement with her oxfords, then clenched her jaw and went in.

In the back of the bar, the policemen huddled with a man who had to be a plainclothes cop. Another uniform stood by with two young men who twisted with anxiety. Behind the bar, the lady bartender was on the phone, talking low. Lennox paused, let her eyes adjust to the darkness, made out a gray-haired woman sitting alone at a table, hands wrapped around a glass of water. The woman followed Lennox with keen eyes and gave a beseeching look to her nod.

Also sitting alone, midbar, was Alfie, the ancient beer drinker. The old man startled when she strode up. Wearing the same filthy waiter's jacket and black sailor's cap, he squinted at her.

"Some trouble here?" she asked.

Alfie blinked. "Davy. Gut-shot."

It would be Davy. Tears streamed down the bartender's face, and she was gulping words into the receiver.

"Poor woman," she whispered. To Alfie, she said, "Is he—"

"Dead. Yup. And Marian won't serve me no coffee."

"You want coffee?"

Making her way down to the end of the bar, washing out a white porcelain cup, Lennox watched the cops at the far end of room. They didn't seem to be doing much of anything, except drinking Davy's mother's coffee. She deposited a cup of burned java in front of the old man.

"Why, thank you, miss." He immediately hunched over to blow the steam.

Leaving Alfie at the bar, she inched closer to the policemen.

One of them looked a little like her old partner, Roger. The gray-haired woman shuffled over, approaching warily.

"You work here, do you?" She had the voice of a woman not used to speaking. Her clothes were clean but off, buttoned wrong. "You know Sylvia. You must. Have you seen her?"

"You've got me wrong, ma'am. I don't—"

"She ain't been home for days, and it's not like the girl. This place"—the woman looked angrily about the dim saloon, the billiard tables, broken stools, filthy floors—"this place done it to her, made her run away. I know it. But I can't get that Marian Esterly to give me the time o' day."

"Her son, Davy," Lennox explained in a soft voice. "He's been shot."

"Here—in this place?" She began to shake. "But my Sylvia, she told me about Davy. He was so nice to her, gave her extra hours because she's good. Oh, she's a good girl."

The policemen were dispersing. The two young men disappeared out the back. The lady clung to her arm. Lennox tried to leave. "I'm sorry. I have to—"

"Tell them, will you? Tell them Sylvia's gone. I can't get nobody to listen. Tell them, will you?" The woman squeezed her fingernails into Lennox's forearm.

She pried off the hand, patted it. "Let me take care of it."

As she walked away, the old woman called, "Anken. Sylvia Anken."

Up ahead, the plainclothes detective and the last uniform stood together. It *was* Roger Carey, late of Sugar Moon Investigations. A lucky break.

"Well, Mr. Patrolman, sir," she said, smiling at the look of him, the cropped blond hair, wiry frame encased in navy blue, with knee-high leather boots, gloves smartly tucked into his belt. It'd been over a month since he cleaned out his desk and put on a badge. "Pardon me. Mr. Wheel Man."

Roger reddened and glanced at the plainclothes policeman. "Dorie. What are you doing here?"

"Just in for some chat and refreshments. Can we talk?"

"You know Detective O'Brian?"

She introduced herself, shook his cold, fishy hand. He spoke to Roger. "Watch the front. No more customers till we're done back here."

Roger snapped his head toward the front door and they walked in that direction. Lennox nodded reassuringly at the old woman, whose stockings now cuddled around her ankles.

They stepped out into the sunshine, where Roger took up his post, face stony, arms crossed, legs spread. Lennox stared, amazed. He had been so carefree before.

"You are a man on a job, if I ever saw one."

He blinked at her. "Did Amos send you?"

"I sent myself. I make my own decisions. It's my investigation, after all, despite the—" She looked harder at Roger. "What do you mean? Has something happened to Amos?"

"You don't know? He's in the lockup as we speak. The captain, his old friend and your uncle, took him in."

"For what?" Roger's lips tightened. His eyes flicked back to the Chatterbox. "For this shooting, Davy Whatshisname?"

"Esterly."

"But he's sick. He's been in the hospital since—"

"Checked out yesterday. On his own, didn't talk to no doctor or nurse."

"What happened here?"

"Fella shot in the guts, back in the alley. Somebody saw Amos's car down at the end, and a medium-sized joe in a gray suit. Word is his gun's fresh, too."

Lennox turned to face the curb. This couldn't be right. *She* was the one who should have been talking to Davy Esterly last night.

"But he didn't know him. He couldn't have."

Roger squinted as she turned back. "*You* knew him?"

She shook her head. "I was tailing this girl, Friday night. She came in here for a few minutes before she did the Dutch act. I wanted to talk to somebody who'd seen her. I talked to the mother a couple days ago, but he wasn't here. His mother said he was working Friday night."

"That bartender?"

"Yeah."

It was almost noon and the pavement was beginning to scorch. From the corner, two farmers, dressed in overalls and work shirts, with a wide-eyed redness to their faces, stumbled toward the Chatterbox. They took one look at Roger's scowl and kept moving.

"Did they charge Amos?"

"Not yet."

"Will they let me see him?"

"Word is even his lawyer's having a hell of a time."

"Who's his lawyer?"

"Who do you think?"

Lennox examined her friend's face. His blue eyes had lost their twinkle since his enlistment in the Kansas City Police Department. But he hadn't forgotten some things.

"Vanvleet," she whispered.

She hadn't been able to reach Vanvleet this morning, either. So Amos and Vanvleet were together, or at least in the same building. It made sense that Amos would call him. Want him on his side. The old man was many things, but he was good.

"Have you seen Amos?" she asked. She had to see him, put this right.

"Been on patrol since eight, then sent over here." He shifted slightly in place, bit his lip. "Most miraculous job, Lennox. Most stinking miraculous."

"So you like the bike?" The Kansas City cops rode Harley-Davidsons with a ton of chrome. It was their best recruiting tool. Besides the plentiful opportunities for graft.

He ventured a smile. "Oh, yes, ma'am. That I do."

She nodded, barely listening. Amos—sick as he was—in jail! The old woman peered out the tiny window glass, bringing Lennox back.

"Who's that?" Roger asked.

"She's worried about her daughter, who works here. Seems to have run away."

"Did you tell her to file a missing persons?"

"Will the miraculous Kansas City Police do one damn thing with such a report?"

Roger's nostrils flared. "Do not malign the name of my employer, madam!" His mouth twitched into a smile. "Damn good to see you, Lennox."

There was nothing else to learn here except the gruesome details of Davy Esterly's demise, which would be screaming from headlines by dinnertime. Talbot might even be writing them. Might be in the alley right now.

Lennox shook her head in disbelief, walking back to the car. Amos in the goddamn KC lockup, and Uncle Herb behind it! What was the world coming to? Maybe it was better with Pendergast; at least you knew who your friends were. Now it was all a crap game. And Amos was on a bad roll.

She slouched in the Packard, trying to clear the haziness in her mind. She flipped the compact open, snapped it shut. Her stomach growled. She looked at the Chatterbox, pictured sitting here on Friday night, Iris going in, coming out. What else? She had the whole damn thing in her mind, tailing the Nash, turning around, watching Iris climb out of the car—again, slowly—and walk into the Chatterbox. She was moving so slowly that night, like she knew somebody was taking her picture. And wanted the picture to be good. Lennox remembered her feeling on the bridge, that Iris had made her, then ditched her.

But Davy Esterly? Was it just dumb bad luck, or did it have something to do with Iris? Did she give him something that night—something that got him killed? What could that be? What had Iris been up to? And how did Georgie fit into it?

She started the car and drove the ten blocks to police headquarters. Their lockup was on the third floor. She had to try to see Amos, see if he needed medical attention. Why had he checked himself out of the hospital?

Uncle Herb's office was on the second floor, in the corner. She knocked and he looked up through the glass and frowned.

"Bad time?"

Herb Warren stood up, pulling his large frame off the chair. "Doesn't matter." He pointed to a chair, but she stood against the wood and glass partition that was his office wall. "You're here about Amos, I guess. I have to tell you, Dorie, it don't look good for the old boy."

"This must be some kind of setup," she said.

"The best kind." Herb's face hung, unsmiling. "They've got a bullet out of Davy Esterly and it looks good for Amos's gun."

"And his car at the scene?"

Herb nodded. "He says you know he hasn't been driving, though."

"I've seen him on the streetcar and I drove us on Saturday." She frowned. "He says he told me he wasn't driving?"

Another nod. She chose not to confirm or deny Amos's statement.

"Is there anything I can do?"

He shrugged. "We're checking his story about collapsing on the steps. Somebody must have seen that."

"Can I see him?"

"Not now, kid."

"Is he okay? He was so sick. Did he check out without his doctor's okay?"

"That's what they say. He looks like hell. Says somebody must've slipped him a Mickey last night. Sick as he is, he's not much of witness, even of his own innards."

Lennox sat down at last, and Herb followed. The silence lasted a long time. Finally, Lennox said, "Shit." Her uncle didn't contradict her.

"Listen, Herb, I gotta tell you about something. You know that jumper the other night, the one I was tailing? Well, she went into that dive, the Chatterbox, just before she went to the bridge."

Captain Warren rolled a pencil between his big hands. "And?"

"Davy Esterly was the bartender at the Chatterbox that night. Iris might have talked to him, or even known him."

"Iris being the jumper."

"Right."

Herb pursed his lips. "So . . . She comes back from the dead?" He flipped the pencil into the air and it landed on his desk in a clatter, then jumped off to the floor. He leaned back in his chair and sighed. "I'll pass it along."

A thought jumped into her head: Iris going in, coming out. "That jumper. Anybody claim her body yet?"

"Nope. Found a suicide note in her apartment, though."

Lennox had her hand on the doorknob. "Oh yeah?"

Halfway to the basement, Vanvleet caught her arm on the stairs. Lennox hadn't even seen him, skipping down the stairs the way she was. She straightened, tried to smile.

"How's Amos?" she asked.

"Holding his own." The old man looked tired. Maybe horse racing had worn him out. "I haven't seen you for a while. I expect a report daily. You are aware of that?"

"Yes, sir." Lennox pressed against the wall to let two detectives pass between them. "I'll have something for you tonight."

"Have you found anything new?"

"Not really."

Vanvleet rubbed his scalp. Even the finely pressed suit and gold watch chain couldn't disguise the deep circles under his eyes and the paleness of his face.

"You'll get Amos off," she said.

His eyes snapped back to her. "Report at six tonight."

A skinny, freckled kid slouched behind the desk at the morgue, reading Dashiell Hammett. He pushed his glasses up on his nose and squinted at Lennox. "Help you?"

"I, ah, yes, that is, I hope not, but—" She gave him her sad smile. "My sister's missing and I *hope*, I hope very much that you don't have her down here."

He put *The Dain Curse* facedown and stood up. "So you want to look at the Jane Does?"

"Are there lots of them?"

He leafed through a couple sheets of paper on a clipboard. "A few. When did your sister disappear?"

"Let's see. Sometime after Friday night. Over the weekend, I guess."

He poked a finger on the list. "Only one to look at, then. The other two been stinking here longer than that." He gave her a devilish grin. "Smells don't bother you, do they, miss?"

Even with the cold air, the overripe odor of the body bloomed from the drawer. It had only been two days, but the deterioration was plain. Lennox didn't have to pretend to be shocked by the appearance of the corpse as the attendant pulled back the cloth.

She clapped her hand over her nose and mouth. The nibbled face was greener, more shriveled and sunken, eyelids a deep gray. The roots of her hair looked darker. Was it true that hair continued to grow after death? Lennox leaned in. Iris's eyelashes were almost invisible, very light. Funny, she'd always assumed Iris was a bottle blonde. There was peroxide in her apartment.

"Smells like dead catfish, don't it?" The attendant was still grinning.

Lennox stared at the dirty, sand-filled hair. It had streaks of dark gold through it, and light brown. Like natural hair. She felt her heart race a little.

"Well? Is it her?" he asked, his grin gone. He scowled at the mangled face.

"Um, can I see down here?" She nodded halfway down the body. "She had a birthmark on her thigh."

"Which side?"

"This side." He reached across the body, lifted the drape that covered the left side of Iris's left torso and hips. Lennox looked at the hands.

The fingers were curled under, fists balled at her sides. Out of sight of Freckles, Lennox pulled out the girl's fingers.

"Do you see it?" he asked.

"I'm looking. It's hard with the skin so . . . you know."

"My arms are going numb, that's all. But take your time. She's got all the time in the world, poor stinking devil."

Lennox touched the nail of the forefinger. Unpainted. Plain. She bent closer, looking for traces of polish. Only broken, dirty, uneven nails. She tipped up the finger. Calluses, old scars on the shriveled fingertips. She looked up at the face again, wishing the fish bites hadn't disfigured it so. But there hadn't been time to take off nail polish. And the peroxide in her medicine cabinet: Iris's hair was bright, like Harlow's. Definitely a bottle blonde.

"Okay. You can lower it."

He dropped the drape. "So? What's the verdict?"

Lennox took a last look at the face, the girl's sunken mouth, the gray cheeks. The tangled hair, the battered neck. Poor unfortunate child. Whoever she was.

"Does she, um . . ." Lennox nudged the corpse's temple away from her, twisting the neck. She bent down to look at the head, parting the pale hair.

"What're you looking for?"

She gave him her sweet look, moved around the drawer front. Another gentle push of the head.

"Hey," protested Freckles.

"Look at that." She pointed to a clotted black tangle of hair. The area around it was angry and dark.

"Yeah, she broke her leg, too." He rearranged the girl's head again. "Is it her, your sister?"

She didn't know much about how a body reacts to a hard slap against the water, but splitting open, bleeding? It was possible. But would the blood have clotted in her hair if it happened in the fall—or rinsed away into the river water?

Lennox stepped back.

"It's not her. No. Thank heavens. It's not her."

Back upstairs, Lennox hunted for her uncle so she could get permission to see the clothes the jumper had been wearing when they fished her out. He had disappeared. She went down to the Property Room and tried to sweet-talk a look at them. But the clerk was a stickler for procedure, a new wrinkle in a department where thousands of dollars in bond money had often disappeared.

"At least let me look at the sign-in sheet. I don't need to see the articles themselves," she said, batting eyelashes furiously. The clerk was a former sergeant, bumped down to the Prop Room and, from the look of it, not happy about it. He took no interest in ocular gyrations.

"Not without an okay from above."

"So call Captain Warren."

He thought about that. "They've got some homicide bust upstairs."

"I heard. They're probably beating a confession out of the criminal right now." She smiled. "I mean, persuading him to see that justice will be done." She hopped up on the counter, sitting pretty for the ugly old sarge. "It might take hours, but I can wait."

A few minutes later, he capitulated, with grumbles, and brought out the small sheet of paper listing the effects of one Jane Doe fished from the river. One blue shirtwaist dress, one gabardine jacket, one garter belt (no stockings), one pair cotton underpants, one brassiere. One torn sheet of music—Cole

Porter?—one matchbook from the Hot Cha Cha Club, one white handkerchief with the monogram *I*.

"No shoes, huh?"

"If they aren't listed."

"No jewelry, either. I suppose the fellas that found her relieved her of her rings."

"This type's hocked it all."

That night at the Muehlebach, Iris had worn gold earrings. But she probably wouldn't have worn them to work. Might have been in her handbag. Where was the jewelry in the apartment? Had she pawned it?

Lennox saw the death mask of the jumper in her mind again. No, she hadn't pawned anything. It wasn't Iris. The old woman in the saloon—her daughter missing. Why hadn't she asked for a description? But old Alfie had mentioned a Sylvia, too, when Lennox had described Iris.

She slid off the counter, head whirling. Iris at the Chatterbox—a switch with same-hair Sylvia, giving Sylvia her clothes, meeting her on the bridge. How had she convinced the girl—money? Sweet, good Sylvia, with the worried mother. A little extra money for impersonating Iris. Easy money, she must have thought.

Then, dead, unclaimed in the morgue.

Matchbook from the Hot Cha Cha, monogrammed hankie. Messages from Iris. Who wanted all to believe she had jumped.

Lennox slapped the list hard on the counter. "Hot damn," she said. Amos would be cleared. By finding Iris, she would do it. The clerk stared at her.

Iris was still alive.

FOURTEEN

THE RAT LEAPT from the third step of the Jayhawker Hotel and disappeared into the alley. Lennox froze at the bottom of the steps, letting cohorts, if any, have a chance to escape. The rat was thin and mangy. He ought to catch a streetcar uptown. The afternoon sun shone weakly through the grime on the hotel's dirty windows. Down the street, a circle of men sat on the curb, playing dice games.

The neighborhood was a little far from the bridge for walking, the farthest she'd tried today. The circle she'd drawn on the map was just a mile in radius—hard to imagine Iris walking too many cobblestones in high heels. The North End and near downtown hadn't panned out, after three hours of hitting the bricks. The West Bottoms was a good place to hide, and only half a block from the streetcar line. The Jayhawker had that affordable look to it, and rats in the bargain.

The hallway was dark and smelled like rot. Like most of the flophouses she'd been in, it wasn't really a hotel, but a converted house with a resident manager. She knocked on the first door. The man who answered wore a sleeveless undershirt and black trousers, and he needed a shave. He blew cigarette smoke in her face. "Yeah?"

She'd given up introductions. "I'm looking for a woman who took a room last week, Friday or Saturday, twenty-five to thirty, nice figure, maybe blond, maybe not. Sound familiar?"

The man scratched his head. She'd interrupted his cocktail hour. "When, you say?"

"Friday or Saturday."

"What's today?"

"Tuesday."

He scratched some more.

Lennox said, "You the manager?"

"Don't remember no broads. Mostly men here. Only an old lady who lives in the back."

"She live here a long time?"

"Who?"

"The old lady."

Lennox knew an act of desperation when she saw it. She knocked on the old woman's faded blue door. She was tired of talking to derelict managers who couldn't remember the day, or their own last name. It took forever for the door to be answered.

The old woman was bent and white-haired. She blinked her crepey old eyes. Lennox looked for a brightness there but saw only fear.

"Excuse me, ma'am. I'm looking for a woman who might have been around this neighborhood last Saturday. She's tall, a little taller than me, nice figure, manicure—"

The old woman slammed the door. The rush of foul air wafted by Lennox's face. She turned on her heel and made her way back to the street and its wildlife. This time, it was stray dogs, sniffing the steps.

Lennox stepped around a suspicious puddle and crossed the street. Last stop in this neighborhood. In the front window of the flophouse, a flower bloomed on the windowsill.

Nameless and narrow, the building was sandwiched between other row houses, done in crumbling brick before the turn of the century. The front stoop was recently swept and displayed a welcome mat. She tried the front door, but it was locked. She knocked.

A small boy wrestled the knob. He peeked around the door at her.

"Is the manager here?" she asked, making him run for cover. In a moment a haggard woman with a large goiter arrived. She was wiping her hands on her apron. Lennox asked if she was the manager.

"This is my house," the woman said. "What you want?"

"I'm sorry. I'm looking for a woman, a boarder. You take boarders?"

The woman looked her up and down. Lennox was too tired even to stand straight in her damp blouse and wrinkled trousers. The woman blew her hair off her face. "You a lady dick?"

Was it so obvious? "This woman's been missing since late Friday. Trying to slip away, you know. Do you take boarders?"

"Now and again. What's her name?"

"Iris Jackson. She's pretty, a bleach blonde last time we saw her, tall, nice hands. She might have come around late Friday or Saturday."

The boy wrapped himself around the woman's leg. She had a hardworking, kind face, despite the neck problem. Even with the insult about the house right off the bat, she still was trying. Lennox felt a rush of gratitude and tried to keep her eyes off the goiter.

"A blonde, you say?"

"Or dyed. She'd be trying to . . . well, look different." Iris wanted to disappear, so she'd engineered her own death. For four days, it had worked like a charm. But being duped by a bar girl, or whatever she was, wasn't going to play. *Not for long, Miss Jackson.* An image of the attacker in her room—it was Iris, had to be. "You know the type. Dark hair maybe."

The woman rolled her eyes. Her unwashed hair was loose from its bun. "We get 'em all down here—you can count on that. Not a blonde, but a gal came around Saturday morning looking for a room. We didn't have any, so I sent her on."

"What did she look like?"

"Pretty, like you say. No schoolgirl, been around some. Fancy manicure. Short black hair, I think. Bangs in front."

"Do you remember her clothes?"

"A dress. Red. Carrying a satchel."

"And you sent her on?"

"No rooms, like I said."

"Did you give her a name of another place?"

"Wouldn't know that, would I? She looked a bit like trouble, if you have to know. Like I'd be sorry I ever let a room to the likes of 'er."

Lennox thanked the woman, patted the boy on the head. Finally, something. She didn't know where Iris was, but the woman's description meshed with the picture she had of her attacker. Iris had changed her appearance.

Back in the Packard, Lennox scribbled the woman's address in the notebook from the glove compartment, and Iris's new description. Iris was close; she could smell her, around the corner, around the block. She would find her.

She smiled to herself, starting the car, and couldn't help whispering, "Curtains, sister." Then knew she was premature. What if there were more than one dark-haired woman? She remembered the words: "Watch your step, Miss Snooper. Because I'll be watching you." She looked in her rearview mirror. The crap-shooters on the corner didn't look so benign. Despite the heat, Lennox felt a chill. Her throat ached a little, remembering the boot's pressure on her neck. Iris wouldn't let a lady dick stop her, or anybody else.

After a quick stop at the Art Institute to get drawing instructor Lorna Hahn to sketch up Iris Jackson's new look in pencil and pastels, using the description and one of the photographs as a guide, Lennox trudged up the stairs to the office in the Boston Building. Lorna had asked about Amos, said she hadn't seen him lately. Apparently, she had missed him. News to cheer up the old soldier. Thinking about him in the slammer—batted about by bulls who believed that a successful investigation added up to one victim, one suspect, and six billy clubs—would he survive that? In his condition? She had to find Iris Jackson.

As she passed the dentist's office, moans mixed with the whine of the drill. She grit her own teeth at the keening sounds, slipped into the office of Sugar Moon Investigations, and shut the hall door quickly.

The receptionist, Shirley Mullins, was on the phone in the outer office. Her eyes brightened on seeing Lennox, and she held up one finger for her to wait. The afternoon sun cut squares in the faded Oriental rug. Shirley chomped her gum, said "Uh-huh" a dozen times, and hung up.

"Your uncle's called three times, looking for you. That was his clerk now, saying that Amos is going to be charged with second-degree homicide. If that new chief don't object. Anyway, they're keeping him there, and he won't confess, so they're throwing the book at him. I can't believe this."

Shirley's eyes were wide in surprise, but more excited than concerned, as if she enjoyed this drama more than the last one, in the hospital room.

"Did they say I could see him?"

"Not as such. Oh!" Shirley stood up, lowered her voice to a whisper. "You have a visitor. In your office. I let her sit down in there, since your chair is more comfortable. Been there nearly an hour." Shirley tried to peer through the milky glass of the door. "She's just sitting there, like a statue."

"Who is it?"

Shirley shrugged. "Mrs. T. she calls herself."

The woman straightened in her chair when Lennox came through the door. Today another stylish outfit, gray suit, with matching hat and gloves. On her face, the strain was apparent.

"Marilyn. How are you?" Lennox sat behind her desk, laid down her handbag, notebook, and keys.

"I could be better. I really could." Her eyes teared.

"Can I get you something, coffee, water?"

"No, no, I'm fine. This has just been so hard for me, coming here, and I planned out what I would say, and then you weren't here and I—" She broke off, stifled a sob with a handkerchief.

Lennox put her hand on the woman's shoulder. "It's all right now. Has something happened?"

"Another call. Actually, two. One I found out about later; the children took it. Richard, he's seven. Always wants to be so important."

"From the same woman?"

"I think so. But I didn't take it, so I'm not sure."

"What did she say?"

"That she was from the bank and needed to verify our account numbers. If I had answered it, I would have known immediately. But I was out, and the housekeeper lets the children run wild sometimes, I swear." Marilyn squinted menacingly. "I think that whore was watching the house. She knew I wasn't home."

"So Richard gave her the numbers."

"He thought he was being helpful. He went into Georgie's desk and got bank statements. I don't know how he found them. He sat at his father's desk, talked to the bank as if he were in charge of everything, and told that woman our account numbers!"

"We don't know for sure it wasn't the bank."

"Oh yes, we do. Because this morning, the bank called me. Wanted to thank me for stopping in and asked if I'd gotten everything I needed."

"And you weren't at the bank."

"Hell no!" she blurted; then her color rose, as if she was flustered that her mask had gone transparent. "Excuse me, I don't do any banking. That's Georgie's job; he's the man in the family, and he provides very well for us when he's—"

When he's not catting around. Well, yes.

"They thought this woman at the bank was you. But you never go in, so they don't know you."

"That's right. I think she wore dark glasses."

"Did you get a description?"

"No, no, I was too upset."

"And you bank at—"

"First Missouri."

Lennox went back around her desk and made a note in her notebook. Another description of Iris wouldn't hurt.

"What did the bank say she wanted?"

"That was the curious thing. She wanted only the balances. She didn't try to forge a check or anything. Just balances on each account."

"How many accounts do you and your husband have, Marilyn?"

Mrs. Terraciano looked up, startled. "I only have the one checking account. That I know of."

"What about your husband?"

"I don't know."

"You've never sat at Georgie's desk and gone through the statements. Like Richard."

"No! I wouldn't think of it. How Richard knew—"

Lennox opened the door, asked Shirley to write up a letter for Mrs. Terraciano to sign, authorizing the agency to take a look at her bank accounts. Marilyn frowned a little at this, twisting her gloves between her hands.

"Is there a problem with that, Marilyn?"

"No. I mean, I just hope Georgie doesn't find out. He's very strict about money. I have to stay within my household budget or he goes through the roof. It's very generous; it's not a problem usually."

"Usually?" Lennox leaned against the side of the desk. "Have there been problems?"

"It must have been my mistake, I added or subtracted or something. I'm not very good with numbers—that's what he says."

"Were you in the red?"

"I didn't think I would be; I write everything down." She clenched her fists. Finally, she whispered, "I know I was right. I know it."

"How much were you off—or they said you were off?"

"Two thousand dollars! How could I make a mistake like that? It's ridiculous. I know, it's a lot, but, as I told you, he's very good to us, and it was time to pay tuition at the children's schools. And then I had to ask the schools to wait. It was so embarrassing."

Lennox walked to the window, listening to the typing slow and end. She opened the window higher. The river, just a sliver through the buildings and trees, glittered in the setting sun. The green of the trees seemed too beautiful, too alive. But someday their time would come. She thought about Sylvia, dead, in the morgue. Of her dear old mother, worried sick. Of Amos, sick and in trouble. And Iris, free.

"Did you find anything out about her?" Marilyn asked.

"No. Not for sure."

Shirley stood in the doorway with the letter, then set it down on the desk for Marilyn to sign. When Shirley had gone, Lennox picked up the letter.

"This is jake?"

The woman nodded. "Find out about the two thousand."

"And the woman who said she was you?"

Marilyn put her hands on her face. Her nails were as nice as Iris's. Lennox squatted down beside her chair.

"I'll see what I can find out. It's possible this woman, whoever she is, is after Georgie's money, not Georgie."

Marilyn dropped her hands, eyes wide, lipstick smeared.

"We'll see what floats up."

Behind her desk again, Lennox folded the letter into her notebook. Marilyn Terraciano took out a compact, dabbed her lipstick smear, stood up. Lennox walked her out in the hallway, where the drill whined, then down the stairs to the sidewalk.

The streetcar was disgorging passengers, others shoving to get on. Quitting time at Eighth and Wyandotte, a hot, cranky time of day. Marilyn paused in the bustle, as if she'd forgotten this many people went to work every day.

Lennox peered at her. "Marilyn?"

A woman in a turban jostled Marilyn, the two of them doing a queer dance step on the sidewalk. The woman took Marilyn's arm as if to push her out of the way. Marilyn's purse landed with a crash, spilling lipsticks and combs and keys onto the Pendergast cement. The woman stepped over the mess and jumped onto the streetcar as it pulled away. The bell clanged.

Lennox stooped to help retrieve the items. Marilyn tilted on the way back to standing. "You all right?"

Marilyn stared blankly down the sidewalk. The bruiser with the tilted nose grabbed her arm. "This way, ma'am." He gently directed her to the waiting black sedan, depositing her in the backseat. He gave Lennox a look as he drove away, as if to say, I wasn't here. You didn't see me. Or maybe, Say anything and you're one sorry Jane. She remembered his laugh and his "Nice try, toots." Who knew with that fella.

Shirley stood in the office doorway with a hand on one hip. "What's all that about, then?"

Lennox sat at the desk. Marilyn and Georgie: O sweet mystery of marriage.

"Isn't that the wife of Georgie Terraciano? Whose girlfriend you were following?" Shirley had on her Irish-mother look. "Are you working both sides of the street?"

"Pretty crooked street."

"I wouldn't cross that Georgie if I were you. He has a hot temper, hotter even than my Bernie. You remember the Pony Jump."

"The what?"

"Five, six years ago? Ach, you were in university then. Well." Shirley sat down, warming to her tale. "Some argument between the North Enders and them Pendergast boys. There was always these tugs-o'-war going on, but this one got personal. Of course, Georgie was a staunch North Ender; all the Italians were, wherever they lived."

"He lives down in Brookside now."

"Their hearts remain in the North End. Georgie was a Lazia man."

"The John Lazia who was gunned down over on Armour Boulevard?"

"The same. Whatever you say about the Italians, they invented loyalty. Course, the Irish ain't been n'better." She rolled her eyes. "Can't say I wasn't too glad to quit making excuses for that Boss o' ours."

"You and every God-fearing citizen. So what's this Pony Jump?"

"Well. You hear how the redskins used to kill their buffalo, run them off a cliff? They say this Pendergast man had it in for Georgie. He took down some sections of fence where Georgie's prize racehorses grazed. Then ran them out the gap, over the cliff, into the river."

"Not a way to Georgie's heart."

"Ooh no. Word was, he tore up the restaurant he was at when he heard. Threw chairs, broke dishes. Then went and cried over his poor dead ponies."

"And then what—to the fella?"

"Broke his legs. I mean it, broke both the poor man's legs. He never walked again. In fact, he died last year of some infection."

"Never caught, I suppose."

"Neither of them. That was the Boss's way. The police were all bought, so what was the point? No justice in this town. So he let the two of 'em work it out to their own satisfaction. I hear he let it be known that enough was enough. He didn't want no gang wars. What do they call it—going to the mattresses?"

"You know more about it than I do, Shirley."

"Aye, I do, child, so don't be crossing that greaser. I don't want to see you with your legs broken. And believe me, neither do you."

At six that evening, Lennox sat uncomfortably on the slick leather chair in the lawyer's office. This room was small, no big window overlooking the city, just the staff attorney's regular mahogany expanse of desk and shelving. The window looked west, at the slaughterhouses and livestock yards stretched along the Bottoms like a Missouri version of hell. But Louie Weston didn't seem to mind. He fingered the cleft in his chin and smiled at the scene, then back at her.

"So I'm to report to you now?" she asked.

"For the time being. We'll see how we get on, I guess. And how Mr. Haddam's ordeal plays out."

"That's one way to describe being arrested for murder."

"Especially when he didn't do it," Louie said.

"You're so sure?"

"Aren't you?"

"I've known Amos a long time." Longer than I've known you, Louie Weston. He was playing the toady, and why? What influence did she have? Where were his plaid pants—there was something so toady about golf clothes. Must be the pink shirts.

The thought of giving him her hard-won information rubbed wrong, very wrong. Especially the fact that Iris Jackson is very much with us, she thought. The moist gleam in his blue eyes, the clear, untroubled brow—had he beat the bricks in search of a dead girl?

If it had been Vanvleet, she wouldn't have hesitated. Although she disliked the old man, she found it impossible not to seek his approval. When this was over, she'd experiment with lying to him, see how it felt.

"So," Louie said, clapping his hands. The awkwardness after the plane ride was forgotten, at least by him. He glanced at her chest and ankles, licked his lips. Lennox squeezed the arms of the chair. "Since I know nothing about this business, how about you filling me in? You were to follow this Iris Jackson?"

"At the place where she worked. On Friday, after a week

of that, she went to another joint, walked to the Hannibal Bridge and jumped."

"Okay. Then what?"

"Then they wanted me to check into her background, talk to her friends, her landlady, all that."

"And so you did."

"Right. I looked at her apartment, talked to the old man downstairs. She left a suicide note on her pillow."

"Huh." Thinking aloud, Louie-style.

"Some longshoremen fished a body out of the river."

"No identification on it?"

"A hankie. And a pack of matches from the club where she worked, the Hot Cha Cha."

"Hmm. I like the sound of that. Hotchacha."

"Used to be a speak called the Tenderloin. Phony butcher in front."

"Anything else?"

She straightened up on the chair, looked him in the eye. "No. That's it."

Easy as that. Lying was so much easier than telling the truth. Must be the key to its popularity.

He slapped the clean desktop with both hands as he stood up. "Let's go get a drink, then. I'll tell you about the weekender a bunch of us took down to Springfield. Landed in a hay field, slept in tents, had a bonfire and a sing-along. Great fun."

Lennox stared at him. "A sing-along? Jeepers."

She stood up. The snowball had a better chance in hell than he did on drinks. But she worked for him now. Make it smooth, she told herself. He had her elbow, guiding her to the door. As he reached around as if to open it, he pushed her backward against the wooden panels, pinning her shoulders. Before she could do more than gasp in surprise, he pressed against her, wedged his knee between her legs, kissing her hard on the mouth. When his hands went to her breasts, ripping open her blouse, she raised her arms and shoved him with all her strength.

"What the hell do you think you're doing?"

"Aw, come on, toots." Face red, breathing hard, he stepped forward again, but when he saw what she had in her hand, he stopped.

"You know what this is?" She had the switchblade, closed, in her hand. "You think I walk around this city unarmed, waiting for some palooka like you to dry-gulch me?"

"Listen, I— Forget about it. I was only trying to be friendly. Come on, toots. . . ." He was sweating now.

"This is my friendly shiv. You should see the unfriendly one." She had her finger on the button. "Hey, *toots*. You want to see how it works?"

"You won't say anything to Vanvleet, will you?" He pushed back his hair and squinted at her. "Not if you want to keep working for the firm, you won't."

She let her hand drop. Her breathing was ragged and fast. How was she going to keep working with him? Think. Anything is possible. You can even work with a man like Louie Weston. Could she use this as leverage with Vanvleet? How? No, it just had to stop, and stop now.

"You keep your distance."

His face twisted into a sneer. "Who are you trying to kid, anyway? You're just like that little round heels, your friend. And she rolled over for a couple beers."

The blade sprang open. She lunged toward him and he jumped back with a yelp.

"Don't you ever say anything about Arlette," she hissed. "You aren't fit to shine her shoes. You say one word about her to anybody and you're ribbons, pal."

Louie blanched, eyes on the long, shiny blade.

She whispered, "You don't know Arlette. You don't know anything."

Words jammed her throat, words to make him feel the pain

Arlette had suffered. But too much time had passed. He would never understand. She watched him sweat. There just wasn't any goddamn balancing scale to make things right. No matter what she said. Things happen and there's no going back.

She found the doorknob behind her, her hands shaking by the time she reached the Packard. She took a few deep breaths. The street was quiet, tired. At least she'd kept Weston in the dark. If she'd told him everything about Iris and he'd done what he did, said what he said, she might have used the knife on herself. She felt the blade in her pocket. No, not that.

Having his number now didn't erase the fact that she had been so very wrong about him in Atchison. Better he had forgotten all that. Being a friend to Arlette was the one thing Dorie had to stand on. Even if her own life had gone to hell in a handbasket after that, she had done what was right, that once.

In the dining room that night, Betty Kimble told another joke. The two shy bachelors slurped their carrot soup. Ilo Gobbs burst into tears and ran upstairs. Mrs. Ferazzi said her boyfriend had run off to Canada to enlist. Winkie Lambert reminded everyone that Boss Pendergast had accepted a medal from Mussolini just last year, and now the wop bastard was siding with Hitler. Mrs. F. shushed her on account of her homeland. The Crybacker twins left early for a polka concert at the Liberty Memorial.

The apple pandowdy was cold.

FIFTEEN

HUNCHED ON THE HARD COT, Amos coughed into his dirty handkerchief. The pain in his chest was familiar, an old friend. He felt warm, damp all over, even though the cell was all cold cement. But that didn't matter. He was struggling to remember every detail that was in Eugenia's notebook. He couldn't believe the two notebooks were missing. But they were. Gone with whoever had doped him and set him up. He couldn't think about that. He had to remember Eugenia. Vanvleet had brought him a sheaf of paper and a pencil, and he was on his third page of notes.

The lawyer had been cross with him about not paying attention to the case. He kept talking about Reggie, the old pantywaist. Amos had worked dozens of cases over the years, and now he was *the case*. It would be funny if he wasn't holed up here, bruises on his shoulders and neck where the coppers had taken their billy clubs to him before Herbert got word in. Oh, Amos expected the treatment; he knew how they operated here, no different from any other police department.

How could he confess? He didn't even know the bloke's name, for Chrissakes. Good thing he'd gotten that letter off to his mother in hospital; now she wouldn't worry when he didn't write for a while. He couldn't very well write that he was in stir. He wondered if they'd started bombing London yet. The papers didn't have anything about it, but their news seemed a trifle stale. He chewed on his pencil, thinking, with a shiver, about his mother, bombs raining down all around her. And him miles and miles away, locked up, sick, and suspect.

And what about Beryl? His sister, living with that bloody farmer in Normandy. Beryl had better get out of there, come over here. He would write to her. Maybe she'd gone home to be with Mum. That little Frenchie probably had her milking goats. He would use simple, earnest Beryl for milking, but he wouldn't marry her.

"Skin like fresh cream," he wrote. "With strawberries. Dove gray eyes; long, expressive fingers with pearl white half-moons on the nails." He wasn't exactly sure if he'd ever written this about Eugenia in the notebook, wasn't really sure if he remembered her fingernails at all. He tried to concentrate. He had held her hands many times. Why couldn't he remember?

He coughed again, a long, exhaustive bout, and when it was done, he saw Lennox standing outside the cell bars. She was trying to smile, and only getting half the job done. Well, what was there to smile about? He struggled to his feet, smoothing his pants. They'd taken his suit jacket—for evidence, they said—and he stood in his shirt and braces to receive her in his new parlor.

"Good evenin', my dear," he said.

The matron opened the door, gave Amos a withering look. He gave her a slight bow, to show her he had no ill intentions. The people who worked here had the most suspicious minds.

Lennox sat on the edge of the cot. Amos leaned against the sink that hung from the wall.

"Nice joint," she said. "Is the food good?"

"A notch below the hospital, if you must know. Quite a large notch."

"I'll bring you something tomorrow; oranges are in at Steiner's." She glanced at the papers on the bed.

He bowed, hoping he looked elegantly cynical.

"We can get a doctor up here, get you transferred back to City Hospital, where you should have stayed."

"Higher priorities."

She sighed. "I was supposed to talk to Davy Esterly. He was the last person who saw Iris Jackson. That was the dive she went into just before the bridge. The Chatterbox. And there's more to it."

Amos wasn't following her very well. He was looking at her hands, wondering if she had half-moons on her nails. She was going on about this Davy character, and that bar girl. Had Eugenia varnished her nails? No, he would have remembered that. He was thinking about how her hands sometimes smelled piney, like turpentine, from her paints.

Lennox frowned at him. "What were you doing here yesterday, at police headquarters?"

"Checking out this gee, Palmer Eustace. Vanvleet set me on him, about the racetrack, then turned around and told me to forget it." Amos shook his head. "I need to talk to Eustace."

"You want me to call him?"

"I don't have a number. Did it all through Vanvleet. Might be I was running up a blind alley, but something seemed queer about the deal."

Lennox went on, jabbering about this Iris dame. Then she stopped talking and looked at him as if he was loopy. He was a little irritated with her, because he wanted to write down the bit about the turpentine before he forgot it.

"Did you hear me?" she said. "She's not dead."

"Eugenia?" A vision of her came to him, waiting at the bottom of a long flight of steps. Older, her hair different. It must have been a dream. He shook his head, trying to clear it.

"Iris Jackson." Lennox stood up, laid a hand on his arm. "Who's Eugenia?" She looked in his eyes. No doubt a frightening sight, Amos thought, remembering his sagging red sockets. "Are you all right?" she asked.

"Everyone knows she wouldn't jump," he said quietly.

She took his arm and led him back to the cot, straightened the sheets of paper. She made him lie down, took off his shoes, and covered him up. It felt good to be looked after.

Lennox patted his shoulder. "Listen now. Iris is still alive, and I'm going to find her. She killed the other girl, the one in the morgue. She found a girl who looked like her, then fed the girl some line to get her up on the bridge." She paused, bit her lip. "She knew I was there, Amos. That was part of it. She knew I was watching. She made me early on. She wanted me to see Sylvia go over. To make it look liked she jumped."

"Eugenia didn't jump. She wouldn't."

Lennox frowned. "Iris. She's cut her hair, and dyed it black. I'll find her, make her pay for killing that girl. And for Davy Esterly, too."

Amos blinked at her. "Esterly?"

"She must have killed him because he saw her at the Chatterbox that night. Knew she'd switched clothes and lured Sylvia out to the bridge. How she got your car and your gun, I don't know. But I know she's dressed as a man before."

Amos shut his eyes. There was Eugenia again, with the short black hair. "Yes," he said, "she cut her hair."

"Did you see her?"

"At the bottom of the stairs. Waiting. Like I waited for her."

"Here? At police headquarters?"

Amos mumbled something he wasn't sure of himself. He didn't want to be here, now; he wanted to go back to the world before the war, when he and Eugenia walked by the sea at Margate. They had kissed only once, but he remembered it all. Lovely warm evening, stars in a velvet sky, mustering out in the morning, orange scent in her hair. She wouldn't have jumped off a ship, killing herself for one kiss. No, it had been a terrible accident, hit her head or something.

"You hit your head?"

His eyelids fluttered open. Lennox still sat there. Couldn't she see he was busy?

"Turn that way." She pushed his skull to one side. "Jeepers, you've got a lump the size of a baseball. Did the doctor look at you?"

"Damn coppers."

"They don't hit over the head like that. That must be from falling on the stairs. Who took you home, Amos? When you collapsed?"

Lennox stood up at last. Maybe she'd let him sleep now.

"Christ. It was her."

He closed his eyes again. "Eugenia," he whispered.

"Iris. She took you home, slipped you a Mickey, took your car and your gun." She bent down over him. "Who the hell is Eugenia?"

Lennox had the matron call the doctor about Amos's head. The way he was muttering and sweating, something had to be done. Whether it was from his lungs or falling on the granite steps or Iris slipping him a Mickey, she didn't know. Hell, it might even have been something this Eugenia did, whoever she was.

For his own sake, she considered reading his scribblings. She had glanced at the sheets and saw the name Eugenia. But she didn't seem to have any significance to anyone but Amos Haddam. Maybe she was someone who existed only in his mind.

The matron returned to tell her the doctor would come as soon as he could. Which could be hours, or tomorrow. Lennox decided to write him a note about Amos's condition, in case the old soldier was too groggy to answer questions. The matron offered her an impossibly small piece of paper and she numbered his ailments, wrote her telephone number at work and at home, and Uncle Herb's for good measure, then shoved the paper back across the counter.

Amos had to get better—and get out of here. There was no other way. And finding Iris was the key.

"Georgie Terraciano. I need to know everything you know about him."

Lennox sat across the kitchen table from Herb Warren, her fingers wrapped around a cup of coffee her aunt had foisted on her. Seeing her aunt Maureen was hard without remembering how much Verna had hated her for her elegant bearing and simple goodness. But then Verna had hated anyone who didn't appreciate her smart mouth.

Maureen had excused herself to escort her elderly mother to bed. The house smelled of peach pie and old times. When Lennox had lived here, all she'd felt were stifling rules and undeserved kindness. Now, in the quiet kitchen, she strained for sounds of cars outside. She was sure she'd been followed on the way over, but nothing had come of it.

Herb sipped his coffee. "You're working for him?"

"Through Vanvleet. But they won't tell me a thing."

"Something happen?"

"I don't trust him. What's happened to Amos—I feel like Georgie is behind all this somehow."

"Don't jump to conclusions." Herb got up to pour himself more coffee. "He's a thug, Dorie. You don't want to tangle with him."

Lennox stared at the black liquid in her cup. Could it be Georgie following her? And would it be worth the thrill to take him on? No, she should be practical.

"Look, Herb. Somehow, Georgie's connected. He says Iris Jackson was his girl. I say it was something else. What's he mixed up in?"

"Meatpacking. Been in that for years, his uncle's business. Squeezed out his cousin fifteen years ago."

"What about horse racing?"

"There've been rumors he put old racehorses into his sausage, but we've never proved anything. He owns a couple ponies. I heard about that when—"

"The Pony Jump?"

"Right. There was always something floating around about his connection with the Black Hand, being Italian and all. Known for a few dark deeds, they were. The Italians had a shaky truce with Pendergast. All Democrats, but not exactly together on things. And there was more than one Italian cell."

"Which was Georgie?"

"There was two families, Lusco and Lazia. He was with Lazia, I think. That whole thing broke down after Johnny was killed."

This name kept coming up. "Tell me about Lazia."

Herb sat down. Out of uniform, he looked like a laborer, in a chambray shirt and big worker's pants, neatly pressed by Maureen. His neck was reddened by the sun. He rubbed the back of it now. "Brother John? He cut quite a figure. Old Tom didn't like him much for that."

"Pendergast cuts quite the figure in prison stripes, I hear."

Herb chuckled. "Tom was thick into horses himself. Nobody knew how thick until it was too late."

She fingered her cup. "Lazia," she prompted.

"Well, Johnny got his first beef for stealing a diamond stickpin. That oughta tell you something. He was like a cat, slinking around in his custom duds. But always the gentleman, polite, a ladies' man. Hard to pin things on a man like that. He wore little rimless Franklins, made him look serious. But he was a sport. Always at the clubs, gambling. Had a big summer place on Lake Lotawana, where he raced speedboats."

"He was a racketeer."

"Oh, sure. Into gambling heavy. Getting rid of gambling is going to make Kansas City right again."

It wasn't the time to get Herb kicking on his high moral horse. "So who killed him?"

"Never arrested anybody. We always thought it was them Luscos. They had it out for Lazia because he was more popular than Pendergast then. They all grew up together down there, in your neighborhood, Little Italy. Lotta violence, fights. Wops hated the colored, used to bushwhack 'em, dynamite their houses. Then somebody'd come down and do the same to the wops."

"How come so many of them got into gambling and all?"

"No jobs for plain laborers . . . well, at least no money in it. They were uneducated, most of them. Johnny worked for a lawyer once; he coulda made it straight. But he wanted it all, fast. The usual story."

Lennox ran her finger around the rim of the coffee cup. "So Georgie was in his gang?"

"If I remember right. Georgie's kept his nose clean the last couple years. I did hear something about taxes."

"Is he behind?"

"Could be, if he's losing racing ponies, or gambling heavy. Or maybe winning big and not reporting it."

"Is he under investigation for anything at your end?"

"If he is, it's not my department." Herb drained his coffee cup. "I'd love to talk about these crooks all night, darlin', but time flies. And soon morning'll be flying in my face."

Lennox looked at the clock, a chicken with wing hands that said 10:30. "Kept you too long. Sorry." Herb gave her a hug, smothering her in his laundry-fresh shirt. He took her shoulders in his hands.

"Only thing too long is the time between visits. Come earlier so we can play cards. The girls love rummy."

"Sure, that'd be swell." Gin rummy with Maureen and her mother, Winifred—she needed that and a hole in the head. Herb kissed her and said good night. At the door, Lennox turned back.

"Does the name Eugenia mean anything to you?"

"Why?"

"Amos mentioned it."

Her uncle took her arm and walked out the screen door and onto the porch. "Before the war, someone he knew. In England."

"But she's—"

"Dead. Some accident before the war ended."

"Long time to carry a torch."

In the thick elms, the cicadas whined like violins in a horror picture.

"Some things," her uncle said softly, "you just never get over."

Forty-first Street was quiet. The big Warren house had been built by Winifred's husband, a banker, at the turn of the century. The trees, elms and maples, made overgrown canopies, shading the elegant streetlamps. Down the steep stairs, Lennox tripped quietly, walking to the Packard.

There was no movement on the street. She shook off her jitters and climbed into the car, thinking of Amos's lost Eugenia. To be haunted by a lost love for twenty years, that seemed cruel. Yet she knew ghosts clung to you, heavy, warm memories, as you tried, night after night, to remember and honor them. And to shuck off the guilt of living when they were cold and gone.

As she pulled out and drove to the corner, Lennox heard a car behind her. Its headlights shone in her eyes. She turned left quickly, trying to see the car from the side. Parked cars and overhanging branches blocked her view.

Myrtle Street was narrow, clogged with parked cars. The headlights came up close behind her. She turned again, bald tires squealing. Thirty-eighth Street wasn't any better. The car stuck. At Benton Boulevard, she turned north. The street was wider but about as well lit as the Hannibal Bridge after midnight. She cursed the city fathers and watched the car come around the corner behind her. It was black, a sedan. Chevy, Buick, maybe a LaSalle.

Lennox floored the old 120 down the Boulevard to Linwood, turned left with a green light. Behind her, the car squealed through on a yellow. Forty-five, fifty, fifty-five miles per hour. The traffic was light on Linwood. The buses had stopped for the night, apartment buildings were dark.

At Paseo, she turned again. In her own neighborhood, she could duck into an alley, get into her building in a flash. She looked at her watch. Almost eleven. Damn, the house will be locked.

The wide boulevard with its grassy median and war memorials was busy. She slowed behind a taxi and a creeping coupe driven by white-haired gent. The black sedan pulled behind her. She edged the Packard forward, hoping the taxi hack would get the message. She honked her horn. He ignored her.

The sedan bumped her, hard. She lurched forward, almost hitting her head on the steering wheel. Son of a bitch! She gripped the wheel. The sedan rammed her again, harder. She jerked the wheel left, but they followed. Then right. The sedan caught her on angle this time, crunching the corner of the bumper, throwing the car sideways.

Wildly, she steered it back into line, throttling hard. She bumped up over the right curb, through a patch of flowers, onto the sidewalk, and off again onto a side street. The black sedan followed, avoiding the flowerbed.

She raced down the street, turning left on Brooklyn and stomping hard on the gas. The sedan never faltered. Who were they? And what the hell did they mean by playing bumper cars? If they were trying to intimidate her, they were barking up the wrong tree. She felt a surge of anger. Damn wops. Why did she assume they were Italians? Shirley's and Herb's words echoed in her mind, their warnings. But what had she done to Georgie? She was working for the sawed-off greaser!

A red stoplight loomed ahead at Independence Boulevard. She looked in her rearview mirror. The sedan was half a block back, coming fast. Lennox plunged out into the intersection. Horns blared; a gray coupe brushed past her. She wove around a maroon sedan, cut the corner, and headed left across the traffic. But before she could look behind her, she realized she'd made a mistake. She was in Terrace Park, on the bluffs above the Missouri. To her right, the lights of the railroad bridge, to the left the ASB and Hannibal bridges. Straight ahead, inky dark. Below, the river.

The curvy park lanes of the Terrace weren't made for eluding black sedans. Her only hope was to zip around and take the first exit. She crouched over the wheel.

The sedan burst into the park and aimed for her. The road ahead curved left. She was going too fast. Blood thumped in her ears. She hit the brakes and the sedan hit her, knocking her off the pavement and onto the parched grass. She clutched the wheel. There—another strip of blacktop. Bumping down the curb onto the other lane, she pulled right, skidding and heading away from the cliffs.

She suddenly began to laugh. If this wasn't some evening excitement! Like bumper cars at Electric Park. Talbot would have loved this: MYSTERY SEDAN SETS SIGHTS ON BULLET-RIDDEN PACKARD. Had she pointed out the bullet holes? Not unusual in cars auctioned at the sheriff's sale. Not in wild and woolly Kaw-town.

The sedan screeched into place behind her. She sucked in her breath. Where had it come from? The car whacked her hard, on the right-rear fender. Glass crunched under rubber. The Packard felt funny, wobbly, and the laugh in her throat melted into a groan.

She hung on to the steering wheel, twisting it left as the car skidded off the pavement again, heading for a clump of lilac bushes. Piloting around them, she got a wild hair, came back up on the street behind the black sedan. Stomping down on the pedal, she grit her teeth and roared up behind them. Two men in the front seat, dark-haired. The driver jerked the wheel and they turned off the roadway onto the grass. She sped past them. Winding around a corner, she slammed on the brakes: There, on her right, was the exit.

Home wasn't far away now. She took Lexington for a few blocks, but it was too open, too bright, so she jammed into the side streets where ragpicker's horses grazed on lawns. Slowing the Packard and her pulse, she turned off her headlights, drove as fast as she dared, crossed Paseo, jogged up to Pacific, and was on Charlotte before her breathing relaxed.

In the alley behind Mrs. Ferazzi's, she pulled the battered Packard to a stop. She got out and stood in the shadows, listening. In the garden behind Poppy's boardinghouse, night-blooming flowers smelled sweet and lush. The scrape of a window opening broke the silence; then the piano player began, melancholy and light. The music lulled her, made her cling to the wire fence too long. Another old song, one from her father's records. Duke Ellington, "Solitude."

The sedan rolled past the end of the alley. Lennox ducked behind the Packard. She waited for the car to stop. When it didn't, she dived across the alley, vaulted Mrs. Ferazzi's picket fence, and ducked around the side of the house. The space between the houses was narrow and dark, the dirt soft and mossy.

Headlights shone across the sidewalk. Lennox squeezed against the side of the house. The lights went out. Inching forward, she peered into the shadows and almost stepped on a body at her feet. Old Jenny, asleep, with her quilts piled around her, her gray head on the wooden sign.

At the front of the house, Lennox flattened herself again. Someone was talking. Two men. She strained to hear what they were saying. They must be in their car, waiting for her. The talking stopped, footsteps on the pavement.

Quiet. The piano player was silent. What about the back door? But she knew Mrs. F. bolted it at night. Was Frankie in there reading? No, the lights were out.

Voices from the alley. Lennox inched to the back. They were getting into the Packard! She drew out her switchblade and opened it at her side. She still held her keys in her other hand, gripping them tightly to keep them quiet. If only she could get inside. Suddenly, Mrs. F.'s rambling wreck was a sanctuary.

The voices were getting closer. Should she go to the street? What if another man was waiting there, by the door? Were there more than two of them? She brought up the blade. She didn't want to cut anyone, but what choice had they given her?

Trying to run her off the road, that was sure provocation. There was a short stretch of tall fence at the back corner of the house. She tiptoed back to it.

The footsteps got closer, went away, came back. A hoarse whisper: "Dark back here."

Brilliant, Sherlock. She readied herself, put her keys carefully in her pocket. She stepped up on the low crossbar of the fence.

A man stepped out from behind the fence. She jumped him from the back, landing like a monkey, wrapping her legs around his waist. He squawked, lurched back into the second man, who grunted and fell to the ground. Lennox tightened her grip on the man's neck and brought the knife around to his throat.

"Hey! Hey!" the man garbled.

"Hey yourself, bruno!" Her arms ached. "Ready for some barbering?"

"M-m-miss Lennox? That you?"

She twisted her head. Luther stood in the yard, dusting off his pants. He was smiling. "There she is, man. She's not lost or n-n-nothing."

Her arms weakened.

"This a game, Dorie?" said the man on whose back she rode.

She wanted to curse. Instead, she pushed off his back and jumped to the ground. She stared at them, panting.

Harvey Talbot was rubbing his neck. "You cook that one up special for us?"

She twisted her neck, looked down the alley. "What are you doing here?"

"Looking for you," he said. "We put the paper to bed, so I came by, but you weren't here. Then these goons roll by, giving us looks like something rotten's about to fry."

"They tried to run me off the road," she said. She flipped her knife shut and slipped it back in her trouser pocket. "When did you see them?"

"Just a few minutes ago. I was talking to this guy who owns the garage."

"Sizz-m-m—m—"

"Czmanski?"

Harvey said, "He's pretty well lit. But he told me I could find Luther round the block."

She looked at Luther, standing awkwardly, barefoot, in the dirty black pants and undershirt. He looked like his old broken self.

"You're all right, then? I'll g-g-go."

Harvey clapped the bum on the back. "Thanks, old boy."

They watched him lope off through Mrs. F.'s dry weeds, out the gate, down the alley. He probably had some cubbyhole like Jenny, a place safe to sleep. She hoped he did.

"I thought you were those goons," she said.

"Don't worry about it. I'll be able to sing in a week or two."

He sat down on the weathered wood steps of the back stoop. He slid to one side and made room for her. She sat down next to him.

The charge of the moment leached away and she felt limp. She lowered her head to her knees. "Jesus H. Christ."

"Who were those guys? In the car, I mean."

"I don't know." She looked up at Harvey. His pale skin glowed in the dim light, a purple shadow against his cheek. "Did you recognize them?"

He shook his head. "What have you been up to?"

"Just the usual."

"Probing and prying where you don't belong, I s'pose."

"The usual."

"I guess I should have been more worried about the goons."

She looked up at the dark clouds. "You would have enjoyed the chase around Terrace Park." She smiled. "Writing headlines on the fly."

"So you missed me?"

She turned to look at him. "Sorry about your neck." Her fingertips grazed his neck; then she kissed him. Her lips felt hot against his, but then Louie came back, ugly and rich. She stood up.

"Dorie," he said, standing behind her. "I'd give anything to erase last night, to pretend it never happened."

She turned back to him. "I wouldn't."

He blinked, confused, an enchanted state in any man.

"Did you hear what happened at the Chatterbox?"

He nodded. "Does it have something to do with Iris Jackson?"

"Oh, I would bet on it."

"Why are you telling me this now?"

"I thought you might want some good headline material," she said. "That's all."

Harvey took her shoulders. "I came over to see if you wanted to go dancing tomorrow night. It's my night off, and I got some tickets from my editor."

"Dancing?"

"At the Kansas City Club. It's Julia Lee. Not as good as big-band maybe—"

"I love her piano. I haven't heard her since she left her brother's band."

"Then you'll go?"

She took his arm and guided them back down the dark side yard, steering around the doomsday lady. At the sidewalk, she said, "That depends."

"On what?"

"On if you can dance," she said.

He pulled her close. "What about that headline?"

"First things first, eh, ace?" She looked up at his chin, then pushed back. "The bartender who was plugged was working the night Iris Jackson supposedly took her brodie off the bridge."

"What's the connection?" He frowned. "What do you mean, 'supposedly took her brodie'? Don't tell me you've forgotten her lovely smell."

"Oh, no. But that's not our Iris."

She gave him the short version on the manicure, the hair, the switch. He folded his arms, nodding, then paced on the sidewalk as he worked it out to his own satisfaction.

"She set the whole thing up? Why?"

"She wanted to disappear, to keep on doing whatever she's doing without being interfered with."

"And what, pray tell, is that?"

Lennox leaned against the lamppost. "Hey, I'm only a private snoop, not a mind reader."

"So she does admit to imperfection."

"Don't tell." She pulled him close. "We still don't know if you can dance, ace."

SIXTEEN

FIRST MISSOURI SAVINGS BANK was a venerable pile of bricks on Grand, wedged between a men's custom tailor and a bookstore. Through the narrow street entrance, the lobby widened and was brightened by a third-story domed skylight. The effect inspired immediate purse emptying, Dorie decided.

She presented her letter to three clerks and a vice president before being whisked into the president's office by a red-nailed polka-dot lover named Patsy. No sign of the man himself. Lennox lowered herself into an upholstered chair in front of a large desk. A fine oil painting—Thomas Hart Benton, if she wasn't mistaken—hung over the sofa. Farmers toiling in tall corn, a good old Kansas-Missouri theme.

The sofa was a lush green velvet, as was her chair. She thought she might never get up: more bank psychology. Before she could fall asleep, the bank president stepped out of a washroom, wiping his hands on a towel.

She stood up and introduced herself. "I have a letter of authorization from Mrs. George Terraciano to look at her accounts."

Mr. President, whose name was Sidney Pitt, took the letter, laid it on his desk, and continued drying his hands. Finally, he disappeared with the towel, returned, shut the door.

"Miss Lennox. After I call Mr. Terraciano, I'll be glad to let you examine the accounts." He folded his short arms. He had a bushy head of gray hair, gold-rimmed glasses, and a somber suit.

"The letter's not adequate, then?"

"In a word, no."

"And why is that?"

He smiled smugly. "You should know if Mrs. Terraciano is really your client. She was here a few days ago and told us to keep the accounts in strictest confidence, that somebody might come around. Mr. Terraciano is an extremely valuable customer to the bank."

"And what if I told you that the woman you thought was Marilyn Terraciano was an imposter. That Mrs. Terraciano has never set foot in this bank."

Gray eyebrows up. "I spoke to her myself."

"Did you check her identification?"

"Naturally." But he blinked and looked away. "Are we quite finished here? I have work to do."

"I do, too. I'll leave as soon as I see the accounts."

"I'm afraid we'll need Mr. Terraciano's okay on that."

Lennox clenched her jaw. "Then at least I can see her own account. That one doesn't need his okay; she writes the checks on it. Go ahead and call her if you want. And I'd be glad to have the real Mrs. Terraciano come down here and present herself."

Mr. Pitt's eyes narrowed. He stared at her for a moment, then stalked out the door. The clock on the wall ticked. Half an hour passed. Lennox hadn't been kicked out of the president's office, and his chairs were cozy. She waited. Another fifteen minutes went by. Then Polka-Dot Patsy came in, led her to a conference room with a cup of burnt coffee and a file folder. When Lennox left a short time later, the plan to keep her pennies in a coffee can behind the radiator had become one of her better ideas.

Lennox walked around the corner to use the pay phone at Woolworth's. Inside the store, the counter was busy with coffee-and-eggers. She edged past the toilet tissue, summer sandals on sale for nineteen cents, and into the booth. But Marilyn wasn't home. Had Pitt called her for an okay? Lennox didn't leave her name. She hung up and called the Chatterbox. Marian Esterly answered. Death or not, back to work. Lennox told her to give a message to Sylvia's mother, should she stop in again. "Tell her to check out the city morgue." It might not have been the best way to break the news, but one grieving mother could surely comfort another.

On the street again, Lennox walked past the bright windows of Emery-Bird-Thayer. The department store was atwinkle in plaids and tweeds and sequins and organza. She stopped and stared at a gray chiffon dress. Would the old blue dress do for tonight? The skirt was full enough for dancing. She wore it when she was trying to impress clients, and probably would have done better had she been wearing it this morning at the bank, instead of the tan trousers and green blouse.

It wouldn't hurt to look around at E-B-T for a minute. It was only 9:30. She still wanted to find out where Georgie parked his company cars, try to find a black one with dents. And there was something going on at the Blue Valley Racetrack. But the stables probably didn't get busy till noon.

Inside the big department store, the effects of the Depression and the desertion of shoppers in favor of the Country Club Plaza were obvious. The high ceiling had a gray cast, lightbulbs were out, and spiderwebs hung in remote ironwork. Lennox remembered coming here once at Christmas with her mother and father—she must have been only four or five; Tillie hadn't been born yet—when the decorations glittered and the smell of hot cider and cinnamon and pine boughs filled the aisles. Today, the old ship of dreams was barely afloat.

She bucked up her spirits for a trip through Ladies Dresses. A few minutes of pawing brought her to the conclusion she couldn't afford a thing. She wandered down to the basement, where the bargains lurked. But disappointment hung like sackcloth down there, and she left in a hurry. The blue dress would do.

On the steps, she looked at the hazy sky. Those maker tags,

the Emery-Bird-Thayer ones. The dresses were full of them. So were Iris Jackson's girdles and garter belts and brassieres. How did a girl get that much fancy lingerie? Sugar daddy? Or—? Lennox walked back inside and found lingerie on the second floor. Camisoles, girdles, full slips, half-slips, bras, garter belts—many with the house label. She was fingering a satiny garter belt with embroidered pink roses when the saleswoman popped up.

"Isn't that the sweetest thing?" she said. She had a toothy smile. "If, for instance, you're out doing the shag, the Lindy, or what all, and your dress should fly up . . . well, it's nice to think you've got something pretty on."

Lennox stared at the garter belt. She hadn't thought about undergarments. She wondered if Harvey did the Lindy. "Isn't there some sort of, um, bloomer?"

The saleswoman, a well-endowed redhead named Joyce, waxed lyrical about the delicate nature of short bloomers for dancing, and at seventy-five cents, Lennox felt she had to have a pair in pearl gray. As the woman wrapped them up, Lennox asked her about the house label.

"All the big stores do it, Saks Fifth Avenue, Macy's. We buy them and put our labels in them."

"So if you work here, you can buy them at discount?"

"Oh, you better believe it." Joyce leaned closer and winked. "I have the most hotcha lingerie in Kansas City, I swear on my mother's grave."

"So you buy them yourself, or do you have yourself a sugar daddy?"

"For shame!" Joyce laughed. "I'm a married woman. Though to tell the truth, the sugar man business is pretty good in here. My husband gets them for me. He gives me the money and I put them on my discount. But he loves to come in and pick 'em out. That's my Ernie."

"This is kinda strange," Lennox said as she took the bloomers, "but do you remember a girl who might have worked here, tall and pretty, nice manicure, maybe a rich fella on the side?"

"Tall and pretty—that's all of us, isn't it?" Joyce winked again. She was a champion winker. "What color hair?"

"Good question. Blond, or black." Or almost any color.

"There was Hildy; she got married last year and quit. She's blond."

"That doesn't sound like her."

"Sorry."

Lennox thanked her. Downstairs, she squirted Chanel No. 5 on her neck and walked past the counters of makeup, jewelry, and gloves. Asking Joyce seemed a little dumb. Iris might have worked anywhere in the store, or not at all. The tags just seemed like a clue. But maybe not.

The store was filling with society women, clerks, secretaries, salesgirls. At the ring counter, a tall dark-haired woman was trying something big and gawdy on her finger. Her figure made Lennox pause.

Her hair was cut just below the ears. Her shoulders were narrow, like Iris's. Her nails were red, immaculate. Her suit had a little peplum that accentuated her waist, and a tight skirt. Lennox stepped up beside her.

The woman turned. She wore heavy eye makeup, her brows arched. Her lined cheeks were dusted with rouge. She parted deep red lips, revealing gray teeth.

Lennox excused herself, then ran out of the store, her bloomers under her arm. On the steps, she scolded herself. It wasn't going to be that easy to find Iris.

The Blue Valley Racetrack parking lot was a sea of scorched gravel. She'd gone back to the office to find Palmer Eustace's telephone number. Then remembered Amos said he'd never had it. Shirley tried to find it but couldn't. She tracked down Floyd Wilson's number instead, in case Lennox wanted to talk to him. At Georgie Terraciano's meatpacking plant, near the stockyards, in a sweet-smelling part of town, cruising the parking lot hadn't turned up any black sedans with dents. Her Packard, rattling and crunched, developed a scraping noise on the drive out from the city. Lennox parked next to fifteen or twenty other cars in the shade of the tall bleachers and walked through the STAFF ONLY gate in the whitewashed fence. She found the horse Smitty's Dream being curried in an open stall. A short conversation with a sullen teenage groom named Darryl was going exactly nowhere.

"You ever bet on Smitty here?"

"Nope."

"He looks like a nice horse. You ride him?"

"Nope."

Lennox pushed back her hair and felt the heat from the moist hay and manure permeate the air.

"Is Smitty running tonight?"

"Nope."

"Another one of Georgie's ponies, then?"

"Dollface."

Lennox blinked, then realized that was the name of the horse. "Where's Dollface?"

He nodded his head south. She wandered down the stalls, checking names beside the gates. When she found Dollface—Fairacre's Tawny Dollface—the stall was empty. Another groom, a teenage girl in riding clothes, led a horse by. Lennox asked her about Dollface and was told she was being exercised.

"Is Georgie Terraciano around?"

The girl squinted. "Who knows? He's around here a lot. Sticking his nose into everybody's business."

"He is a busybody, isn't he?" Lennox fell into stride beside the girl and the chestnut horse.

The groom had a blond braid down her back. She tossed back her head. "Just because he's had a couple winning horses lately, the man thinks he hung the moon. He's over here telling me and Darryl how to exercise our mounts, as if we were his employees."

"You aren't?"

"Heck no. I work on Brick Rogert's horses, not his."

"So you don't work for the track?"

"Oh, we do. But we're also paid by the horse owners. The trainers choose the grooms, just like jockeys."

"Do you see the track owners very often?"

"Mr. Wilson comes to the races. He's a nice man, but he doesn't know squat about horses. And the other bird, no one's seen him at all. Never comes out. Somebody said he was here opening day. Up in the owners' box."

"You know Mr. Terraciano's jockeys?"

"Not the new ones."

"New ones? He just hired them?"

The groom glanced at her, then away. "Uh-huh."

"Because he fired the old ones?"

She shrugged, petting the nose of the chestnut.

"Why were they fired?"

"I wouldn't know. I'm just a groom." Her voice was harsh.

Lennox patted the horse's neck. "But was there a problem?"

The girl led the horse on. "Listen, I have to get to work."

Head down, trying out theories, Lennox went off in search of a pay phone. Georgie was up to something out here, and it stunk. Had Amos gotten too close? Although Shirley had done it already, Lennox dialed the operator and asked for a listing for Palmer Eustace. Still no go. She couldn't very well ask Vanvleet, could she? He ordered Amos off the case. But she had Floyd Wilson's number. She dug out more nickels and rung him. A butler or somebody said for her to wait. No problem. Waiting was her middle name.

Five minutes later, Wilson answered the telephone. His voice wavered like an old man's.

"If I could have a few minutes of your time, Mr. Wilson," she said. "I'm a colleague of . . . Dutch Vanvleet." She had almost said Amos Haddam. She wasn't sure old Vanvleet's name would get her any further.

"What about?"

"The racetrack. But nothing like the auditor and all that. That's been resolved."

"Resolved? What the hell you mean?"

"Dropped. Over. Finis."

"The lawsuit's been dropped? That what you're telling me?"

Lawsuit? Lennox swallowed hard. "I can't tell you that. But I do have some other information for you. About your partner."

The old man sniffed. "My partner. Who you kiddin'?"

"You do have a partner named Palmer Eustace?"

There was a pause. When the voice came back, it was subdued, wary. "Yes."

"Then can I come talk to you? Say about four o'clock today?"

Floyd Wilson agreed, in his new odd tone. Lennox wondered who he thought she really was. G-man, cop, revenuer? She smiled. She could be anybody he wanted as long as he answered her questions.

She found her way out of the stables and back to the parking lot. Georgie Terraciano was winning big bets, long shots, with those new jockeys. Had anyone else's jockeys been fired? Were they fixing races? Did Floyd Wilson and Palmer Eustace know about it? And what did the track have to do with Iris Jackson?

Lennox wove around bumpers gleaming in the sun. Was Palmer Eustace colored, like the *Star* reporter'd said? What was this lawsuit?

She didn't see the man who jumped her. He pinned her arms behind her. Shock gave way quickly to rage and she kicked him hard with her stiff oxfords. He grunted but kept hold. Another man jumped up to clinch her ankles tightly under his arm. With his other hand, he searched her pockets, dumped everything on the gravel. Lennox screamed for the grooms, but before anyone could come, she was thrown in the back of a black sedan. Of all things.

A very small man sat on the backseat next to her, a thin smile on his lips. His short legs dangled off the floor like a child's. He wore a tiny black suit, black shirt, and white tie, like a midget movie gangster, or a miniature Georgie Terraciano. On his very small hands, he wore very small black leather gloves.

The two big boys got in front. She straightened her blouse and glared at the midget. "What the hell is this?"

"Behave yourself, Miss Lennox, and this ride will be over soon." His voice was nasal and rough, but childlike. "Misbehave and . . . well, there's no promises then."

"You in the promise business?"

He smoothed his slacks and gave her another enigmatic smile.

"Who are you? What's going on?"

The sedan moved out of the parking lot as Lennox wrestled with the door handle. Locked again. This black sedan kidnapping routine was getting old. No more was said until the sedan pulled off the highway in a grove of willows along the creek and stopped.

"Now we'll talk, Miss Lennox." The midget crossed one tiny foot over his knee. His lilac-water scent was nauseating. "What do you know about the financial dealings of one Georgie Terraciano?"

"Nothing."

"Oh, come. You work for the man."

"That doesn't mean he tells me anything." She tried the door again. "You work for him, too?"

"If we did, Miss Lennox, would we be here?" The midget scooted closer. The driver got out of the car.

"If I knew who you were, I could better answer that."

"You were at his bank today, looking at his accounts."

"They wouldn't show them to me."

The driver opened Lennox's car door and pushed her to the middle as he hopped in. She was wedged now between the heavily muscled thug and the flower-sweet, pint-size Pretty Boy Floyd.

"Listen, fellas, if I knew anything, I'd tell you. I don't like Georgie any more than you do." She hoped they really didn't work for him. "Look, what do you want know, specifically? Ask me. I'll tell you what I know."

The midget took her right hand as the thug twisted her left behind her. She stiffened, arching her back.

"Such nice hands. Precious little fingers." She tried to pull her hand away, but the thug held her elbow, too. She could feel his hot breath on her neck.

The midget broke her little finger so quickly, the pain came after the audible snap. Her body hardened and she let out a groan.

"Now, my dear, tell us everything."

Lennox heaved for breath. Pain shot up her arm to her shoulder. The finger lay at an odd angle in the midget's palm. "Okay, okay. He's got racehorses; you know that."

"Yes, dearie," the midget squeaked.

"And I think he's got money troubles, taxes. So maybe he's fixing races, betting on them and winning big."

"Very interesting. Do go on."

"I don't know anything else, honest." She watched with horror as he picked up her next finger. "Aw, come on. I don't."

"What about the suitcase money?" He lifted her finger.

"What? I don't know anything about suitcase money."

The midget snapped her fourth finger between the knuckles. He did it so quickly, she was grateful. Except for almost passing out.

"Enough fooling, girlie. The Truman money. Where is it?"

She tried to clear her vision. Smarting tears ran down her cheeks. "Truman money? You know more about this than I do, short stuff."

The midget bared his baby teeth and slapped her, the leather glove stinging her face. He kept at it, back and forth, the tiny hand connecting with one cheek, then the other. It hurt but it took her mind off the racking pain in her hand.

Finally, the thug spoke up: "She don't know nothing, boss."

The little man sat back but kept his hand up and ready. The tiny paw packed a pretty good wallop for its size. His nasty little face was red with fury.

"Dump her," he said.

SEVENTEEN

AT 3:45, Dorie Lennox let out the clutch and let the Packard lurch to a stop in the middle of the street. Charlotte Street lay rancid in the afternoon heat. Luther approached from the shadows, his head tipped in question.

"Sumpin' wrong, M-m-miss Dorie?"

She pulled herself out of the car. The drive back from the track had been slow in second gear. She couldn't get the Packard to shift to third without passing out from the pain. She held the maimed fingers against her stomach.

"Watch the heap, Luther."

She ran up the boardinghouse steps. She had to go talk to Floyd Wilson. A few choice words about midgets slipped out on the way up the stairs.

At her door, she fumbled in her pockets. Thank God she still had her blade, that they'd only dumped her stuff in the gravel. But she'd left her keys in the car. She was locked out of her room. Back downstairs, she poked her head in the kitchen. Frankie was bent over the kitchen table, rolling out piecrust.

"Got any cloth down here, gauze strips?" Lennox asked.

Frankie stared at her red sausage fingers. "Lordy, girl."

"Fast, Frankie, I gotta be somewhere."

The girl looked frantically around the kitchen, rolling pin in hand. Then her face lit up. "Come on, back to the house."

Frankie led her across the yard, out the gate, into the neat, well-tended vegetable garden with its rows of tasseled corn, pole beans, okra and beets, up the wooden steps. They entered a dim kitchen, scrubbed clean and smelling of simmering collard greens. Frankie took Lennox's good hand and pulled her through a hallway. From another room, a clunk, then an awkward plunking of piano keys. They went into a bathroom and shut the door. The room was a recent improvement, with white tile on the floor and a big porcelain bathtub.

From the cabinet over the sink, Frankie took out a tongue depressor and a roll of gauze. She turned on the cold water and filled the basin.

"Stick 'em in there for a sec, get the swelling down."

"I don't have time, Frankie."

"How'd it happen? You fall down?"

"Just wrap 'em. Please."

The girl gave her head a shake and sat Lennox down on the edge of the tub. She splinted the fingers and bit off the end of the gauze, tucking it under the bandage. She made Lennox wait while she wet a washcloth and cleaned her face of road grime. The walk back to the racetrack had been dry and long. Lennox thanked her.

On the way out of the house, she paused at the sound of the scales. "Who's playing?"

"My nephew, Sonny."

"Is he ready to join a band?"

Frankie smiled. "Soon. He's already five years old."

Floyd Wilson lived on Stateline, on the Missouri side, but in sniffing distance of Kansas. Lennox snarled to herself. Back in golf course country. She might have known by that sneer in the old man's voice. He would probably be missing his afternoon game.

A thick belt of trees hid the brick house from the road. Lennox steered the Packard up the circle drive. She'd never seen this house before. Nor so much grass in one place. The man could have a golf course in his own yard.

He answered the door himself. Thin, with a shock of white hair, Wilson had once been tall, but now was stooped. Close to seventy-five, she guessed, following his tilted gait into a parlor stuffed with modern furniture. The sleek shapes of the sofa and chairs, the steel and glass of the tables—all looked incongruous in this old house. She eyed the old man. Who else lived here?

Wilson pointed to a strange laminated-wood chair for her. It was surprisingly comfortable. He lowered himself onto the edge of the deep red sofa. His navy duck pants looked more suited to yachting than to golf.

"What's with the hand?" he demanded.

"Accident."

He frowned, then, after some discussion within, agreed with himself. At least his eyesight was still in order.

"Who did you say you were again?"

Lennox wished she'd changed her dirty clothes. "Doria Lennox. I work with Amos Haddam." No use lying, once you're in the door.

"That bag of bones?" Wilson sniffed again. He and the winker ought to get together and start a vaudeville act. "So, what's this about?"

"Your partner, as I said on the phone. Palmer Eustace."

"Never met the man, if that's your question. Dutch set the whole thing up himself, found me a partner, formed the corporation. And now he's trying to set me up for something, but I can't tell what. I used to trust the man."

"You don't have meetings?"

"Phone calls, that's it. We have a track manager; he takes care of things. Or he's supposed to."

"What's his name, this manager?"

"Vance Moore."

Lennox would have written it down, but writing was out for a while. Instead, she repeated the name.

Wilson looked at her oddly. "You all right, miss? Need something for that hand?"

The pain waxed in a flash, as if gratified by the attention. Lennox winced and the old man trotted off somewhere. In a minute, he and a young woman were back with a towel full of ice. The woman clucked around, found a china bowl, set the towel and Lennox's hand in it, and put the whole thing in Lennox's lap.

"Thank you," she said, trying to smile at them.

"This is Gertie," Wilson said, nodding at the woman.

"His wife," Gertie said, smiling. She looked half his age, dressed in a stylish shift, but with her dark hair long and straight, tied loosely with a ribbon. She was barefoot.

"Don't know what I was thinking. Must've been the sun," Wilson said, then smiled at Gertie.

"We met on a sailboat, back on Nantucket." Gertie sighed. "And here I am."

"Landlocked," Lennox said.

Gertie and Floyd laughed. She grasped his hand, tapped his old chin lovingly, and skipped back to where she'd come from. Floyd watched her go for a long minute, as if she might disappear forever.

"Pretty girl," Lennox said.

"Too pretty for an old codger. I know it." He sunk into the red sofa. "Bought her all this new stuff. I hate it."

"You've lived here long?"

"Most of my life. My father built this house just before he died. I moved in with my first wife forty years ago." He looked around. "Great old place, isn't it?"

"Beautiful. Your father must have been very . . . creative."

"Rich, you mean?" Another sniff. "Started three banks. Two in Missouri, one in Kansas. Only one left now, but it's enough."

"Enough to start a racetrack from scratch."

"Oh, that. Not my own money, and barely have half interest. And we got plenty of county bond money, you know."

"So it's leveraged. Is that what you call it?"

"Mortgaged, leveraged. We don't own it outright. That's foolish in business."

"How so?"

"You don't want to lose your shirt. Seen enough of that, haven't we? So if the thing goes under, the bank ends up with it. I should know. We foreclosed on plenty of farms and businesses."

"Is the loan through your own bank?"

"Of course. It's my own personal loan."

Sounded like he couldn't lose. "And what bank is yours, Mr. Wilson?"

"First Missouri Savings." He grinned. "You want to open an account? We welcome all, big or small. That's our motto."

Lennox put the bowl of ice on the floor. Her hand was numb now. "I know that bank. Downtown." She smiled at Wilson. "Georgie Terraciano is one of your customers."

Wilson blinked. "I don't do day-to-day business anymore. I let Mr. Pitt take care of that."

"You know him?"

"Terraciano? We've met."

"Out at the racetrack?"

"No. At some society functions."

"He doesn't seem your type."

"How clever of you, Miss Lennox." He stood up; his stooped yet regal bearing was back. "I'm sorry I can't help you with Palmer Eustace. I have to say, I've always been a little curious myself." He led Lennox to the front hall. "Do you suppose it's Dutch Vanvleet himself?"

Lennox smiled. "He is a sly one, isn't he?"

On her way to Brookside, Lennox wondered where all this racetrack business was leading. Should she have mentioned the suitcase money to Floyd Wilson? The mysterious Palmer Eustace had her dander up. Was he a sham, an alias made up for the racetrack corporation? Was he Dutch Vanvleet's alter ego? She was curious, yes, but was it important? What she needed was something on Iris, where she was staying, what she wanted. And who had contracted the midget to lean on her? The thugs were new to her, as was the midget, although his methods had been around the block a few times. Her hand throbbed inside the splint and she tried holding it at various angles, none of which helped the pain.

The Terraciano house was also brick, with a green lawn about an eighth the size of Wilson's, manicured shrubs, and a large screen porch on the side. The Brookside neighborhood was respectable and proper, everything Georgie aspired to. His tots took their lessons from nuns; his wife had her own car and driver.

Lennox had stopped at a drugstore in Brookside to use the telephone, so she knew Marilyn was home and Georgie wasn't. But the meeting would have to be short, as it was close to six now. The door was opened by a Negro housekeeper, a stout, bright-eyed woman. She let Lennox in, eyed her bad hand, and disappeared.

Dinner smells came from a far room. The hallway was small with a crystal chandelier and a vase of white roses. Marilyn came from the direction of the delicious smells, wiping her hands on a pink apron. She shooed Lennox into a den and shut the door. Not the first time clients had been embarrassed to be seen with her.

Mrs. Terraciano didn't ask her to sit. She walked to the window overlooking the side yard, where two boys played on a swing set. "So what is it? What have you found out?"

Lennox leaned against the back of a leather chair. "The bank wouldn't let me see all the accounts. Claimed that you had told them not to, but that, of course, was the other woman. They did show me your own checking account."

"Did I make a mistake?"

"Two thousand dollars was withdrawn by bank draft two days before you tried to pay the school's tuition."

Marilyn looked sharply over her shoulder. "Who made the draft?"

"A bank official. He transferred the funds. So they probably went into another account."

"One of Georgie's, you mean. So he did it. He put the money in for me, then took it back out." She marched to the small white fireplace and turned on her heel. Her eyes snapped with anger. "What now?"

"I don't know if there's anything that can be done about that, Marilyn. But if you want to know about the other accounts, you'll have to go to the bank yourself. It'll take some convincing that you're the real Mrs. T., but if you have identification, they should show you the accounts. They showed them to the other Mrs. T., so why not you?"

"The other—*Who is this woman?*"

"I'm working on that."

"What's her name?"

"She's using bogus names now."

Marilyn untied her apron, balled it up, and threw it into the leather chair. Her heels clicked across the wood floor as she went to a small walnut desk, pulled a checkbook from a drawer, and scribbled on a check. She handed it to Lennox. "There. Two hundred dollars. I know I've got that much in there. I want to know who she is, where she lives, what she wants."

"Your husband is already paying me, Marilyn. It's not necessary."

"Take it."

Lennox took the check, folded it into her pocket.

Marilyn crossed her arms, seemed to focus on Dorie's bandages, then frowned. She turned toward the window and was quiet for a long minute. Then she whispered, "You have to go."

Lennox walked toward the door. "I'll call when I find out any more about her."

"No." Marilyn spun around. "I've changed my mind. I won't need you anymore."

Mrs. Terraciano stood stock-still, hands locked on the back

of the leather chair. She pulled her eyes off Lennox, looking back at the children outside. Lennox saw that the anger had gone out of her. Outside, a boy played, a boy who must be Richard, the seven-year-old.

"I see."

"Do you?" Marilyn said, her voice both hard and full of regret.

The Packard jumped the curb on Charlotte Street in front of Joe Czmanski's garage. Marilyn's turnaround was swift but understandable. No woman wants to know everything about her husband. Knowing what's necessary for children, food, and shelter generally satisfies. Knowing too much can sour things, make love difficult, partnership impossible. Dorie's own father had remained a mystery to her mother until the day he packed up his accordion and Jelly Roll Morton records and skipped town. Only then was it all too obvious that the man wanted more than children and Atchison and a WPA job sweeping the streets.

Joe stuck his scarred face out from the depths of the small garage. He was wiping his hands on a greasy rag as she kicked the car door shut with her foot.

"The old boiler sounds bad," he said. "Want me to look at it? Do it for nothing, for you, Dorie."

The pining in his voice cut her. Best not to take a hard look at Joe, with his hair gone and one side of his face scarred over from the explosion. Two years since the car blew up, everybody was used to his face. But still hard to take a close look.

"Look at those cars, they're lined up waiting for you."

"Let me look right now." Before she could stop him Joe had the hood open and was poking around. Lennox slumped against the car. She shouldn't be doing this. She had a million things to do, calls to make, notes to write. How was she going to report to Vanvleet tonight, with this hand?

She pulled herself up, holding the bad hand in the other. "I'm sorry, Joe, but I gotta go get this looked at."

"It's all right, Dorie. I know you got better things to do."

"That's not it, Joe," she said, trying to explain. "My hand got—my fingers—" She stopped herself. "I'm sorry, Joe. I've got this date tonight."

He was bent under the hood, fiddling, and said nothing as she backed away. She crossed the street, feeling like a shit, until the pain and the dirt and the heat got her.

In the boardinghouse, supper was being served in the dining room, with the radio playing. Everyone was bent over soup bowls, listening to "Jack Armstrong, All-American Boy." Jack would soon have to put away his football and pick up his gun. No one gave her a second look, or even a first.

She slipped through to the kitchen, where she chipped off a hunk of ice from the block in the icebox, wrapped it in a dish towel, and climbed the stairs. On the landing, she scrounged in her handbag for a nickel and dialed Vanvleet's office. It rang without an answer. She slammed down the receiver and was glad. She wasn't going to scour the city for him again.

With some difficulty, she unlocked her door. At least it was still locked. All she needed now was Iris to jump her. On the floor was a note from Mrs. Ferazzi in her crabbed hand under the heading *Sunny Farms Chemical Fertilizer*. "Working late. Meet me at the KC Club at nine, Harvey."

She felt her shoulders sag. She'd have to retrieve the Packard from Joe, then drive it with the bad hand. Talbot couldn't even pick her up. She crumpled the scrap of paper in her good hand. She had half a mind to stand him up. She shouldn't be going dancing anyway, not while Amos was in the clink.

Angry, puffed skin poked out of the bandage. She contemplated unwrapping the gauze, taking a look at it, then decided she wouldn't like what she saw. She lay back on her bed, set the hand on the chunk of ice in the towel, and tried to close her eyes. But every time she did, she saw that awful little man and his tiny hands and heard the sound of bones snapping.

Amos Haddam watched his lawyer and his oldest friend walk side by side into the cell. He blinked. There was a strange spot in front of his left eye. He rubbed it, but the spot remained. He slumped on the cot as they all said their howdy-dos.

Herb looked at him, squinting his eyes. "How's my favorite limey holding up?"

"Don't look at me," Amos said. "I'm not Wallis Simpson."

"Wallis is no limey." Herb looked at Dutch Vanvleet. "Has his sense of humor at least."

Dutch raised his eyebrows as if to say, He's going to need it.

Amos felt he should stand up, but his legs felt like custard. "So who died?"

"Well, that's the problem, Haddie," Herb said, hooking thumbs in his belt loops. His uniform was so crisp, you could play table tennis on it. "Davy Esterly is dead."

"We've been through this, haven't we, old boy?" Amos said.

"Get on with it, Captain." Dutch looked at the wall.

"All right," Herb said. "We thought the bullet looked too big for your thirty-eight. Now they're telling me it's in a hundred pieces and they'll be no matching it to any gun."

"That's good news, then," Amos said. The pillow never looked finer.

"Not really. Because your gun was recently fired. Your car was at the scene. A man your size was there in the alley, running away from the dead man."

"And you've got no alibi," Dutch said.

"You're some kind of counsel, counselor." Amos looked at Herb. "That's all you got, copper?"

Herb shrugged, rubbed his bald head. "It's enough for the prosecutors. In the mood Chief Reed's in."

"Bloody rabid G-man," Amos muttered.

"He should be in the hospital," Dutch said suddenly, as if he'd just joined the party. "Your quack won't even come up and look at him. Look at the back of his head, will you? He's a sick man, and you know it, Captain. Put him in the hospital or charge him with something, but don't just hold him here. It's inhuman, and what's more, illegal."

Amos sat up straight. "That's my boy. Yessir."

Herb Warren looked at Dutch, then at Amos.

"What's more," Vanvleet continued, "he saved your life—how many times? Don't forget that Kentucky moonshine raid, Captain, where the hillbillies came out of the hills with shotguns. Weren't you covered with buckshot? Didn't he drag you to the car, save your life?"

Amos dropped his head to his chest. "Don't bring up ancient history, Dutch."

"Chief Reed tells me the physical evidence is here," Herb said. "I don't have a choice. The arraignment is in the morning."

Dutch Vanvleet jerked his briefcase off the floor and held it to his chest. Amos stared at him. Was this a new defense strategy—the temper tantrum? Vanvleet went to the cell door, motioned for the matron to let him out. He left without saying a word to his client.

Amos felt weak. "He thinks I'm fried."

Herb frowned. "You okay? I'll get that doc up here. I'll lean on him. And it's not that bad. It's not over yet."

Amos lay down on the pillow and shut his eyes.

"Do you know anything about Georgie Terraciano, Amos? Does he have it in for you somehow?"

"Gorgeous Georgie. Swell guy." Amos smiled, his eyes still shut. "We're pals. Nothing but pals."

"Dorie thinks he's tied in because of that joint the Chatterbox, and the dame she was following. The one who jumped."

"But she didn't jump. Lennox told me. She's still alive. She's going to find her." Amos opened his eyes. "Herb?"

"Yeah?"

"I'm going to sleep now."

Lennox jerked, shaking her head to clear the sleep. The ice had melted onto the bedclothes. She sat up in a panic, looking at her watch, then slumped back. She'd slept for only fifteen minutes.

Her dream clung to her. In it, Harvey Talbot was making love to her in a swimming pool. She floated in the water in the moonlight. His hands felt like moths fluttering, their soft wings searching, searching.

She stood up and stripped off her trousers and blouse, her socks, underpants, brassiere. She wrapped her mother's old Chinese robe around her, difficult business with one hand. She felt filthy from the dumping by the willows, the trudging back to her car. She didn't want to think about Harvey and how the night was now ruined. But still, she had to take a bath. She kicked Winkie Lambert out, ran water, and sank into it while keeping the wrapped hand above water. As long as she didn't touch it, bump it, or use it, the hand felt all right. Not good, but within the bounds of human endurance.

She was angry at herself, at her body, which had let her down again. If she were a man, she could have muscled out of the goon's clutch, shot him in the foot, punched out that midget. Humiliating business there. She railed silently in the bath at crooked Georgie Terraciano and aloof Vanvleet, at Amos for leaving her to deal with everything alone, at Harvey for the damn note, at Hitler for the stupid war.

And Iris Jackson! That bitch. What the hell did she want?

By the time she got into her blue dress, fixed her hair, and put on a little makeup, she was too mad to put on stockings. Besides, she didn't have any without tacked-up runs. And her hand made everything hard. She put on anklets, the bloomers, and scuffed shoes that she gave a quick spit polish.

She looked ready for dancing. But it was the last thing she wanted to do tonight.

EIGHTEEN

DRIVING DOWNTOWN calmed the inner storm, so that Lennox had second thoughts about the anklets. Maybe she'd spring for a pair of stockings. She had tucked Lorna Hahn's sketch of Iris into her bag, an ulterior motive as she parked near Emery-Bird-Thayer and climbed the steps into the department store.

The store was quiet, minutes to closing. Sweet perfume smells floated on the still air. Up the stairs, in Lingerie, Joyce and another saleswoman chatted over the cash register. Joyce looked up, surprised.

"Look at you! Got those bloomers on?"

The older woman, short and plump, let out a chuckle. Joyce explained about the dancing bloomers.

"Got a question for you ladies," Lennox said, pulling out the sketch. "This is a woman who I think used to work here. Same one I mentioned earlier, Joyce. Do you recognize her now?"

The older woman sported an elaborate permanent wave on her graying hair. She pulled up glasses resting on her bosom in order to look at the picture.

"In this department? No, I don't remember her," the plump one said. Her name tag read CLARA. "Worked here twenty years. I think I'd know her if she worked here."

Joyce shook her head. Lennox lost her enthusiasm for stockings.

Clara looked at her bandage sympathetically. "Why don't you ask Gloria up at the credit counter? She knows everybody."

The credit counter was tucked back into a corner of the third floor, behind men's socks. Gloria Mulder, head cashier, according to the nameplate, was busy stacking receipts and punching an adding machine. A pale, thin-faced woman with straight brown hair tucked behind her ears and a lace handkerchief pinned to her chest, she had a large rubber thimble stuck on her thumb.

"Help you, miss?" she asked without looking up.

"I hope so. Clara in Lingerie sent me over." Lennox pushed the sketch across the counter, into Gloria's line of sight. "She thought you might remember this woman, if she worked here in the past."

"In the past? That's a big country." Gloria peered up over her half glasses. "How long ago?"

"I'm not sure. Within the last ten years?" Still pretty big country.

"Hmmph," the cashier said, rotating her bony shoulders and laying a knuckle on the sketch. "Looks like a girl worked here. I remember her, pretty in a cheap sort of way. In Men's Furnishings, sold shirts and garters and ties." Gloria raised her eyebrows. "Men liked her."

"You don't say. You remember her name?"

"Rose Schmidt, easy enough. Won some dance contest years back, at the Muehlebach. One of those dance-till-you-drop things. That's where somebody got the idea to hire her."

"Rose Schmidt. You're sure, are you?"

"Oh, yes. The artist caught that slant of her eyes perfect, didn't he? Her hair was longer then, but with the bangs across."

Lennox pulled the sketch back. "Remember where she was from?"

"A little town around here. Lots of girls came in looking for work back then. They still do, but back then, it was a flood. She was one of the lucky ones."

Lennox waited for more memories. Then said, "Yes, ma'am. Thank you."

She was walking away, repeating the name in her head, as

if she would ever forget it, pressing through black socks, silk socks, tennis socks, working her way to men's shoes, oxfords and patents and tap shoes, when Gloria hailed her.

"Miss! It was 'Raytown Rosie'—that's what they called her, the fellas over in Men's Furnishings. Raytown, that's the place."

On the street, still in ordinary anklets, Lennox twisted her wrist-watch around her arm with the good fingers of her right hand. She'd stopped long enough on the first floor to buy a cheap blue-and-white scarf to drape over the splint. She had just enough time to visit Amos. She'd been neglecting him.

Catching a bratwurst at the sidewalk vendor, she gulped it down in her car, managing to keep mustard off dress and bandages, then drove to police headquarters. The matron let her into the cell. Amos was up, pacing like a caged animal.

He ran a hand through his greasy flop of hair. "What's going on? Where have you been?" He sat heavily on the cot and held his head in his hands.

"Sorry. It must be awful," she said.

He looked up at her, the lines across his forehead etched deep. At least he wasn't coughing. "Where you think you're going?"

She ignored that. "Did the doctor see you?" She sat next to him on the cot. "The last time I was here, you were in pretty bad shape."

"He's been here. Herb got him on the horn. The lump's gone down." He rubbed the back of his head gingerly. "Still got the most bloody thumping headache." He glanced at her dress, the scarf on her hand. "What's this, then?"

"A date."

His eyebrows danced. "With a person of the male persuasion?"

She felt her face heat up. At least his eyes looked clear now. "I have to tell you what's going on." She stood up and faced him, good hand on her hip.

"What happened to that?" He pointed at the hand.

She pulled off the scarf. "You ever hear of a midget who likes to break fingers?"

Amos blinked a few times. "Were you offering them as love objects?"

Down the hallway the matron read an issue of *Weird Tales* and pretended not to hear. Lennox ignored Amos's remark. "Iris Jackson isn't dead. Do you remember me telling you that?"

"Yes, dear, I remember."

His voice mocked her, and she felt like smacking him.

"I found out her real name. It's Rose Schmidt. She worked at E-B-T, the big department store, back some years, and moved here from Raytown."

Amos was quiet. She turned finally, to see his fingertips digging into his patrician forehead. He looked up, eyes bright now, and said, "She shot the bartender, this Davy fellow. Her name's Rose Schmidt."

"And she threw Sylvia Anken off the Hannibal Bridge."

"She killed Davy because he saw her with Sylvia. But why Sylvia? Oh, right, she looked like Iris. Or Rose." He smiled, twisting his fingers in the air. "Nice touch, the flower names."

"Did they—have they told you about the bullet they took out of Davy?"

Amos frowned. "Splintered. A million pieces."

"So they can't tell if it's from your gun."

He stood up and began pacing again. "Doesn't matter to them. I'm as good as hung." He stopped and stared at her. "Why did Iris have to disappear?"

Lennox shook her head. "Wish I knew. The midget said something strange. He wanted information on some suitcase of cash. Something called 'the Truman money.' "

"What the blazes is that?"

"That's what I told the midget, but he wasn't listening."

Amos stopped pacing. "I knew a midget once. Nasty kid. Only he wasn't a kid. Brought up mean with circus folk."

"Where'd you meet him?"

He rubbed his forehead. "Can't remember. Oh, yes. Working for Vanvleet, years ago. One of his clients wanted his cousin out of the business. I wouldn't do what Vanvleet wanted, so he brought in this midget. I had to brief him on the layout."

"Was it Georgie? He ran his cousin out of the meatpacking business."

"I can't remember. Years ago." He took her damaged hand. "Does it hurt horribly?" She shook her head. He touched her chin. "Knocked you around some, did he?"

"At least I don't have a concussion."

He let her hand go. "The least of my worries. My head is too hard to break that easily." He gave the ceiling a strange look and sat down.

Lennox rubbed her cheek, feeling again the sting of that little hand. "Do you think Georgie is after this money? That this midget works for him?"

"Last I checked, *we* worked for Georgie. You haven't ticked him off, too?"

She thought about Marilyn, and wondered what Georgie knew about that. She hadn't actually seen the Italian since Saturday, except from afar at the racetrack.

"I think Georgie's fixing races out at that track."

"You got evidence?"

She shrugged.

"We got enough trouble."

Lennox said, "What about Palmer Eustace? Who is he? I talked to Floyd Wilson, and he's never met him."

"Vanvleet never gave me his number. Never met him." Amos looked up sharply. "Don't let Vanvleet know you're sniffing around Eustace. He told me to quit on it."

"What did the old man tell you about him?"

"That he was the silent partner, the one with the money. My guess is that he made his money booting hooch in from

Canada. Now he owns a bottling plant, Dutch says, down in Tulsa."

"Tulsa. I'll try to check that out. Why were you working on that track thing?"

"Vanvleet said Eustace thought he was getting gypped out of the profits, that his money had lined somebody's pocket. Which was probably true. How else do things get done in this town?" He cocked his head. "And there was something else. He also wanted me to look up this old chippie nobody'd heard of for years. Curious those two requests came in at the same time."

"You think the chippie is related to Eustace somehow?"

"Didn't think of it till now. The woman disappeared, changed her name, died, who knows what."

"What was her name?"

He rubbed his forehead again, kneading the thoughts. "Edna. Damn. My notebooks were stolen. Both of them." He concentrated. "Edna Klundt, that's it. Piss-poor name for a chippie, I remember that. Klundt."

"Edna?"

"Does it mean something to you? I couldn't find fur nor feather of 'er."

"The woman who tossed my room—I told you about that, didn't I?"

"I might remember something like that, lass."

"It was Saturday, after I came home from the hospital. You were in a fever the next time I saw you. She said to tell you to stay away from Edna. That had to be Iris. I'd been following her all that week, only on Saturday, I thought she was dead."

"Did she hurt you?"

It was injuries ago. "Mostly held me down on the floor to give me this message."

"That I should clear off Edna."

"What does that mean? Should I try to find her?"

"I looked everywhere. She's gone. But I suppose Iris giving

you a warning for me means I might have been close." Amos shook his head. "Sure never felt like it. But what about that racetrack? Where would Eustace's money have disappeared to?"

"I'm not sure *his* money went anywhere."

"Obviously, they built the track with it. But his partner, that Floyd Wilson, seemed on the up-and-up. Opened the books, showed me everything."

"They built the track with county bond money. Wilson told me he has a loan for his share through his own bank. Where Georgie banks, too, by the way. Nobody put up any real money." Lennox leaned against the cool bars. "Georgie's fixing races, I'm sure of it."

"Can't say I care. From where I sit, more power to him, I say." Amos lay down on the cot, wearing the same white shirt, now smudged and stained, the same braces and trousers. He linked his fingers over his concave chest. "My, my, my. Georgie's been a busy boy."

Lennox felt a sting from his words. She hadn't been busy enough, finding Iris, clearing Amos.

"I'm working on it, Amos. I'll get you out of here."

He looked up at her from the cot, his eyes dull and resigned.

"I promise," she whispered.

When she'd left, her blue dress swinging across her athletic calves, making his heart ache a little, Amos stared at the ceiling. No, his head wouldn't break, but his heart felt beyond repair. He'd spent all last night, awake and alert at last, scribbling out chapter and verse about Miss Eugenia McAughey. It had come into his mind, after feverish hours of writing, that he was mourning his own youth, health, homeland, things that would never be again. He could no longer grasp even the tiniest clear image of the girl. Sweet Eugenia. She was nothing but a vapor, a dream. As if she had never existed at all. And that filled him with a deeper sorrow than he'd never known.

Caged, inert, he felt as if he were evaporating. Like Eugenia, he would simply disappear, and only a few people—certainly not someone like himself, a clinging vine to memory—would occasionally speak his name, smile at some witty remark ascribed to him, recall one charitable moment. That would be all.

It was the war. Almost every man in his first platoon died, in the trenches, in airplanes, from disease. He should have been one of them. There was no reason he should have survived the plane crash, or all that followed behind the lines. Yet for no good reason, he had.

He sighed on the cot, closed his eyes. Where was that girl going tonight, dressed in her best clothes? In spite of himself, he began to picture her dancing with a tall stranger, twirling to the sounds from the bandstand, the man's hand on her waist, her feet light. Her life would go on. There would be happiness for her, and laughter, and children. A smile crept onto his mouth.

By God, his heart might mend after all.

Lennox didn't hurry to the club. She found a parking spot a couple blocks away, put on lipstick in the car by streetlight, and rearranged the scarf around her hand several times before giving up on a disguise. She got out of the car with the blue-and-white flag tied to her handbag.

Rose Schmidt, Rose Schmidt. Lennox wanted to go straight to Raytown, shake her out. Could Iris be hiding out there with her relatives? The sidewalk cracks told her nothing. And who was this Edna Klundt? Was she a friend of Iris? Somebody she wanted protected, yes, but who? Someone who would know where Iris was?

She rounded the corner of Twelfth and turned onto Baltimore. The sky was a slate color, with stars popping out in the east. Across the street, the Muehlebach Hotel glittered, the fancy restaurant on the corner all silver and crystal. She'd been so close to Iris in the ladies' lounge there, so close, she could smell the woman's skin, see the fine pores of her face. If only she had taken her arm, made her talk.

The Orpheum next door was playing *Pirates of the Skies,* along with a Peter Lorre picture, *Mysterious Mr. Moto.* Above the titles, the marquee read LADIES! CUTLERY OR LUNCHEON-WARE WITH 20 C ADMISSION! CARTOON REVUE! Couples lined up at the ticket window for the second show, arms around each other. She put her head down and walked to the corner to wait for the light.

Across the street, the Kansas City Club stood venerable and proper, an odd place for "race music," as some people still called jazz. There was Talbot, leaning against the doorway, slapping the tickets against his palm. He looked up and saw her. His eyes moved to her legs, her face, then to the bandage.

She stopped in front of him. He took her arm and led her inside, past the elegant gentlemen's lounges, the library, the dining room, to the stairs. As they climbed, he said, "I was beginning to wonder if you'd changed your mind."

Her knee hurt on the stairs. All the pains of the week rushed back, the knee, the back, the ribs, the knot on the forehead, the hand: a conspiracy of hurt. She said crossly, "You're not the only one who works."

At the top of the stairs, Talbot handed the tickets to a young man dressed to the nines in baggy trousers, patent-leather shoes, fancy satin vest and shirt. They found a table in the ballroom with two reporters and a man from a music store. Lennox sat down as Talbot got them cocktails.

"She hasn't started yet?" Lennox asked Landon, who was sitting next to her, soft and round and wearing glasses. He worked at the music store.

"Not unusual. Creative types."

Bob, one of the reporters, leaned forward. "I hear there's a special guest tonight. Somebody big."

"You say that every time."

"This time, it's true." Full of energy, Bob bounced his fingers against the edge of the bare tabletop like a drummer. "Cripes, I hope there's some good-looking ladies here tonight."

"All the good dancers are over at the Jitterbug Jamboree," Landon said. "That's where you should be, Spence."

The other reporter, Spence, sipped a whiskey sour. He slouched in a blue jacket. His brown hair was slicked back. "I'm not that good, Lan. I went over there last week. They are *swing cats.*"

The three described their best moves—an over-the-shoulder throw, through-the-legs twirl, roundhouse—as Lennox listened. She didn't know most of the moves, and it worried her. Harvey set a gin and tonic in front of her. He went to work on his own drink, a martini in a tall-stemmed glass.

The ballroom had a domed ceiling over the wood dance floor, with a raised bandstand at one end. A grand piano sat in the center, several music stands, an upright bass, and a drum set. The curtains behind the bandstand were a faded violet and the walls were lit with uplights, making splashy V's at intervals. The ring of tables was bare-bones—no tablecloths, no candles, just round wooden tables and chairs.

The crowd was fancy, but she'd expected that at the KC Club. Three tables over, a group of well-dressed men and women in satin and sequins huddled together, laughing. The men wore respectable suits, the women stylish, fancy dresses. Lennox checked their stockings and high heels and tucked her feet under the table. In the society group, a man rose to clap another on the back. It was Reggie Vanvleet. He was smoking a cigarette with a holder and wearing a tuxedo, overdressed again. She watched him for several minutes, the way he touched the girls' shoulders, the way he tipped his head back and drained his glass. Which one was his wife? His voice was loud. He asked a woman about her diamond, told someone about a deal he'd made that would make him millions.

Lennox turned her glass around a few times on the table.

She'd never called him after he gave her his card at the country club.

"Don't you want your drink?" Harvey asked. His martini was almost gone.

She picked up her glass and sipped. She should ask him about work, what story he'd been so busy on tonight that he couldn't pick her up. But she didn't. Talbot slouched in his chair, long legs splayed. She took another drink and the crowd began to cheer and clap as Julia Lee, small and elegant in a long black dress, stepped up to the microphone and welcomed the crowd. Behind her, the drummer and bass player took up their positions.

The first song was one made famous the year before by Ella Fitzgerald, "A Tisket, a Tasket." Harvey drained his martini glass.

"Want another?" She shook her head. He stepped away to the bar.

The audience was all white, even though the performers were colored. Private clubs like the Kansas City Club would be the last to let in Negroes. Colored folks could spend their money on clothes or books or farm equipment, but they couldn't even buy a Coke in the tea room at Emery-Bird-Thayer. On the dance floor, a few couples were swaying to a slow tune.

An hour of Julia Lee's piano and song went by. The men at Lennox's table discussed big bands and swing records. They read jazz magazines and listened to broadcasts of Chick Webb from the Savoy Ballroom and Count Basie from the Famous Door. Bob asked a girl at the next table to dance. Harvey concentrated on his martinis. The men avoided asking her any questions, she noticed, as uncomfortable with her as Harvey seemed to be. She wondered why she'd bothered to come.

Julia Lee took a break, the reporters went for drinks, and Landon went outside for a cigarette. Lennox got a Lucky out of her purse and fumbled with the matches. Harvey made no attempt to help. She smoked her cigarette angrily.

"I should go," she said, killing her cigarette in the ashtray.

She stood up, draping the scarf around the bad hand and heading for the door. Harvey just looked at her.

A clot of people at the entrance to the ballroom slowed her down. She held her hand close to her body. Better this way, without any scenes or regrets. There was a jot of relief. This is the way things always turned out, sooner or later. So it was sooner. It didn't make any difference.

In the hall, at the top of the stairs, he caught her. He held her arm, swung her back toward him.

"Wait, Dorie." Talbot ran his hand through his hair, only making it more unruly. She looked at the stairs. "I've been an ass, I know. This story tonight, a boy down by the river, and they think his mother put him in a sack and drowned him. I had to go down there and talk to that woman. She was—" He had to stop. He looked at the ceiling and gave a bitter laugh. "Now I know how you feel about rivers."

Lennox looked at him.

"You see things in this job and you wish . . . you wish you'd gotten there earlier, instead of after all the—Aw, hell." He leaned against the wall; she stepped out of the crowd next to him. "Let's forget about it. That's what I wanted to do tonight."

"You seemed well on your way."

"I was trying, wasn't I?" He leaned close to her and rubbed his knuckle down her jawline. "I was hoping we could dance. But what's this?" He took her wrist.

"I got on the bad side of a Munchkin. I may never find the Wizard now." She took her hand back. "Listen, I'm sorry about . . . the story and all."

"A Munchkin?"

She waved her good hand, seized now with her news. "I found out her name, Iris Jackson's real name. She worked at E-B-T. And lived in Raytown, so I'm going out there tomorrow."

"She's a shop girl?"

"Was. They say she won a dance marathon once. It's not much to go on. But I've got her name. I'm going to find her."

Harvey opened his mouth to speak as shouts in the crowd

rolled over them. Excited scuffles and yips then shoving and pressing back into the ballroom, then the magic words: "The Count." Lennox looked at Talbot, saw he had heard it, too, and they joined the rest, who were stomping out cigarettes, throwing down drinks, piling back into the ballroom.

The crowd was on its feet. The cheery round face of Count Basie stood at the microphone on the bandstand, waving as people began to chant, "Count Basie, yeah, Count Basie, play it, Count Basie." Lennox recognized Lester Young behind him, and wasn't that the famous drummer Jo Jones? The Count gave up trying to speak over the noise and sat down at the piano. Jo Jones counted out the beat and they began to play. The crowd continued their chant until the men grabbed their girls and ran to the dance floor.

When the intro finished, the Count said in his sweet voice, "Good to be back, my friends. So. Do you want to jump, children?" A cheer rose from the crowd as he trilled out the first bars. Then the band swung into "Jumpin' at the Woodside," fast and hot.

"Well, child?" Harvey said, his face lit up. "The Count requests your presence."

Lennox felt the energy down her back, into her legs, the rhythm full of something so close to pure delight. Her toes twitched. She had told herself the night was ruined. But the hard feelings turned to jelly inside her. "The hand."

He stepped close to her, put his hand on her waist. She had to crane her neck to see his face. The smell of gin and hair oil and sweat was curiously sweet. Around them, couples were throwing partners from one end to the other, the beat moving them, laughter, joy on their faces. It was a miracle, the way the music just captured people, made them happy.

Harvey took her handbag, set it on the table, then put her broken hand on his shoulder, took the left one in his. He leaned down, touched his cheek against hers.

"Let's forget," he whispered.

Later, as they walked through the street, the buzz of the music hummed inside her, an electric charge that wouldn't quit. There was nothing like Count Basie for swing. He was the cat; that's what Landon had said. She'd danced with Landon, too, and Bob and Spence. Right at the end, Count Basie's group played "One O'Clock Jump" and she and Harvey had danced like demons, forgetting all about Iris, Sylvia, and rivers, forgetting everything.

The sky was a pale midnight blue, washed with city light. The stars were faint, but she counted seven before the ache in her hand brought her back to earth. She held it close to her ribs. The bandage was dirtied with spills; she'd managed to dump over her gin and tonic in her fierce thirst after dancing. The fingers had gotten bumped so much they were almost numb. Harvey was whistling, hands deep in his pockets, tie and collar loose.

Keys in her hand, she walked around to the driver's side. Harvey leaned over the roof of the Packard. "Can I come?"

"It's awful late."

"Just let me get in for a minute."

He was a little drunk. The effect of the martinis had worn off from dancing, but he'd had another just before leaving. She slipped behind the wheel and put the keys in the ignition. He got in beside her and moved close.

"Down, boy."

He lay his head back on the seat. "Why didn't you dance with me more? I had to dance with a fat girl from the mailroom because Bob bet me a buck I wouldn't. And who was that swag in the penguin suit?"

"Are you complaining?"

He sighed and closed his eyes. She ran her good fingers along the steering wheel. Reggie Vanvleet asking her to dance hadn't quite surprised her. She knew he'd seen her, she just couldn't figure out what he wanted. It was a slow dance so they had to make conversation. He smelled like bourbon. After a fascinating discussion of his hole-in-one at the Mission Hills Country Club, he brought up Georgie Terraciano.

"I thought we were going to work together," he said, gliding her around the room.

"Your dad might not have approved."

Reggie did the silent laugh. "My father doesn't tell me what to do. You don't believe what those little twists around the office say, do you? I'm my own man."

"Does your wife let you go out dancing without her?"

"My wife lets me do anything I want. She's dead."

Lennox looked for regret, sorrow, anything on his face. But the bourbon had erased everything. She said, "I'm sorry."

"Don't be. I'm not." He smiled his movie-star smile. "Now what about Georgie? You going to fill me in?"

"You first." She was sure he knew nothing about Georgie's activities. Dutch was too smart for that. "What do you know?"

"He's got some hatchet men that look like trouble to me. I'd like to know why a meatpacker needs that kind of goon. What's he up to?"

"Heck if I know." Lennox watched him look at her bandage. "Smashed them in a car door. Can you believe it?"

He didn't look like he did. "Where've you been flopping? You laying down for Georgie?"

"Don't be a bunny, Reg. He's a client. He already pays me."

"That so? But for what?"

"I'm checking out his dead girlfriend. But don't tell the missus. Hush-hush."

Reggie's eyes widened. He tried for more information, but he seemed satisfied with that tidbit. Lennox told herself the information was bogus anyway, so it didn't matter. But by the time the dance was done, she still wished she hadn't told him.

She looked over at Harvey Talbot in the car. His profile, so close, made her nervous. "Don't you know Reggie Vanvleet? Worthless heir to my sometime employer."

"The lawyer? Son of a son of a bitch?" Harvey turned sideways, leaning his cheek against the seat back. "Did he step on your feet?"

"Like you did?"

He reached a finger to trace down her nose, lips, chin, neck. She almost stopped him at the neckline of her dress but sucked in her breath and let him go, down between her breasts, then flattening his hand against her stomach. He pulled her toward him then and kissed her.

She moved away from him, sat with her back against the door. She licked her lips where his had been, tasted the gin. He was gently poking her bandage. She'd told him the whole story about the midget.

"I have never met anyone like you. Who are you, Dorie Lennox?"

"Just a peeper with broken fingers."

"I want to know everything about you," he said hoarsely.

"We'll have to be much more sober for that."

"Come on. What are you afraid of?"

She looked out the windshield. Clumps of dancers, some still jitterbugging, laughed on the sidewalks.

"It's late, Talbot." His eyes bored into her. She knew she ought to tell him everything. She liked him. She wasn't afraid of any man, only river snakes. "Okay. Ask."

"Where're you from?" He was slurring. He wouldn't remember this tomorrow anyway.

"Atchison, Kansas, home of Amelia Earhart and sixteen hundred head of cattle on shipping day."

"All of whom are dead now."

"Give the man a prize."

"What about after Atchison?"

"I came here."

"What's the worst thing you ever did?"

She could lie to him; she'd done that before. But eventually, it came around to a moment like this. It'd been a short romance, if that's what it was. But what choice was there? She was going to pretend to be a good little girl from a fine, upstanding family?

She took a deep breath. "Stole a car, went to Beloit, let my mother drink herself to death, and killed my baby sister."

Harvey put his elbow up on the seat back to hold his head up. "Whoa, whoa, slow down. Start over."

She leaned over the steering wheel, hooked her chin over the top. "Stole a car."

"When was this?"

"I was fourteen. I stole the landlord's Buick and drove to Kansas City. Got caught and sent to the girl's school in Beloit. Garden spot of Kansas, you know it?"

He looked sober now, eyes wide. "You must've had a damn good reason."

"Of course."

"Then what?"

She looked at him. "Reporters are ghouls, aren't you?" She took another breath. "While I was vacationing in Beloit, my little sister had nobody to look after her. But that didn't stop my mother from calming the nervous fears of Atchison's married men. Tillie got into some matches. She was burned real bad." She looked at her wristwatch and tasted the bile in her mouth. "There's more, but it's late."

She hoped Harvey didn't take too long getting away. He was groping for her good hand. She yanked it away. Why was he taking so long? He took her arm then and pulled her into him, wrapping his arms around her.

"You better go now, Talbot," she said over his shoulder.

He laid his cheek against hers.

"Talbot. Time to go."

She pushed him back, turned the ignition. The Packard roared to life. The worst part was the pity. Remember that, she scolded herself. "I'll drive you to your car."

"Why didn't you tell me this before," Talbot said as he directed her around the corner.

"So you could feel sorry for me? At least my mother didn't put me in a sack and throw me in the river."

"No, I—" He pointed at the Chrysler under a streetlight. "There."

She put on the brakes and rattled her good fingers on the steering wheel. "Good night, Talbot."

"Look at me," he said.

She turned. His face was half in shadow. Dark hair flopped over his eyebrow. "Look, no hard feelings," she said. "I try to forget it most of the time."

"Like dancing."

"Right. So, thanks for the dancing. The talking part isn't ever so good."

"Come to my place. We don't have to talk."

She felt her breath lighten, a laugh percolating up from a place inside her that didn't care about the past, about guilt or misery or responsibilities to the dead.

She looked at him, his profile blushed in blue light. "I'll bet."

He slid close again and put his lips to her ear. "You haven't asked about my secrets."

"Last of the Romanovs, are you?"

"Come up and find out."

"You'll bare all, I suppose."

"And then some."

She kissed him right there, double-parked, until somebody honked their horn. Then she followed his Chrysler to an apartment building on Baltimore near the Plaza.

He undressed her carefully on the bed, taking extra time around the damaged fingers, kissing the dirty bandages to make her laugh. There was a hardness to his body that she marveled at, the lean torso, the sparse black hair, the ribs. He moved inside her, kissing her neck, the tender, soft inside of her arms, taking everything so slowly, she wanted to pull out his hair. He made her forget. He made her glad. Glad, actually, didn't describe it.

"So, tell—" she began as they lay close on his narrow bed. But he covered her mouth with his finger, then his mouth.

"No more questions tonight."

NINETEEN

THE DIRTY THIRTIES weren't kind to Raytown. With Kansas City not ten miles to the northwest, the village had no claim except as a stop on the Rock Island Line. In recent years, small suburbs had cropped up for people who liked the low prices of the land or worked on the railroad. Their houses sat in sad rows, all dingy white, the residents apparently never having heard about fierce funnel clouds that drop out of the sky.

Limestone cliffs buffered Raytown from the metropolis. Entering through natural gates in the cliffs was like being transported back to Atchison, where there was nothing to do and nobody to do it with. Lennox felt something like a headache between her eyes. Maybe talking about Tillie last night. That always did it.

Even with little sleep, she'd beat Winkie Lambert to the bathtub this morning and rewrapped her splint by breakfast. Gulping down Poppy's flapjacks had helped and she felt strong, and eager to find Iris today. When she got home at four o'clock that morning, she felt so strange that she sat on her bed and cried for a minute. Thirty-five seconds, actually. Then she washed her face and tried to sleep. Harvey Talbot had an odd effect on her. She felt insanely good, and also very bad. As if she had betrayed something, or someone.

The piano player was making his music somewhere and she had listened in her room, a night full of music in her veins. Maybe the piano player was a dream. She lay on her bed, in and out of sleep, until she figured she might as well get up.

It was barely nine when she parked the Packard in front of the tiny Carnegie Free Library just off Raytown Road. She climbed the granite steps in the late summer air, the cottonwood tree beating its leaves in the breeze. The boxlike building had heavy, imposing doors, but inside, the single, high-ceilinged room with dark red carpeting revealed good intentions and little else.

A white-haired lady sat behind the circulation desk, working through a card catalog box. She looked up sharply at Dorie Lennox's entrance, her fingers stuck in the cards.

"Good morning," the librarian said, her voice pinched.

"Ma'am." Lennox dropped her keys in her trouser pocket. "Do you have a Raytown telephone book, by any chance?"

"Of course." The librarian tucked a card sideways in the box before rising. From a nearby shelf she pulled out a small booklet. Lennox took it, opened it: just five small pages.

"Something else?" the old lady asked, adjusting her glasses back to her nose. Lennox shook her head and sat down at a dark wood table.

Going quickly through the *S*'s in the booklet, it was soon obvious no Schmidts lived in Raytown. She checked the booklet's cover and saw it was dated September 1937. She cleared her throat and asked the librarian if there were any older or newer telephone books for Raytown. The old woman got up again and delivered another small booklet to the table with a slap.

This booklet was dated September 1935. No Schmidt's. It was possible the family had no telephone; many didn't. She looked up Klundt in both directories, but struck out again. She carried them back to the circulation desk. "Shall I put them back?" she asked. But the librarian held out her hand and placed them next to her on the desk.

"Would there be any other listing of residents?"

The old woman pinched her eyebrows together. "There's always the county land deeds in Independence."

Lennox thanked the woman and stepped back into the sunshine. It was unlikely either girl owned property, although the parents might. She took a deep breath. The county rolls were torturous business, and she knew no one in the courthouse there.

For two hours, she strolled through stores, seizing lulls in business to quiz store owners and wizened citizens, young paperboys and bored clerks. By then she was beginning to doubt the memory of Gloria Mulder. *Raytown Rosie.* Maybe it was Rockville Rosie, or Rolla Rosie, or Richmond Rosie. Maybe it wasn't even Rose Schmidt.

Lennox sat at the polished steel counter in the Starlite Fountain and debated questioning the pimply soda jerk. It seemed futile; he was too young and didn't look particularly bright. She ordered a malted instead, chocolate, and swung around on the stool as she waited for him to blend it. The café was nearly empty, only an old man drinking coffee and reading the *Star* in a far booth. He got up as the blender whirred, folded the paper, and set it on the counter. As he left, she jumped up to grab the paper.

Talbot's story was on the second front page, under the headline BODY OF BOY, 3, FOUND IN RIVER. No catchy header this time. A sorry tale, and Talbot's dry writing of it barely hid his outrage. On an inside page was a tiny picture of a small boy, grinning, sawed-off hair across his forehead, and the information about his funeral. She'd been trying not to think about Talbot this morning, and the search for Rose Schmidt had been useful that way. But now she remembered the look on his face when he'd told her about the mother by the river. Rivers were just too damn convenient.

On the front page, a headline read LONDON, PARIS BLACK OUT. She scanned the other stories, Roosevelt again trying to calm the jitters, Ambassador Kennedy sending missives back from London about Neville Chamberlain, Hitler buttoning up Poland. Another story about the track. No byline, but it had to be Russell. This time, the city was considering annexing the land around and including the Blue Valley Racetrack. Owner Floyd Wilson was said to be opposed. She decided the time had come to find out something about Palmer Eustace. She got up and dropped a coin in the pay phone in the booth at the back of the store.

The operator at the *Kansas City Star* was a little miffed by her asking for "a reporter named Russell."

"Last name or first name?"

"Not sure. How about the city desk?"

In a moment, a gruff voice announced the city desk. "Is Russell there?"

"He's not around till deadline. Whatcha got?"

"Just want to talk to Russell. When is deadline?"

"Three o'clock. Check back then."

When she got back to the counter, the soda jerk set down the huge malted in front of her, the frosty glass brimming with creamy chocolate. He had put whipped cream and a maraschino cherry on top. He laughed at her expression of awe.

"We aim to please," he said, Adam's apple bobbing. "Couldn't help noticing your hand there. What'd you do to it?"

Lennox spooned whipped cream and malted into her mouth. "Clumsy, that's all," she said.

"Funny, you know," the boy said. "My neighbor had the same thing happen. Broke the same two fingers just last week."

"You don't say." The malted was delightful, cool and sweet. It had been ages since she'd sat down long enough for one.

"He's just an old man, full of wild stories. I bet he just fell down, too. Or slammed 'em in his door."

"What did he say—a pixie jumped on his hand?"

"That's close. He says a midget broke them."

She set down her spoon. "A midget?"

"Ain't that rich? 'What,' I says, 'is the circus in town?' "

"Was it?"

"Hell, no. The man's off his nut."

"Could I bother you for this man's name? It's just curiosity." She held up the bandaged fingers. "Fellow war hero."

The soda jerk squinted at her, then shrugged. "No skin off my nose. His name's Grady. Lives next to me on Olive. Little green shack with big lilac bushes in front." He slapped his rag on the counter and leaned in. "Don't say I didn't warn you. He's off his nut."

She finished half her malted and paid the soda jerk, and tipped him, too. As she got up, a group of kids came in, laughing and talking, carrying schoolbooks. Lennox paused at the end of the counter, turning to the soda jerk.

"Say, you ever hear of a Rose Schmidt who lived around here? Or an Edna Klundt?"

"Nope, sorry," he said.

Lennox thanked him and turned to go. A girl in a too-tight cotton dress and saddle shoes stared at her, mouth hanging open, like she'd never seen a woman in trousers before. Small towns. Lennox smiled and the girl blinked her round blue eyes. Down the street, at the Packard, Lennox stopped. She should go back and question that girl. It wasn't the trousers. It was the names. She knew something.

But back inside the Starlite Fountain, the girl was gone.

Lilacs were a favorite on Olive Street, but there was only one green shack. She knocked at the door with her left hand. After three knocks, a short old man opened the door, his slumped shoulders making it difficult for him to look up at her.

"Mr. Grady?" She introduced herself. "Your neighbor boy at the fountain told me about you. I think we have something in common." She held up her broken fingers. "A midget did this to me."

The old man brought up his broken hand, streaks of purple bruises covering it. His splint looked more professional than hers, but the crippling looked worse.

"Who was he?" Grady croaked. "I never did nothing to nobody."

A state of grace she had no claim to. "Mine wore little leather gloves and rode in a black sedan."

"That's him, the little fucker."

She smiled. "My sentiments exactly, sir. Could I ask what he said to you?"

"Made no sense."

"Like what?"

Grady looked at her for a moment, then over his shoulder into his house. "Can't ask you in. Place is a dump." He stepped outside and shut the door. "Come over here."

He shuffled across the dried grass toward a wooden bench set under the lilac bushes. She sat down carefully. It was a primitive affair, but it held her. The old man lowered himself, stretched out his legs.

"Nice day." He looked at the cloudless sky. "Fall's really coming now."

"You were going to tell me what he asked you."

"Oh, Lordy, yes. Wanted to know about some money. Something he called 'the Truman money.' They tore up my place looking for it. I never heard nothing about it—that's what I told him, but he broke my fingers anyway."

"Do you know why he might ask you that?"

"Haven't a notion. Loony little shrimp. Those tiny hands." He stared at his own big, battered hands. "Who'da thought it."

"Tell me about yourself, Mr. Grady. Have you lived here all your life?"

"Oh, no. I worked the railroad, moved around a lot. Settled here after I retired, to be close to the family. Wife died about ten years back. I was a conductor. Saw all the West. Something in those days."

She was silent a moment. "You never had anything to do with Harry Truman? Worked for him or anything?"

"Voted for him, I did. He's a war hero."

She tried to think. "Have you ever heard of a man named Georgie Terraciano?"

The old man shook his head. "One of them Italians? Al Caponee?"

"Sort of. From Kansas City. Did you ever know a girl from here named Rose—Rose Schmidt?"

"I knew some Schmidts in Illinois. But not here."

"How about Palmer Eustace? That mean anything?"

"Nope. That the midget's name?"

She shrugged. Could it be? "How about Floyd Wilson?" He shook his head again. What else should she be asking? What was she missing here? What connected her to this old man besides a nasty midget? She stood up. "Well, thanks for your time, Mr. Grady. Someday we might find that midget."

He struggled to his feet. "You have my permission to pinch his little balls off. You can tell him it's a message from Ed Grady."

"Okay, Mr. Grady. I'll remember that." She said good-bye and ducked her head to find her way out of the bushes, back to the car. Might as well go back to the city now. She'd go talk to Russell at the *Star*, bargain for more information. Call Tulsa. Maybe she'd go talk to Amos again. They might come up with something together. She paused at the street, then turned back. Mr. Grady was framed by the huge bushes.

He peered through the leaves. "Forget something?"

"One more name, then I'll go." She stepped back toward him. "Does the name Edna Klundt mean anything to you?"

He blinked, ran his tongue over his dry lips. "O' course. She's my granddaughter."

They sat on the bench as Mr. Grady told her the sad story of Edna. Named after him, she had been a favorite grandchild, pretty and attentive. But after the crash, her father took off for California and never came back. Mr. Grady's daughter, Louise, struggled to keep the family together, but Edna ran off to Kansas City when she was seventeen. Word was, she came to no good. Louise remarried. She hadn't been visited by a midget, but her husband had scared off a couple of heavies with his shotgun last week. Edna hadn't been heard from in more than seven years, and her family feared she was dead. Grady showed her a picture of a pretty girl of ten or eleven with sweet bowed lips, a large nose, and a short neck. Her hair, Ed said, was strawberry blond. Disappointment struck; it wasn't Iris. Lennox squinted at the round cheeks. She saw something there. But what?

Lennox drove back to Kansas City with Edna's last known address and a warm feeling for an old man who wanted nothing more than to see the lilacs bloom in the spring and that a certain midget got what was coming to him.

In town, she drove by the address, a boardinghouse near Troost, now boarded up. Another dead end. What did Edna mean to Iris? Were they together in this—whatever *this* was? Is that what Iris's warning had implied?

Lennox killed a couple hours in the Kansas City Public Library, a much bigger affair than Raytown's, but just about as helpful. Librarians were scarce and city directories no help. Schmidts were too common, Klundts too few.

Out on the street again, she found her car being ticketed by the city's finest. The cop gave her a stern lecture on driving with her lights broken out. Told her she should be ashamed of herself for the way the Packard looked. She assured him she was.

She drove south to the *Kansas City Star* at Eighteenth and Locust. The outside was impressive, but inside, the low rumble of machinery and ever-present coating of grease meant business. She found the city editor, who told her Russell was still not in. Then he blew cigar smoke in her face. She decided on another tack: the morgue.

"No, you can't go back and look yourself. Some floozy off the street. Are you kiddin', sister? We don't even let the blasted reporters back there."

The *Star*'s morgue was cheerier than the city's, but just as poorly lit. The basement clipping library was run by a man of Ed Grady's age named Folsom. A most unwilling old bastard.

Lennox tried smiling more, but her face hurt. "What else are you doing? Come on, how about a buck or two?"

"Look, go away, okay, girlie? I don't want your filthy money. I got work to do, and I can't do it with you here sitting on my desk."

"Mr. Folsom. I'm a busy person, too. I can understand that. Maybe I can help you, get you some lunch?"

"I had my goddamn lunch. Breeze off, chickie." He was a wiry little man, straighter in posture than Grady, but with the same white tufts of hair over his ears.

She watched him work his old lips. "Did you know Ernie Hemingway when he worked here?"

"Just another son of a bitch reporter," he grumbled. "Nothing special."

She was trying to remember how much money she had in her wallet, when Harvey Talbot rounded the doorway from the hall, head down, and stopped dead when he saw her. He worked his hand through his hair.

"What are you doing here?" Harvey said.

"Bothering me," Folsom replied. "Get rid of her, would ya?"

"Sure, but—" His voice was soft, almost breathy, so unlike the way he'd acted the first day she met him, brash and unstoppable. "Did you want something out of the morgue?"

"Dance marathons," she said. "I thought there might be something on Iris."

He took her arm. "Come on."

Spread out on Talbot's desk were six articles, some with pictures. They dated, he said, from 1930 to 1933. Iris Jackson wasn't mentioned in any of them.

"How about as Rose Schmidt?" Lennox asked.

He shook his head. "But look at the pictures."

The newsroom was a huge open room with a low ceiling, filled with wooden desks and scattered with newsprint, clacking with the sound of typewriters. Most of the desks were empty. Still no sign of Deadline Russell. She leaned over Talbot's desk, bringing her face close to one grainy photograph after another. In one, four couples danced, arms hanging limply at their sides, heads resting on each other's shoulders. In another, a girl lay flat on the floor, a doctor checking her pulse. Lennox peered closely at a couple who held up a trophy, smiling after all that dancing. Buck teeth—no, not her, unless she'd been to a bunch of dentists.

"Don't they keep the original photos?" she asked.

"Yeah, way back in another part of the morgue."

She picked up a clip with a photo that had only a caption. In it, a girl danced alone. Presumably, her partner had given up the ghost and she had gone on without him. She was barefoot, wore a simple shift dress, and had one hand on her stomach, the other held out, as if holding a partner's hand. She smiled for the camera. A ratty square of paper was pinned to the hem of her dress with the number 12. The caption read:

This plucky marathoner participating in the popular Muehlebach Hotel dance event has captured the fancy of many onlookers, including Democratic leader John Lazia, left. The dancer's partner collapsed due to exhaustion five days ago—on Day 23—but the lass refuses to quit. She is going all the way, she told a reporter. The grand prize in the "Endless Starlight" Muehlebach marathon is $500.

"Which one's Lazia?"

Talbot leaned over her shoulder and pointed to a man in a dark suit, with slicked-back hair, rimless glasses, and a big grin, standing by the bleachers, clapping. Yes, the neat clothes, the specs, just how Herb had described him.

"Is that her?"

"The clerk said it was at the Muehlebach."

She stared at the fuzzy, smiling face of the dancer, then shut her eyes, picturing Iris that night in the ladies' lounge. The same smooth skin, the same facial shape, but the hair was different, dark and stringy. She looked thinner, scrawny even. But she'd been dancing for a month. The date of the clipping was July 12, 1931.

Lennox bored into the grainy photograph. What was she missing? There, the earrings, the gold hoops! Iris still had those; she'd been wearing them that night in the satin dress. Lennox felt her heart race. It had to be her.

She set the clipping back on his desk. "When was Lazia killed?"

"Thirty-four. Is it her, then?"

"I think so. Do you think she and Lazia were an item?"

Talbot rubbed his unshaven chin. "Because he's in the picture?"

"She had a lot of fancy underclothes from Emery-Bird-Thayer, old things. Like somebody bought them for her. Her sugar daddy."

"Anybody coulda bought them. Her mother."

"Not this kind of underwear. I keep stumbling over Lazia's name. Georgie worked for him back then." Lennox looked up. "Can you get Lazia's file?"

It took Talbot fifteen minutes to go back to the morgue and return with the fat file of clippings about John Lazia. On top of the stack were the stories about his sensational daylight murder on Armour Boulevard. A photograph of his wife at the funeral, along with numerous city and county officials, and, yes, Pendergast, too, caught Lennox's eye. Other clippings, other photos. She scooted them over to Talbot.

"Recognize any of those people?"

While he frowned at the photos, she picked up the next clipping, Lazia's obituary. He had been on a number of boards and committees of a civic nature, parks and streets and planning. The board of directors of the Boy Scouts. Now that was fitting. Probably helping an old lady across the street when he was chilled off.

"Here's Harry." Talbot pushed over the photograph. A shot through a car window showed Mr. Truman, then just a candidate for the Senate, his head bent reverently.

Lennox looked up at the reporter. She hadn't told him about the Truman money, whatever it was. How was Harry Truman connected to Lazia? Was it politics, or was it something deeper, more bent?

She looked back at the obituary. At the bottom, a boldface poem had been inserted, courtesy of Mrs. Lazia.

Wherever you are, my lost lamb,
There will be stars burning.
One of them, twinkling high
Above your head, is me.
My love that sputters and flares but never goes out.
Steady, love. Take care, my lamb.
We'll be together soon.

"Look at this."

She pushed it across the desk, swung it upright for him. He put a finger on it and frowned.

"Here. This poem or whatever it is. That's what Iris said in her phony suicide note. Same lines. She was writing it for her lost love, John Lazia." Lennox felt a surge of excitement, then tried to bring it down in order to think. "You aren't going to write about this now, are you?"

"This doesn't prove he was her man."

"Look at that picture, Talbot." She pointed at the marathon shot. "Must have gone over good with Mrs. Lazia. Look. He's nuts about her."

"I have to talk to you, Dorie."

"We are talking." She laughed, looked around the newsroom again. Several rows over, greasy Russell stared at them over his typewriter. She waved and he ducked his head. Iris and Lazia, the lost lamb. Edna and Rose. She felt giddy.

She looked back at Harvey. He seemed tired and his eyes were hot. "Not now, Talbot."

Russell punched his typewriter keys, hunting and pecking. Lennox stood in front of his desk, tapping one foot. The reporter didn't look cleaner or dirtier than he had the other day. Same shirt, same sweat. She was glad for the distance.

Finally, he stopped, one finger poised in midair, and cocked his head.

"Howdy, Russell. Remember me?"

He looked her up and down. "What do you want?"

"You sound suspicious, Russell." Lennox smiled. He was wearing the rope belt again. Tops on the newshawk's guide to glamour. "Can I sit down?"

She pulled a chair over from another desk and sat down at the end of Russell's. He pushed back from his desk and folded his hands, squinting at her. "What's going on?" A glance in Talbot's direction, also squinty.

"Information, Russell. That's all." She looked at Talbot. He stood over the clippings about the dance marathon, staring at them. "Don't tell Harvey," she whispered.

"Tell him what?"

"I'm trying to find out some information on one of the partners at the Blue Valley Racetrack. You've been writing about it. A lot."

"No more than any story."

"What's your interest? You think it's a scam or something?"

"Maybe. What's your interest?"

She sighed. "Client privilege. But this Palmer Eustace is a slippery character."

"Slippery as smoke."

"So he is colored?"

He squinted again, calculating. "What's it to you?"

"Nothing. I got nothing against colored folks. I just want to know if you can say for certain he's colored. Like you've met him. Because if you have, and you can give me some information on him, maybe I can help you out."

"With what?"

"Information. Savvy?"

Russell's chair creaked under his weight as he leaned back to think. He scratched under one arm. Bit his lip. His eyes darted around the room; then he leaned forward. "What you got?"

"A little life story."

"From who?"

"His mouthpiece."

"Vanvleet? That shyster?"

Lennox raised her eyebrows. "You know where he's from? How he makes his money?" She watched him. "I don't have all day."

"How do I know you ain't stringin' me with Talbot?"

"Talbot—that nance?" She smiled over at Harvey. "You don't. But I'm not. You've got something I want. Or do you?"

He laced his fingers over his belly and gave a small nod.

"Then it's a deal?" He scratched and finally nodded again. Lennox pulled her chair up close and got a good whiff. She said it fast. "Word is, he's from Tulsa. That he owns a bottling plant there. Some think he smuggled in hooch from Canada, made his money that way."

"Tulsa?" He nodded to himself, leaned over his desk, scribbled some notes onto marked-up sheets of type. She let him go a few minutes on his own, then cleared her throat. He ignored her and kept scribbling.

"Your turn, Russell. Spill it."

He glanced at her, then back at his papers. He stood up suddenly, throwing his chair back. Lennox was up in a flash. "Where you going?"

Russell waved his left arm vaguely. "I gotta—" He stepped away, but she was on him, digging her heel into the top of his right foot. He groaned and pulled on the desk with both hands. She grabbed his filthy shirtsleeve and held tight.

"We had a deal, Raunch."

He wriggled out from under her foot. Lennox caught the rope belt and tugged it hard, pulling his feet out from under him. Russell landed back in his chair, then bounced to the floor. Before he could scramble away, Lennox put one foot on his shoulder. "A deal's a deal, Russell."

He grimaced under her heel. "Okay, okay. Let me up."

"You gonna make good?"

"Yeah, yeah. Let me up."

She stared hard at him. "I've got a blade in my pocket. And I'm not afraid to use it." He flattened out both hands, palms up, in surrender. She slowly removed her foot. He pulled himself up to the chair, his face red and sweating.

Talbot stood in front of the desk. "What's going on?"

"Russell was just helping me out," Lennox said. "Weren't you?"

"Ain't your business, Tall-butt. Buzz off."

Talbot scowled at them both and backed away to his own desk.

"Okay," Russell said, watching Talbot's distance. "I got a photo."

"Of Eustace?"

He nodded. "I've been after that shyster for weeks to set me up with Eustace. Told him I thought the man was nobody, a phony, a front. And if I didn't see a photo or meet the cat, I was going to print it that way."

"So he sent you a photo?"

Russell looked around the newsroom suspiciously, pulled a string of keys from his trouser pocket, and unlocked a bottom drawer, to the desk. From the back of the drawer he pulled a file folder, and from the folder, a small two-by-three-inch photograph. Russell sat down and hunched over it. Lennox sat next to him.

"Let's see it," she said.

Russell held it out but didn't release it. He whispered, "My place was tossed. They been following me. Yesterday I saw—" He swallowed hard.

"A midget?"

He let go of the photograph. "How'd you know?" He stared at her bandage. "What'd they do?"

Lennox pressed the tiny photograph onto the desktop. Two men stood in an office overlooking the city. Vanvleet's office, she thought. One was a light-skinned Negro, dressed in a satin vest, starched shirt, snap-brim hat. She didn't know him. He wasn't smiling, just looking at the other man—who was Louie Weston.

"Damn."

"You know him?" Russell whispered.

"This one. Louis Weston. In the firm with Vanvleet."

Russell was scribbling again. "You vouch for him? He's jake?"

She shook her head and stood up. Handed the photograph back to Russell. He stared at it hard, trying to get it to release more secrets.

"Looking forward to your story, Russell," she said, backing away. "Hey, get that shirt washed. Send me the bill."

Lennox drove to a diner. With her notebook in front of her as she ate the blue plate special of pan-fried chicken and mashed potatoes with gravy, she made notes, ideas, everything about the case. She put her own ideas about Palmer Eustace in a separate notebook, trying to work out what was going on but getting nowhere. Louie Weston knew. That fact grated on her. Anyone but Louie.

Up at the county lockup, Lennox waited in a hard chair to see Amos. The matron moved as if through molasses, but she finally ushered Lennox through the dim hallway to his cell. He lay on his side, staring at the wall. They'd taken his clothes now and given him gray cotton pants and a white shirt. He didn't turn as the matron unlocked the door.

"Amos?"

On the floor were the scattered pages where he'd scribbled out "Eugenia" and "England" and "war." Lennox stopped, not wanting to step on them. "Hey. You okay?"

He rolled over and sat up. His face was thin and drawn, washed out by the gray walls and single bulb. "Dandy." He rubbed his eyes and coughed. "You?"

She wanted to tell him about John Lazia and Iris. About Raytown and Edna. About Georgie and the racetrack. He lay back on the cot and stared at the ceiling. "What's the weather like, then, lass?" he asked.

"Still hot. A little breeze, though."

"A breeze. What's it smell like?"

"Um. Hay, the river, dry fields."

He closed his eyes.

"Amos? Can I bring you anything?" She remembered suddenly she'd promised him oranges. She hadn't brought them, or anything. "Are you all right?"

He didn't answer. He laced his fingers across his ribs. Lennox backed out, walking away while the matron turned the key in the lock.

Where was Iris? She had to find Iris.

Lennox drove to the office. Again she had the feeling someone was following her, first a black sedan like the midget's, then a blue coupe, then another black sedan. Too many cars for a tail, she thought, but lost them in the Market anyway. At Shirley's desk, she typed up a report for Vanvleet. It was slow with one hand. But she had to turn it in today. That meant seeing Louie, too. Not much choice in that.

When it was done, she sat at her own desk and looked out over the city. The streetcars followed their neat tracks up the hill and out of sight. She looked through her notes in the other notebook and found the name of the racetrack manager.

"Vance Moore, please." The switchboard operator told her to wait.

Another woman came on the line and Lennox asked again.

"He's not in. Can I take a message please."

Lennox looked at her watch. "When does he come in?"

"Today, I'm not sure. Usually, he's in by noon."

"Is there somewhere else I can reach him? It's important."

In the pause, she could hear a pencil beating against a desktop. *Tap-tap, tap-tap.*

"Miss? Can I reach Mr. Moore somewhere else?"

The secretary sighed. "He's probably at his other job. Which is at Overland Meatpacking, if you must know."

Lennox had been to Overland Meatpacking before. It was Georgie Terraciano's business, only a short drive down the hill to the Bottoms from the office. She found a small office annex on the far side of the parking lot from the slaughterhouse. It looked like a plain shingled cottage, painted appropriately blood red and remodeled for business purposes. She pushed open the door and waited by an empty desk inside a front room.

Somewhere in the back of the offices, a radio was playing band music. Lennox sat down on a wooden chair. It was four o'clock. She had the report in her handbag, ready for Vanvleet. She wanted to ask Vance Moore about Georgie Terraciano, but now she knew she couldn't. Moore worked for him. So she would ask about the racetrack, about Palmer Eustace and Floyd Wilson and the audit Amos had supervised. Anything, to get him talking.

A man came in, glanced at her before looking for something on the vacant desk. He wore a bookkeeping shade, small glasses on his nose, and garters to hold up his shirtsleeves. His fingers were stained with ink. He nodded at her, then disappeared again.

Lennox got up and opened the outside door. Where was the secretary? The smell on the breeze down here was a far cry from dry fields. The stench of the slaughterhouse was rich. She shut the door and sat down again. It was 4:15. She couldn't wait forever.

The back hallway was unadorned, the wood floor scuffed. She followed the sound of the radio to an open door. The nameplate on the man's desk read ELMORE CURTIS. The bookkeeper.

He looked up at her knock. "Can I help you?"

Lennox stepped into the room. The bookkeeper stood up, his look wary. "I hope so. I'm looking for Vance Moore. I was told he works here."

The man's coffee-colored skin set off his white shirt and yellow satin tie. His wavy black hair stood stiff above the green eyeshade. He glanced nervously at Lennox, then came around the desk. "I don't know about Vance. Where he is. Hasn't Ethel come back?"

"No, there's no one—" Lennox stared at the man. "You're Palmer Eustace."

"I beg your— My name is Elmore Curtis."

"Right. And also Palmer Eustace. When it's convenient."

Curtis smoothed his pencil mustache nervously. "If you're looking for Mr. Moore, I can take a message."

"Did Vanvleet put you up to this? No, it was Georgie, wasn't it?"

"Please. You must leave." The bookkeeper stepped to the door of his office and pointed the way out.

"I saw your picture. With Louie Weston at Vanvleet's office. You're fronting for Georgie as the racetrack owner."

Curtis began to shake. "Please. Go."

"What is he paying you to front for him? I hope it's a lot, because he's making a bundle. That track brought in two million last year. And he's betting on his own horses, and ya know what? They're winning. And the worst of it? If something goes sour, the books get audited—I mean the real books this time—

then the G-men come sniffing. Who do you think he's going to let go down for this?"

He blinked, taking this in. His eyebrows jumped. He went back to his desk and sat down, as if acting in a dignified manner would make everything right. "But . . . the paper said half a million."

"Don't believe everything you read in the paper." Lennox looked at him, huddled in his smudged starched cuffs. So eager to believe. If he bought Georgie Terraciano's line, who wouldn't he believe?

"I don't know anything about the track," he said quietly.

"I need your help, Mr. Curtis. I need evidence on what Georgie Terraciano is up to."

He ran a hand over his hair. "I only know what he tells me."

"Did he ever mention a woman named Iris Jackson? Or Rose Schmidt."

He frowned. "No."

"What about something called 'the Truman money'?"

"The senator?"

"Only Truman I know. Ever hear of a stash of his money?"

"No. What's this about?"

"What about John Lazia? What did Georgie do for him?"

He blanched. "Who told you that?"

"Seems it's common knowledge. Georgie was one of his lieutenants. Do you know what he did? You worked for Georgie back then, didn't you?"

"I knew John," he said carefully. "Everybody did. I'm not sure what Mr. Terraciano did for him."

"Come on," Lennox hissed. "Don't give me that crap."

The man laid his hands carefully on a ledger on the desktop. "I have a family. I have a job. Are you the police? Because Mr. Terraciano has friends, see?"

"No, I'm not the cops. And Georgie's friends may not be so friendly anymore. And you, Curtis?" She leaned over his desk. "You'll have a job breaking rocks if Georgie lets you take the fall."

He squirmed on his chair. The radio announcer launched into a commercial for Anacin. They listened to the jingle.

"I tell you, I don't know anything about the track." Curtis glanced at her bandaged hand. "Who are you working for, then?"

"Somebody who wants Georgie stopped."

Curtis clenched his jaw, dabbed sweat off his eyebrows. Finally, he sighed. "This was years ago. It ended—everything ended—when Lazia was killed." He lowered his voice to a whisper. "Georgie ran Lazia's book back then. Took all the bets, made the payouts. He was the top man behind Lazia. When Johnny was killed, Georgie thought he was gonna take over. But Lazia's bodyguard, Freddie Salvatore, he got the job."

"Freddie got indicted."

Curtis nodded and swallowed hard. He glanced up at Lennox as if he was thinking about indictment himself.

She said, "Does Georgie still work for the organization?"

"Freddie busted his chops when Lazia got snuffed. Didn't want Georgie muscling in, so he got rid of him. Cut him out of the action."

"Then Georgie gets his own action going, ponies, racetrack, betting. Even fixing it so his own horses win."

"I don't know anything about that. I stay away from the track. As a matter of fact, I'm allergic to horses." He smiled lamely.

Lennox examined his patient, frightened face. "Does Georgie have a girl on the side?"

"There's been stories. Some cigarette girl from one of the casinos, women like that."

"But nobody permanent, or visible."

He glanced at his watch. "The shift will change in a few minutes and the parking lot will be crawling." He stood up, took off his eyeshade and garters, and hung them on a peg. He put on a plaid sport coat and shot his cuffs. He took a snap-brim hat off the rack.

Did he know more? In his position, she would try to be involved in the boss's shenanigans as little as possible. Just enough to hang on to the job.

He positioned the hat on his head. "Best if you go first."

Lennox drove up out of the Bottoms and back to downtown. She should have called the law offices first to let them know she was coming. That way, she might have bypassed Louie Weston and talked to Vanvleet. She wanted to ask the old man about Amos, too, and his defense. But now there was no time.

It was hot and stuffy in the Packard. The wind had picked up, catching skirts and hats. Children played ball in the street. She parked the car on Tenth near the New York Life Building. She chucked her blade into the pocket of her gray trousers and took off down the street.

Pushing open the heavy brass doors to the building, she patted her windblown hair as she waited for the elevator to descend. Should she go back to Amos tonight and tell him about Palmer Eustace? Would Amos think that was an important break? So Georgie was having his bookkeeper front for him as owner of the track. So what? That would be Amos's reply. He had bigger fish to fry.

With a clunk, the elevator doors opened. Louie Weston and Reggie Vanvleet were laughing with Sam, the operator. Louie called out her name.

"Everybody's gone home, Dorie." Louie put his arm around her shoulders, turning her around in the lobby. She twisted out from under it. "You got a report for the old man?"

"Has he gone?"

"Your partner's keeping him busy over at the courthouse all day," Reggie said. "Nobody's seen him since the morning."

Lennox frowned. Vanvleet wasn't at the jail with Amos. Making a deal with Herb somewhere? "I should go up and leave the report with his secretary." She turned back to the elevator, but it had closed and gone. Fifth floor, the needle showed.

"She's gone, too," Louie said. He smiled at her, and she wondered what she had ever seen in him: a slick, lying sharper. Was that something she'd aspired to once? Someone like Georgie Terraciano? Reggie looked a little off balance, into the tiger's milk again. They were a pair. No better than the criminals they served.

"What's that on your hand, a butterfly cocoon?" Louie asked.

"We're headed over to the University Club, Miss Lennox. Care to join us?" Reggie offered his elbow.

Louie exploded with laughter and punched Reggie playfully in the shoulder. "Come on, old boy. Don't be daft."

Jumping over the streetcar tracks, Lennox held on to her hair as the wind swept in from the west. She was relieved that Louie had dragged Reggie off to the club. She didn't have to make any excuses. She didn't even care about his insult that she wasn't University Club material. She was past caring about Louie.

At the corner, the wind was calmer. The air smelled better up here. Not for Amos, she thought. She would come by the office first thing in the morning and drop off her report. It was done. She felt good about that. Iris wasn't found, not yet, but she would be.

The knee felt good today. Lennox flexed it as she walked to the Packard. Maybe because it was almost fall, and that brought memories of school days, or maybe it was the giddiness she felt at the *Star,* but she thought about running again. She gauged the distance to the corner, a hundred yards, maybe more, and wondered what her time would be now. Dismal no doubt, especially in creaky oxfords instead of cleats, on Pendergast cement instead of the track.

A man lounged in a doorway ahead, smoking a cigarette. The bend of his hat was wrong, too low, his movements too jumpy. She reached for her switchblade. Her heart sunk. She'd put it in her right pocket and the bandaged fingers made extracting it next to impossible. She slowed her pace, looked back at the traffic, readying to cut across. And never saw the man who jumped her with the soaked cloth for her nose and mouth. She struggled, gagged, tried to scream, thought she kicked him.

But it was too late, and too dark, for that.

TWENTY

INSIDE HER HEAD, the horses took off, thundering hooves, pounding earth. She opened her eyes to keep them from exploding through her ears.

The room was dark as pitch. Was she blindfolded? Lennox blinked, her eyes refusing to focus. Her neck was bent at an awkward angle. Heat blew against her cheek. She pulled her head up and felt the steam thick in the air. She tried to move, but her hands were bound behind her back, her ankles tied against chair legs. The shuffling of feet not far away sent a shock wave through her.

Then a door opened, a shaft of burning glare. The yellow light framed a man. There was talking. She felt like a stick of wood, solid, dull, heavy. The smell of wet laundry was in the hot air, cotton, moist.

More shuffling toward her, the light gone. Then the beam of a flashlight knocking her back. And the voice.

"You awake now?"

She squinted at the glare.

"Turn on the light." An overhead bulb ticked on; a room of fog glowed under it. And a goon with a flashlight, and Georgie Terraciano, in a blue silk shirt and a pinstriped sack suit.

"Hello, toots." Georgie leaned his face down to her level. "You don't mind me calling you toots, do ya? Seems like you got some information we ain't been getting from ya. Things you been snooping about that aren't getting back to us. What you got to say to that?"

"You're doing the talking, toots," she said, her tongue thick and dry.

"No, no, no. You're wrong about that, Miss Lennox, 'cause you'll be talking. You'll be telling us everything that ain't in that report." He waved the folded sheets, four in all, in front of her. "You think we buy this is everything? You got another think comin'."

The goon was the older boxer, the one she'd biffed in the jaw that day with Marilyn. Great, just great. He looked at her with an expression of bland disgust. She felt the same away about herself.

Georgie paced in front of her. "Hit her, Tarp."

The boxer stared at Georgie. "Aw, boss."

Georgie gave him a sour look and took a step back. Tarp stood between her and Georgie. She held up her head to give him a good shot. "I'm sorry about this, miss."

"It's all right, Tarp. Sorry about the knee."

"That's not the same. I—"

"Do it, Tarp," bellowed Georgie.

The slap was an openhanded hit, and it gave her a crick in her neck. Her stung. She looked at Tarp, trying to communicate something, anything. He frowned and rubbed his hand.

"Now, talk." Georgie stepped back into the friendly circle. "What have you found out about Iris Jackson?"

"It's in the report. All of it. Her real name is Rose Schmidt."

"No, it ain't. No such person, in Kansas City or in Raytown."

So they had been to Raytown. With their trained midget. "Well, maybe she lived somewhere else. A woman at Emery-Bird-Thayer identified her as a Rose Schmidt. That's all I know. I couldn't find her in Raytown, and I guess I wasn't the only one looking."

Georgie rubbed his chin. "So where's the dough?"

"Dough?"

"The Truman money. Why do you think we're looking for

the dame—'cause I need to get laid? She knows where the money is."

"I don't know anything about any money, Georgie. If you'd told me this earlier—"

Georgie slapped her himself. Other cheek, harder, more stinging. Possible tooth cut.

"Don't lie to me. You're after the money yourself. You weren't going to tell me about your extracurricular projects with my wife, were you?"

"What does your wife have to do with it?"

"You know, I hate know-it-alls more than I hate liars. Hit her again, Tarp."

It was softer this time, and she tried to thank Tarp with her eyes, but he kept his averted.

"You think I don't have my people at that bank? My wife goes waltzing in there big as life to see my bank accounts, I hear about it."

"That wasn't your wife; that was Iris Jackson."

"The hell. My wife told me herself—she went down there and made a big scene, showed 'em our marriage license and made 'em open the books."

"Marilyn did that? Good woman," Lennox said. She spit blood.

Georgie pulled his arm back to hit her again, but Tarp put his in the way. "You want her to talk or not, boss?"

He lowered his arm and glowered at her. "What else haven't you told us?"

"That you own a racetrack and are making a killing out there. Let's see. That Reggie Vanvleet owns his own tuxedo."

"About the money, you dumdora. Where is the money Lazia gave her?"

Lennox ran her tongue along the cut inside her cheek. *Truman.* Nineteen thirty-four, the year Truman was elected to the Senate. *Lazia.* Also the year John Lazia was gunned down. *Money.* The essential ingredient in the triangle. If Lazia wanted to make a big contribution to the campaign, maybe even an illegal one . . . But he got shot, and Iris was his girl—

"She's got it hidden somewhere. She came back for it."

"There you go." Georgie was smiling. "Come on. Where'd she hide it?"

"I don't know. Give me some time. Maybe with that Edna Klundt."

"So where's she?"

Lennox shook her head. It felt clearer, but the rope was cutting into her wrists and ankles. Her neck hurt; her lip was swelling. The heat wrapped everything in a smothering dampness. "Maybe dead. Who knows."

"Don't give me your bushwa. I been following this dame for weeks, long before you came trottin'. But you're the pro—that's what Dutch tells me. Trust the professionals; they'll find out where she stashed the money. But I need that money now."

She looked closely at his swarthy face. "You scared Iris, didn't you? She had to disappear."

Georgie paced angrily. "I never talked to her."

"But you followed her. She saw you, didn't she? She's not stupid. She made me, too. I was set up, the witness to the jump."

"So what? What I want is the money. I don't care about the broad."

"She killed that girl, the one who looked like her. And the bartender who saw the switch. She might come after you, too, Georgie. You better watch your step."

"Yeah, right." Georgie picked up a jacket from the doorknob. She could see his face glistening with sweat. "Tarp here's going to look after you till I get back. Hit her if she acts up, Tarp. You—" he pointed at her—"you and I will talk later."

The boxer watched Terraciano leave. He turned to her, leaned against the cavelike wall, crossed his arms over his chest.

"Warm in here," Lennox said, looking around. There were

only the slimy walls, the single bulb, and the heat. "Where are we?"

Tarp looked her over. "Power plant."

"Ah. The steam." She felt her blouse sticking to her chest, looked down. The fabric was translucent with moisture. Tarp was looking, too. "I'm sorry I hit you the other day. I didn't know you worked for Marilyn."

"And Georgie, too," he said.

"Right. That must be tough, the loyalty thing. But I guess you don't play favorites."

He blinked, looked away. Minutes passed. Water dripped. Lennox sweated. Tarp sweated. The steam swirled.

"Is there any water?"

The big man pushed off the wall, stepped outside the door, and returned a few minutes later with a paper cup full of water. He held it to her lips. She washed the blood off her tongue. The water dribbled down her chin into her lap and onto her blouse. "Okay?" Tarp said.

"Do you think . . . Oh, never mind."

"What?" He stood over her in his double-breasted suit, wide shoulders not needing padding, legs like tree trunks.

Lennox looked up at him and smiled. "I just wondered if you had a handkerchief."

He pulled a red silk square out of his pocket. "Want I should wipe your face?"

"Please."

Awkwardly, he got down on one knee and patted her forehead, picking off a stray hair with his fingers. Then her cheeks; then she closed her eyes and he dabbed her eyelids. "I appreciate this, Tarp," she whispered. He wiped her chin and the corners of her mouth.

Before he could stand, she said, "What if you untied my legs. I'm getting cramps in my thighs." She tried to raise her thighs a little and saw him swallow hard. As if maybe he was getting his own cramp.

He stared through her blouse at her bra and her breasts as his big fingers fiddled with the ropes at her ankles. "Just for a minute," he said. "So's you can stretch."

"I really appreciate this, Tarp."

Lennox took slow, deep breaths. She watched the door through the misty air, and the top of Tarp's head, his small bald spot surrounded with curly black and gray hairs. His pushed-in nose and scarred eyebrows. She tried not to think about how big he was, and if he had a gun. Where was her switchblade? She looked at the trousers stuck against her legs. It was gone.

"There now." He stood up. "Stretch 'em out for a minute. Then I gotta put 'em back."

She moved her feet forward, and it did feel good; the knee released its grip. She said, "Ah," and smiled. "Thank you. Say, got a cigarette?"

He pulled a deck of Camels from his jacket and lit her one. The end was damp when he held it to her lips. She puffed on it a few times and he pulled it away.

"More?"

She shook her head. Tarp finished the fag and rubbed it out under his shoe. He held the ropes nervously. "The boss'll be back."

"Where'd he go?"

"His kid had some school program. Marilyn couldn't go."

Lennox squinted at him. "Did he beat her up?"

The big shoulders jumped.

"That son of a bitch," she whispered. She caught a trail of sweat with her tongue. "You married, Tarp?"

"Not no more. She run off with the milkman. You believe that?"

"I bet he wasn't as handsome as you, Tarp."

The boxer's lips turned up in a smile. "Plug-ugly."

"Bet he doesn't satisfy her like you did," Lennox said. *Easy, girl.* Tarp gave her a side look and hitched his pants. "I bet there's nobody who could."

His hands strung the rope out. "You better stop, uh, that talk."

"Is Georgie going to be back soon?"

"Not for an hour, I guess."

She stretched her legs long and tipped her head back. "An hour. Oh, that feels good. But you know, Tarp, I still have that cramp in my thigh. Do you think you could massage it a little?"

He debated with himself, tugging on the rope, glancing at the door. Lennox worked her shoulders around, over the top of the chair back. She urged Tarp over with her smile and a toss of her head. Behind her back, her hands were slimy with sweat, the bandage on the bad hand limp with moisture. The slats of the chair back felt solid, but her grip on them was none too.

"Come on, Tarp. Just a rub. It doesn't mean anything, does it?"

"Well. A kinda rubdown. Like the trainers used to do before my fights."

"That's right, a rubdown. It's my right leg, just above the knee."

He got down on one knee again, in front of her, and dropped the rope. His fingers touched her leg gingerly, just the tips against the gabardine fabric of her trousers. "Harder, Tarp, harder," she whispered. "Oh, yes, up just a little."

Tarp swallowed, licked the sweat off his lip. He kept his eyes on her knee, except when they couldn't help going to her filmy blouse. She let him knead a little, watched the sweat roll down his temples. "What about my calf, Tarp? Just below the knee."

He bent farther, and as he rearranged, one hand on the floor, she pulled her feet back and brought the chair around to the left in a sweeping arc. He brought his head up, mouth hanging open in surprise. The edge of the seat connected with Tarp's skull in a thud; he froze in place, eyes rolled back, then slowly toppled. She held the chair aloft, ready for another blow. Her breath came hard and fast in the heat. But Tarp didn't move, and she lowered the chair.

She dropped to the moist cement, wincing as she wiggled through her arms to get her hands in front. Her mangled fingers shot with pain. Kneeling next to Tarp, she patted his pockets, found her blade, and sawed furiously through the rope. In a moment, she was at the door. She flicked off the lights and looked back.

A lump was forming on Tarp's skull. Lennox stepped back inside and felt his wrist for a pulse. He was still alive. She patted his cheek and whispered, "Sorry about that, old boy."

The halls of the power plant were dimly lit, one bare bulb a stretch, suffocating with heat and slimy with moisture. They all looked alike, tunnels under the earth, miles of them, slick stairs and moldy walls, distant clanking of machinery and hiss of steam. She ran, trying one hall, then another, until she was frustrated and lost and wondered if she was going to run smack into Georgie.

Lennox leaned against a wall, wiped her face with the back of her hand, and caught her breath. There had to be a way out; she had to think. She noticed a slope to the floor. If she went up, she would eventually get to the surface. She ran, checking her balance at intersections, picking turns willy-nilly. At the third intersection, standing on one foot to see which way was up, she heard voices. They came from one of two uphill hallways. She listened hard but couldn't pick out the hall. She turned and backtracked. If you can't go up, you go down.

At a crossing, she stopped to catch her breath in the heavy air. Her fingers throbbed and she tore off the bandages and threw away the splint. Her body was drenched in sweat. She couldn't believe what she'd done to Tarp—not whacking him; that was nothing. But seducing him; she hadn't known she had it in her. She felt a curious freedom, until she remembered she was stuck in this maze. She kept going, running her hands along the dim hallways, feeling the moss and fungus growing there.

The voices startled her again. She sank into the shadows. They got closer, footsteps approaching fast. She slipped off her oxfords, tied the laces together, and slung them over her neck. And ran again, in the other direction from the voices.

Around a bend, she suddenly smelled clean air. Her heart lightened—a way out. Natural light seemed to come from another hallway. She crawled through a high square on the wall and found herself in a round culvert running parallel to the tunnel. The voices were sudden and loud in the hall she'd just left. They echoed against the rock. Angry—that was Georgie. He was cursing. She flattened against the rounded wall and listened as the clattering faded. Her heart was in her throat as she inched down the culvert toward the light.

She could almost stand in the big drainpipe. Warm water sluiced along the bottom, an inch deep. The shoes swung in front of her. She stepped on a bolt, winced, went on. The culvert turned, went another ten feet, and stopped.

In the dark tunnels, like in hell, time was endless. Outside, it was daylight, the sky still light, blue with clouds. It hurt her eyes. She could see the Hannibal Bridge up to the right, looming. She stepped to the edge and looked down. The culvert emptied over a limestone cliff that dropped straight away from the lip. Below, the rock was etched and brown from the runoff from the culvert, pocked with tiny holes in the ancient layers of ocean bed. Fifteen feet down, the trickle widened into a waterfall that spread into a spray and disappeared as mist.

Below that, the river.

She took a step back.

An oxbow bend off the main channel swirled brown and languid below, undercutting the limestone. The brown Missouri water was straight down. Lennox caught herself on the walls of the culvert. The breeze felt clear and cool against her skin, drying her sweat. But the drop to the river? Forty feet?

Holy Mary.

She turned back to the dark hole. The footsteps were distant now, a shout unintelligible. She could retrace her steps. Theoretically, yes, if all the halls didn't look alike. If Georgie and Tarp and who knew who else weren't looking for her. She faced the river again, a shiver passing over her damp back, the sticky blouse clinging to her ribs. She thought of Sylvia falling like an angel in the night air, of Melva with nowhere to turn. *Don't think about them. Do something right for once.*

How deep was the water down there? What sort of animals lived in that muddy sludge? *Crawdads, pinchers, slime.* The drop wasn't nearly as far as off the bridge. She eyed the old iron monster high above, the cars whizzing by, the train level empty. On the far side of the river, an airplane took off, its tiny roar carrying across the water, a passenger plane with its steel body gleaming in the setting sun. She watched it rise, ached to be on it, to be airborne. It went up, and up, then was gone.

She was sucking air, her chest heaving. *Snakes, Amelia, hopeless endings.* Her toes curled over the edge of the culvert. *Biting things, razor teeth, catfish jaws.* Taking her shoes from her neck, she held the strings by her side, tucked her bad hand into her shirt.

Hell or high water.

She looked down once more and thought, This is going to hurt.

TWENTY-ONE

THE MARSH went on forever.

Dank, muddy, with cutting reeds and stagnant sinkholes: the interminable marsh. Lennox had scrambled out of the river as soon as she could—the oxbow was barely four feet deep—to examine the raised red marks on her arms and ass and legs. The hit from the water had knocked her senseless for a second, but the putrid water brought her to. The trousers had helped, cushioning her skin, but now they were heavy with water and mud, dragging her down with every step. She put on her oxfords but the soft ground sucked them off her feet. She wedged them out of the mud, tied the laces together again, and trudged on.

Under the bridge, she began to look for the fishermen's shacks as the light dimmed to a shadowy purple. She crossed the railroad tracks, three sets. The sun had set and a gloomy stink rose from the earth. A path appeared, used by fishermen to reach the river, and the going was easier for a while. Then the path petered out and she pushed aside cattails and weeds, turning her ankle in puddles, cursing the swamp.

She reached the top of the bank at last and caught her breath on the sidewalk near where Talbot had parked his car that day. What time was it? Her wristwatch had disappeared. Setting her shoes on the pavement, she sank down to examine her feet.

Her socks were torn, covered with muck and algae. She stripped them off. A few cuts, but nothing serious. She tried to wring out her wide-legged trousers at the hem, and she let out a small scream when she saw the leach on her calf. She picked it off and heaved it into the bushes.

A wild dance then, patting and wriggling and yelping. People in cars were staring at the dripping, hopping, cursing woman on the sidewalk. She wanted to strip off her trousers, right there, but settled for a quick hand down her waistband, here, there, up there, down here. No more slimy animals. She relaxed and picked off one of hundreds of half-inch-long strings of algae that clung to her skin and clothes.

Lennox didn't want to think about her hair. Tucking wet strings behind her ears, she walked barefoot the six blocks to Charlotte Street, keeping her eyes down. As she rounded the corner to her street, she bumped into Jenny.

The old woman let out a mewly howl. "Eeeuw. Don't touch me, girlie. Oh, it's you. Got a smoke?"

Lennox pushed past her. If only she could get a bath. Get clean, get this swamp muck off. She concentrated on that. *Then this nightmare will be over.* She walked up the steps to the front door. That goddamn fussbudget prig better not be in the bath.

"Miss Lennox!"

A cluster of residents, and Harvey, huddled near the bottom of the stairs. Mrs. F. wore her cleanup apron with its big Hawaiian flowers, the twins sensible suits. Betty and Ilo were half up the stairs, but they turned and stared.

She nodded at their wide-eyed looks, lowered her head, and circled them. *Just let me get up the stairs. Just let me get in the bath.*

"What's happened to you, young jouster?" one of the twins asked.

"Look at your clothes!"

"Oh, dear, that smell," said Mrs. Ferazzi. "Bring those down right away, dear, and I'll wash them up for you."

"I'm burning them," Lennox said, mounting the steps.

"Oh, no," Ilo said softly above her. "Those were my favorite trousers."

"I certainly don't have clothes to burn," Betty said.

"Dorie?" Harvey called. "Dorie, wait."

The voices began to rush together and she felt smothered by them. "What a stink." "Did she jump in the river?" "Winkie's in the bath again." "Let us help." "She's barefoot." As she reached the landing, Lennox turned, covered her ears, and yelled, "Leave . . . me . . . alone. All I want is a bath. So leave me alone!"

At the second floor, she heard his heavy steps come up behind her. "Don't, Talbot."

"Wait, will you? I've been looking all over for you. Some things have happened." He grabbed her arm and she winced. "Are you all right?"

"I'm just . . . filthy. So let me go, all right?"

"Come with me. To my mother's place. She's got a big tub. Lots of hot water." He took her shoulders. "You sure you're all right?"

"What—don't I look like my usual million bucks?"

He touched her cheek. "Did you get sunburned?"

She pulled away. She felt a last jag of anger bubble up and pop. Harvey took her hand, her bad hand, and she made a low cry. He switched hands, led her down the stairs. Outside, he put his arm around her waist. In the Chrysler, he said nothing about the smelly stain she was making on the upholstery.

Lennox fell asleep in the bathtub. Mrs. Talbot came in and helped her wash out her hair. A grown woman needing help bathing. Ridiculous. But the old woman was so kind, round-faced, double-chinned, the type who bustled and cooed and clucked and brought soft, sweet towels from a cupboard. Lennox was sure she was dreaming.

The house, she knew. It was the mansion by Loose Park where they'd swum. Talbot had fibbed; didn't want his family to make a difference, he said. So this was his secret. He was rich. Inside, the house was expensive without being stuffy, with soft chairs and family portraits, and warm shades of red and yellow. In one of Mrs. Talbot's terry-cloth robes, Lennox sank into a soft chair in a sunroom off the kitchen. Harvey brought her a cup of cocoa, something she never drank, didn't like, but which she gulped down greedily now.

"What about a sandwich?" Mrs. Talbot asked from the kitchen. Harvey sat in the chair opposite her, staring at his knees. "Is tuna salad all right?"

"No fish," Lennox said.

"How about that roast beef from last night, Mama?"

Mrs. Talbot puttered around the kitchen. Lennox ran a comb through her hair, tucking her feet up under her. The slap marks, both human and river-inflicted, had faded. She wondered if Harvey could see the handprint on her cheek. Her bottom lip was still fat. She looked at him over her mug.

"You call your mother *mama*?"

"Why, what did you call yours?"

She noted the past tense. "Verna. Or 'you slut.' "

He squinted, half smiling. "You keep trying to test me, don't you?"

Mrs. Talbot brought out the sandwich on a little tea tray and placed it in Lennox's lap. The bread was hearty, the mustard thick, the roast beef delicious. She tried to keep up the jive, ask him why he'd never told her about this house, his family, but her mouth was too full. Mrs. Talbot brought lemonade, freshly made. So this was what it was like to be rich. You take long baths and people bring you food and you eat good.

Harvey pulled his chair up closer after sending his mother on to bed. "I know you're going to tell me what happened today, and I want to know. But some big stories came through the newsroom today."

She drank lemonade so she could speak, but he put up his hand. "Just sit tight. For a change." She made a face but kept quiet, popping the last of the bread crust in her mouth.

"The feds are onto Georgie," he said. "They're investigating him for tax evasion. They think he's got sources of income he isn't reporting."

"The fixed races?"

He shrugged, examining his palms.

"Talbot, listen. I talked to Palmer Eustace today. Or the man calling himself Palmer Eustace. He's fronting as the racetrack owner. He works for Georgie." She leaned forward. "He told me Georgie was Lazia's right-hand man, that he worked all Lazia's book."

Harvey sat back, frowning. "I don't know who this Eustace character is. But that isn't true. My father was a lawyer, one of Lazia's lawyers before Johnny bought it. He knew Georgie. Georgie was a thug, a low-level operator. He wasn't Lazia's second. Maybe that's the story he spreads around, but it's not true."

Lennox drank more lemonade. She wasn't sure what difference that made. Georgie had heard about the Truman money—whatever that was—through Lazia. She was sure of that.

Harvey continued: "A fella at the city desk says Georgie is in debt to some big-time Chicago trouble boys and he's trying to hide his assets. They put a lien on the meatpacking plant today."

She wiped her mouth on a napkin. "All this happened today?" No wonder he was around the bend.

Harvey searched her face with his eyes. "Did he do this to you?"

"Don't go into your Captain Avenger act, Harve."

"You called me Harve."

"That doesn't mean I'm going to call your mother mama."

He smiled. "At least you're all right. How did you get all wet and—"

"I don't want to talk about it, not tonight. Is that the end of the news, ace?"

"There's one more story, but you'll have to wait until the morning paper for that one."

"That's teasing. Is it about Georgie?"

"No. And I can't tell you anything. Except that it'll knock your socks off."

"You are a cruel, cruel man."

She put the tray on the floor and grabbed his foot. Like a good boy, he had taken his shoes off at the door. She clamped his socked foot under her arm, tickling viciously. "I told you not to fuck with me, Harvey."

"Stop that! Hey!" He laughed, struggling halfheartedly to get away, until he grabbed her bad hand and the game was over. She bent over in pain, cradling the hand. He put his arms around her, whispering apologies. She rocked on the edge of the chair for a minute as the pain subsided.

His lips pressed on her neck. She felt his warmth, smelled his cinnamon breath. To fall into bed with a man once, that was excusable. They'd been riled up by close dancing, tipped a few. But she was sober now. It would mean something. And it wasn't something she could deal with, not now. She recognized the fear in her, and she hated the feeling. But it stuck on her, the feeling that knowing Harvey too well would be courting a bitter finale. He was too good for that.

She stood up. "I better go to bed." The rush of energy coursed through her. After nightmare tunnels and a river dunking, she felt so alive. But she said, "It's been a doozy of a day."

Mrs. Talbot had laid out a gauzy nightgown, tissue-thin, with smocking across the chest. It bunched around her legs, trapping her as she rolled across the soft bed. She straightened it out and lay on the downy mass of pillows, staring at the lacy canopy. She would think about the case, about Amos. No, not in this decadent room, not Amos. Just the case, Iris Jackson, aka Rose Schmidt, aka . . . Was she really from Raytown? With somebody searching for Edna Klundt, breaking Ed Grady's fingers, she had to be. They must have been friends. But where was Iris now? Where was Edna? She was no closer to finding either of them than she'd been days before.

Lennox threw back the covers. Moonlight poured in the window. She needed air. The window was painted shut. Grabbing the terry-cloth robe, she tiptoed into the hall. In the living room, moon shadows streaked across the floor. She peered through the dining room at the pool. It lay still, twinkling, beckoning her outside.

Lying on her stomach on the brick patio, she watched her reflection in the cool, still water. In the stillness, she heard Tillie's high-pitched voice singing: *Come sit by my side if you love me. Do not hasten to bid me adieu.* A flush of sadness filled her chest. She was alone in this world. They had all bid her adieu.

The pool shimmered, blue, dots of silver, aqua shadows. She trailed her fingers along the surface and wondered about the depths, if anyone compared the water at the top to the water at the bottom, the same clear water that never got to see the stars. Unfair that the water shivered and swirled like liquid metal and still some water remained at the bottom, held down and unable to breathe night air.

She rolled over and looked at the stars. Amelia Earhart never let anybody keep her on the ground, never let them tell her no. Amelia, the wags in Atchison said, had a mother who let her play in bloomers at boys' games. Verna had never made Dorie be girlish and prissy. She'd let her run full tilt, all over town, muddy, dusty, devil-may-care. So why blame Verna for everything? Why couldn't she let Verna go?

The door opened.

"Everything all right?" Harvey asked.

She stood up, the robe untied, her legs, her dark nipples outlined in the tissue gauze. She looked at her blue bare feet against the gritty brick, then up to his figure, shirtless in the moonlight. He was just a man. A man in striped pajamas. The pajamas looked silly and endearing. There would be men in her life, Verna alive or dead, Tillie, too. She had to believe that.

"No," she said. "Everything's not all right. Come here."

In the blue ether moonlight, she slipped the robe off her shoulders, pulled out of the nightgown, and slid into the water. He came to her, soundlessly through the wet. They moved deeper into the slanted far end, down where a person could drown, down where the bottom slipped away, and she kissed him and held on.

The dream returned that night, the argument on the bridge. She woke to birds and thin gold light. Strange this time, like she knew she was dreaming inside the dream, manipulating the people, herself and her mother. Verna looked tired, worn-out, not the way Dorie liked to remember her. And the words said, angry, sad words, words that finished it, whatever it was. A stillness fell on the bridge, like morning mist.

Harvey snored, his left arm around his head. Something rattled in her mind from the night before, something about Iris. Georgie getting the squeeze was well and good, but Amos remained in the hoosegow. What about Iris? She rubbed her forehead, trying to think. The thought floated just beyond her consciousness.

Clanking sounds in the kitchen meant Mrs. Talbot was up. Lennox slipped out of bed and into the robe. Coffee perked on the stove. The widow looked up from the table where she sat in a housecoat, gray hair down in a braid, chins smiling, reading the morning paper. "Sleep well, dear?"

"Yes, ma'am."

Mrs. Talbot said to help herself to coffee, so she poured a cup and sat at the old farmhouse table that anchored the bright modern kitchen. A red geranium sat by the window. Mrs. Talbot talked of rain pounding on the roof last night, but Lennox had heard nothing.

"And Harvey, is he up?" She poured nearly an inch of milk into her cup.

Lennox sipped coffee. "Didn't see him."

The widow adjusted her bifocals and snapped the paper back. "Monarchs won last night, nine to three. Do you follow the Negro League? Harvey takes me out now and again when he gets tickets. Maybe you'd like to come along."

"Is he your only child?" She surprised herself. She hadn't even known she was curious.

"Oh, no. Three girls, all older. Busy with their own families now."

What had he meant about the surprise in the paper this morning? She scooted the front section over, twisted it around. "May I?"

Lennox spread out the front page and looked for his byline. War news, more war news. London possibly bombed already. A small article on Georgie, just as Harvey'd said. Investigation by revenuers, lien against the meatpacking plant. He would be desperate, running scared from both the G and the trouble boys. She shivered. Would he come back for her? Would he keep looking for the money? She needed to find Iris—and the money—then this business would be over, nobody would be after anybody.

She looked for a story by Russell, or the picture of Louie Weston and Palmer Eustace. Nothing. She was ready to turn the page, when she saw Harvey's byline in the center bottom column.

**Vaudeville Piano Player
Living on Street in Market**

By Harvey Talbot

Fifteen years ago, Augustus "Gus" McElheaney played with the best, playing piano for silent movies and traveling shows, backing up entertainers like Katie Krippen, Fats Waller, and Alberta Hunter, touring the burlesque circuit of sepia performers.

Today, he lives off the kindness of his neighbors in the Market area, a broken man but still a remarkable talent.

Now using the name Luther Hanes, Gus McElheaney

has hidden his past well. Few of his neighbors know about his education at the Tuskeegee Institute, or even that he plays the piano. He lives, according to his friend Poppy Henderson, a simple life.

Things turned sour for Gus McElheaney in 1927. He injured his right hand in a brawl in a speakeasy in St. Louis and was unable to play the piano. Not long after that, his wife left him, taking their three children. Soon McElheaney frequented the speaks, gambled, and was often fired from bands.

In September 1929, he was arrested in Kansas City for the crime of a piano heist. He was found entertaining a crowd in the middle of the intersection of Eighteenth and Vine, playing Piney Brown's baby grand piano, which he had wheeled into the street without permission. McElheaney spent six months in jail. When he was released, the market had crashed and he had lost a piece of himself. He hasn't worked in music since.

But late at night, near Poppy Henderson's boarding house on Cherry Street, the sound of tripping ragtime and sweet blues falls and rises in the air, and you know Augustus McElheaney is back at the ivories, working his magic.

"Good morning, dear," the widow said.

Lennox looked up from the paper, to find Harvey standing next to her chair. He squeezed her shoulder, then his mother's, and poured himself coffee.

"It takes my boy a couple cups to wake up," Mrs. Talbot said. "You might put clothes on with company here, Harvey."

He was wearing the blue-striped pajama bottoms. His eyes sparked at Lennox over his coffee cup. She gulped coffee and concentrated on the newspaper.

"When did you find out all this about Luther?"

"A couple days ago. Finally got Poppy Henderson to spill."

He sat down and checked the headlines, pushed the paper away. "Very protective, she is. But Luther inspires that, I guess."

"Augustus McElheaney," Lennox mused. "That's a mouthful."

"Who's that?" Mrs. Talbot asked.

"Fellow who lives down by Dorie. Piano player."

"He's the one I hear at night." She frowned. "Augustus McElheaney—was that his stage name?"

Harvey nodded, fetched the coffeepot and poured for all. Lennox spun the strange name around in her head, trying to reconcile it with the man she knew as Luther. She hadn't even known his last name, Hanes. Names, such a funny business. Take Iris. Or Rose. Or—She shook her head.

"Can't fathom it?" Harvey asked.

Lennox put her forehead into her hands. That slippery thought about Iris Jackson—where was it?

"You ought to get those fingers looked at by a doctor, dear," the widow said.

"She's right," Harvey added.

The fingers had streaks of purple over the knuckles. The swelling was ugly. "I guess I should. Haven't had the time."

"What do you do, Dorie?"

Lennox frowned. She always hated this part.

Harvey turned to his mother. "She's a mortician. Odd profession for a girl, I know. But Dorie has a strange fascination with the dead."

Mrs. Talbot eyed her, curious, but one lip slightly curled. "Is that so? An undertaker?"

Verna and Tillie flashed through her head. A strange fascination for the dead. Had she talked in her sleep? Or was it just a joke? Was being a snoop the lowest of professions—even worse than embalming?

She squinted her eyes at him as he drowned a laugh in his coffee.

TWENTY-TWO

IN HER ROOM in the boardinghouse, Lennox peeled off the stiff, filthy trousers. They would never be the same. Mrs. Talbot had washed her blouse by hand and ironed it this morning. Still, she stripped it off, took another bath, and rewrapped the bad hand. She found a pair of trousers with only one bad stain, and a beige sweater.

Downstairs in the hall, Betty, Ilo, and Mrs. Ferazzi huddled over the newspaper. Betty saw Lennox and cried, "Dorie, look. Luther was a piano player in St. Louis."

Mrs. F. held the paper in her fist. Her eyes were wide. "I can't believe it."

"Now I know who to thank for keeping me awake with that piano music," Lennox said. She edged around the group. She wanted to look for Iris. She had to find her.

"Wonder why he changed his name," Ilo said. She smiled and rolled his name on her tongue. "Augustus McElheaney. I like that."

"It's a mouthful, that's why," Betty said. "Imagine having to write that out. It's like your name is John Jacob Jingleheimer Smith."

"Changing your name is a way of hiding," Mrs. F. said. "You're ashamed of who you are, or what your family was. I knew a family who changed their name after the war. Didn't want to sound German anymore."

Lennox stood at the door. The hazy bit about Iris was back

in her mind. The compact. Some letter, then R. H. She turned back. "What did you say?"

The three women looked at her, a tableau of frowns. "Who, me?" Betty said.

Mrs. Ferazzi turned to Lennox, smoothing her apron. "I said this family I knew changed their name after the war. My friend's name was Franz Koberstein. Then he was Frank Kober."

"That's silly," Betty said.

"Not if boys who lost a brother are beating you up every afternoon," Mrs. F. said.

Lennox walked over to her landlady, took her shoulders, and, before Mrs. F. could get out a word of exclamation, kissed her on both cheeks.

The librarian in Raytown didn't look happy to see her. She frowned over her glasses. Lennox asked for the telephone directories again, and she ignored the librarian's stare. Her new theory, that Rose Schmidt's real name was Xxx Rose H (xxx)schmidt, was ready for testing. She had written herself a note in the Packard before she came in. With her bad hand, it looked like chicken scratchings. She smoothed the note on the library table and sucked in her breath.

She worked through the most recent edition three times before giving up. There were no (xxx)schmidts at all. She scoured the *H*'s, but to no avail.

The 1935 edition, the same. Nothing even resembling a Blankenschmidt.

The skies over Raytown were brighter than her mood. Back at the Starlite Fountain, Lennox had a hot beef sandwich and a glass of milk. The soda jerk remembered her, but she didn't feel like talking about her broken fingers anymore. But he did remind her she had one more lead.

Ed Grady was working in his yard, raking out a flower bed that had gone the way of all green things. He stared at her as she walked up the flagstones, until he saw her hand.

"Fingers! You find him?"

"No, sorry." She smiled at him. "Mr. Grady, I got a favor to ask. I need to talk to your daughter."

The house on Blue Ridge Avenue was white clapboard, a bungalow with a handkerchief porch crammed with pots of summer flowers. In the open garage was parked an old black coupe. Lennox rang the doorbell and eyed it. There were so many old black sedans and coupes.

The woman who answered the door peeked through the curtains first. She opened the door two inches. "Yes?"

"Excuse me. Are you Ed Grady's daughter?"

The blue eyes looked her up and down, staring at last at the bandage and the purple-hued hand.

"My name is Dorie Lennox. I'm looking for a woman who may have been a friend of your daughter Edna's. Can we talk for a minute?"

The door opened wide enough so that Lennox could see the woman's white knuckles against the door frame, her washed-out calico dress, apron, wary eyes. She looked behind Lennox, up and down the street.

"He told me about you, and your fingers. Same as him," Louise said.

"He's a good man. I'm looking for a girl who might have been friends with Edna. I think they knew each other in Kansas City."

"I don't know who was her friends there. She never come home."

"This woman was from here, I think. She calls herself Iris Jackson now, but her name in Kansas City back then was Rose Schmidt. Now I think that's short for something—"

"Gladys Rose Hammerschmidt."

Lennox blinked. "Excuse me?"

"Gladys. Her mother's name. She hated it. She was a couple years older than Edna. A wild one. Not surprised they took up in the city. She came by here last week, talked to my husband for a minute while I was out."

"Hammerschmidt," Lennox muttered. Of course. "She was here?"

"Wanted to find Edna, same as you. My husband told her we hadn't heard from her in years. She got riled up and Dan had to shoo her off."

"Does she have any family left here?"

"Her mother, she's remarried. Or maybe just lives with the man." Louise made a sour face. "Some bum fell off the Rock Island."

"Do you know his name?"

"It's a small town, honey. Jimmie Nagel. Out on Davenport Road in a little hardscrabble place, chickens and pigs. Can't miss it—it stinks to high heaven."

Lennox found the Nagel place down a dry, rutted road. She rolled up the windows of the Packard to keep the smell out and parked in the ditch. Red chickens scattered and squawked as she opened the picket gate.

"Anybody home?"

A rumble and sudden lightening of the air foretold rain. She'd asked Louise for a picture of her daughter. She hoped for a more recent photograph of Edna than Mr. Grady's. Taken when she was sixteen, Louise said. A full-cheeked young woman whose auburn hair had darkened. With her lips well painted and her eye makeup thick, the connection finally clicked. Edna Klundt, cleaned up past and present, was now married to one of Kansas City's finest jugglers, whose balls were now crashing to the ground. Her name was now Marilyn Terraciano. Lennox hadn't had the heart to tell Louise.

The old cottonwood tree in the Nagel yard rattled in the wind. A ramshackle barn, once painted white, sat to the north of the one-story farmhouse. It, too, could have used paint. Sadly plain, without shutters or porch; all the curtains were closed.

Lennox called hello again. Pigs made their pig noises in the shade of the big tree.

A woman in farm pants, rubber boots, and plaid shirttails tied at the waist came out of the barn carrying a shallow bowl. She picked up a handful of grain and began scattering it for the chickens as she made low clucking noises. Lennox walked toward her slowly, trying in vain to avoid several varieties of animal droppings along the way. Ten paces away, she cleared her throat and said good morning.

The woman looked up, stock-still. Her dark hair was pulled off her face into a bun. Her arms and face were tanned from outdoor work, but she had Iris's beautiful face, older, sadder, but the same face.

"Mrs. Nagel?" The woman stared, silent. "My name is Doria Lennox. I'm here from Kansas City and I hoped we might talk about your daughter Gladys Rose."

For a moment, the older woman just stared. Then she snapped, "What's she done?"

"I just want to talk. That's all."

"You don't look like police."

"I'm not. But I've been looking for your daughter, ma'am."

The woman dumped out the shallow pan, set it by the barn. "I can't pay you nothing."

"I don't want money. I just want to talk."

Mrs. Nagel looked her over again. "Better do it now, before Jimmie gets back."

Lennox sat at the kitchen table, which looked a lot like Mrs. Talbot's, only this one was in a real farmhouse and had names, dates, and sayings scratched into its sticky surface. The kitchen was cluttered with pots and pans and dirty dishes, and feathers from a plucked chicken that lay in the sink. Mrs. Nagel ran water in small jelly jars and set one on the table.

"So what's she done? I know it's something to bring you out here."

"Have you seen your daughter recently, Mrs. Nagel?"

"Not in five or six years. I think she took off for Chicago."

"When was that?"

"She had some boyfriend problem, couldn't stay around. In a panic, she was."

"Did she say who this boyfriend was?"

"For all I know, she had dozens. All the boys was after her. She and Jimmie didn't get along; he said things—that's why she took off for Kansas City. No jobs here anyway."

Lennox drank the rest of her water. "Did she leave anything behind when she went?"

"I never saw her; Phylly did. That's my other daughter. She'd meet Gladys Rose in Kansas City once in awhile. She never would come home." Mrs. Nagel blinked, looked away from the window, remembering the question. "Some old clothes, that's it. I left them in the attic, no need for fancy duds. Edna brung 'em over. You know Edna?"

"I talked to her mother. That's how I found you."

"Louise All High-and-Mighty. Hmmph." She slammed down her glass and frowned. "Married to my cousin until she run him off."

"What did Edna bring over exactly?"

"A case, I told ya, with clothes in it."

"You still have this case?"

"Somewhere, I guess. What business is it of yours? You looking for Gladys Rose—why? What's she done?"

"I'm afraid," Lennox said, "she may have done many things."

Mrs. Nagel sat down at the table, head in hands.

"But if we can find her, we can help her." Lennox laid out her bad hand for sympathy, but the woman didn't notice. "Could I take a look at that case?"

It took half an hour and considerable grumbling for Mrs. Nagel to rummage through the debris in her attic and come up with the suitcase. If it hadn't been for the imminent return of infamous Jimmie, it might never have happened at all. The case was wedged under a pile of old drapes and a baby carriage. It was small, with frayed leather straps, and heavy. Sweating in the attic heat, they laid it on the bare wood floor at the top of the stairs.

The case was locked. A small but sturdy padlock held the clasp secure. Mrs. Nagel and Lennox stared at it.

"Edna never said anything about a key," the older woman said.

"We could break this with a hammer and a screwdriver." Lennox rose to go back downstairs. "Come on, show me."

Mrs. Nagel frowned. "All right."

Lennox looked back at the case, irritated and eager. She'd found the Truman money, she was sure of it. Now for the final step, using it to find Iris. How was she going to do that?

Three steps down to the back hall, Lennox stopped on the rough-hewn stair. She looked back again. Beside the case sat her handbag. She grabbed it and snapped it open. With her left hand, she pushed aside her keys, a comb, her notes, pencils, bobby pins. There. Iris's keys.

She pulled them out and showed them to Mrs. Nagel. "These were in her car." After a few minutes of struggling, she groaned and gave up. "They don't work. She wouldn't leave behind such important keys."

Mrs. Nagel looked at her crossly and held out her hand. "Let me."

The woman had delicate hands like Iris's, with long fingers. No manicure, plenty of calluses and scars. This is what Iris escaped, a farm life of feeding chickens and pigs. Hard, dirty work that went on, day after day, week after week, the only change the seasons.

Mrs. Nagel looked at the smallest key. "These always come in twos, you know." She pushed it into the padlock, squeezed the lock with her other hand. It clicked and sprang open. The woman smiled at Lennox. Then she sat back on her heels, a terrified look on her face.

"Open it," Mrs. Nagel said.

Lennox sprung the latch. She opened the lid. A jumble of clothes there: dresses, blouses, nightgowns, old stockings. Lennox pushed them aside. A panel divided the case. She turned the brass knobs and lifted the thin petition.

The money lay in bundles secured with paper straps. Bundles of bills. Hundreds. One of the straps was torn, bills missing. Three packets were missing from one row. The rest were intact, five deep, six across, fifty bills to a bundle. One hundred and fifty thousand dollars, less a few. Mrs. Nagel stared at the money, hands tucked around her as if she might touch it and it would vanish. She glanced nervously down the stairs.

"Is Jimmie coming?" Lennox moved her hand over the money, feeling the quality of the paper. She took a bill out, held it up to the light from the dusty attic window, smelled it. "Mrs. Nagel?"

"He pulls in from the southern run today. But he stops in town for a while before coming home, usually."

"Does Jimmie know about this?"

Mrs. Nagel chuckled unhappily. "I wouldn't think so."

"Do you want him to know?"

The woman looked up, nerves twitching her mouth. She looked pretty in this dim light, the woman she was before Jimmie Nagel, before all of it. She wore a defeated look, as if this, too, would be taken away.

They drove to Independence and put the money in a safety-deposit box in the name of Gladys Hammerschmidt. In her city dress and heels, her hair combed into a twist, wearing lipstick, she looked different, but still afraid. They stopped at a roadhouse on Highway 71 and had a chicken salad sandwich. Lennox sat in the dark, cool café and examined the face of the woman.

"You look like her. Your daughter."

"Everyone always said so," Gladys Nagel said. "You look like your mother?"

Lennox blinked and shook her head.

"You don't get along? No shame in that. I should know. Gladys Rose and I, we fought all the time."

Thoughts of Verna were the last thing she needed. The dreams were enough. The tangle was deep, unresolved even by death. That much she'd learned.

"She was the sweetest thing, Gladys Rose."

"Until she turned thirteen?"

"Twelve. She had that figure then—and learned what it did overnight."

"A quick study."

"Sharp as a tack. I always told her to stay in school, be a nurse or something."

Lennox pushed back her plate. "But she didn't?"

"Run off when she was sixteen. About a year after Jimmie moved in. They fought like cats and dogs. Of course, he wasn't her daddy, but he'd been gone five years and . . . well, sure was quieter after she left." Gladys sipped her tea. "I hated her gone. She was too young."

"Did she find work?"

"Nightclubs for a while. She'd send a few dollars back to Phylly. Then she had a bad patch, until she got on at a big store. How she sweet-talked that one, I'll never know. But that's my girl." She smiled. "Always lands on her feet. She's special, that one."

Gladys Nagel never asked where her special daughter scared up 150 large. Some questions were better unasked.

They rode back to Raytown in silence. Lennox was thinking about Jimmie coming home, and how she hated leaving Gladys there alone. She knew men like Jimmie Nagel, who thought nothing of knocking around the wife at the end of a long shift and a tear in the gin mill. But another sight changed her thoughts as they rounded the last corner onto Davenport Road.

"That Jimmie's car?" A late-model yellow coupe was parked in front of the farmhouse.

"No. Never seen it."

"Okay, listen, I'm going to drive by, but slouch down a little and don't look at the yard. Then I'm going to drop you off down at the crossroads. You stay there. All right?"

"In the bushes?"

"In the bushes."

"There's been a car come by real slow. An old Nash. It bothered me, but I never wanted to say nothing to Jimmie about it."

Lennox didn't look at the yellow coupe, kept going to the crossroad. "Blue?" She made a U-turn and stopped.

"You know who it is?"

"Get out here." Lennox waited while the woman climbed out, shut the door. Then she waved her behind the bushes. The car and farm weren't visible from here, and Lennox drove around the intersection onto Davenport Road and pulled in behind the yellow coupe.

There was nobody in it. She stepped out into the dirt and dry weeds. Her oxfords, so carefully cleaned by Mrs. Talbot the night before, were dusty now. She strained, looking into the afternoon sun, trying to make out a figure in the dense cottonwood shadows. She had an idea who would drive a fancy coupe like this. She inched forward to the coupe's door, looked on the seats. Nothing. She reached in the open window and pulled down the visor on the driver's side. Nothing.

She had qualms then, thoughts of Jimmie Nagel's bookie stopped in to get his due, or the extension agent coming by to check for pig diseases. But a prickling on her neck told her no. This was not a business call.

Lennox could see Gladys Nagel peeking through the weedy shrubs at the crossroads. Whoever was here must be in the house. She hesitated, though she had her switchblade handy in her pocket. This was a man's car. A desperate man.

She made herself go through the picket gate, shooing chickens with her foot. She walked to the barn, peeked inside the hay-strewn depths, shadowy and thick with the smell of whelping sows and Rhode Island Reds. At the large door of the barn, she turned to face the house. Better not to surprise him, to let him come out, even though it was a coward's way. She didn't have a gun. He was a man. He would.

Lennox jerked as the front door cracked open and the tall man appeared. He didn't see her as he clomped down the two steps to the dirt yard. Halfway to the picket fence, where the Packard came into view, he stopped.

She walked toward him. He turned, his face set in malice.

"Nice day for a drive in the country."

Reggie Vanvleet's face reddened as his jaw worked furiously. His hands flexed and opened. He wore a purple shirt, its neck open, a satiny black jacket, gray trousers.

"What are you doing here?" he said, almost growling.

"Visiting a friend. You?"

She stopped five feet from him. His eyes looked wild, darting, searching. Dust streaked his jacket. For a moment, he might have been acting, but he wasn't; this was too real. He turned toward his car.

"Looking for someone?"

He mumbled something over his shoulder. She skipped to catch up. "What?"

"I said, you know right well enough who I'm looking for." He stopped, turned, beet red now. "Iris Jackson, or whatever her name is. You led me here, but it seems I'm a little too late." He looked away down the road, his noble profile draining of color, hair flipping in the wind. Thunder rumbled from the clouds building to the west.

Reggie turned and stepped close to Lennox. "Tell me where she is. Where the money is. I'll give you a cut of it. That's what you want, isn't it? More than Georgie would have given you."

"I don't want a cut of it. It's not mine."

He tried to laugh. "Possession is nine-tenths of the law. That's what the old man says."

"Well, I don't have it. So it's not mine."

"Who does?" He took her shoulders and shook her. "Where is it, blast it? Why is everyone so goddamn closed-mouthed about it?"

"Could it be they don't want you to get your mitts on the money?"

He let his hands drop. "Who lives here?"

"A fellow named Jimmie Nagel. Railroad man."

Disappointment creased his face. He rubbed his forehead. "Goddamn it!"

"Just go home, Reg. Talk to your old man about it."

"Too late for that. I got debts, see? They're leaning on me. If I don't get it . . . I told the old man, and you know what he said? Give a man enough rope, he'll hang himself." He looked at her desperately. "My own father."

"He won't abandon you. Ask him again."

Chickens pecked at the tassels on his loafers, beating their russet wings against his trousers. He stared at the clouds, enjoying his pitiful despair, blaming his problems on his father's heartlessness. Ever the actor, his expression calculated to rouse sympathy. Lennox felt the bile rise in her throat.

But she looked at his pockets for heavy instruments just the same. Was Reggie man enough to use a gun? Hell, I've known midgets with more guts, she thought. But what kind of a man did it take? Only one who didn't consider the consequences. That breed wasn't rare.

"It's too late now. Too late for anything." Then he suddenly grabbed her again. "Where is it? I need that money. Can't you see? I'm the one, *I'm the one* who needs it. My father won't give me anything. He blames me for not being Dick, for not being the lawyer—"

A voice caught on the wind, a lost word. Then the sound of the car, *tat-a-tat* against the gravel, a throaty roar. Their heads turned together at the sound and they saw the blue car coming toward the farmhouse, and the woman running after it.

"Gladys Rose! Stop, baby, stop!"

Reggie spun and ran for the road. Lennox was right behind him. The man tried to hurdle the low picket fence, caught his trouser cuff, and fell over into the ditch in a heap, losing a loafer. The blue Nash kept moving, passing the Packard, then the yellow coupe, the black-haired woman looking at them, at the rearview mirror, then she hit the gas.

Lennox was through the gate and running for the Packard. Gladys ran up the road, waving her arms. As Lennox turned the key, the woman jumped into the car. Down at the crossroads, a yellow school bus let out a plump girl in saddle shoes. The Packard backed, swerved, and tore against the dirt ruts as Reggie threw himself into his coupe.

The Nash put up a cloud of dust. It was easy enough to follow, but not to catch, even with the Packard's getaway guts. They bounced on the deep, hard ruts, Gladys grabbing the dash. Behind them, the yellow coupe roared up close. They were in the center of the farm road, where the ruts weren't as bad, but Reggie was going to pass. Lennox rolled down her window.

The shot rang out. Gladys squealed and ducked. Lennox looked in her mirror and saw Vanvleet's arm out the window, the pistol in his hand. Left-handed, on a dirt road, from a moving vehicle. He'd be lucky to hit a barn on purpose. But she eased the Packard right, into a new set of ruts.

The engine of the coupe purred as he passed them, his head out the window, pistol outstretched, hair flying. His perfect white teeth were going to catch bugs. Holy Mary, he was enjoying himself.

With the cloud of dirt behind the coupe, she had no choice but to slow and let him get a lead. Gladys began coughing and rolled up her window. The air inside the car was stuffy and full of dirt. Lennox wiped her eyes and kept driving.

"Who is that man? Is he going to kill Gladys Rose? Is that the boyfriend she ran away from? Oh, Lordy, he's going to shoot her."

The coupe and Nash had turned left at an open crossroads and they watched as Reggie blasted with the gun again. A ewe in the pasture dropped to her knees. They screamed past a farmyard, rusty Model T's and ancient tractors in the tall dry grass, then another where a woman was hanging laundry on a line.

"He's seen *Gangbusters* one time too many," Lennox said.

"Who is he?"

"His name's Vanvleet. Seems he was on the scent of that money, too."

"You knew about that money? I thought you came looking for Gladys Rose."

"She's been looking for it, too. So if I found her—"

"But she ain't been to the farm. Not in years."

"She didn't know it was there. She was looking for Edna Klundt."

The woman held on to the door handle as they made the corner. "That Edna Klundt hadn't three ounces of brains. And I'm not saying that 'cause of Louise. That girl was stone-dumb. She told me when she came out that she was a hatcheck girl. I didn't believe her, but she was dressed nice. I knew, though. She was a lady of the evening."

"People change, Mrs. Nagel." The Packard and its bald tires wouldn't go more than thirty-five on these ruts, and she was losing them.

"My Gladys Rose never did nothing that low. I brought her up right. She might have been starving and broke, but she never laid with no men for money. Not my girl."

What about John Lazia? Her daughter might not have laid with men for money exactly, but there was worse, like heaving a poor innocent girl off a bridge in the middle of the night.

The yellow coupe was closing on Iris. They turned right, out of sight behind a line of poplars. A blast was followed by a pop.

When they turned the corner, the blue Nash sat listing in

the ditch, its left rear tire blown. The string-bean poplars had stopped the car. The yellow coupe sat half off the road, door wide, as Reggie ran, pistol in hand, toward the Nash. "Oh, Lordy," whispered Gladys Nagel.

Lennox pulled in behind the coupe and shut off the engine. She jumped out and let the door fly, then stopped. Reggie had Iris by the collar, dragging her from the car.

"Let her go, Reggie," Lennox said. He stared at her for an instant, then went back to venting his anger on Iris. "Reggie!"

He finally stopped shaking the woman. Lennox stared at her black hair. It was her—Iris: the creamy skin, the crimson nails, right down to the red dress and the platform shoes she should have been wearing when she went off the bridge. "She doesn't know where the money is. She would have taken it and run if she did."

Iris seemed to wake up, getting her feet under her and twisting out of Reggie's grasp. Her red dress was torn. One eyebrow was split and bleeding. She turned to run, got five steps, and stopped.

Gladys Nagel stood next to the Nash. Her daughter froze as if caught in the headlights.

"Gladys Rose?" the mother said. She stepped closer, her voice wavering. "It's been so long, child. Let me look at you."

"Don't call me that." Iris's throaty voice clinched it for Lennox. Disgust and despair mingled on her face. Then she turned away. Could this frigid article be crying? This would have been Reggie Vanvleet's cue to grab the girl, but he was transfixed by the drama, moving his gun from one to the other.

Tears streamed down Mrs. Nagel's face. "Come here, child. To your mama."

"I don't have a mama." Iris turned back, tears on her cheeks, but her face twisted in a vicious sneer. "My mama gave me up when she took up with Jimmie Nagel."

"Don't say that, child. I did what I had to. I never gave you up."

"Oh, yes, you did. Every single night."

Confusion wracked her body. "How can you say that?"

"The truth is easy enough even if you're full up to here—" Iris put her hand across her bloody eyebrow—"with lies and liars."

Gladys stepped closer to her daughter, reaching out a hand. "What truth, darlin'? I'm listening now."

"*Now?* Ten loused-up years later?" Iris looked wild. "Why do you think I never came back? Why do you think I had to get away? To get away from Jimmie Nagel."

Gladys swallowed hard but kept her eyes on her daughter's face. "What?"

"Oh yes. Good ol' Jimmie. Midnight was his favorite time, but he wasn't particular."

"Baby—" Gladys held her ribs as tears streaked down her face.

"And now all I want is to get away from all of this, from you, all of you. If you'll just give me the money."

Reggie stepped beside her and grabbed her arm. "We can split it, huh, sister? How much is it exactly? Half a million? Fifty-fifty will leave us each plenty, huh?"

"Put the gun down, Reggie," Lennox said. Her voice sounded strange to her, twisted on the wind. She thought about the switchblade in her pocket, but with her bad fingers and his gun, it was a ridiculous notion, a provocation. She felt calm and knew she shouldn't. But she'd found Iris, and the money. Iris would talk. Amos would be cleared. He would recover. Everything would be all right.

"This is over now," she said, hoping she was right.

Iris looked at Reg hovering next to her like a bloodsucker, then gave him a sharp jab of the elbow to the solar plexis. He doubled over with an *oof* as Iris bolted for the road, running hard. The sirens started then, as if switched on by the woman's desperation.

Lennox dove for Reggie's hand with the gun, but he saw

her and stepped back as he came up, still gasping for air. He wheeled around toward the running figure. Lennox tried again, succeeding in pulling down his outstretched arm, until he gave her a swift kick behind the knees and she lost her footing. Above the dry grass, he squinted against the purple clouds, aiming at the fleeing streak of red.

He squeezed the trigger. A shot roared over the ditch and made a dull sound in the dirt. Lennox struggled to her feet. He aimed again. A hand from behind pushed her aside. Gladys Nagel leapt at Reggie, screaming, *"No!"* covering his arm with her body as the gun discharged.

The sirens were close now, wailing in the stillness. Lightning flickered as Lennox knelt over Gladys Nagel. A ragged red hole in her chest gushed blood. Thunder rumbled. Lennox pressed the heel of her hand against the wound. The pulse grew fainter. She pushed back the woman's hair, which had been loosened by the wind, dusted with road dirt. Her eyes were open, glassy.

"Easy now," Lennox whispered. "Easy."

Above them, Reggie Vanvleet was taking another shot and cursing. Lennox looked up, felt a careless despair. They were all fools, fools for money. Sirens filled the air. Sheriff's deputies and Highway Patrolmen on motorcycles screeched against the gravel, produced dozens of firearms, and shouted down Reggie.

Lennox stood up in front of him, took out her switchblade. Shouts came from behind her to get down, get out of the way.

"Put the gun down, Reggie. It's over. They'd just as soon clean your clock with lead as spit on you."

Vanvleet's chest heaved. His nostrils flared, eyes darting at the fleeing girl, the cops, the wounded mother. Lennox saw the violet sky in his eyes as he pointed the gun at her chest and pulled the trigger.

The click rocked her. He stared dumbstruck at the silent gun. In that clear second, the birds fell silent in the poplars. Lennox put her hand to her stomach, but it was already covered with Gladys's blood. She thought of Tillie, in the ground. She gasped for air, felt it fill her lungs, heard a high-pitched wail from somewhere.

Lennox grabbed the barrel of the gun, pushed down his arm. She jumped close to him, put her blade tip to the collar of his silk shirt. The point stuck his thin skin. A dot of blood grew. It was red, alive, and she surprised herself by loving it this time. *Your blood, Reggie.* With your blood, you pay.

His taut figure went limp as the cops ran forward, pulling off Lennox's arm, slapping down the pistol, spinning him around, snapping on handcuffs. A deputy in motorcycle dress glared at Lennox until she closed the switchblade, put in her pocket.

It began to rain, fat, angry drops. Lennox crouched beside the dying woman. She leaned close, sheltering her from the storm.

On the wind, one of Tillie's songs: *Go in and out the window, go in and out the window, as we have done before.*

"It's all done now," Dorie whispered. Her face was wet with rain and tears. "She's safe."

TWENTY-THREE

LENNOX WALKED out of the Methodist Church in Raytown, glad to see the afternoon sun. The service for Gladys Nagel had not been well attended, although cousin-in-law Louise did make an appearance. Young Phyllis sat with a very old lady in the front row. The hymns were dirges, lying in the stomach like an overcooked meal.

People clustered on the sidewalk at the bottom of the steps. They stared at her, a stranger, alone. They whispered behind their hands. They had read the paper; maybe they blamed her for bringing Mrs. Nagel to the scene of her violent, senseless death. Maybe they blamed her for mucking with their dull lives. Maybe she didn't care.

Maybe she did. Lennox felt bent and old as she trudged down the sidewalk toward the Packard. In a yard next to the church, a small dog came yapping up to the fence, beating down the cosmos and the last of summer's daisies. She paused to admire his energy, his flying fur and squeaky voice, leaned down to pick a daisy that poked through the pickets as the black sedan slowed next to her at the curb.

Later, she wasn't sure if the woman had even seen her, if the slowing was intentional. Then she was sure it was, sure the woman had wanted her to turn, to notice the light blue gloves she held tensely on the steering wheel, the hat with the veil pulled low over her brow. Marilyn Terraciano never looked Lennox's way. Sunglasses, hat, and veil shielded her face. She tapped one gloved finger as if impatient, then sped away, through the parked cars and mourners, out of Raytown for good.

Lennox hadn't mentioned Marilyn Terraciano to the cops, hadn't told anyone who she really was. She'd chosen her life, molded it from scraps of nothing into something better—if not respectable, then at least something worth saving. Lennox admired her for that; it was no mean feat. What could the cops pin on Marilyn but a ruined life? Georgie was probably going up the river soon, and being married to Georgie was punishment enough.

Back in Kansas City, Lennox decided to skip Sylvia Anken's memorial service. She could still see her silver hair flying as she fell through the night air, still remember the pale, ghostly figure floating facedown in the Missouri. That would be memorial enough, and someday it might block the memories of her in the morgue drawer.

Lennox drove to the office and straightened her desk until there was really no more straightening to do, no more reports to write, no phone calls to answer, and it was time to go home.

The sun was going down over the Boston Building as Dorie Lennox climbed down the narrow, worn stairs and felt the heat rising from the pavement on Wyandotte. The streetcar was pulling away. Amos Haddam looked up and smiled.

"Got 'em back. They were in the girl's car." He waved two small booklets with leather covers. He opened the black one and sighed. "Can't believe I got her back."

Lennox fingered her new splint. It was awkward and heavy. The sky was clear again, no more thunderstorms. The air smelled sweet with alfalfa and clover. Amos gave her a long look, and she had a feeling he wasn't looking at her.

She shuffled on the sidewalk, swinging her keys. "The past doesn't come back, Amos. You don't get another chance."

He squinted at her. "But it's a part of you. Like it or not, it stays alive inside you. You can't change that. You can regret it, you can wish it'd been different, you can even try to forget, but you can't change the way it's changed you. All we are, lass, is a ratty little bundle of our past."

Not that she wanted to be reminded. "That's comforting, Dr. Freud."

He smiled. "You'll be in tomorrow, then? We'll catch up on the paperwork."

"I think I'll take the day off."

He squinted at her. "They find the girl yet?"

The dragnet had come up empty. Iris could be anywhere by now. Lennox wasn't sure how she felt about that. Iris should be caught, punished for what she did to Sylvia Anken and to Davy Esterly. But it'd been a hard life, and freedom was just about the only thing Iris Jackson had going for her. Maybe she deserved just one break. She would never get her hands on Lazia's money. It had taken the feds a matter of minutes to determine it was phony, to link it to a counterfeit scheme from five years back, when Lazia had used it for gambling payouts. Harry Truman wouldn't have been amused. The younger daughter, Phyllis, she could have used that dough; it might have made a difference. But Phylly wouldn't get it.

The person Iris Jackson owed her life to would never get it, either. For Gladys Nagel, there would never be an even break.

Driving home, Lennox suddenly wanted to be alone, to lie in her room at the top of the boardinghouse, not talk to a soul. Drink a little gin, play a little music, and forget.

When she rounded the corner onto Charlotte and saw the large group in the middle of the street, her heart lurched. An accident, Jenny or Luther, hit by a car, passed out from hunger. But no—people were laughing, cheering. There were the two bachelors from the second floor, legendary grumps now grinning. Mrs. Ferazzi in her flowered apron, even Tony, hollering and throwing up a fist.

After parking the car, she approached the crowd slowly,

wishing she could slip by but knowing it wouldn't happen. Energy filled the street, a strange and jubilant feeling. As she got closer, she saw Betty Kimble and Harvey Talbot each with one of Luther's arms, pulling him toward the center of the circle. Luther's face had darkened and he shook his head violently, digging his heels into the cobblestones.

In the center of the circle sat Mrs. Ferazzi's piano. Joe Czmanski struggled to push a wedge under one leg to keep it steady on the cobblestones. Winkie Lambert and a new beau in a streetcar hack's uniform egged Luther on, calling for him to play. Across the crowd, Poppy and Frankie stood mutely, worry clouding Poppy's motherly brow.

Harvey and Betty had pushed Luther up to the piano, but he grabbed onto the back side of it and refused to budge. Betty put her hands on her hips and started a harangue in the vein of "all we've done for you." Harvey smiled at the man, tried a man-to-man approach. Neither attack worked, and Luther's refusal to play sent up jeers from the bystanders. They had all helped carry the damn piano into the street, it seemed, and were expecting some payment in music.

A large Plymouth came down the street behind them; the driver laid on his horn. Winkie's beau stepped back to give the man directions to turn around. Harvey saw Lennox and waved her over. "He said he'd do it if we brought the piano out," he said. "Talk to him."

Luther had broken out in a cold sweat. He held his head in his hands, elbows on the back of the upright, and looked like he might cry. Lennox didn't know what to say to him. Whose idea was this? She looked back at Talbot and frowned. He urged her on.

"Luther?" she said softly. "Remember when we planned that picnic by the river?" He moved his hands, eyes fixed on her face now. "I didn't tell you, but I'm afraid of the river, of the snakes and fishes and water. I didn't want to go there."

"You dint?"

"Nope. The river scares me."

His eyes darted around the street, lighting on faces, on hands, on windows bright with the rosy flares of last light. Then back at his own hands, graceful and brown.

"So I was happy when we didn't have that picnic," Lennox went on, her voice low. "I felt like that man in the book I gave you, that I'd gotten free of something, gotten away. But I was wrong."

Luther rubbed his fingers into his eyes, wiped sweat dripping off his eyebrows, stared back at her.

"The fear stays inside you until you let it out, let it go free. I had to do that with the river."

"Whacha do?"

"Jumped right in. I was scared, but I did it anyway. After the first splash, it was fine." It was a sham. But for Luther, she would do anything, even tell lies.

She saw him looking at the ivories. She leaned close. "You have the most beautiful hands, Luther."

He dipped his chin, a tiny smile on his lips. He stretched out his fingers on the top of the upright and the talking in the crowd hushed. He lifted his head up and rounded the instrument. Joe Czmanski pushed the apple crate forward, centering it in front of the keyboard. Luther grabbed it, held it close for a second, then straddled it, extending his arms from one end of the ivories to the other.

In a bar or two, Norma and Nell were bobbing their heads, Betty and Ilo jitterbugging. Mrs. Ferazzi rocked on the balls of her feet in time to the music. The piano was woefully out of tune. No one seemed to care. The ragtime music sounded tinny and dated, but he played it so neatly, his fingers tripping over the keys, light as air. For a moment, time stopped and they were back in New Orleans, St. Louis, Charleston, in a speakeasy, nothing but music and moonshine and smiling.

Frankie's braids bobbed in time. Poppy's worry still clung, but she was smiling now. As one song ended and the clapping subsided, Luther started up again, a Jelly Roll Morton song, "Kansas City Stomp." When he hit the high trills, Lennox could see her father and mother dancing close in the apartment over the drugstore, and she felt a shiver run up her back.

Harvey appeared at her shoulder, leaned down to whisper in her ear, but gave her a small kiss instead.

"Hey, Dorie!" Frankie touched her arm. "I wrote my paper about that book, and I think I figured out what it means."

Harvey moved around the piano. He looked back at Lennox and winked, then leaned an elbow on top of the upright.

Lennox turned to Frankie and smiled. "I'm glad."

"You wanna hear what I said?"

With the limp daisy in her fist, Dorie closed her eyes before answering. The vibrations of the piano thumped through her. The bridge—there was Verna walking away into the twilight. And Tillie. Singing. Something sweet and high and pure. The evening light, lavender and misty, began to pale. The river disappeared, and Verna took Tillie's tiny hand in hers.

Dorie's eyelids began to burn. She let the image go and opened her eyes. She looked at the people, her friends, with their happy, rapt faces, and knew she would never be one of them. But maybe this was enough. Joe's ravaged face, the bachelors who barely spoke, the old woman lost in a dream of salvation, the twin sisters with their caring hearts, the single girls searching for adventure. Harvey Talbot, who . . . was Harvey. Poppy, who finally told the story of a broken man. And then Amos and his lost love. The future looked full of war, suffering, losses. But what choice was there? The past was full of ghosts.

She took Frankie's arm in hers. Luther pounded on the keys and grinned up at them.

"Yeah, Frankie, sure," she said. "I want to hear it. But can you tell me later? I love this music."